QUEEN
OF
MERCY

ALSO BY NATANIA BARRON

Queens of Fate
Queen of None
Queen of Fury

Love in Netherford
Netherford Hall
The Viscount St. Albans
The Game of Hearts

The Godlings Saga
Pilgrim of the Sky
Gods of Londinium

These Marvelous Beasts
Frost & Filigree
Masks & Malevolence
Time & Temper

Rock Revival

QUEEN
OF
MERCY

NATANIA BARRON

SOLARIS

First published 2025 by Solaris
an imprint of Rebellion Publishing Ltd,
Riverside House, Osney Mead,
Oxford, OX2 0ES, UK

www.solarisbooks.com

ISBN: 978-1-83786-065-4

10 9 8 7 6 5 4 3 2 1

A CIP catalogue record for this book is available from
the British Library.

Designed & typeset by Rebellion Publishing

Printed in Denmark

For Liam and Elodie.
May you find joy and peace—even when there is pain—
and always love where your hearts lead.

"Again I hold thee to my heart, Morgane;
Here where the restless forest hears the main
Toss as in troubled sleep. Now hear me, sweet,
While I that dream of yesternight repeat."

Madison J. Cawein,
Accolon of Gaul, with Other Poems (1889)

The island of apples, which is called the Fortunate
island, has its name because it produces all things for
itself... There nine sisters give pleasant laws to those
who come from our parts to them, and of those sisters,
she who is higher becomes a doctor in the art of healing
and exceeds her sisters in excellent form. Morgen is her
name, and she has learned what usefulness all the herbs
bear so that she may cure sick bodies.

Geoffrey of Monmouth, *Vita Merlini*
(trans. Emily Rebekah Huber),
via The Camelot Project

Yet some men say in many parts of England that King
Arthur is not dead, but had by the will of our Lord
Jesu into another place; and men say that he shall come
again, and he shall win the holy cross. I will not say it
shall be so, but rather I will say: here in this world he
changed his life.

Sir Thomas Malory, *Le Morte d'Arthur*,
Volume II, Book XXI, Chapter VII

CHAPTER ONE

MORGEN

THE NIGHT VYVIAN du Lac died, a late summer storm fell upon Carelon, hail rattling the windows like thieves clawing through an abandoned grave.

A bell tolled in the distance, Arthur's new Christian chapel clanging in the midnight hour, and my beloved aunt closed her fever-bright eyes, breathed out, and was no more.

For a woman possessed of such power and magic—and, some might say, legend—Vyvian du Lac departed the realm of the living with no celestial dazzling rising from her small, sturdy body. She did not even utter a prophecy or impart upon me words of wisdom. No, her spirit left without fanfare, as natural as the sun setting or a leaf falling. Inconsequential. Mundane, even. But that is so often the face of mortality, as I have learned many times over.

I do not think Vyvian du Lac was afraid of death, for it surrounded her for decades. Like so many of us, Vyvian lived a life forever adjusting to the whims of war, revenge, and power, most often wrought by men of power and consequence: Uther, Merlin, Arthur, Lanceloch... their names go on and on.

My grief was fueled by fear of losing her. She was the last, great woman of a generation now gone, her depth of knowledge beyond even my own. Vyvian, my mother's sister, keeper of our fragile, brutally powerful line, forever changed by the House of

11

Pendragon. And I, remaining behind, the next matron of this power we had all built.

And I had not even been able to walk her through to death, as I had with so many others in my life. Somehow, she had gone alone across that threshold, leaving me with nothing but all the love and gratitude I could no longer express to her.

Once, perhaps, she would have been attended by a dozen priestesses of Avillion, singing her to her end with Iaia's lamentations and psalms. We would have burned incense and recounted Vyvian's great deeds and trysts, drunk sacred honey wine, and walked her through into the beyond.

Instead, she had only me. Morgen, called Le Fay, last pupil of Merlin and once priestess of Avillion, daughter of death who hadn't even known when her beloved aunt had actually perished, even after holding vigil for days. I felt both a poor reflection of my inheritance, and a meagre witness to her greatness.

Vyvian slipped away so swiftly I'd not had time to fetch anyone, not even my sister Anna, who had been sharing the vigil with me. Her son Galahad and my daughter Llachlyn were due soon at court, and I hoped Vyvian would hold on long enough to see them. Especially for Llachlyn, who had grown close to her through letters—closer than I was, I knew. So few of my family extended kindness to Llachlyn, and taking Vyvian from her would be a blow, indeed.

Standing over Vyvian's bed, I tried to utter Iaia's blessings, tried to remember the correct cadence and tune, but all I could manage were strangled whispers. I pressed a kiss to her already cooling forehead and arranged her hands. Then, I pulled the sheer silk veil of Vyvian's death shroud, woven from my sister Anna's own hands, from the chest at the foot of the bed, and covered her body, standing in silence as the storm went on.

"I'm sorry," I said to Vyvian as I took the ring from her thumb, the ruby signet emblazoned with two intertwined dragons, and prepared for my duty. "As ever, Carelon demands progress."

I knew I must speak with King Arthur and inform him.

* * *

I FOUND MY brother Arthur, High King of all Braetan, alone in his study. He was poring over a stack of ribbon-strewn correspondence, the light of a fragrant beeswax candle illuminating his face. He wore his simple robes and a heavy, fur cape, the gold clasp glinting as he turned to see me.

"Morgen," he said, making to rise. "I didn't hear you come in."

"Please, sit," I said, wanting to cause as little distress as possible. "The weather is bad enough on my bones, let alone yours."

Arthur was not well. Despite my medicinal regimen, his body was wracked with aching, swelling, hives, and persistent melancholy.

Arthur gave me a tiny nod, then gestured to the seat across from him.

But I did not sit. I advanced, my hem scratching across the thick carpets, and placed Vyvian's ring on the scribe's table before him. It wobbled a moment, then was still.

We did not need words to explain. The ring had once been Merlin's and was Vyvian's sometime after his death. I always found it curious how Arthur bequeathed the role of High Counselor to Vyvian without so much as an argument, given her long-standing feud with Merlin. Perhaps he saw Merlin's early death as a personal slight, and trusting Vyvian as an act of rebellion. I never asked.

Arthur reached out to touch the gold band, gently, almost reverent. "After Merlin left," he said. Merlin *was* dead, but Arthur never said the words if he could help it. "Mordred found this in the earth below the great oak tree just a few days later. Did I ever tell you that?"

"A few times," I replied.

"I thought it a miracle, a portent, an omen—this small boy had stumbled upon one of the greatest symbols of power, handing it to his nurse as if it were just another acorn in the ground. He could have eaten it, you know. He was such an impulsive child."

He sighed, shaking his head at such notions. Mordred was no longer an impulsive child, but a reckless, impulsive adult. "Now, I do not think it a miracle. Just a coincidence."

Ever trying to be profound, Arthur left the ring where it was and glanced up at me with a sad, thoughtful look. With his beard grown long it was easy to see the resemblance to his father, Uther Pendragon, but thankfully tempered with our mother's softness and beauty. Age fell upon Arthur with a surprising delicateness, narrowing his features and sparing him the deep furrows of other men of his age.

"Perhaps," I said. "Vyvian would say it was the gods' way of telling us to move on after Merlin."

"She always knew the right thing to say. I appreciated her directness, where Merlin preferred riddles. I will miss her greatly. Did she go quietly?" Arthur turned back to his correspondence.

"She did. The sickness was brief, and I do not believe she suffered much. Death came swiftly, in the end. One day she was at her forge, a week later she was gone."

"I will send Gareth to see what can be salvaged from her workshop. I do not think our aunt would like to think of her masterworks left unattended," Arthur said.

Ah, Arthur. Ever with an eye toward swords. Vyvian had made him many in her time, but he always coveted another. Though Vyvian insisted her weapons were not magical in nature, I had my doubts. Even so, the value of those left after her death would be immeasurable. Llachlyn, who had apprenticed from a distance in small trinkets and jewelry, would want at least some of what remained.

The fire hissed across the room, flames guttering, and rather than call in a servant, I went to tend the hearth myself, adding another log to the embers.

I felt Arthur's eyes on me as I moved. After that single fateful night nearly twenty years before, we never felt the pull of desire, nor spoke candidly about its repercussions. But that union had

14

brought about my daughter. It was not, as the stories say, a passionate affair; no, I am certain Merlin's magic moved our steps, as a punishment for refusing the conjuror himself.

Merlin said Arthur's firstborn child would shatter his rule. Perhaps even take his life. The prophecy spoke of doom, and Merlin insisted the words spoke of my child. Our child.

But prophecies are rarely so easy to interpret. Vyvian, one of the very few who knew Llachlyn's parentage, believed the prophecy a three-pronged echo of Fate, spinning outcomes for Mordred, the changeling boy and child of Arthur's heart; Loholt, his bastard; and Llachlyn, our daughter. Mordred was not his child by blood, but Arthur was unaware. He knew of Llachlyn and Loholt, and Loholt was the eldest—though Arthur did not recognize him as legitimate. He was still favored publicly at court, far more than Llachlyn would ever be.

Vyvian believed each of them were capable of breaking Arthur's reign, of throwing the Round Table, and all we had worked so long for, into chaos. *Prophecies are as fickle as fish in the shadows of the lake*, she told me once. *One must not get lost in the pool's reflection, for the truth always lies deeper.*

It is why I sent Llachlyn away to Elaine, why I removed myself from her upbringing as much as possible. I never taught her the old ways, never put a sword in her hand, simply gave her a peaceful, loving upbringing in the sweeping fields of Gaul alongside her cousin Galahad. I visited her often—both when she could see me and when she could not—and watched her grow from a precocious little sprout to a headstrong, wild young woman with a propensity for making all manner of jewelry in her little forge.

Arthur never asked after Llachlyn; I never mentioned her. But despite Queen Mawra continually pushing back against the influence of Avillion and the old ways, Arthur protected Vyvian, Avillion, and me—even though he had taken the vows of the Christ and pressured his knights into doing the same, especially the sons of Anna du Lac. It had worked with Galahad and Gaheris, at least. Gareth and Gawain, I suspect, would not be so easily moved.

My half-sister Anna remained unchristened, but she was no Avillion maiden, fathered instead by Uther Pendragon after he burned down half of Braetan to steal my mother from my father, Gorlois of Cornwall. My sister Elaine of Benwick had raised Llachlyn for me, and I would be forever grateful, even if she had turned her back on our faith and proclaimed herself a Christian.

Anna and I shared the old powers, secret powers, but we were part of an ever-dwindling number, and her skill far lesser than mine. There were others skilled in sorcery and divination scattered to the fringes, but most kept far from Carelon for their own safety. We had forged our own way to communicate, but I feared our days were numbered.

"I would like a small, private ceremony for the burial," I said to him, turning around. The warmth of the fire lingered only a moment, cold rushing as I walked from the flames.

Arthur, to his credit, did not hesitate. "That can be arranged easily."

"I will have her ashes brought to Avillion, afterward."

"Yes. Of course."

"And I suppose I shall be the one to perform the death rites."

"If you wish."

I rubbed at my forehead, an ache building between my brows. There were so many threads between us, lines of Fate pulled through Carelon and across the entire country, and I was weary from having to tend to them, to have to hold so much of the burden alone. To know so much and have to keep it inside. I could feel Vyvian's absence, now, the warp and weft of the Path straining to hold.

So many secrets, so many barefaced lies. For I had done much magic, and dark deeds, indeed, at the behest of Merlin and of my own free will. Perhaps this was my penance, watching Carelon crumble before my eyes. The whole kingdom was held together with spidersilk, and I could feel the winds blowing, sense the blades coming that would tear us all asunder.

"Someone ought to tell Lance," I said, half to myself. I did not like bringing up the man before Arthur, but Vyvian had raised him from a boy, and it would have been an unkindness to her memory had I not informed him. He had not tended her death bed, even when it looked dire, nor cared to speak with her when she was hale save for when duty and courtesy required. They had quarreled long ago on matters of faith and had never healed the rift.

"Perhaps his wife is best suited," Arthur said, his voice low. "Though I rarely see her haunting the corridors these days."

"Is there anything else, Your Majesty?" I asked, not wishing to enmesh myself further in my siblings' fraught relationship

He took a deep, steadying breath, as if steeling himself. Then he said: "Morgen, you should take the ring. By rights, it should be yours. I still need a High Counselor, and I can think of no one better."

By rights, Arthur would have declared me his High Priestess immediately, not a vague title like High Counselor. But our world was not what it once was, and I did not expect him to understand.

"I have no desire to wield such a symbol. But thank you, Your Majesty." I could not stomach wearing that vile ring, as I remembered it on Merlin's hands, and recalled where his hands roamed, and how I had been defenseless to stop him.

The King did not argue. "Very well. Please, get some rest, Morgen," he said. "Thank you for telling me about Vyvian. I will miss her. The whole family will miss her. She is the last of Mother's generation. 'Tis a stark reminder we are next."

CHAPTER TWO

LLACHLYN

LLACHLYN LE FAY sat on a bench in a crowded receiving room—packed with herbs, barrels, bolts of cloth, and dusty paintings—gazing up at two of the most intimidating people she could recall seeing in her short life. Both her mother and her aunt Vyvian had told Llachlyn about her cousin, the famed Sir Gawain, of course. So she had some expectations of his size, given his reputation and adventures.

Still, he was something else altogether in person.

Legend aside, the most important element her mother had stressed was that he and his wife, Dame Ragnell, could be trusted, if anything were to befall her.

"She's my cousin, my love," said her enormous cousin to his wife, Dame Ragnell. At least, that's what they *said* was her name. People also said she was so hideous Gawain could not take her to court, but Llachlyn had snuck up on her while she was picking apples in their orchard, and although furious, Dame Ragnell was far from ugly. *Beautiful* did not begin to describe her, really.

Dame Ragnell's eyes were pale brown, nearly amber, filled with a deep knowing that reminded Llachlyn of her so recently departed Aunt Vyvian. Uncanny eyes. Her long red hair fell down her shoulders like unspun silk, and tall as she was, she stood with the presence of a goddess.

This was in contrast to her husband, who was twice as wide as Llachlyn, his features bold in their angles, as if he had been hewn from a great tree. Like his wife, his hair was red but touched with pure white at the temples and beard. His face bore the scars of a lifetime of war, but it was still kind in its expression.

It was very difficult to imagine he was Galahad's half-brother, so far apart were they in age and bearing.

"You're Morgen's daughter," Dame Ragnell said, gently. "Llachlyn."

"Yes," Llachlyn said.

"How old are you?" Gawain asked, squinting.

"Eighteen."

Gawain counted out years on his big fingers, then made a grunting noise which probably meant frustration. Llachlyn could not be certain.

"The last time I saw you," Gawain said, running his hands down his red-bearded face, "you were still cutting teeth."

"And the last time I saw you, you didn't walk with such a limp," Llachlyn said.

Dame Ragnell chuckled. "I like her."

"Were you not brought up at court, lass?" Gawain asked, giving his wife a patient but purposeful look. "Had you no one else to turn to? Someone closer, perhaps, rather than wandering all the way up here?"

"I was born at Carelon," Llachlyn explained. "But when I was seven, Mother sent me from Carelon to Kerduel. I spent most of my time with your youngest brother, Galahad, and our Aunt Elaine and Sir Hector de Mares, in Benwick."

"But Elaine sent you back to Carelon recently?" Dame Ragnell asked.

"Sir *Hector* sent me back to Carelon, since Aunt Elaine has no real interest in me these days, along with Galahad and—and a squire." She had to try to keep Percival out of it for now. "After Lady Vyvian's death, you see—we were meant to arrive in time for the funeral, but our ship was blown off course."

By the time they arrived at court, not only was Vyvian two weeks dead, but Llachlyn's own mother had vanished without so much as a word.

Llachlyn swallowed back on a hard pebble of emotion. She did not want to weep like a child before Sir Gawain. Though she and her mother were not close, Llachlyn still felt the sting of her disappearance deeply.

No, weeping would not do. Small as Llachlyn was, everyone expected her to be weak, sweet, and meek. But there was steel in her; Aunt Vyvian had always said as much.

Llachlyn continued, filling up the silence. "It was important for Galahad to be there, since his own father was raised by the Lady Vyvian. And sure enough, he got all the attention the second we got there. He's very good."

"Good at what?" Gawain asked.

As if he didn't know. Llachlyn snorted. "Oh, *everything*. But especially the Tournament. Better than Lanceloch, I think. Son of Lanceloch this, son of Lanceloch that. You'd think they were planning to erect a whole bloody monument to him the way they've all gone on about him. It's a bit nauseating."

"Now *I* like her," Gawain said to his wife.

Finally, they were warming to her. Llachlyn found the more honest she was with the thoughts in her head, the more people trusted her. Or, at least, the more she could figure out if *she* could trust *them*. That was how she had become such close friends with her aunt Vyvian. One letter, cordial and proper, had eventually turned into a short lifetime's worth of correspondence, and trust. And true, glimmering friendship, bolstered by their common love of smithing.

But she was gone now. Gone forever. All Llachlyn had left were the small trinkets she'd learned to forge with Vyvian's instruction and occasional gifts of ore from Carelon. They'd only seen one another four times since she'd left for Kerduel.

Llachlyn turned the ring on her finger, a rather rustic band she had made and laid with a small green peridot. The feeling of the rough metal under her thumb was a soothing balm when she was most anxious.

Dame Ragnell leaned forward, her shining red hair slipping down across her shoulder. "Do you mind telling us what happened—how you ended up all the way up here and without proper escort?" Her voice was low, smoky. Llachlyn quite liked listening to her.

Llachlyn took a deep breath. She didn't want to talk about this part, but honesty built bridges. "When we finally arrived at court, Mother was gone. She left no notes, and no one had seen her since the night after Vyvian's funeral."

"Morgen le Fay is missing," Dame Ragnell said softly.

"Did you go to the King?" Gawain asked, a little stiffly.

Of course they would know. Everyone knew. Everyone whispered. Llachlyn was certain her own parentage was the very reason her mother had sent her to Kerduel. Her own existence was the King's greatest shame.

"I could have, but you see, I was dressed as a page to Galahad, so no one knew who I was. At least, not at first."

"So you were purposefully hiding from everyone at Carelon?"

"It's easier, sometimes, not being who you are. At least for a while."

Gawain and his wife exchanged a glance at each other. "But that couldn't last forever, could it?" he asked.

"One day, Queen Mawra recognized me, and she was so very angry. She said I should have been put in a nunnery a long time ago, that I was a demon—that my mother was a succubus, and worse. She was so angry, the vein in the middle of her forehead was pulsing."

For some reason, this made Dame Ragnell cackle.

Llachlyn continued. "She had guards and priests, and I knew I was outnumbered. So I pretended I might consent, but when she got close to me, I bit her—which when looking back is probably not the best choice to prove I wasn't some sort of demon. Anyway, that's when she threw me in a cell."

Dame Ragnell bit on her lips to keep from laughing. An odd reaction to just admitting to savagely attacking the High Queen of all Braetan.

"How did you escape the cell?" Gawain asked. "I can't imagine it was easy."

Llachlyn grinned. "I am resourceful, and I do have friends. So, when I escaped, I headed north. Mother and Aunt Vyvian said if I was ever in peril I should come here. So that's where we went."

"We?" They both said it at the same time.

"Us!"

Percival's blond head rose just above the wavering glass. His face was still smeared with blood from their last encounter with the wolves, and his eyes went wide when he realized everyone was looking at him. This was not his cue, and Llachlyn had to roll her eyes at his ridiculous entrance.

"They're spreading. Like wild hares in the spring," Gawain groaned, and went to the window and pulled up Percival by the collar, dragging him inside as easily as if he were a sack of hay.

Llachlyn had never seen a show of strength so impressive. Of course, she'd heard the many tales of Sir Gawain, but, like many, hadn't really believed them. They said her mother had black wings and snakes in her hair, after all, and she knew for a fact neither was true.

Gawain glowered. "Any more of you, or is this the extent of your little band?"

A gangly thing with pale hair and bright eyes, Percival made no real attempt at fighting back, but crumbled to the floor near Llachlyn, breathing hard. He may have mumbled a few hasty words of apology, but none of it was particularly clear.

"Tell us who you are, boy, and why you've attached yourself to my cousin," Gawain said, towering over Percival.

"I'm Percival of Pellam," he said from the ground, hands held protectively over his head. "Son of Pellinore."

"A prince?" Dame Ragnell asked. For the first time since Llachlyn met her, she was truly surprised.

"Ah, perhaps in name, but not in deed," Percival said, finding his charm once again. He could talk his way out of nearly anything. "My father is loyal now to the High King and neither I nor my siblings stand to inherit those titles. And even if I did, there are seven other brothers before my claim, most far older and more accomplished."

Gawain stretched out his massive hand and helped Percival stand. Llachlyn had always thought Percival was tall, but he looked like a child next to her cousin. "That's not necessarily a bad thing. But you have a significant amount of explaining to do, and fast."

Percival looked over to Llachlyn and she nodded to him.

"Gawain, my love," she said to her husband, putting her hand gently on his chest to get his attention. It worked. The look of fondness in his expression was enough to make Llachlyn's own heart ache. "We ought to feed our guests before we are accused of a lack of hospitality. Clearly, they have been through a great deal to get here, and we can certainly spare some hot water and fresh clothes. I will have Prydwen put together an afternoon meal before our discussions."

For a moment Llachlyn thought Gawain would protest, but he softened further under his wife's touch, and relented.

CHAPTER THREE

GAWAIN

GAWAIN'S WIFE WAS angry with him, and likely, the world. And she had every right to be.

They had been enjoying a deep autumn harvest day, preparing for the onslaught of apples coming into the barn to be pressed and stored for the long winter ahead. Though they had been married for over a decade now, they still found comfort in the simple tasks of running the manor of Thistlewood and its surrounding land and villages. Theirs was no longer a life of adventure—at least, not visibly so—but it was happy and peaceful and comfortable. He loved and treasured every moment.

But escaped young folk from Carelon—that did not bode well. Indeed, it threatened the safety and secrecy of Thistlewood. Their marriage was not one sanctioned by Gawain's uncle, King Arthur. Dame Ragnell was far more than she seemed. Oh, Thistlewood was hers by right, but only because her own mother, together with Gawain's mother, had arranged their forbidden union right under Arthur's nose. If the King knew Gawain had married Hwyfar of Avillion, the sister to his own Queen Mawra, the consequences would be dire. Such flagrant disobedience would be seen as treasonous and a sincere blow, not just to Arthur's already tenuous hold on his knights, but to the very lines of succession.

Hwyfar paced their hall as servants came and prepared the

massive, oak-hewn table for a sizable meal. Almost no one came to visit Thistlewood, save Gawain's brother Gareth and Sir Palomydes, and though he felt an air of excitement in the house, it was mingled with unease.

Just like before a battle, Gawain realized, as he lowered himself into the chair at the head of the table. Today, his knee didn't hurt as much as it sometimes did, but his back was another story. If it wasn't one thing, it was another.

"I'm not upset about hosting family, Gawain," Hwyfar said, pausing by the hearth to lay her hands upon the mantel. "But I am fretfully worried about the timing. Morgen has never been gone this long, and if she was missing from Carelon since Vyvian's death, then I do not know what to think. Without her…"

Her voice trailed off and Gawain's heart sank for his wife.

Hwyfar practiced the old ways. Her methods of communication with her fellow priestesses were far more complex than just sending letters back and forth: it was a vast network of mirrors and spells stretching across the kingdom and beyond. He'd seen a magic mirror, once, in his mother's room, and understood their significance. Hwyfar used a scrying bowl to speak with her small and fierce group of women, and until recently, all had been well.

Gawain watched as his wife worried her full, pink lips between her teeth. That was mightily distracting. "She has gone away before, but not to send word to Llachlyn seems more than cruel. Unless…"

"I don't like that word. Unless what?"

"Unless Morgen no longer trusts the Circle of Nine." Hwyfar dropped her voice. "With Vyvian gone, there could have been some conflict I was not aware of. Modrun has been erratic at best, and Elayne does not always do as she's asked, especially when it comes to her treasures. Vyvian told us Arthur was again looking for the *graal*."

The Circle of Nine was a secret society comprised of the most powerful sorceresses in the realm. They were united in their mission to preserve the old ways and keep the *graal* from Arthur. He had supported Hwyfar in her connection to them, feeling she was safer for their collaboration. Never had he imagined that one among their ranks might resort to treachery.

Gawain's skin crawled with the idea that any of those women, his mother included, might have brought their secrets to Arthur.

"That is a grave thought," he said.

"She could have been happily ensconced in Cornwall if your uncle hadn't disinherited her years ago," Hwyfar snapped. "His own sister! All because the King is afraid of ghosts."

"Arthur is not afraid of ghosts, but he is afraid of the political ramifications of drawing attention to Tintagel. That's different."

She leveled a scathing look at him. "And that is only due to Merlin's damned prophecies and Uther Pendragon's incapacity to keep his prick in his—"

"Yes, yes, I know. Our fathers and our father's fathers are all monsters. I cannot disagree with you there. But that has nothing to do with Llachlyn."

"Doesn't it?" Hwyfar dropped her voice and strode toward her husband.

Gawain swallowed back the uncomfortable feeling, the rising tension between them. Both he and Hwyfar had lived in Carelon when Llachlyn was born, when her mother Morgen had fallen pregnant. The rumors, they suspected, were true: Llachlyn was the unfortunate child of a union between Morgen and King Arthur. Hwyfar insisted there was some sorcery involved, but frankly, Gawain didn't like thinking about it, magic or not.

Hwyfar kneeled before her husband, putting her hands on his knees, and gazing up into his face. It was hard for Gawain to focus on anything else when she did that, so enraptured was he with her. Just the feel of her hands on him was a greater comfort than a warm fire or the finest wine.

"Llachlyn was kept from court, swept away to Kerduel," Hwyfar said.

"Fosterage is no unusual thing," Gawain said, trying to make light of Hwyfar's inescapable logic. They had spoken of this in the past—who among their family hadn't? But Gawain had never expected Llachlyn to appear at their doorstep like this. A woman grown, and with those *eyes*. He knew those eyes as he knew his own face. If Arthur *was* her father, the poor child would need their protection.

Hwyfar tried again. "Queen Mawra hates her. Tried to ferret her away to a nunnery. The daughter of Morgen le Fay! That alone should tell you there is a far more insidious reason for her distaste. For Queen Mawra to behave so recklessly does not bode well—unless she is not afraid of Morgen's intervention at all."

The servants were bringing in more food, the aroma of bread and cider wafting up toward Gawain, making his stomach twinge in anticipation. But his wife was right.

He pulled Hwyfar up, bringing her knuckles to his lips and kissing her gently. Though she was still frustrated, she relaxed somewhat. He loved that he could still do that, give her peace amidst her fury.

Gawain lowered his voice. "We will take one mystery at a time, my love. It may have been a misunderstanding. She's a headstrong girl, just like her mother. And there's the lad to consider in this, too. He's a king's son. Surely Arthur ought to have kept a better eye on him."

"Arthur has a long, sordid history of not taking care when he ought, especially when young women are involved," Hwyfar said. She reached for Gawain's cheek and cupped it, tenderly swiping her thumb across his beard. "Sometimes negligence is a message unto itself. I should know better than anyone."

CHAPTER FOUR

HWYFAR

AT LEAST THE two young runaways cleaned up well. Hwyfar had to give credit to Prydwen and Alwine for their quick attention to the new and extremely unexpected guests. It was difficult to believe they were children of court at first, what with all the scrapes, blood, and tattered clothing. Good soap and water, however, did miracles to reveal the pink, freckled skin on Llachlyn, and Percival's riot of golden curls and quick, almost familiar smile.

Llachlyn was small for her age, but sprightly, her hair a sooty kind of deep umber, straight and slick. Percival was all height and bones, but already filling out in the way boys his age seemed to do overnight. With the right training, he could be rather formidable. Except Hwyfar had the sense the boy was far more suited for the scriptorium than the battlefield. He had the most delicate hands, and curious, warm brown eyes.

Just as the first bread was passed about, Hwyfar decided she ought to begin the conversation.

"Where I'm from, we believe there is a certain power in eating and discussing matters at the same time," she said to Llachlyn. "It is said we think with our hearts far more when we are gathered around sharing food, and therefore have more honest conversations."

Percival took a tremendous bite out of the braided bread he'd been given, eyes closing in unrestrained enjoyment, and let out a long, contented noise before going for more.

Llachlyn laughed through her nose. "If that's the case I'll do all the talking. Percy barely stops breathing when he's eating. Which is quite a welcome change from his endless prattling."

Percival frowned around the mouthful of bread. He'd already proven Llachlyn's point, however, and so he simply went for some wine instead.

"My husband is of a similar inclination when it comes to enjoying a meal," Hwyfar said, with a look over to Gawain. He, too, enthusiastically sliced a slab of cheese on his plate, which was already fit to bursting with bread and fruit.

"I do, too, stop to breathe when I eat," Gawain said, jaw set in defiance. Then he gave her a wolfish grin. "Though, when I'm enjoying some *particular* dishes, you do complain piteously when I come up for air."

Hwyfar was not the kind of woman easily embarrassed by such a comment, but that sort of banter was best kept to their more comfortable guests, or in private. She glared momentarily at her husband before rearranging her knife and composing herself.

Thankfully, neither Llachlyn nor Percival seemed to notice, so intent they were on the steaming creamy onion soup Eadgyth ladled onto their plates.

"All that to say," Hwyfar said, voice as smooth and welcoming as she could manage. She poured herself a glass of the manor's own fresh cider. "The table is yours. Please, if you would, share your adventures."

Llachlyn glanced at Percival, then puffed out her cheeks as she let out a long breath. She may have been eighteen, but her size and her expressions made her seem much younger. "Well, if I recall, the last you heard was I narrowly escaped going to a nunnery. We must go back to why."

Percival froze, soup halfway to his mouth, then put down the spoon and set it aside. "The soup is delicious," he said. "And I must apologize. I should have come straight in rather than let

Llachlyn do all the talking, but I was a bit worried that without ties of blood you might consider my motives untoward."

There was something so familiar in his mien, and Hwyfar could not say what it was.

No matter: it would have to wait.

"*Are* they untoward?" Gawain asked. The way he leaned forward in his chair, commanding his side of the table, was a threat in and of itself. There were few men in the whole kingdom who could rival her husband for size and strength, and he knew how to use them both. She did love when he did not hold his stature back. "I've met many a prince in my day, and I'm ashamed to say it did very little to confirm their honor on the whole."

"No—no, Sir Gawain, I promise you—we are great friends, and that is all," Percival said, hands flapping as if to save himself from Gawain's mere presence. "But I do owe everything to Llachlyn for rescuing me."

Hwyfar stifled a chuckle. "I know all about rescuing princes. This one needs it more often than he would like to admit."

Gawain scoffed at his wife. "It was just a few times."

What Hwyfar wanted to do was go to her husband and have him wrap his arms around her as they slowly made their way back to their room and reveled in the feeling of their bodies together in passion and power. It was how they spent most of their evenings, unconcerned with the tangled web of court politics and gossip. This long decade had been the happiest of her life, happier than she could ever imagine—happier than she thought possible in matrimony, of all things.

Alas, Hwyfar knew their peace was a borrowed one, even if she had hoped it would linger longer. These young folk were sweet enough on the outside, but her magic—though muted since Vyvian's death—prickled in warning. She did not have the Sight, but she knew a shifting of the winds of Fate when she felt it. And these two brought with them a tempest.

"If I hadn't helped you out of those brambles last week, you'd likely still be there," she reminded Gawain. He relented, folding his arms. "But we digress. Percival was telling us his tale."

Percival looked back and forth between Hwyfar and her husband before swallowing and folding his hands over his stomach. "I was sent to Benwick a few years ago, to train alongside Galahad in the summers, since we're close enough in age—that's where I met Llachlyn. Then it was decided I would go with them both when Galahad was finally presented at court last month. Except, no one knew about Llachlyn when we arrived. We called her Godric, and it was a merry ruse. With a slouched cap and a bit of a stoop, she did look the part."

"How were you found out, Llachlyn?" Gawain asked his diminutive cousin. "You didn't speak to any others in the family? My mother still lives there, and surely, she would have recognized you."

Llachlyn frowned, just a little, and Hwyfar could tell she was sifting through her thoughts, deciding exactly what to share. "I was Godric to just about everyone. Who remembers Llachlyn, anyway? The last time I was at court, I was still small enough to fit in a cupboard."

Hwyfar did not press, but she could just imagine how difficult it would be to arrive at Carelon with Morgen missing. Arthur had never formally acknowledged Llachlyn, and she had no other contacts at court. Lady Anna was a commanding presence, but rarely left her chambers. Vyvian was dead. Llachlyn would have been utterly alone; far better to hedge her bets as Godric, protected by her cousin and Percival, than among the women of Mawra's court.

Hwyfar took a large platter of poached eggs and partridge cakes from Eadgyth, then passed them to her husband. "I can somewhat understand Queen Mawra's impatience for Llachlyn. She's never liked it when people, especially young women, behave outside of what she deems appropriate, not to mention those outside the faith. Impersonating a man would be an affront to her."

She would have liked to explain she knew this from very firsthand experience, but unfortunately neither of their guests knew the extent of her relationship with Queen Mawra. Alas, the idea of the Queen imprisoning two young folk, both with ties to the crown, did not seem as improbable as it ought. In recent years, Queen Mawra had grown ever more paranoid and officious. Especially where religion was concerned. Or so Palomydes had reported, and Hwyfar trusted him entirely.

And as Llachlyn was the daughter of Morgen le Fay, she very well could have considered her a threat. A demon, indeed!

Hwyfar's heart ached. Llachlyn ought to have gone directly to Avillion instead of Gaul. She ought to have been able to communicate easily with her mother, her aunts, her family. Hwyfar could not understand Morgen's intentions at all. She was owed an inheritance of power and a good deal more instruction for surviving court, no matter her rumored parentage.

"We were just being foolish," Percival said morosely.

"Being foolish? You're of an age where foolishness is nigh on a requirement," Hwyfar said with a laugh. "Did you say anything to offend the Queen?"

Percival rubbed at the back of his head, wincing as he did so. "It's a bit of a ridiculous story, really," he said, glancing again to Llachlyn for support.

"Go ahead, boy," Gawain said. "We are here to listen. You're safe from the Queen here." Hwyfar could tell her husband's impatience was rising, though. He was no friend of the Queen's as it was, and she stood accused of maligning his family member. Try as he might to live a life apart from court politics, the man could not let family insults go.

Percival licked his lips, his gaze darting from face to face around the table. "It all happened so fast. There we were, celebrating Galahad's good week in the sparring ring."

"Celebrating a little too much," Llachlyn said.

"We were *very* drunk," Percival said sheepishly. "Galahad, Llachlyn, and I, we were careless and loud... There's a balcony, just outside Galahad's quarters, and we did not realize how far our voices carried."

"My old room. Yes, I spent more than one drunken evening there in my day. It's best to shut the windows, though," Gawain said, trying to keep the conversation as comfortable as possible. "Go on."

"One of the Queen's own, Sygremors I believe, overheard us referring to 'Godric' as Llachlyn. And then she nearly fell off the balcony. After that, they rounded us up and threw us in the dungeon to teach us a lesson about temperance. It *started* as a few hours, but then, when we failed to show how sorry we were, she extended our tenure." Percival shivered and added, "She said drunkenness was a sin, that we were an affront to Christ. The Queen has her priest spies everywhere."

"In her defense, we were *very* loud," Llachlyn said with wide eyes.

"I hardly think some drunken antics would be enough to convince her to keep you in the dungeon," Hwyfar said. "You'd hardly be the first to behave in such a way."

"When the Queen came to us and realized just who we were—particularly who I was—she became incensed. That's when she threatened to send me to the nunnery, and I bit her." Llachlyn did not seem bothered one mote about her behavior, and Hwyfar had to admire her pluck. She'd had much occasion in life to wish she could bite Mawra, too.

"Galahad was there with us the first night," Percival continued, looking longingly at his plate. "The cells are dark and dank, and they kept us close together. Maybe that explains it."

"Explains what?" Sir Gawain asked.

"We weren't really in trouble until we all had the same dream," Llachlyn said, her green eyes flashing under her bold, dark brows.

"All three of you?" Hwyfar asked. She could feel the tingling pressure of her magic waking again, a sense of foreboding in the air. Gawain met her eyes, concern in his expression. He could feel it, too.

Percival nodded. "Yes. We began talking about it, first thing in the morning as we nursed our headaches. The guards, apparently, were listening and went straight to the Queen. That's when they dragged us back, bodily, to the Queen's apartments and questioned all of us. We described what we saw in detail, not knowing the significance, and Her Majesty became even more furious. But when the Queen asked Galahad, he…"

"He said it was a vision from God, a *miracle*," Llachlyn finished, making a face like she'd just drunk sour milk. "We knew better, of course."

"What did you all see, lass?" Gawain asked. He was sitting eerily still. Battle hardiness was still part of his body's memories, Hwyfar knew. No doubt, he was struggling to keep his temper in check.

Llachlyn stabbed her quail with a fork. "A shield. A glowing shield, made of pale metal and gleaming with red stones, rising from the middle of a lake."

"Not just a shield," Percival said, with that scholar's air in his voice again. He held up an instructive finger. "A *graal*."

CHAPTER FIVE

MORGEN

I NEVER RELISHED speaking with Lanceloch du Lac, but I knew my sister Anna needed my support given the current circumstance. Though they were married some fifteen years now, their relationship was as cold and dead as Merlin's stones. What began as a marriage of convenience, once holding some promise of love—and indeed, which gave them their son Galahad—now was barely concealed hatred.

So, rather than force Anna to speak to Lanceloch, I decided to bring the news of Vyvian's death myself.

I did not have many friends I could trust, nor did I often rely on the kindness of others. It was better to be beholden to no one; besides, I have always found far more comfort in wresting control of situations myself. Then failure is mine alone.

Still, I was fiercely protective of my little sister, and glad to save her the heartache of enduring Lanceloch's moods and whims.

After some significant searching, I found Arthur's prized knight alone in the armory, bent over a worktable with a full suit of armor before him. Though no smith himself, having been raised by Vyvian but never apprenticed, he was still fastidious about armoring details. With Galahad preparing for his next tournament, I imagined his father wanted to ensure he had the proper equipment.

I was not surprised to recognize the 'sword as cross' sigil Lanceloch had adopted since his conversion some years before upon the gleaming breastplate before him. Though the cross predated the Christians by a considerable amount, he and Arthur were forever seeing crosses and symbols on every corner. Especially when it came to swords.

In the years since I'd known him, Lanceloch had retained his vigor in an almost uncanny way. Though his temples were grey, and his eyes lined with the passing of time, he was still as spry and lean as when he first appeared at court.

And nearly murdered my nephew Gawain in the tournament. That detail was hard for anyone who had seen it to forget. I never let go of the knowledge, knowing for all his professed gentleness and temperance, there lay a murderous monster inside of him, incapable of mercy—and rarely let out.

"She's gone, then," Lanceloch said, not looking up at me.

That prescience startled me, but I made no indication of my surprise. Instead, I sat down on one of the smooth wooden benches across from him and spoke softly. "I wish I had better tidings. But yes. Vyvian du Lac is gone."

He was not simply adjusting the leather findings on the breastplate before him, I saw now. He was embossing the leather with little designs, too small for me to see. I could not imagine how he could do such delicate work in the dim light. Except he was Lanceloch du Lac, and he thrived on adversity.

Lanceloch sighed deeply, splaying his hands upon the wooden surface of the table before looking over at me. His eyes, a strange honey hue, were dark in the candlelight. "I would be happy to arrange a Mass for her."

My stomach roiled at the thought, defensiveness rising in me like a sudden tide. I kept my composure, though. "I doubt she would have appreciated it, but you may, of course, mourn in your own way should the need arise."

"What does that mean?" He cocked his head at me, assessing me as a predator watches his prey.

I glared back. I might not have been a warrior of brawn, but I was no trembling hare. If Merlin was an owl, Vyvian was a

36

hawk. And I, though smaller, was yet a crow. Small, canny, and clever. And more resilient than the rest put together.

"You know what it means," I said. "Vyvian was a priestess of Avillion, as were her sister and mother before her. Your religious pageantry did not impress her in life and would be an insult in death."

He took a deep breath, nostrils flaring. I avoided speaking to Lanceloch about faith whenever humanly possible, but in matters of death and respect it was inevitable. We shared a home by necessity and a family by marriage. That was plenty for Fate to connect us time and again.

"Morgen, you are outnumbered here in Carelon. I said as much to Vyvian the last time we spoke. If everyone else can see it, why can't you, given your wisdom and power?"

I did not want to have this conversation with him. I did not want to have *any* conversation with him. "Lanceloch, not everyone is moved by the stories of your priests."

"They are not stories. They are guides to a happier, more complete life. Forgiveness. Peace. Contentment. And release from the torment of Hell. It is perplexing to me how you would side with such ill spirits, and continue in your denial."

This, coming from a man who had once pledged his body and soul to Ayr, living a vow of chastity. A man who now, despite his professions to the contrary, regularly tupped the Queen, and who had once loved the King in the same way.

"I do not need a religion bent upon self-hatred and the snuffing out of all other beliefs. I am as the goddess made me, and that is complete and whole. And she most certainly does not threaten us with an eternity of hellfire to terrorize me to belief."

No, I did not know precisely what awaited me after death, but I knew the borders of it—the shape of it. I had stood upon the threshold of death and carried others across for decades. I had held dying babes while their mothers bled their last; I had watched children pass suddenly, while the old lingered. And all I knew was that dying, when it came, was as natural as living.

Lanceloch sneered, flapping his hand at me. "You're as impossible as Vyvian is—was." I saw that his eyes danced with tears; so, he was not entirely without a heart. "I will add her to my prayers, and perhaps I may spare her some eternal torment."

Never, in all my years, had I flaunted my power before Lanceloch. Mine was not a magic of extravagance as Merlin's had been, but one of private study and connection. Yes, the old conjurer had added to my knowledge during my time under his tuition, but I also held secrets old and strange, and the magic in my blood was as rare and powerful as any. Magic he never bothered to learn, believing it the purview of women and the weak-minded.

Perhaps it was my grief that led me to such a careless action, but upon hearing his judgement of Vyvian—the woman who had raised him for two decades during her own imprisonment and then, when exonerated, dedicated herself to Arthur's court upon Merlin's death—I pulled the flames on all the torches in the armory, suffusing them with a twinkling emerald hue. They looked like claws of fire, reaching for Lanceloch, and reflecting in my eyes.

I was the abyss. I was death. I was the end.

I always had been. Call me demon, call me damned. I cared not.

Lanceloch crossed himself furiously, but did not flee in fear. Nor had I expected him to.

"If I ever hear you speak of Vyvian in such a way again, I will unleash far more than these theatrics," I said, leaning over on the table and speaking calmly, coldly, to him. "You dishonor her here, and you dishonored her before. She loved you like a son, cared for you, gave you joy and freedom and built your strength day by day when she could have rejected you, rejected your mother's plea for her help, rejected Merlin's portents. By all accounts she should have."

A fleeting look of shame passed his features, his lips pursing under my verbal assault. "I'm sorry. That was ugly of me. I know you loved her, too, Morgen. I simply thought I had more time."

"Only a fool ignores time."

"Then the greatest fool am I." Lanceloch turned back to his work.

The fires dimmed and I, exhausted, fell back a step. I could not look at him, could not tolerate his constant emotional jostling. As ever, when confronted with his temper, Lanceloch turned inward, blaming himself. No doubt he would bruise his own soul with self-hatred for days.

"I will be holding a small ceremony in the crypts," I said, forcing myself to say the words though I wished I did not have to. "At sunrise. The day after next. Should you decide, you may attend. Arthur will be there."

He nodded but gave no indication one way or another. I hoped it meant he would stay. The idea of him postulating and proselytizing at her funeral made me incandescent with rage.

I made to leave, and he stood, drawing my attention away.

"He will not be able to protect you forever, Morgen," Lanceloch said, voice cold and almost apologetic. "Be careful with your so-called *theatrics*. There are many at court far less tolerant of your ways than I."

"I am quite capable of protecting myself," I said, gathering up my skirts, and departing as regally as I could manage, back to the fresh air of the courtyard and sparring ring.

Once outside, my breath came in heavy, gulping rasps, and I fell to my knees, stifling the sob that needed release by biting the thick wool of my cloak. Grief fell over me, inexorable and heavy as a lead coffin.

Vyvian was gone, truly gone, and the world simply plodded on without her.

For the first time in ages, I wished I could speak to Merlin, to ask him what it was all for. Could he ever have foreseen this great change at court? Did he know I would live to see the slow, painful dismantling of all he had worked for? See my sisters scattered to the winds? Every day I heard of more violence against them, and I was powerless to help. I had no love for Merlin, but I had once believed in his vision. Peace, unity, a banner of common purpose. Even if the Pendragons had bought it with blood, rape, and deceit.

All the things I had done for him and for Arthur, and for what? The dark deeds in the shadows, bribery and blackmail. No, I had not twisted the knives myself, but I had sharpened them and placed them in hands that could. I could not enumerate all my deeds even if I tried to. I had forgotten half of them already.

Galahad would arrive at court soon. And Llachlyn with him. She was a woman grown, now, and they were fast friends. Such bonds gave me hope for the next generation.

For the future looked bleak. The Sight was dimming across the land, and temples fell to give rise to new chapels and churches, even while we fought to preserve the vestiges of our power.

And I was getting older.

She is the last of Mother's generation. 'Tis a stark reminder we are next.

I RELIEVED THE young priestess holding vigil for Vyvian, now accoutered with the implements of preparation of the body, in her old chambers. I brought herbs and water from Iaia's Well, perfumed oils, and hawk feathers. I also brought Vyvian's own sword, the battered and unembellished weapon she had used to train Lanceloch. Perhaps she would not be remembered as a warrior, but given she had trained the greatest warrior of the age, I felt it appropriate.

How many bodies had I wrapped in their final weeds? Too many to count, some so small they'd breathed but once before going to the gods. Or not at all. It had become as welcome and expected as birth, as each new season, familiar to me as the sound of my own heartbeat.

Yet this time, it was different. I could not banish the memory of my mother's body; how I, a girl of barely fifteen, had kept watch over her, day in and day out, until she was gone, while my own sisters were too afraid to sit with her. How I kept watching her chest, hoping she would breathe again upon her royal bed, dying, counting down my heartbeats until the silk stopped rustling.

Who would I go to, now Vyvian was gone? She was the eldest and wisest of all of us. Keen and clever and loving, ruthless when she had to be, and a skilled smith the likes of which we would never again see. When I was tired, Vyvian told me to rest; when I was morose, she showed me the joy of working with my hands to till the soil or to stoke the fires in the forge. When the burden of my gifts felt too great to shoulder, she let me sleep in her room and brought me tea and told me stories.

And yet I could not help but be angry, too. For Vyvian had left us just as we needed her most. Arthur was closer to the *graal* than he ever had been, while Avillion was fading to the mists. Over a dozen priestesses of the Isle had already converted to the new faith, and fewer and fewer came to learn, despite our efforts.

No matter how often I had tried to push Vyvian, to warn her about what was happening, she was not moved. Though powerful, her guidance to Arthur in the last years had been far more diplomatic than supernatural. She had said it was my inheritance, not hers, to define what power meant for the next season.

But I felt detached from the world around me, and utterly helpless to fight the oncoming storm.

The door creaked open, and I turned to scold whoever was intruding upon me and my thoughts, but I stopped.

It was Anna, my sister.

"I came as soon as I heard," she said, sweeping into the room and taking in Vyvian's unmoving form.

"You don't have to be here, Anna. I can do this on my own," I said.

My half-sister Anna du Lac stood far taller than I, thanks to the blood of Uther Pendragon in her veins, but had grown painfully thin over the years, a result of melancholy and the price of magic. Of all my sisters, we, together, had worked the most powerful spells, even though she was no priestess of Avillion or otherwise trained. Anna still possessed great gifts bestowed by the gods, strange and subtle but never to be underestimated.

After all, without her, Merlin would yet live. I had wanted him dead nearly as much as she had, and indeed I had given her the keys to that careful vengeance; but I wondered often what price we would pay for our treachery, especially regarding Prince Mordred and Percival of Pellam. Only we knew that Percival was Gweyn's natural son, begotten by her paramour, Sir Lanval; Mordred was the true son of Anna's handmaiden from Orkney and, I guessed, the result of a ravishment at the hands of Lot of Orkney. She had assisted me in switching them at their birth, at Merlin's request, to appease one of his long-reaching prophecies and to hide Gweyn's infidelity.

It had not been difficult to convince King Pellas he had another bastard; he had so many already, some even knights of the Table Round. That man seemed to collect them like a magpie collecting baubles. That had been the easiest part of the entire ruse, and all to further twist Merlin's attempts to change Arthur's fate—*The first child born of Arthur shall bring his end*. Merlin believed it was a threat, and he was obsessed with thwarting it—even using it against me, when Llachlyn was born.

Still, of all the sins in my life, all the desperate and premeditated alterations of fate I had committed, this one, above all, bothered me. For Percival had found his way to Gaul, where he was squire to my nephew Galahad and friend to my daughter Llachlyn. And it had been Vyvian who'd arranged it, without my knowledge. Now, they were all fast friends—if one could call Llachlyn and Galahad friends, what with their competitive natures and uneasy childhoods—and I knew Fate would not hold back the tide of that truth forever.

I looked over at my youngest sister, noting her hair, now white as my own, and the intricate braids twisted about her head reminded me, indeed, of the threads of Fate all around us. She wore simple clothing but of sumptuous make, her bony hands protruding from the edges of the fabric at her wrists, glittering with golden rings.

Anna moved slowly, brushing her fingers across the shroud as she came around the bed, thoughtful and measured. How rarely her mask slipped, her carefully maintained visage of imperious calm.

Then, with a cry, she fell to her knees before our aunt, overcome with emotion to see her body so displayed. Grief was like an assassin to the heart, sometimes. I let her weep alone, giving space to the mourning. We had not just lost a member of our family, but also of our sisterhood.

"I don't think she ever warmed to me," Anna said, looking up at me with her pale eyes, red-rimmed. "But she helped me, anyway. Despite what Merlin had done to her, despite my fumbling attempts at magic. She trusted me. She saw something in me, no matter my murderous father."

"I think she saw some*one* she loved, and cherished, and grieved for," I said, putting my hand on Anna's sharp shoulder. Goddess, the woman was so slight. "There is much of Igraine of Avillion in you, Anna, and Vyvian never stopped missing her sister."

"I can't understand how she could have come here, how she could have lived in this castle knowing what had happened to Mother," Anna said. Her voice was so small, ragged with anger and sorrow. "She lived among the wolves, every day."

I thought of that often, too. Perhaps more than most, as one of Igraine and Gorlois's daughters doing the very same. Our answer has been simple: conformity was safety. We all knew what could happen to women who resisted. My beautiful, powerful mother served as a warning to all. And was my life so terrible? I had given much, suffered much, but I had more power and influence than any woman of my age.

I walked to the basin and straightened my implements once again, breathing in the deep mint and earthy musk of the herbal mixture. Memories of dozens of rites, performed in just this way, flitted through my mind. They were with me, now, keeping me company.

"Vyvian once told me she wished to wreak vengeance on Uther Pendragon, to curse his family and generations to come," I said, dipping one of the long silk cloths I'd brought in golden oil, smelling lavender. "But Arthur was born, and then you, and to curse the generations to come would have meant doing so to her own flesh and blood."

And some of us were cursed enough, as it was. At least I had been spared the agony of an early marriage, but Anna had not. At twelve, she had been sent to marry Lot of Orkney, and though she never told me precisely what had happened between them, I had helped her rid the world of his pestilence. Never have I regretted it a day.

Just another murder I coaxed along the web of fate.

"Gawain has Uther Pendragon's eyes," Anna said, taking Vyvian's hand in her own. "Gooseberry green. I cannot imagine looking your nephew in the face as she did and seeing the man who raped your sister and broke a kingdom to keep her—No. We are not merely who we are born; we can be made again. We can choose otherwise."

I let Anna sift through her emotions. It was not uncommon for those in the throes of grief to move from one feeling to another; goddess knew, I had over the last few hours.

But now I was Morgen, daughter of death. Merlin had never ceased to remind me.

Your power is great, but fairly useless. It is a magic that slips into the shadows, unseen and unfelt. You will impress no one with such darkness, daughter of death, unless you push yourself to learn more.

"Gawain is proof of that," I said to her gently. "He is a good man, but he was not always so. Given his father and grandfather, it is no small feat. He chose otherwise—he chose our family."

"Yes. But he has also given up so much, suffered so needlessly. If the world was fair, he would be here, as he ought to be, at Arthur's right hand—and Hwyfar with him," Anna said, dropping her head. "Carelon is not the same without them."

"You have given them ten years of happiness," I reminded her. "That is not without value."

"I know. And some days I wish I had not. Of all my children, he…"

She had been scarcely thirteen when Gawain was born and had thrown her focus in life to raising him, protecting him from Lot of Orkney, and fashioning him into a peerless knight.

"We do the best we can for our children," I said. "Vyvian and Llachlyn had quite the bond, you know. I've put aside many of her scrolls so Llachlyn can learn from them. It seems we have more than one smith in our line, though her creations are far smaller. I fear she will never work iron."

"Llachlyn is blessed to have found her own path. I only wish Gawain's had not been at such a cost to his body," Anna said.

Gawain, like so many, fulfilled his use for Arthur as his body faltered in the wake of his many campaigns. It might have broken another man to be cast aside so carelessly, but Gawain found a way out. And found love, even if it was forbidden and hidden from Arthur. The boy was lucky he had powerful, clever women in his life. We'd formed the Circle of Nine and provided protection around him and Princess Hwyfar; she, too, was one of us. Her power, her fury, gave me hope.

"I look forward to seeing her and Galahad both," I said lightly, trying to turn our conversation to lighter, more hopeful pathways.

"Galahad wrote and told me they will be traveling with Percival of Pellam, as well," Anna said, measuredly. "He describes him with little detail, as my son is far from the poet, but it sounds as though young Percival very much takes after his mother. I only wish…"

Wishing, alas, was a shadow of hope. And in some places, hope was too dangerous a candle to light, for fear of what it might reveal.

Anna looked away from me, swallowing back the words of our shared treachery, and took Vyvian's hand. Silence fell over us both as I began the final preparations for Vyvian's body.

UNSETTLED, ANNA AND I finished preparing Vyvian for her funeral. There were not many knights I would trust with transporting the body, given how much had changed in Carelon, but I was very relieved to see Bedevere arrive with Palomydes in tow. Bedevere was Anna's lover and had been for time out of mind; Palomydes was Gawain's greatest friend and confidant, born in the distant East and far more accepting of old magics than half the rest of court.

"Lady Morgen," Palomydes said, always so courteous and genuine. "We are here to provide strength and assistance in bringing the Lady Vyvian to her eternal rest." There were tears in his eyes as he spoke, freely grieving as we were.

Bedevere embraced me, and I was so surprised I barely managed to return it. "This day came too swiftly," he said, his beard scratching my face. "The Knights of the Table Round all mourn with you. You are not alone."

They were both accoutered in plain grey robes and tunics, free from the burden of armor and the trappings of war. They did not even carry their swords, a sign of respect for the dead—and, indeed, in recognition of Vyvian's remarkable skill as a smith.

Would that I had my own priests to take her, but they were close enough.

Quickly and efficiently, Palomydes and Bedevere bound Vyvian's body onto a painted board, built for such transportation, the cords giving shape to her wrapped form. They would bear her to the crypt together and begin the long vigil.

I wished I could wail, tear my hair, scream my grief to the goddess. But I was a priestess and a sorceress, the daughter of death, expected to carry out this duty with calm and grace. Vyvian would have scolded me for such emotion and sent me out to meditate on the coming winter and its lessons of death, reminding me that life was a circle, and death merely a new beginning.

And I could accept death, even my own. It was an inevitable dragon awaiting my soul, an indescribable end every being must face.

But living in a world without Vyvian, where so many secrets lingered at the edges of our lives, felt more than I could bear.

CHAPTER SIX

PERCIVAL

EVERYONE IN THE room went completely still when Percival announced they had all seen a *graal* in their dreams. Of course, he didn't know what it was right off. Only Galahad, as per usual, had the answers to their questions when it came to miracles and wonders.

So much had happened that night. So much, so fast.

He was being pulled apart by Galahad and Llachlyn, one day at a time. They would not stop arguing with one another, not stop bickering. And then bickering turned to drinking, and drinking turned to carelessness. And then he'd almost kissed Galahad, right in front of Llachlyn.

Thankfully, she'd nearly toppled into the courtyard and interrupted them.

"*Graal* is an old word," Dame Ragnell said. "A powerful word. A promise."

Percival turned to her, struggling to meet her intense eyes. They were deep amber, rimmed in dark lashes, and he wondered if she could see directly through to his soul. Llachlyn said she didn't know precisely who this woman was, but she suspected Dame Ragnell was considerably more than she appeared. Her accent was vague but clearly from the South, and she had poise one could only attain at court.

Clearing his throat, and seeing as Llachlyn was, once again, entirely unhelpful, Percival continued. "Yes. Purported to be the lost implements of magic, uniting all three kinds of power from the gods. Or perhaps even *before* the gods. Forged by smiths of old—twelve or thirteen in all. Most of them have been lost to time, or else destroyed for their magic within. Their mystery is part of the gods' gifts, though."

Llachlyn snorted. "Or, if you're Galahad, you think it has to do with their baby tree god and his blood. Which is both gruesome and implausible."

"I take it Galahad is a devout Christian," Gawain said, unable to keep the slight note of disdain from his voice.

"He always has been," Llachlyn said. "Aunt Elaine never pushed me—I think she feared Mother's fury—but Galahad was trained half as a monk."

"Galahad believes God has blessed him with purpose," Percival said. Even though it wasn't a lie, saying so made him feel traitorous. Galahad was Gawain's youngest brother, though, even if separated by a generation. "And now, so does the Queen. And that news, of course, aroused a fervor among all the knights. Arthur has declared a *graal* quest beginning at Pentecost, and close to a hundred of his best knights will be searching the whole realm."

Dame Ragnell's eyes blazed, now, and for a brief moment Percival worried she might have a sword, or an axe hidden in the folds of her gown, and would rise and hew the mighty oak table in half. Sir Gawain rose and walked over to her, slowly, as one might approaching a she-wolf. When he touched her on the shoulders, she closed her eyes tight and grabbed his hand as if it tethered her to the world.

Saints, they loved each other. It made Percival's heart ache with longing to see such tenderness, such voiceless connection between them. His own father and foster-mother had loathed one another with a palpable hatred, though they were the picture of joy before their guests and at feasts. He had scarcely ever dreamed he might love another in such a way. Sir Gawain was surely the richest man in the realm to have a wife such as she, matched in every way to him.

"It isn't the only reason they kept Percival in the dungeon," Llachlyn said, her raspy voice breaking the thick silence.

This was the worst part. The part that made Percival want to run into the woods and never return. Well, he'd done half of that already. He hadn't ruled out the other.

"I panicked, and I am a terrible diplomat," Percival admitted. "They'd taken Galahad, and I truly couldn't think of anything else to do."

Llachlyn let out a long breath, irritated. "I told you not to say anything. I told you to pretend it never happened. But no. You had to go spouting secrets."

Percival mustered his thoughts, trying to sound as measured as he could. In the moment, it had seemed his only choice. "I thought to bargain with the Queen. She was furious with Llachlyn and was going to take her away if I didn't do anything."

"You should have let her," Llachlyn said. "I'd have escaped a nunnery, anyway. I know more than how to forge locks, after all."

"Bargain with the Queen?" Dame Ragnell asked. "What on earth could a slip of a squire have to bargain with the Queen over?"

Percival wished he hadn't eaten his soup so fast. Or perhaps it had been those three slices of bread doused in butter and berries. Or the eggs. Either way, his heavy meal pooled in his stomach, churning as he worked his mouth.

"I feel like a gossip," he muttered. "Truly, Llachlyn, this part of the story doesn't need to be told."

Llachlyn glared at Percival, and his heart skipped in response. They had promised to share this part. They had to share it with *someone*.

"I promise you, we will say nothing. You are safe here, far from court," Sir Gawain said, the fire behind him setting his red, curly hair ablaze. He looked like the god of the forge come to life, Percival thought. And yes, it did make him feel safer than he had ever been in his life. It was hard to see any of Galahad in his eldest brother, but Percival found himself wishing fiercely for a sibling so fierce and protective. He had siblings aplenty; just none who cared about him in the least.

Percival summoned his strength and continued. "Not long after I arrived at Carelon, Galahad sent me back to his rooms to collect a change of clothes for him. He's always being invited to feasts and meetings, and he couldn't very well go in what he was wearing at the time since it was covered in sweat and—"

"The point, Percival," Llachlyn said.

"Right. The point. I…" Why was everyone looking at him? Why was the room so very warm? "Galahad had shown me the quicker passages I could take to and from his room, and I noticed one he had not pointed out before. Easy to miss, really, since it was behind an old rolled-up carpet. I can never leave a thing alone when it starts tapping at my mind, and so I took a detour."

It had smelled sweet, like roses, not like he'd expected. He'd pushed the carpet away and seen the soft glow of candlelight in the distance.

Percival took a deep breath. "Someone else had been using the passageways. There were signs of a struggle, the ground upturned. I should have gone back, but I was worried someone might be in trouble. When the cries became too loud, too angry, I hid, waiting. Two figures came my way, and I recognized one as the Queen. The man with her—I know not who—was angry, threatening her.

"'I will charge you and du Lac before the whole court,' he said to her. 'And every hand will turn against you both for your transgressions of the flesh.'

"I had never seen Queen Mawra afraid, never heard her voice as anything other than certain and commanding. I couldn't hear all the words, but I remember her saying:

"'I swear to you, if you so much as threaten me, Lanceloch will cut every last soldier down. They will drown in their own profane blood, and if God deems it, we will rule together over their corpses.'"

"My gods," Gawain said. "You have a good memory."

"Hard to forget words like that," Percival said.

Dame Ragnell put a hand to her heart as if it would help soothe her emotions. Her face was still a mask of fury, but her shoulders had softened. "You tried to blackmail Queen Mawra with her infidelity and treason."

"I did," Percival said. He couldn't look at them anymore. His cheeks burned.

"Ah, you daft, stupid boy," Sir Gawain groaned, covering his face as if he couldn't bear to look at Percival.

"You must understand, Sir Gawain, Llachlyn and I—we have no one at court to speak for us, no allies. With Morgen gone and Vyvian dead, I feared the Queen might kill us. I was the first of any of Pellinore's bastards to make it this far, so I didn't have brothers or uncles or anyone," Percival tried to explain, but his argument sounded very thin. "And Galahad was no real help. He wanted to believe his own legend so thoroughly, he half forgot we were alive."

"She very well could have taken your lives then and there," Dame Ragnell said softly. "Part of me is surprised she didn't. But Percival—threatening the Queen with such a thing openly— by the goddess. Being Pellinore's son is likely the only thing that saved you."

It was strange to think, given Percival was the youngest of so many siblings and bastards, his father's blood would do anything to help him. It had never been of any assistance before. No, he thought the Queen had simply drawn a line at outright murder.

Dame Ragnell looked thoughtful, ruminating on all this information. "Let me piece together this tapestry you have woven for us: You were drunk and roused the Queen's ire. She threw all three of you in the dungeon to teach you a lesson. You woke that morning, in the dungeon, having all dreamed of the *graal*—but the guards overheard your loud mouths, and when the Queen found out, she decided to use it to Galahad's advantage. Galahad, Gawain's brother and Lanceloch's son, because he is a convert, and you are both unchristened."

Percival nodded. "That is correct."

"Then," Dame Ragnell continued, "when the Queen threatened to send Llachlyn to a nunnery, she bit the Queen and, in a panic, you tried to blackmail her. So, she went into a fugue and kept you both in the dungeon."

"Essentially, yes," Llachlyn said.

"There is one detail missing," Dame Ragnell said, leaning forward. "How did you get out?"

Percival and Llachlyn exchanged looks. Then, at the same time, they both said, "Galahad."

CHAPTER SEVEN

GALAHAD

THE ROAR OF the crowd finally relented, and Galahad limped his way back to the armory and training grounds just outside the tilting field. His blood still pounded in his head, his hands still trembled from gripping his sword so long, and his heart...

His heart was still shattered, God help him.

For a moment, Galahad thought he could see Percival's mop of curls in the corner, but it was just a trick of the light on one of the practice straw men.

And the only person greeting him was his father, face cut with a grin so full of pride Galahad immediately felt guilty.

Guilty, guilty, guilty.

"Galahad. I did not think you could do better than last time, and yet, your form—it improves every single fight," he said, taking his son in a crushing embrace.

"Thank you, Father," Galahad said, his armor rattling as his father slapped his back. "I've been working to strengthen my offensive attacks, keep them far more varied, rather than falling into a pattern. I tend to do that."

Sir Lanceloch du Lac, Galahad's father, was no stranger to the tilting fields. In his day, he had been the most celebrated and decorated contender, even besting Sir Gawain of Orkney. And though they had not lived much of their lives in the same place and were in some ways still just getting to know each other, Sir

Lanceloch had attended every single tilting lesson, spar, and tournament without fail since Galahad had arrived at court.

He didn't usually meet him after, however. That was typically Percival's job, and Llachlyn's, if he was lucky.

And now they were gone.

"The King even watched from his window; did you see him?" Sir Lanceloch asked, eyes expectant.

Galahad made his way across the room as a pair of squires arrived to help him change out of his armor. He didn't want to look at them. He didn't want to acknowledge them. It meant Percival and Llachlyn were really gone.

"I did," Galahad said. When a squire pulled too hard on his pauldron, he yelped. That shoulder was far worse off than he thought, having received the brunt of Sir Brandalis's mace during the last stage of their combat.

"Are you hurt?" Sir Lanceloch crowded in.

"No more than usual," Galahad said. One of the young apothecaries was already fussing over his arm, applying cooling salves to the skin without his asking.

Annoyed, Galahad wrenched back his arm. "I can manage from here, thank you," he said to the small cluster of attendants. He could not bear the feeling of them pressing around him, tutting and pulling and prodding. It made him feel less like a human being and more like a prized stallion.

That was the worst thought.

Sir Lanceloch, clearly understanding his son's frustration, helped to usher the group away. He was always doing things like that, trying to anticipate Galahad's needs. As if he knew him at all.

Galahad did favor his father somewhat, at least in terms of his build. He'd never reached the stature of his older brothers, who were the tallest of Arthur's knights, instead growing lean and strong and fast. But he had his mother's coloring: fine grey eyes and his hair a rosy blond. Indeed, of all his brothers, he looked most like their mother.

He often wondered if his twin sister, the one who'd died when they were both born, would have looked like Lanceloch.

"Are you well, son?" Sir Lanceloch asked.

Galahad gave him a smile, because smiles were the best kind of lies. Even if his insides curdled when Sir Lanceloch called him *son*. "Of course. Just tired. And I've asked them not to send a whole retinue out when I'm coming off the field. It makes me feel uncomfortable. I need time for rumination and prayer, not fussing."

Sir Lanceloch nodded, clasping his hands behind him as if he knew not where to put them. "That is prudent. The Lord values humility and prayer. But if you are open to my suggestion, I've a little secret that may well help you."

"You do?" Galahad asked. He really did not want to talk with his father any longer than he absolutely had to. Every minute was torturous.

"I suppose I ought to ask first: Have you ever found the way to the hot springs?"

That got Galahad's attention. His shoulder spasmed in anticipation of relief. "Hot springs? Here?"

His father nodded. "Indeed. A hidden wonder of Carelon. Ah, it's not easily accessible for those who don't know where to look, though. But I can take you there." There was a curious, almost mischievous look in Sir Lanceloch's eyes.

"Very well," Galahad said, too tired to fight against his father's hope. "Lead the way."

Though he had been at court, officially, for the last month, Galahad's exploration of Carelon's grounds was sincerely lacking. Percival and Llachlyn had managed far more in terms of their wanderings, but they didn't have the exhausting schedule of a newly-dubbed knight. If Galahad wasn't practicing or training, he was fighting; if he wasn't doing either of those things, he was sitting at Mass or attending his uncle Arthur or visiting his mother Anna, or perhaps his brother Gaheris. Everyone expected so much out of him all of the time, and he had no time to himself. The few evenings he'd managed to escape with his friends had been the most treasured moments.

And now it had come to an end.

Sir Lanceloch brought Galahad about a mile from the tilting field, through a great vined archway nearly obscured by vegetation, and into an open area. The remnants of a temple lay off to the side, carved straight into a rock face. In front of that, deep blue pools steamed in the chilly air.

Galahad was awestruck at their crystalline waters, even though plenty of bracken still lay about. It was not difficult to imagine how beautiful it must have been in its previous incarnation, as glimpses of mosaics and glass caught his eye.

Joy. He felt joy the closer he got, his muscles aching with anticipation of their relief.

"What was this?" Galahad asked his father.

Sir Lanceloch knelt down and put one of his hands into the water, smiling serenely as his fingers met the warmth. "This was once a temple to Lugh."

"As in Lugh of the tournament?" Galahad asked. He wasted no time stripping off the remainder of his fighting gear, unceremoniously throwing them to the uneven stone ground. He was suddenly certain of one thing in the entire world: that he was getting in that water, and the sooner the better.

"The very same. Though we no longer call it Lugh's Tournament. It's the King's Tournament, of course."

Galahad could barely hold a conversation, so elated he was to meet the spring. Percival would know about Lugh; Llachlyn would want to explore the mosaics. But Galahad was ever a man of flesh and feeling, and he could spare no more time in idle chatter.

Sinking down into the hot water was a revelation to Galahad's sore and aching muscles. He thought his soul might take flight with relief. The waters smelled of minerals and just a touch of sulfur, but he would gladly tolerate worse smells for a chance to soak for an hour. Plus, there were no flower bits or perfumes like the baths back at Carelon. He was forever finding rose petals in his bed linens after a bath.

He took a deep breath and let the water rise to his shoulders. "Perhaps it's called that now, but half the knights still forget and call it Lugh's. They're not yet used to how things have changed."

"God will move their hearts in time," Sir Lanceloch said softly. "You see how swiftly these false gods fall before the faith."

"Not the springs, though. Thankfully." Galahad closed his eyes and thought of Llachlyn. She was forever prattling about springs and streams and little gods and big gods. Though certainly no witch of Avillion, she'd still never adopted the new faith, not even with all of Aunt Elaine's gentle teachings.

Well, he supposed, the daughter of Morgen le Fay may not be tamable.

"Did you and all the other knights come here after a tournament?" Galahad asked.

Sir Lanceloch sat across from Galahad, one hand dipping into the water now and again. "That would be a tale to tell, but no. Even in my time at the tournament, this was a secret place. Vyvian told me of it. I—I had an affinity for Lugh, once. And I had more time here at Carelon than most of the other knights, so I would visit often. I found the waters restorative to body and soul."

"Time alone? I thought surely you'd been away on campaign plenty," Galahad said, watching his father with sudden curiosity. "You're of an age—a little older than Gawain, and he was at the front at fifteen. And my brother Gareth fought against Ryence in Avillion."

The smile on Sir Lanceloch's face was strained, Galahad thought. He did not know his father as well as he ought, but he was aware of having stumbled into an uncomfortable subject.

"Gawain and Gareth are storied warriors indeed," Lanceloch said, stiffly. "But no. I stayed here, though. Not because I didn't want to fight at the front, but…"

"I didn't mean to pry," Galahad said quickly, fearing he might have upset his father.

"It isn't prying. It's a good question. No, after I married your mother, I remained here. The King has always given me the task of maintaining peace at Carelon, and I have given many years to that duty."

It was a strange answer, but Galahad was too warm and tired to think much on it. "Ah, yes. And we all know Sir Cai needs all the help he can get."

Sir Cai was the seneschal, technically, and Arthur's first friend. He had been raised in fosterage for a few years with Sir Ector, Cai's father, and their family. But Sir Cai was the most irascible man Galahad had ever met—stubborn, impatient, and sometimes even cruel, especially to new arrivals to court. Aunt Elaine had said, once, that Cai's early wounds from his first campaign had taken a part of his soul that would never heal.

There were many elder knights at court, but it was only Sir Bedevere Galahad felt most comfortable around. He was so intelligent, so kind, so full of information about how court functioned, and especially keen with the sword and shield. Perhaps Galahad ought to have asked his own father for advice, but he never could get the words out. Sir Bors, Sir Palomydes, and Sir Bedevere had been constant in their martial and brotherly support.

But every time Galahad ended up alone with Sir Lanceloch—his *father*—their interactions were strained and uncomfortable.

"Indeed, Sir Cai is not known for his diplomatic finesse," Sir Lanceloch said.

Sir Cai had actually struck Percival in the face when he'd found them all drunk in the armory storage room. Percival had dared to stand up for Llachlyn, who Sir Cai had called a bastard and implied both Galahad and Percival ought to spend time with more worthy friends.

They were very good at both getting drunk *and* getting caught, and that had been the end of everything.

By Christ, Galahad missed his friends. It hurt, right in the center of his chest, whenever he thought about them, like a perpetual bruise. He should have gone with them, escaped. He should have left to go see his brother Gawain in the North.

But the problem was, Galahad was both a Pendragon and a du Lac. He had a duty, not just to the King and his parents, but to God. That was something neither of them understood.

The first week after their escape, Galahad had kept expecting to see Llachlyn's face in the stands or catch Percival climbing up the terrace to his window with apple wine strapped to his waist. Now it was like they had never even been friends at all. Llachlyn had been like a sister to him. He had a responsibility to her. And Percival had been a friend like no other. But he had betrayed them—for what? For his faith? It seemed to him it was a fickle, fragile faith that would put him up to such actions.

"You seem deep in thought, son," Sir Lanceloch said. "If you—if there is anything you'd like to speak about..."

Galahad wanted to tell Sir Lanceloch he missed his friends, and it was his and the Queen's fault they were gone in the first place. He wanted to shout how he had freed them both, and he knew Sir Lanceloch and the Queen were not only sharing a bed but sharing potentially disastrous plans. More than anything, he wanted to shout at him for never being there for him, for tossing him away and not writing and having to endure Aunt Elaine for so long.

But Sir Lanceloch had not been part of any of Galahad's recent scandal, at least not directly. His friends' incarceration and subsequent questioning had been under Queen Mawra and Sir Fergus, mostly. Galahad was terrified of them both, and their priests. He knew he had done wrong—so much wrong. But he simply could not implicate his friends and could not stand by while they were being treated so poorly, not when he was being touted as a saint for his vision.

It was *their vision*. Their shared vision. Every night, Queen Mawra would find him and ask him if he had seen the *graal* again in his dreams, and every night he would answer the same. *No, milady. If God wills it, I shall see that holy artifact again soon.*

And that part was not a lie, at least. But his compliance had meant their capture; at least he'd had the courage to free them before it was too late.

"We're planning a feast in your honor tonight," Sir Lanceloch said when Galahad did not reply. "The King is announcing his plans for the *graal* search. I suspect he will want you to be at the heart of it. I am so proud to know God is speaking to you through His great miracles."

Galahad swallowed, his mouth suddenly sour with the thought. "If the King wills it, I will do as he commands."

"I'll leave you to your rest," Sir Lanceloch said, standing with a bit of a groan. "If you need me, just whistle."

God, grant me wisdom, grant me peace.

And as he sat in the deep, warm springs, for a moment he did feel both of those things.

CHAPTER EIGHT

MORGEN

THE NIGHT AFTER we sent Vyvian's mortal remains to the goddess, I was awoken from a deep, dreamless sleep by a feeling of utter dread. My skin crawled with it, my heart sluggish yet pounding in my ears, as I rose from my bed and reached for my slippers and shawl.

Glancing around the dark room, I saw nothing amiss, and fumbled to light a candle with my magic.

Nothing happened.

I let out a bitter laugh and focused my thoughts, concentrating on the nature of flame as I had been taught: heat, ash, fuel, light.

Still nothing.

Cold dread coiled tight around me, and I thought I saw a flicker of light under the door.

I lived alone in the tower. It had been Merlin's command, years ago, when I returned from my travels. Once, I had thought I would marry a man in a far-off kingdom, thought I might have found happiness, but that brief delusion only fortified my resolve. The tower was mine, even though it was meant as a mark of shame by Merlin. I made it my own.

Though I had guards at times, and more so lately, no one visited me without express permission. I had cast wards through every inch of the place. My tower was my safety, my place of retreat and rumination. It was my solace.

Failing again to light a candle, I instead went to the hearth and found the still warm embers there, as well as an old lamp. I would not go blindly into whatever awaited me. After a few attempts at lighting it, the lamp gave me a clear view of my room at last, gold light casting long shadows around me.

Pushing open the old door carved with the interlacing knots of Avillion, I looked down the short hallway. Below me, I saw nothing, heard nothing. But as I walked toward the upper staircase, I saw again a flicker of firelight, beckoning.

Closing my eyes, I reached for my power. What answered me was cold as death, fathomless and empty.

What was I without my magic, but an aging old woman many feared was some demon or devil? My power gave me purpose, and not a little pride. And perhaps, I thought, a false sense of safety.

I could alert my guards—Dodinel and Sir Lucan—but I risked losing track of this presence. Besides, if I ran to them like a frightened maiden and we only discovered owls in the belfry, they would think me slipping into madness.

No, I was Morgen le Fay, and I did not balk at shadows. I lived in them.

Shivering, I began my ascent. All that lay above me was the small room where I kept the mirror which allowed me to travel the Path or to project myself across a distance. Vyvian had forged it, and together with the Circle of Nine, I had perfected it.

I felt a presence there, heard creaking.

Alarm climbed up my spine as I began taking the worn steps two at a time, mouth dry and skin pimpling with gooseflesh. I tried to keep my senses, to approach with calm and focus, but in all my years in Carelon, none had ventured into my tower without my express permission. And the closer I got to the strange presence, the more I believed someone, or some*thing*, awaited me.

As I crested the landing, my ears began ringing, and my teeth rattled. The room opened up before me, just a simple circular space with the mirror in the middle, the floor covered in thick carpeting and rushes.

The pain in my ears did not abate, and reaching up, I found the warm, sticky wetness of blood cascading down my jaw and neck.

An overwhelming pressure took me, then, slamming me to my knees as if I had been struck from behind. My lantern went flying behind me, clattering down the stone stairs, glass shattering in its wake before its light guttered and died.

Dragging my head up, my neck screaming in pain, I tried to claw my way toward my mirror. There was a twin to it in the castle, in Anna's quarters, but it did not have power in the same way as this. Accessing the Path was just one part of what this particular artifact could do—it was an amplifier to my own power, necessary for maintaining the balance between Fate, Power, and Prophecy.

I did not believe in demons, nor the God of the Christians, but I knew the power here was greater than any I had ever encountered, strangling my magic, strangling the very air out of the room.

Iaia, Mother, protect me.

From what? I could not say.

Training my eyes upward, I spied dozens of crows ringing the room, wings out as if preparing to take flight, moving sluggishly as if under water. They'd not been there a moment before, though I often invited them in. If they made noise, I could not hear it, only see their shadows in the moonlight creeping through the small windows high above.

I crawled forward, feeling as if my body weighed six times what it ought, my muscles screaming in protest. I had to protect the mirror, my doorway, my duty. We had worked to build the Path again, to draw power together across the realm, and here, in Carelon, that power was concentrated even in the face of our dwindling faith. This pressure, this power, was capable of breaking all of that.

I saw, rather than heard, as the glass surface began cracking. The power of the mirror was not in its reflective surface, but the forged frame and shape. It stood taller than me, the silver edges cold and so far from my reach. I had to warn my sisters, the other priestesses of the Conclave—Anna, Hwyfar, Elayne, Ahès, Tregerna and more besides—but the pain and force of this strange magic would not relent.

Black feathers fell before me, cascading down so much slower than they ought, as if the very air itself had thickened. Perhaps it had.

Enough.

Vyvian told me my power was unlike any sorceress, bard, or priestess to ever tread upon the earth. Merlin had honed me into a weapon of cunning, magic, and illusion. Then I had woven my own learning as an herbalist and midwife and part of the Circle.

I opened my inner soul, the place where my power lay. This depth was dangerous, unstable, and deadly. It was there, more than anywhere, I knew the truth of myself. Though I had read prophecies and cast charms, felled beasts and tamed the winds, nothing compared to the power at the center of me.

It was when I'd accepted this part of me, when I'd shown Merlin the shadows within me, that he'd rejected me wholly. He'd claimed giving it up was the only way to avoid my fate and Arthur's doom.

But I was Morgen le Fay, daughter of death. And I did not push away gifts from the goddesses for power and safety. I lived and died by my own choices. For I had turned down the hand of kings and princes both, refused corrupt magics, and helped forge a kingdom of prosperity.

The abyss yawned wide in my mind, and I pulled from it with great draughts of power, and it made my body burn and freeze. Where my fingers had touched the carpet, the fibers began to wither, to decompose into its barest components. My nails ached with burning cold pain, and I cried out.

I crawled forward and found the pressure abating slightly,

recoiling as I started to move again. I still pushed out those shadows, still drank from the maw wide open at the center of me, gaining a few feet before I watched the mirror shake and tremble.

The crows began swooping before me, a flurry of snapping beaks and black wings, gently caressing my face. Each crow carried a wisp behind it, the mark of death, helping to clear the way toward the mirror.

I was so close. I just had to touch the edge of the mirror, to send out a warning. Something was coming, great and terrible and unseen—a power Vyvian had been holding at bay, I was certain of it.

I thought of my daughter, in that moment, as I watched the shadows burn the tips of my fingers black. I thought of her place in all this, and my cowardice keeping her from her true inheritance.

The guilt was my downfall. I lost the grasp on the maw of death and the mirror before me flashed a deep crimson, thousands of tiny cracks appearing all across the frame. It was as if an invisible forge had roared to life, melting the metal and sizzling across the mirror's surface.

And in the mirror, I saw Merlin's face, alive and terrible, looking upon me with judgement and disgust.

Here you lie now, alone and whimpering upon the floor. You submit to me at last, daughter of death, came Merlin's voice.

"Never," I croaked.

I reached desperately, the heat of his power burning my face. I needed only a handspan more to touch it—

I felt the oncoming explosion and knew, with certainty, I was about to die. Time slowed around me as the mirror shattered, frame and all, and molten hot shards flew in every direction.

Bracing for the inevitable pain, I gasped to see the crows intercepting the barrage. Their wings kindled when they collided with the smoldering metal, and they puffed away into ash that rained on my face. It smelled of the air after a lightning strike.

And wings. So many wings. A dense flurry of black feathers, surrounding me, carrying me, saving me…

WHEN I OPENED my eyes, I saw mist. Overhead, massive trees swayed with the weight of my crows. I could hear them clicking to one another, calling to me, chatty and concerned.

It was early morning, and the first rays of sunlight split the roiling white clouds around me. Ferns rose out of the fog, their stalks withered and brown as they prepared to go dormant for the season.

My whole body stung, and my bones cried out in pain as I tried to move my hands and lift myself up. Closing my eyes, I fumbled for my magic and found nothing but the empty maw of death. Just a doorway to the unknown, empty as a starless sky.

It was no use. Exhaustion settled over me, and try as I might, I could not rise, nor fight my eyes from closing.

I FELT HOT breath on my face, smelling of rotted meat and, strangely, wintermint. When I opened my bleary eyes, I was greeted with the golden stare and magnificent whiskers of a lion's muzzle. He was pinning my body in place, one great limb on either side of my arms.

Fumbling for my power to defend myself, I came up empty again, only an echoing strain deep inside my mind. I cried out, my head singing in agony, preparing for an attack.

"Melic! Off!" A man's voice, low and full of whispers.

I did not die, then.

The lion merely leaned forward and nuzzled me, his immense wet nose dragging down the side of my face, and then he pounced away with all the agility of a house cat. The ground shook in his wake and I forced myself upon my elbows, looking around frantically for a way to protect myself.

Without my magic, and despite my years and my training, I still remembered the terror of knowing I was alone with a man I did not know. The sharp bite of that fear helped propel me backward.

The mists persisted, and the lion gamboled around me as the man approached. He moved with an eerie grace, not unlike a cat himself, and wore a cloak of deep grey wool, strapped with leather. He carried an elegant bow and quiver, as well as at least four knives strapped at his hips and thighs. When he saw me, he cocked his head like a curious bird and then squatted down, one hand upon the ground, as if to make himself less threatening.

"Thank you, Melic," he said, to the lion, who was now enthusiastically rubbing his head against his shoulder. He turned his attention toward me. "You do not need to be afraid of me right now. How come you to this wood, woman?"

Woman, indeed. It was the words 'right now,' however, spoken in his whispering deep voice, which made me second guess his meaning. Indeed, I had no doubt about the man's prowess. I had spent my life around men trained to kill and I recognized such power in him immediately, even without the many weapons.

"Which wood is this?" I asked, skirting the question.

The man let out an irritated huff. "The big one."

"That is not remotely helpful," I said, wincing as my muscles reminded me just how much I had endured recently. My hair hung limp around my face, and when I looked down at my fingertips, I noticed they were still black. I must look like a drowned hag to him. Not that I cared. Perhaps looking like a hag would help protect me. Men did not like crones, after all.

He relaxed slightly, leaning back on his haunches. "Hmm. Well, I don't have to be helpful to trespassers, now do I, Melic?"

Melic stopped his incessant nudging to glare sidelong at me, as if he understood the question. Without looking at him, the man reached up to scratch the lion's chin affectionately.

My heart held a little hope: if this dangerous man could show an animal such camaraderie and love, he might pity me.

"I assure you, I did not mean to trespass," I said. I wished the crows would return and whisk me away again so I could ignore this infernal conversation, but I couldn't very well share such information with him.

"No one ever does," the man replied. He had a dry, unbothered way of speaking that was both comfortable and curious. "Until recently, trespassing here would be punishable by death."

I swallowed back my fear—not of death, but of what could come before it. "I'm sorry. If you direct me toward the nearest village, I will make haste and not return. It is a grave matter indeed."

The man stood up, brushing the front of his leather armor. "Very well. Keep going west for about two days. Then, if the forest wills it, you will be allowed to leave."

Then he started to walk away. The lion stayed a moment longer and then began to pad away after his master.

Damn the man! I had no weapons, no magic, and no good shoes. I was already freezing cold down to my bones, and though I was certain I could find food, it had been ages since I'd stayed outside for any length of time.

So, summoning what strength I had and pushing down my pride, I stood on wobbly legs and staggered behind the man.

"Sir—if I can take just a moment more of your time," I called after him, hating the pleading note in my voice. Morgen le Fay, begging a forest bandit for help. Goddess help me.

The man took a few more steps before coming to a stop and then turning slowly. The light had shifted, and I finally glimpsed his face: handsome, angular, with pale blue eyes and dark hair pulled back into his hood. Perhaps of an age with my nephew Gawain, or a little older.

I knew him. I just couldn't say from whence. That unreachable memory made my heart hurt, like a long-forgotten wound.

"I don't wish to be involved in"—he shook his gloved hand at me to indicate my entire being and sorry state—"whatever this is."

Part of me wanted to declare my status and call down a curse upon him. Yet even if I frightened him, even if he believed who I was, I could not follow through. I was useless. Just a powerless, aging woman, with white hair and black fingers.

"I'm lost," I said, trying to make myself as small as possible. "I need to figure out where I am and how to get home. It is a matter of immense importance to the realm."

His dark brows slid down over his eyes as he scowled at me. "You said. Yet the thought of assisting you is both inconvenient and unattractive."

I bristled, despite myself. "Once it was every man's duty to come to the aid of women in distress. I did not think the world had changed *that* much. Or were you raised without thought or care for those less fortunate than you?"

He eyed my embroidered hems, the lush silk hemming my shawl. Though I was undoubtedly dirty and had dried blood on my face, it was clear my means were not less fortunate than his.

The man stood preternaturally still, and I watched as he pursed his lips together, teeth clenching as he battled with whatever thoughts flitted through his head.

"Fine," he said at last. "I'll take you to a place you can rest. But then you must be on your way."

With no further word, he began stalking away through the dense forest.

I limped behind him, choking back tears of gratitude. Blessedly, one of the trees provided a limb as a decent walking stick, and this allowed me both more support and a way of testing for unsteady ground. I offered up a silent prayer to Iaia, even if she did not answer.

"May I give you my thanks properly? I do not think you gave me your name," I called after him. "It seems strange I know your lion's and not yours."

Clearly irritated that I continued to speak, the man paused briefly and looked over his shoulder at me. "He's not *my* lion. He's his own lion."

"Very well," I said.

He began stalking away again as he said, "I'm Yvain." He spat on the ground. "And I know exactly who you are, Morgen le Fay."

CHAPTER NINE

LLACHLYN

THOUGH SHE HAD been intent on disliking her cousin, Llachlyn found it quite difficult to do so. He was gregarious, attentive to his wife, he listened well, and he provided Percival and her with a substantial bit of apple wine even after they'd dined. Although it was clear their arrival at Thistlewood put them in imminent danger, Gawain and his wife did all they could to make them feel comfortable.

They even gave them a bit of space.

The second floor of the manor house at Thistlewood had a small balcony. At first, Llachlyn thought Dame Ragnell had placed Percival and her in rooms so far from one another out of a desire for propriety, but she realized it was not so. There were simply no other rooms available to them, as the others were used for storage or clearly had occupants. This was a working farm, with rooms not for impressing guests but for clear purpose. It was a real, thriving, home, lived-in and ragged about the edges, but so cozy Llachlyn wished she could stay forever. No wonder Sir Gawain had left Carelon. Thistlewood was a treasure.

As for her cousin and Dame Ragnell, their rooms were on the first floor and had a terrace and garden, giving them considerable privacy from the rest of the house.

So, after their long, meandering dinner, Llachlyn and Percival found themselves wrapped in thick blankets, drinking apple wine, their legs dangling down through the balcony railings, looking over the twisted branches of the apple orchard under the stars. The mountains in the distance looked like darker smudges against the star field, a void at the edge of the world.

Neither of them was as drunk as they wanted to be, but at least, Llachlyn realized, she felt safe for the first time in ages.

"I wonder what he's doing right now," Percival said.

"Likely stuck at Mass," Llachlyn replied. "And basking in the glow of being Galahad."

Percival tore his gaze from the horizon and turned his attention back to Llachlyn. He had such a steady, honest way of looking at a person and it always made her feel both inferior and guilty for letting her mouth run away without thought.

"You know he's not," Percival said. "Don't be an ass."

"I'm not an ass. *You're* an ass."

"What a riposte. I am wounded by your boundless cleverness, Mallow."

She smiled at the use of her nickname. They'd called her Mallow ever since she'd tripped into a swamp during a chase and come out covered in bog mallows, furious and embarrassed.

Llachlyn almost giggled. But then that ever-present cloak of sadness descended upon her. "I'm just glad we made it here. I wasn't certain the horses would make it."

Percival shoved her shoulder gently. "We *stole horses*."

"*I* stole horses. You fell off one into a ravine," Llachlyn said. She pinched his cheek. "And the scratches are still there."

He reached up and touched his swollen face. Nothing had required stitches, but it never ceased to amaze Llachlyn just how much the human face could bleed. When she'd first reached him, she thought he might have lost enough blood to be in real danger.

Percival took a deep breath. "Thank you, Llachlyn. For all this."

"You're so insufferably insipid when you're drunk," she complained.

"I am *not* drunk. Though I will admit to being insufferable. That is simply a product of being one of so many bastards. I had to come up with some way of being noticed. Otherwise, I'd have slept with the pigs every night."

Llachlyn took another swig of her apple wine, letting the cool, sweet sting course down to her stomach. She wanted to tell Percival there was no way he could go unnoticed, that being next to him was like knowing the Lodestar was always overhead. She wanted to tell him she was glad it was him and not Galahad who had come along on this adventure, and she felt disappointed, in a way, that their time alone together had ended. Even if it meant they were safe, for now.

However, Llachlyn said none of those things. She was not the kind of person who allowed such professions out of the realm of her thoughts. It was better to keep them tied up, tamped down, unspoken. Besides, she didn't want her words misconstrued. She loved Percival deeply, but not in the way of romance. She adored him. But she was jealous of the attention he paid Galahad. Because they shared something she could not.

You are meant for greater things, her Aunt Vyvian would tell her in her letters. *Do not let the distractions of youth allow you to stray from the path of your fate. Especially where men are concerned.*

It still hurt.

Because Galahad loved Percival, and Percival loved Galahad. And even if he would never admit it, Llachlyn could never compete. Would not *allow* herself to compete—would not even want to, really. She didn't think of young men in that way. Even if Galahad was feted and adored, even if he was the best knight Carelon had ever seen—or perhaps *because* of all of those things. Galahad got everything he wanted. The attention, the fame, the best cuts of meat, the most ostentatious finery—their whole childhood, she'd gotten his dregs. Did he have to take Percival, too? Wrap him up in desire, where she could not follow?

Still. She had Percival *now*. If they ever got home, if the world ever righted itself and she had a place at her mother's side, maybe then Llachlyn could think of what, and who, she wanted.

If only her power was not so pitiable. How laughable that the daughter of Morgen le Fay couldn't even convince a candle to burn brighter.

"Speaking of pigs, it is a shame Galahad will have to spend so much time with his father without us distracting him," Llachlyn said coyly.

Percival gaped at her. "You dare to speak of Sir Lanceloch so."

"Who says I was referring to him? Galahad is a pig sometimes, too."

"Only you would utter such foul words against the realm's most honored knight."

"Honor? Hardly. Lanceloch may have gotten all the attention for his deeds upon the tournament field, but he never once stepped foot in a war. He stayed at Carelon in every major battle, while better men—like Gawain in there—fought and sometimes died to bring Arthur's vision of Braetan to life."

"War isn't what makes a man worthy," Percival said softly. "And not every knight is allowed to fight."

"Of course not, but you know there's more to it. Especially considering what we heard. I still think we should have told Galahad about the passageway."

"I don't think he'd have handled it very well. He doesn't love his father, but we'd have put him in an impossible place. His family—"

"It's my family, too," Llachlyn reminded him.

"Yes, but he's got a different set of expectations. It eats him up inside. Knowing his father was openly plotting with the Queen…"

Bristling, Llachlyn raked her hands through her short hair. "Lanceloch du Lac. I never liked the man. Even before I found out he was scheming with the Queen. Sir Hector always said he was too powerful for his own good. And besides, imagine if he *had* been gone during the wars. All the Queen's priests would never have had such a foothold at Carelon. Which means we wouldn't have been treated the way we were, and maybe Aunt Vyvian and my mother would still be…"

Oh, goddess, Llachlyn was crying. Her thoughts had spilled out of her mouth and now they were *real*. The weight of everything that had happened in the last few months came upon her like a hammer upon an anvil, welcomed by drink and exhaustion. She had not wept once—not upon hearing of Vyvian's death, not after learning her mother was gone, not after being thrown in the dungeon, and not even after Queen Mawra had called her a child of the devil.

But now, after an evening of kindness and *hope*...

Percival's arms were around her and he smelled of the smoky tallow soap they'd used to wash, and apples, and wool. She wrapped her arms back around him, encircling his waist, and let herself sob into his chest, her own tears cold against her face.

When she pulled away, Percival pressed his forehead to hers and spoke softly. "I'm sorry you're stuck with me. I'm sorry it feels like everyone wanted us to fail, like what happened was what they wanted all along—to get Galahad to themselves and to be rid of Lady Vyvian. But both she and your mother gave you this gift, at least, of your cousin's hospitality. Morgen le Fay is the most powerful sorceress in the realm. I am certain she'll find you again."

Llachlyn swallowed and nodded, angrily wiping her face with her palms. "It's her power that worries me. Queen Mawra called me a child of the devil. What does that make my mother?"

"A threat to Queen Mawra," Percival said, lowering his voice. "She is the old way, and Queen Mawra is the new. The Queen seeks to strangle out anything that comes in the way of her faith."

"But why?"

"Why do people like her do anything? It's power, Mallow. It's who gets to tell the story after it's over. If Queen Mawra had her way, then we are *all* the devils and she and Lanceloch are the angels come down from high. And Morgen? Perhaps she is the worst of all."

"But—the Queen wouldn't dare come after us, would she? Mother is—"

Llachlyn knew who her father was. Percival and Galahad did, as well. It was a secret she had held onto until they had formed their bond, the three of them, summers before when they'd first met. Galahad claimed she had misunderstood her mother, but Percival knew better. Percival knew what it was to be seen as less than. He was a bastard, too.

Though *his* parents were not half-siblings.

"Your mother is protected by the King," Percival said, and his words soothed the storm inside of her. "There is no safer place to be."

"Well, so much for that. *He* didn't come to help us," Llachlyn said, not for the first time.

"I must believe the King didn't know," he said. "You weren't even Llachlyn. You were Godric. Besides, it was three days. Three days! We've been gone far longer before, and no one's raised alarm."

"Three days to ruin our lives," Llachlyn said.

"Or to give us a chance to start again. You really think anyone is going to try to bother us here while we're with Gawain of Orkney? Did you see the size of his arms?"

"Did you see the hitch in his step?"

Percival gave her an exasperated sigh, then handed her clay cup to her. "Drink. You're being morose, Mallow."

Llachlyn drained her cup. "I'd put my money on Dame Ragnell," she said. "Even if she's clearly not—well, whoever she says she is."

"She reminds me of Queen Mawra, somehow. But, you know, without the look on her face like she's just stepped in shit."

They both started laughing, and before long they retired to their rooms and slept deeply, heads throbbing with apple wine and momentarily free from the worries that had followed them so far.

CHAPTER TEN

HWYFAR

"COME TO BED, love. No amount of pacing is going to solve our troubles tonight," Gawain said from the bed.

Hwyfar stood at the window of their bedroom, looking out across the view she treasured so dearly: the orchard, the mountains, the stars. Never in her life would she have suspected she'd enjoy working the fields and pressing cider and picking insects off the trees. But neither had she imagined loving a person as fiercely and terribly as she did her husband.

Even if no one knew. It mattered not. Theirs was a connection forged with magic and love and fate, built on the threads of *carioz*, an ancient connection between two souls. Rare and powerful and blessed. A fate, above all, they had chosen, together.

"I am unsettled, my love," Hwyfar said, pulling the thick curtains over the window and going to sit on the bed next to Gawain. Their bed was a marvel of carpenter's art, constructed to hold the both of them through sleeping—and their many other, more intimate, encounters in the room.

She slid her hand over the brocaded coverlet and Gawain reached out to clasp her fingers in his hands, so warm and solid and sure.

"Talk with me, Hwyfar. Let me in," he said gently, his voice rolling over her and comforting her.

"It's bad enough what those children discovered—"

"They're *not* children. They just haven't experienced the kind of world we did at that age." Gawain was adamant about this. Every time Hwyfar worried they needed coddling, he would insist on her using different words. "They're a man and a woman, and this has been the hardest time of their entire lives. At eighteen, you'd already been—"

"I know where I was when I was their age," Hwyfar said, batting away her husband's hands. He'd started tracing little circles on her thigh, and it was maddeningly distracting. "Which is part of what worries me."

"Oh, indeed. And I remember you at that age," Gawain said, closing his eyes and folding his hands across his belly. "Gods, the way your hips swayed when you strode across the hall…"

"And I do not sway so tantalizingly now?" She had to rise to the bait, just a little.

He grinned, the lines around his eyes deepening. "Mmm. You'll have to remind me. Perhaps you can stride across the room one more time and I'll pass my judgement."

Oh, how she wanted to laugh, to cover him in her kisses and feel him inside of her.

But the world was breaking, and Hwyfar was growing more concerned by the moment.

"Morgan's disappearance coincides with the Path falling silent," Hwyfar said. "I would have thought, if she knew aught was wrong, she would have told us. We have protocol for such things. She visited me just after Vyvian died and I—" Unexpectedly, Hwyfar swallowed back a lump in her throat. Vyvian was Gawain's aunt, but had also been a mentor to Hwyfar, one of the few people who knew where she resided outside her more visible duties in Lyonesse. And her own mother, Tregerna, was not far from crossing to the realm of the dead, either. It reminded her that nothing, not even their carefully hidden world, could remain untouched forever.

Gawain's eyes mirrored her tears. "There will never be another like Vyvian du Lac."

Hwyfar stilled her breathing. Gawain reached out for her hand again, and she clasped it. "You cannot travel the Path, but I can. I could, until just after Vyvian's death. I thought, initially, it was me—my grief was somehow preventing me from traveling. I should be in Lyonesse right now, and the Path has always allowed me."

The Path connected Hwyfar to the Circle of Nine across Braetan to Avillion, Lyonesse, and Ys. However, only Hwyfar, Morgen, and Elayne of Astolat could travel the Path corporeally. The rest could send illusions of themselves across it, over vast distances, but always remain where they were. It was how Hwyfar had managed to balance her life at Thistlewood, as Dame Ragnell, and her duties as heir to the throne of Lyonesse.

"Give it time. Losing Vyvian may have repercussions no one fully yet comprehends," Gawain said.

"And these children," Hwyfar said, rubbing her jaw. Her whole body was tight and strained.

"Not children," her husband corrected.

"These *naive young people*," she said.

"We already went over this. We all know who Llachlyn's father is."

"That means—"

"That *means*," Gawain said, rising up on his elbows. "She's almost as close to me as my own brothers. Closer than—well, I can't do the sums right now because I'm tired and I have a lot of brothers. No matter. She's my blood and I will protect her."

"And the boy—" Hwyfar rolled her eyes. "Percival."

"What of him?"

Hwyfar had watched Percival during dinner, and then after as they spoke of their family ties and childhoods abroad. Percival had lived with his father King Pellinore, and Pellinore's extensive family of bastards. He was one of the youngest, and clearly overlooked. He'd been sent to Benwick to train with Galahad during the summers, and the three had formed an inseparable bond.

It was only... the color of his hair, and the way he tilted his head when he was thinking. The *gestures*.

"He reminds me of someone, that's all," Hwyfar said at last, not wanting to meander down such dark hallways of thought.

"He reminds you of Gweyn."

Gawain was not often the most observant of men, but he had loved Gweyn as dearly as a sister. And she *was* Hwyfar's sister. Gone, now, fifteen years.

"He does," Hwyfar said, running her hand through Gawain's tangled curls. She would have to get the comb out, and some hair oil.

"Well, half the Knights of the Table Round are my cousins to one degree or another. Pellinore was Arthur's first cousin, I believe. So that makes me—well, related. You're probably just seeing my beatific features in his angelic face," Gawain said.

"I need to speak with your mother. We could go to Carelon, together, to see for ourselves."

"Absolutely not." Gawain sat up in bed, the wood creaking under his considerable weight.

"Gawain, we may have no choice."

Gently, Gawain took Hwyfar by the shoulders and turned her toward him. "No. We can't risk what we have. What we have built."

"We may have to. You know our quiet joy here—it can't last forever."

"It will if I can help it."

Her heart broke at her husband's stubborn faith in her, in their life. Ten years they'd had outside the politics of Carelon, the scheming and machinations. But the news there had only become more and more concerning with each passing season. With Vyvian gone and Morgen missing, the Path broken and priestesses diminishing, there would be no anchor for Arthur. And given the rumors of Lanceloch and the Queen, no doubt it would fall before they could intervene.

Hwyfar took her husband's head in her hands, staring into his expressive eyes that gave everything away: every emotion, every thought, every desire. "If what they say is true, your uncle will need you more than he ever has."

Gawain tried to wrest his head from her grasp, but she steadied him. Their *carioz* was such she could use his own strength against him, if it was required. Not as she once might have been able to, when their connection was unaltered, but it served as a reminder.

"Hwyfar, my love, I chose you. I chose this life. Over him, over my brothers, my mother, over *everything*. I will not go back to that, not now," he said, his voice cracking with emotion.

Her heart felt run through with thorns, but she would not break his gaze. "If Lanceloch is involved with what the children suspect, and if Queen Mawra gets her hands on the *graal*, the fragile world Arthur built will fall apart. The world that still protects women like me. And Morgen. And your mother." She took a deep breath, steadying herself. "My sister is a viper and Lanceloch is a zealot. Together, and with such power, they could be devastating. I cannot stand by and see Avillion fall. It is my inheritance, my duty. And if Avillion falls, what of Lyonesse? Or Ys? When will they stop?"

She thought he would fight her, but instead Gawain relaxed his shoulders.

He grabbed her around the waist and hoisted her upon his lap. "You're stronger than I have ever been," he said to her, burying his face in her bosom. "And I will follow you into the Underworld if you ask. Only promise me…"

"Gawain." His name was a whisper against his lips as her own passions rose and his hands slipped up under her long sleeping shift.

"Promise me you won't leave my side. When Arthur finds out—when he discovers what we've done…"

"If you do not run," Hwyfar whispered into his ear.

"I will not falter," he finished.

Their magic mingled as their lips crushed together, half a day of distraction finally destroyed in the melding of their bodies.

Hwyfar let Gawain peel off her shift, his hands tracing the lines of her body with reverence, planting soft kisses all along her neck, down her chest. She sank her hands into his russet curls again, hearing him moan in reply.

Goddess, she loved to hear the sounds he made when she moved over him.

She sank down into his lap, feeling his need just below her own, as he took one of her pink nipples into his mouth and bit down gently. A thrill of pleasure wound across her body and down to her core, her heart pounding along in concert.

"Always so ready," Gawain said, his hands now tracing the lines of her rear, finding the little indentations. "Gods, I can feel the heat of you, woman."

Hwyfar grinned at him under her lashes, tossing her long braid over her shoulder and then sliding herself over his hard rise.

"And lo, husband, I can tell you were thinking of this precise arrangement for half of dinner," Hwyfar said, rising to her knees so she was poised just above him.

"On the contrary, love. I was thinking about dessert," Gawain grunted, his head going back as she reached down between them and squeezed.

"Liar." She pulled on his hair with her other hand, hard.

He grabbed her chin and kissed her deeply, ravenously, teeth and tongue vying for attention, breaking away only to breathe. With a mischievous glint in his eye, Gawain asked, "Who says *you* aren't dessert?"

Hwyfar laughed breathily and then, in one perfect motion, slipped over his proud length and enveloped him wholly.

CHAPTER ELEVEN

MORGEN

YVAIN. OF COURSE. How had I forgotten about Yvain and his lion? Further, how could I have missed the similarity of features he shared with his father, King Uriens of Rheged? King Uriens and I had nearly married, once. Perhaps, in another lifetime, we had.

Though born out of wedlock, Yvain was a prince of Rheged. Once, I had studied my family lineages every night, ensuring I knew precisely how our court and its allies were connected, helping Merlin infiltrate every noble house in the realm. I should have guessed far earlier. I was losing my sharpness, as if I needed the reminder.

More importantly, once, I had been in love with King Uriens. Or as I knew him, Coel. Not the childish love of a young girl, but the powerful, steady love of a woman grown, who for one sweet season saw a glimpse of what her life could be without the shackles of Carelon. And I had walked away from it.

Well, I couldn't chastise myself too harshly. When I had last seen Yvain, he was scarcely Llachlyn's age and accoutered in full armor at Carelon. And he did not have a lion with him.

He was no mere king's bastard, though; he was Modrun's son, and her demesne was Brocéliande, the great forest at the center of Avillion. The greatest forest in the realm, redolent with ancient power even greater than I could wield.

Brocéliande, the forest where we stood.

'The big one' indeed.

How I had gotten to Brocéliande, however, was a much more troubling concern than how much Sir Yvain had changed in the last twenty years. Typically, as he had intimated, trespassers in the forest were dealt with harshly and effectively. Though Modrun was part of our Circle of Nine, she mostly kept to herself unless we absolutely needed her assistance. Her magic was wild, protective, and fierce in a way the rest of ours were not. She had also endured hardships most of us could not comprehend.

And Yvain, well. I knew the comings and goings of most of Arthur's anointed knights of the Table Round, and Yvain attended his sovereign when duty required. However, he had been in Brocéliande for the majority of the last ten years, sending occasional missives and regrets, but never in attendance.

The crows, or so I theorized, had carried me from my tower in Carelon across the sea and here, to the outskirts of Avillion. There was no precedent for such power, no way for me to make sense of it, especially considering that my own magic—save for the heart of death I carried with me—was yet unresponsive. That vision of Merlin haunted me, still. I could not understand why the goddess had sent me here.

By the time we reached the small cottage Yvain claimed was his winter home—he said little else other than this during our entire walk—it was dusk. My feet were numb, and my face burned from the wind and chill. If Yvain noticed my discomfort, he said nothing.

Yvain barreled through the front door of his moss-covered cottage, Melic bounding away into the snow rather than going inside. Without a glance my way, Yvain began taking off his cloak and weaponry, throwing them on a small, rickety table near the hearth. What remained was a lithe, but surprisingly broad, frame, and long, crow-black hair, held back with a simple leather lace. Though he sported no beard, he was nonetheless at least two days away from having shaved.

He was captivating. Or would have been if I wasn't in so much confounded pain. I saw both of his parents reflected in his movements, but the whole was completely his own. How he'd remained unmarried and hidden here for so long, I did not know.

The cottage had just one chair and table, one bed, and a wall of drying herbs and meat. I noticed a small cabinet by the hearth held a variety of implements for sharpening knives and fletching arrows, as well as poultices and salves.

He also had a vast number of books, mostly strewn about or piled upon one another.

"Sit, if you want," he said, as I closed the door behind me.

I did, gladly, while he went about stoking the fire. I'd not noticed the brace of squirrels he'd brought in with him. Once the fire was warm, he got to work dressing them, throwing their pink little bodies into a black pot, and then swinging the cauldron onto the fire.

Just as I was about to start peeling the slippers from my raw, bleeding feet, he placed a small pot of salve on the table beside me and then poured me a glass of dark wine.

"That should help," he said.

"Thank you," I said.

I took a deep, grateful gulp of wine and then started when he threw a pair of thick wool stockings at me.

He gestured to them. "For after."

I hissed as I pulled off the silk quilted slippers, my blisters and abrasions having long ago stuck to the material.

Without my magic to dampen the sensations, the pain was breathtaking. The salve helped soften my skin, but the only solution was persistence. I lost track of time as I worked, and when Yvain set a bowl of stew beside me, I almost retched at how similar the dressed rodents were to the color of my raw skin.

"Do you have the means to warm some water?" I asked through gritted teeth. "I—I'm sorry, but I am at your mercy, Sir Yvain."

"Yvain. Just Yvain." I thought at first, he would ignore my request, but then he went to put another pot on the fire, already filled with water.

I was shaking so violently when my feet hit the water that I worried I might swoon before him like some fragile maiden. Just as I thought I could handle no more, the pain began abating.

Yvain went to his wall of herbs and grabbed a couple of handfuls of agrimony and comfrey, which he crumbled in the water. Again, I fought back tears at even this small gesture. When I tried to speak, I could find no words, and so I drank more wine.

Then he sat down on the floor and began eating his stew, eyes never leaving me. His mistrust lingered between us, a palpable thing.

"I don't get many visitors," Yvain said.

I cleared my throat. "I am grateful for the exception."

"Initially, I assumed you were lying to me. About being lost. Given you're a sorceress." It sounded like an accusation. Yet he was the child of a witch. Curious.

"What made you change your mind?"

Yvain tilted his head toward me again. "I know pain, and you aren't faking. Living here has eroded my trust and my manners, somewhat. I should apologize for making you walk so far without good shoes."

"I am indebted to you, still."

He glowered. "No. That's not how it works."

"Not how what works?"

"Just because I helped you doesn't mean you owe me anything. I prefer not to deal in such things."

"Well, we have that in common," I said.

Slowly, carefully, I took my feet from the water and flexed my toes, gazing at the lacerations in wonder. It had been ages since I had been unable to heal myself with magic. Yvain threw a cloth at me, and I dried my feet, then applied more of the salve and, eventually, pulled on the socks he'd given me.

The relief was beyond compare. And once I had eaten enough stew to settle my stomach and meld with the wine, I was so sleepy I began falling asleep sitting up.

I snapped awake and saw Yvain directly before me, staring into my eyes as if I were an irksome child. I started at the hostile look in his expression, but then he backed away.

"You really have no way of protecting yourself, do you?" he asked, straightening up.

"I—well," I said, fighting back the embarrassment both of falling asleep and being so very helpless. "No. No, I don't."

He nodded, as if it confirmed everything for him. "You can have the bed."

"There's no need," I said, making to stand, but falling back into the chair with a gasp.

Yvain simply scooped me up and set me upon the bed as unceremoniously as a sack of grain. Even so, I was a grateful sack of grain.

"I beg to differ, Lady Morgen," Yvain said, crossing his arms and looking down upon me. "You need to rest. In the morning we can discuss more."

"Why not now?" I asked, tugging the coverlet up over my legs, but keeping my feet clear of the weight.

Yvain rolled his neck, then sat down on the chair. "Because the things we need to talk about are best spoken during the daylight."

With that ominous statement, I settled on the bed. I must have dozed quickly, for I started awake to see Melic, stretched out by the fire, and Yvain leaning upon his great flanks. The firelight behind them obscured most of the detail, but I was quite certain Yvain was reading one of his books.

"For such a small person, she has quite large feet," Yvain said to—apparently—his lion.

I was going to add a retort, but sleep pulled me back in. As I sank into the darkness, I recognized the bitter taste of corna, the prickly poppy, and valerian. The strange knight had, apparently, dosed my wine without my notice. But I was not angry. I needed the rest, and he must have guessed at my stubbornness.

THE NEXT MORNING rose blue and cold. When I awoke, I was alone. The pain in my feet had lessened significantly, but the rest of my body screamed in protest. Beside the bed I found a small bucket of water and a sponge, and, after smelling the contents—it had a hint of rose to it—I went to work washing the blood from my face and the dirt from my hands.

My fingers remained stained no matter how much I scrubbed, the fingernails purple and glossy and strange to me. It could have been a trick of the light, but I could swear the bruising was spreading past my knuckles now.

Closing my eyes, I sent a prayer to Iaia, but heard no answer: nothing of her warmth in my heart, no resounding response. The maw of death, however, was ever-present.

Had I truly seen Merlin in the mirror? Was this blight upon my hands some sort of curse from him? Was my death imminent?

I contemplated what it might take to make a tisane for myself, given all the medicinal herbs about.

The door thundered open, rattling on its iron hinges, as Yvain burst in, head down, a sack on his back. He looked up at me, displeasure written across his features.

"You're still here," he said.

So much for pleasant morning conversation.

"I am afraid I wouldn't be able to get too far on my own at present," I replied.

"But you're standing. And talking. Let us thank the gods for that," Yvain said, tone dripping with sarcasm, as he moved past me and to the small table.

In the daylight, his cabin was, dare I say, almost quaint. I had not noticed the woodwork along the beams, painstakingly carved into dragons and bears and, of course, lions. It was sparse but remarkably clean. It seemed a contrast to his continually surly temperament.

I tried to calm myself and not rise to his deeply unchivalrous attitude, but jumped as he threw the sack to me. I just barely managed to catch it, and glancing down at the worn leather in my hands I was surprised at its heft.

To my unspoken question, Yvain said: "A spare cloak. Traveling tunic. Basic supplies." He pulled out an apple from the folds of his own cloak and took a messy bite. "Some apples."

I pulled out the clothes, running my hands over the thick wool plaid in deep green and warm brown. Once, I had traveled the whole realm with Merlin, wrapped in similar clothes. I was younger, then, and dependent on the old bard in ways I did not like to remember. When I had told him I had been reading of a forgotten web of power between priestesses, he'd laughed at me. He had not laughed when I'd shown him the face of his death, though.

I pulled the cloak around me, settling into its warmth. "May I ask you a question, Yvain?"

"You just did."

I stilled my breath. The man was maddening. Or mad. Or both. "How did you know who I was?"

Yvain scratched the side of his face with his long, agile fingers, his icy blue gaze moving over my face and body. It was not an assessment of my womanly form, no lecherous catalogue of my breasts and form; I was long past being seen in such a way. Yet it was exacting, still, and made me feel laid quite bare.

"I grew up in Carelon before being sent to Avillion. And one does not forget the face of Morgen le Fay. Unless they are an idiot." He took another bite of the apple and then said through a full mouth, "Though there are a great many idiots in Carelon, so I suppose your question is valid."

I had to laugh a little, and it warmed my heart, even if the knight did not join in. He just looked at me, an expression between pity and disgust flitting across his features.

"On that, you and I are most certainly in agreement," I said. Goddess, I was tired of the politics and alliances and masks I had to wear every day at court.

Yvain walked across to me and drew one of his daggers from his hip. I started backward, and he sank it into the table beside us, the blade ringing as he released it.

Absorbing my expression of terror, he raised one eyebrow and then snorted. "For the apples."

I ate the apples, sliced them with the dagger he provided. When Yvain went out to collect more snowmelt for the water,

I changed into the clothing he had brought me. With the belts and leather lacings, I was able to assemble a passable traveling ensemble far more appropriate for the weather.

When he came back in again, he had a pair of boots for me. They smelled of fresh cure, the edges still pink from cutting, the stitches white and gleaming against the bark brown of the leather.

"Did you make these?" I asked him.

Yvain seemed to have some sort of routine in his cabin and I, of course, was interrupting everything. "Yes. Contrary to popular belief, Brocéliande does not grow boots upon the boughs of her trees."

The socks gave enough cushion that, upon slipping my feet into the boots, the combination relieved even more of the pain. I had not worn such comfortable footwear in an age, and though they were far from what one might consider court appropriate, I had no doubt they would last a long time.

"They are very fine," I said, standing in the middle of the small cabin, looking about me. "You have done more than enough, and I appreciate it. I suppose I have everything I need to start my journey west."

A look of annoyance again. "Lady Morgen."

"Morgen is fine."

"*Morgen*," he said, with an exasperated sigh. "You were correct last evening. I should, by my birth and my training, provide more to you than I did. My concern was not so much with your survival as your magic, which I frankly do not trust."

I went to make some feeble argument when he took a step toward me, holding up his hand.

"Whatever you're going to say, don't," Yvain warned.

To speak to me in such a way! Insolent, maddening man. If I had my powers, I'd have cast an illusion of carnivorous beetles on him so completely believable he'd be checking his crotch for weeks.

Yet I complied. For now.

He continued once I was silent. "You are dangerous. But you are powerless. And though I am not a good man or a chivalrous

89

man, I am yet a practical man. Letting you run wild through my forest, bleeding and flailing like a rabbit stuck in a snare, would certainly cause your death and then, by simple logic, bring blame on me and mine."

"Your mother—"

Yvain bared his teeth at me like an irate wolf, and all the words I had dried up. The gall. For his part, Melic just sat by the hearth, flicking his tail now and again, clearly bored with our argument. Useless creature.

"My mother, yes. My *mother*." There was no softness in him now, as if a great sharp shadow had fallen over his soul. "Indeed. Before we do proceed, we must speak to my mother. And that, Morgen, is the worst part of all of this."

"I know your mother, Yvain. She has helped me—and so many others. She will tell you I am safe, I am to be trusted."

"No one knows Modrun. Not even me."

"Let us go to her. Surely, she will assist me, and you can be rid of this burden, and I can leave."

"Ah, so simple." Yvain gave a bitter laugh. He gestured around the cabin, the windows, the hearth. "What do you see here, Morgen?"

I glanced around the room again, looking for a nefarious sign. I found nothing. Without my magic, I was lost. "It is a comfortable cabin."

"It is a *prison*." Yvain leaned close, poking me in the chest. If I was not afraid of him, if he did not have so many weapons upon his person, I would have bitten his finger off. "My *mother*, your *friend*, has kept me here in the confines of Brocéliande for ten years. Ten. Years."

"Yvain—I didn't know," I whispered.

"Now you do." He called Melic to his side with a high clicking sound, and the lion stretched and meandered over to him. "So, if you have any hope of leaving here, and fixing your most important matters, you will need to do what I—her own flesh and blood—have not been able to do. Convince her to take down her wards. Otherwise, this is where you will die."

CHAPTER TWELVE

GAWAIN

THISTLEWOOD HAD NEVER been a place of gathering, by dint of necessity. Only a precious few visitors ever came to stay, and thereby his and Hwyfar's secret was kept safe. But gods, how Gawain had missed the rowdy commotion of people in the home!

He and Hwyfar were awoken at dawn by footsteps above them, followed by laughter and then a great crash. Gawain went to get out of bed, but his wife had put a hand on his arm and reminded him they were *not* children, and more assuredly could manage whatever consequences they had wrought.

"The twins were like that," Gawain said, settling back down into the bed. Hwyfar nestled into his shoulder, and he traced the rise and fall of her arm across his stomach. "Early risers, late to bed. Ready to crack the bones of the world and suck the marrow before the sun even crested the horizon."

He thought of Gareth, ever loyal and a pillar of connection to the world. And of Gaheris, the one who he had never managed to reach, the one who was slipping away more and more each time he saw him.

Gawain and Hwyfar had no children of their own, not out of choice but necessity. It was a pact they'd made together in the early months of their union. Any child of theirs would have a claim to too many thrones—Carelon through Gawain, and

Lyonesse and Avillion through Hwyfar—and would never truly be safe. Even here.

Still, child or not, they knew their choices would bring them, ultimately, back to Carelon.

The line of succession was clear. Mordred stood to inherit the throne once Arthur… Gawain could not think of these things. Not now.

They had guests. And he could smell fresh bread already wafting through the house.

Hwyfar pulled his chin toward her, a wicked smile upon her lips. "I do have something in common with them, then, being quite fond of waking and sucking the—"

Pulling her toward him, Gawain covered her mouth with kisses and tried to smother the growing sense of unease within him.

Gods, he loved her. He needed her. And for all they had endured, these years of living together in quiet simplicity were a blessing beyond measure. No single day did he take for granted. No single moment of being in her arms, or between her legs, or listening to her play her harp and singing under the apple trees.

The idea that their long charade might finally come to an end terrified him. He should have been preparing himself for this all along.

"Gawain, where are you?" Hwyfar smoothed his furrowed brow. "You went away."

"Ah, love, I never left."

Sometimes Gawain did go away. It was not often, and it was not predictable, but on occasion his mind fell into a cold, fathomless ocean of numbness. At the bottom of the waters, he saw the faces of those he had lost, those he had killed, rotting and deteriorating, their hands reaching for him.

But she would always find him.

"We need to tell them," Hwyfar said gently. "About me."

"Aye, we do."

"That is not all that's troubling you."

"No." He sat up and, grunting against the pain in his knees, set his feet on the floor. "But if what Llachlyn and Percival say is true, my troubles are naught compared to theirs."

"It doesn't make them any less painful."

He reveled in the warm press of her arms around his neck, her breasts against his back, her gentle honeysuckle scent wrapping around him. "They seem so much younger than I was at that age."

"They are," Hwyfar said. "They are children of peace and prosperity, raised in warmth and comfort. You had stared down the face of death at that age, endured the merciless abuse by your father—you had seen the world for what it is."

"And now, seeing them, I feel so much older than my years," Gawain continued, rising and pulling on his morning robe, letting the cool velvet wrap him in its familiar touch.

Hwyfar's hair fell down her breasts like a goddess incarnate, and she was surrounded in fine linens and furs, though nowhere near as fine as she deserved. "We are," she said softly.

He went to smooth her lovely cheek, and she kissed his palm. "*I* am. You are still as ripe and lovely as the first day I saw you. But you're right, you know."

"I very often am."

No amount of strength could make the words easy to say. "The right thing to do is to take them back to Arthur. To offer them our protection when they face him. They are frightened and up against so much. And with Aunt Morgen gone—Well. What kind of knight, or kin, would I be to do aught else?"

"And I will only be able to offer them the protection of Lyonesse and Avillion, and challenge my sister, if I stop hiding," Hwyfar said, her eyes filling with tears.

Fuck all the gods, Gawain's heart bled when he saw Hwyfar cry. It was worse than being gored by a boar. And he'd experienced that at least twice.

"It's been a long time since we had an adventure of our own," Gawain said. "Are you certain you're up for it?"

"Me?" She furiously wiped at her tears, laughing. "You're the one who's the fondest of staying home and avoiding travel. I don't suppose you think we'll pull you along in a cart."

"A knight in a cart! The mad things you come up with," Gawain said, trying to laugh along with his wife.

But as he made his way to the hall for their first meal of the day, he could not shake the gnawing dread from his bones or the pain from his body.

GAWAIN WAS GLAD to see a bit of lightness in his new guests as they gathered around the table to eat, shoving one another out of the way to get to the warmest bread and plumpest fruit. They argued like cousins might, but theirs was a deceiving age, when the demands of one's body and mind are not always aligned.

Were their responsibilities not as they were, Gawain could have watched and listened to his young guests all day. But a look across the table from Hwyfar encouraged him to ask for quiet and attention.

He felt like the castle tutor, just then, striking the table to make them focus.

"Llachlyn, Percival," he said, acknowledging each in turn. There was much last-moment stuffing of faces, but they both settled. "My wife and I have had a chance to discuss the matter of your escape and the information you brought to us. I thank you for your candor and trust."

"We thank you for the food, especially," Percival said, eyes alight over the bountiful table.

"And the hospitality," Llachlyn added.

"And the wine."

"It is our duty and our pleasure," Hwyfar said.

Gawain cleared his throat. This was not exactly a speech suited for his fellow knights or to court, but he had managed more difficult audiences before. Still, he was rather nervous.

"First," Gawain said, "though we are relieved you have come to us here, we have decided the best course of action would be to return you both to Carelon."

Immediately, Llachlyn was on her feet. "No! We can't!"

"Llachlyn, please." Percival pulled at her tunic, but she snapped her hand back. "Let him speak."

"I will not. They're going to send us back to our *deaths*," Llachlyn snapped.

"No one is going—" Gawain tried to interject, but Percival now stood next to Llachlyn, looking down at her, wagging his fingers and heat rising in his cheeks.

"This is why you're always getting in trouble!" Percival cried. "You never let people finish what they're saying, and you assume the worst."

"I'm looking out for us," Llachlyn said. Gods, but she was ferocious, just like her mother. "You wouldn't notice because you're so busy sharing every secret you've ever had with the entire realm whenever you get a chance!"

"Enough!" Hwyfar's voice echoed through the hall, commanding and irrefutable. "This is not up for debate."

"How could one knight possibly protect us from the Queen's guards and her wrath?" Llachlyn demanded.

Gawain dabbed at his sweaty brow, glad for a moment that he did not have children of his own. "I am not just any knight, Llachlyn. I am Arthur's first nephew, and I have many friends at court."

"And I am not just any country wife," Hwyfar said. "I am the Queen's sister."

Both Llachlyn and Percival stopped their bickering and stared down the table where Hwyfar stood. She had planted both of her hands on the edge of the table surface, leaned forward, her braid cascading down her shoulder, and her eyes burned with fury and passion and gods above, Gawain loved her.

"Told you Dame Ragnell wasn't her real name," Llachlyn said.

"Your… Highness?" Percival tried.

Hwyfar laughed, deep and musical. "If we are being formal, I am Hwyfar of Avillion, Crown Princess of Lyonesse, Lady of Orkney, and Dame Ragnell of Thistlewood. But most everyone, including Arthur, has no idea Gawain and I are married."

Llachlyn looked impressed, sizing up Hwyfar with new eyes. "How did you manage such a ruse? And why?"

"I believe it's time for a story, love," Gawain said, settling back down in his chair.

Hwyfar told most of the tale: how she had been Arthur's intended, but he'd fallen in love with her sister Gweynevere instead. Then how Gweyn had died, and how both Gawain and she had mourned apart, not knowing they had individually held her dear. She walked the guests through the days of her loneliness and isolation from court, how she'd eventually been called back to Avillion to care for her infirm father when her other sister, Mawra, had married Arthur.

"Avillion was under great strain then, and I had no army," Hwyfar said. "So, with your mother's help, Llachlyn, I convinced Arthur to send knights to the Isle."

"And I was among them," Gawain said, remembering seeing her again arrayed like a warrior queen. "I was told to stay well away from Hwyfar, but one look at her—ah, I was doomed. The King forbade our union, even so. He meant to force Hwyfar to marry one of his knights in exchange for his assistance, but Queen Tregerna of Lyonesse, Hwyfar's mother, got dispensation when she named Hwyfar her heir."

"Did that change Arthur's mind about you?" Llachlyn asked.

There was so much more to the story, but these were the important parts. Gawain continued, "Not at all."

"Did you truly behead the Green Knight?" Percival asked.

How the story had changed from the brutal reality of Ymelda's beheading, he did not know. "No, the Green Knight is a friend. They yet live. Ymelda, Queen Tregerna's consort, did not."

"But you said you left Avillion after Arthur arrived," Llachlyn said. "How did you marry her in secret, and yet receive the King's blessing?"

"I left Avillion believing we would be kept apart forever. But our mothers conspired to influence Arthur to allow me to marry a woman with considerable land and inheritance in the North.

She was not comely, they said, nor was she healthy enough to visit the courts, but I could live out my days in peace."

"My mother owned these lands," Hwyfar said. "Gawain arrived here, prepared to meet a woman he did not know or love, but found me instead."

"For ten years we have resided here, save a few visits on my part to Carelon for feast days. Hwyfar, however, maintains more frequent contact with Lyonesse where her mother and uncle currently rule together."

"How could you be in both places? Surely someone would note your comings and goings," Llachlyn said.

"I am part of rather secretive group, and I have been working with your mother and Aunt Anna, Llachlyn, and many other similarly talented women, to keep our secrets and ways safe. I am one of very few who can travel the Path, a kind of magical road, which connects us all," Hwyfar said, then turned a bit more thoughtful. "Until Vyvian died, at least."

"A magical road would be immensely helpful right about now," Percival said, clearly captivated by the story. "But why can't you use it?"

"We do not know," Hwyfar said. "I thought, at first, it was my doing. But I have heard from another of my sisters, and she has confirmed the entire Path is inaccessible. Gawain's mother, Anna, is the best to discuss the matter with, and I will need to speak to her in person."

"But what about what Percival heard?" Llachlyn asked. "How can we be safe in Carelon when Queen Mawra knows?"

Gawain was not a man of complex thinking, and he certainly did not like the way the world was shifting. Carelon was deteriorating—it always had been, to some extent, but now it was more than surface cracks. The plaster was flaking, the beams rotting, the very foundations shaking. It had never been a place of one kind of magic, or one kind of law. Arthur, for all his faults, had built an egalitarian approach to his rule.

Gawain had long suspected Queen Mawra and Lanceloch

were involved intimately, but had never had direct proof. Very little would have ever convinced Gawain to go south again, to work to repair the relationship with his uncle. To see Lanceloch fall would be worth every painful mile.

"We will say nothing," Gawain said, staring straight at Percival. "You will be staying with us, under our protection, and only if and when we find evidence. I will speak with Arthur, as it is a matter of the crown—infidelity of this sort is nothing short of treason."

Everyone looked at Gawain, the whole room hushed but for the crackling fire and faraway chatter in the kitchens.

"Meanwhile," Gawain continued, "Hwyfar will learn all she can from my mother—and, hopefully, Morgen, once she returns—concerning the *graal* and Queen Mawra's aims."

"Our focus must be on you both returning. The Queen acted unacceptably," Hwyfar said. "She is not infallible, she is not well liked at court, but she is very clever. If she behaved in the way you say, she was afraid, perhaps coerced, into such action. My sister would not act so recklessly unless she was indeed desperate."

Llachlyn went pale as they discussed matters, focusing on her uneaten breakfast rather than interrupting again in conversation.

"Llachlyn, cousin, I know this is not the news you were hoping for," Gawain said. "And it is not the news I wished to bear. But you are right. I am just one knight, and one who has more dents than a pewter mug thrown down a flight of stairs. There are knights I trust in Carelon, knights who will protect you because I ask. If any of them find out what the Queen did to you, they would riot."

The young woman blew out a long breath, shaking her head. "I believe you. I'm just terrified."

"Nothing worth fighting for requires anything less," Gawain replied, holding up his cup. "We leave the day after next."

CHAPTER THIRTEEN

PERCIVAL

OF COURSE LLACHLYN planned on running away. That was her solution to just about every problem she ever ran into. How many times had she run away during their summers in Benwick? Too many to count. And no matter how disastrous the outcome had been, every time, she would do it again.

Percival knew she believed she didn't fit in anywhere. He felt the same way. It's why they got along so well, in ways Galahad never would.

It wasn't that Llachlyn ever said anything bad about her mother, Morgen. In fact—surprisingly, given her age and temperament—she had never uttered one criticism. Because, Percival realized, Llachlyn only had a handful of experiences with her mother. A visit here, a tour there, but never for long and never with the kind of depth she deserved.

Gawain and, well, Crown Princess Hwyfar—Percival was getting used to saying it—had a great many chores about the house to do before their trip, including visiting the local merchants and arranging for someone to bring in the rest of the harvest, not to mention what to do with the animals. There were an absurd number of animals at Thistlewood. And they seemed to follow Gawain around, in particular, with great interest.

It was a goose, though, chasing Percival at present, and he, in turn, chased Llachlyn across the fields. Though it wasn't quite raining, it wasn't *not* raining, either, and he most certainly didn't appreciate the erratic pelting across his face and the way it seeped into his clothing.

Well, not precisely *his* clothing. Hwyfar's. Because Percival wouldn't have fit in any of Gawain's trousers, let alone manage one of his cloaks. He would look like a tentpole under a canvas.

Llachlyn's short legs were quick and sturdy, and Percival was trying to both avoid the goose and all the various animal droppings in his way. Not that it would matter soon enough, if Llachlyn had her way; they'd both be back in the wilds again.

Scrambling over a stile, Percival caught a glimpse of Llachlyn's blue scarf just as the rain really started in earnest.

Frustrated and more than a bit defeated, he called out after her. "By the goddess, Mallow, will you slow down?"

"We don't have time to slow down," she called over her shoulder. "If you want, you can stay here and make eyes at the princess all the way to Carelon. I'll be leaving."

"Where exactly?" Percival asked, clutching his side. He would have thought, after days of hard travel, he'd have gotten used to running after her. "We already came here. This is where we're supposed to be."

Llachlyn tore at her hair, one step away from stomping on the ground like a petulant child. When she leveled her green stare at Percival, her cheeks flushed red.

"My mother is never coming back. If Hwyfar doesn't know where she is, then I might as well give up hope. Arthur is too sick and too distracted to even care. So I'm going to find my other family," she explained.

"You're going to walk to *Cornwall?*" Percival asked dubiously.

"If I have to. Preferably I'll steal a horse, first."

"Llachlyn, please."

He'd finally reached her, and saw now how red her eyes were from crying. When the tempest rose up in her like this, it got so hard to talk with her, so impossible to help her see through the roiling emotions.

"My grandfather's people are there," Llachlyn said. "Not many of them, but enough that they'd know me and take me in."

"Cornwall is a very long way."

"We rode here just fine."

"That's one way of putting it. But you can't seriously think you'll be going without me, can you?"

She wiped her nose on her sleeve, face bunching up against more tears. "You'll be with Galahad again. Everything will be fine for you. You're not the King's bastard. You belong with the knights—you should be one."

Percival, of course, had always dreamed of being part of the Table Round. And though he trained with Galahad, his talent certainly did not lie in the sparring field. He was a decent bowman, but no other weapons came naturally to him. It's in the realm of knowledge that Percival was best served, with his ability to remember almost anything by just seeing it once. That could be immense help on a battlefield, or the diplomatic table.

And Galahad... Gods, but Percival wished he could make sense of it all. Not just how he felt for Galahad, which was certainly more than common brotherhood, but of Llachlyn's searing jealousy on the matter. Could they not all just be friends?

"I don't want to be with Galahad right now," Percival said. He kept his voice calm, even. "I'm here with you."

"You're probably already planning what it'll be like to be back at Carelon, and all the stories you'll be able to tell him," Llachlyn said, turning away from him.

She was right, of course. He would be so excited to hear about their fights with the wolf, their battles against the elements, and meeting Gawain. He'd likely leave out the part about falling down the ravine, though.

"Galahad isn't with us," Percival said, finally managing to put his hand on Llachlyn's shoulder. "Whatever happens in all this, he will stand with his father."

"But he helped free us," she said.

"He let us go because we're his friends, not because he agrees with us," Percival said. "He doubts Arthur and he believes the *graal* belongs with the new church. His faith is complicated, but it is part of who he is."

"How will we endure it?"

Percival didn't know. For all the many things he understood in life—had read in books, had heard in conversations—how to come together across the growing chasm between them was not one of them. The deeper Galahad went into his faith, the more it seemed they were on opposing sides.

He reached out and cupped her cheek, wiping away the tears pinking her skin with his thumb. She was so fierce and so wild, and he never quite knew what to make of it.

"We'll endure it together," he said.

What if he kissed her? What would it feel like? Her dark hair was plastered to her forehead, the curls like ancient whorls, and her green eyes burned with so much emotion in her face it was like gazing through stained glass.

No, she did not desire him that way. Nor anyone, he didn't think. He could love her, if that was what she wanted, but more than once she had expressed she wanted only friendship, not romance or sex. And he didn't want to push the matter. But she was jealous, because whatever he and Galahad shared encompassed romance and desire. He didn't know how to manage them both; he couldn't bear to lose either of them. For now, he had chosen Llachlyn, his dearest friend—but what would their future at Carelon look like?

The trees behind them shook, their boughs bending, and a massive creature approached, limned in mists and obscured by the continual downpour. Percival jumped back, grabbing for his knife.

Llachlyn gasped as the mighty beast burst through the greenery, the branching horns upon its head all encrusted with moss and lichen. It was a stag, if something so grand could be so called, but easily twice as big as those Percival had seen in the King's wood. Its hooves thundered upon the earth, and its wide, black eyes surveyed the two of them with regal indifference.

Clouds of moisture plumed from its nostrils as it snorted.

The whole of its body was slightly green, not just its horns, as if it had sprung from the lichen itself.

"I see you've found Bredbeddle," came Gawain's booming voice behind them.

The knight pushed aside a dead tree as easily as if it were made of twigs, and then strode past Percival and Llachlyn with the help of a carved blackwood cane.

Immediately, the stag turned his attention to Gawain, lowering his head so the knight could pet him.

"You have a tame stag?" Llachlyn asked.

Gawain gave her a disappointed look, one eyebrow up. "Does this majestic creature look in any way *tame?* Oh, nay, lass. Bredbeddle is no pet."

Percival could not stop looking at the stag. The little mossy bits on his horns had all sprouted delicate flowers he could have sworn were not there to begin with. And every time the stag looked at him, Percival could feel something inside of him rise in recognition and fear. Or not fear, exactly—perhaps it was awe.

"I've never even heard of such a creature before," Percival said. Llachlyn had found her way back to his arms, and he gave her a squeeze. "Not even in all my books."

"Books can only take a person so far. Bredbeddle is an emissary of sorts, from a friend of mine," Gawain said. "His presence here is a good omen."

As Percival looked at Gawain, he thought for a moment his eyes were the precise hue of the moss upon Bredbeddle's horns, and faintly glowing. But then he blinked, and the light was gone. He decided he needed better sleep, less wine, and a hot bath.

Llachlyn's mouth worked, but no words came out.

"He's beautiful," Percival said.

Bredbeddle took a few booming steps forward, then bobbed his head up and down as if in acknowledgement.

"Vain creature," Gawain scolded. "Percy, you need not indulge him so. But I suppose you're right. He is a marvel, indeed." The knight turned to them, then, a glint of mischief in his eyes. "I certainly didn't expect to find you both out here, though. And in this weather."

"I was going to run away," Llachlyn said.

"Of course you were," the knight replied.

Percival had to laugh, and Llachlyn elbowed him in the stomach. "I was trying to stop her," he said.

"Sounds about right," Gawain said.

"How did you know I was here?" Llachlyn asked her cousin.

Gawain walked by them, mussing Llachlyn's hair as he did so. "Because running away is exactly what I would have done at your age. Come, now, you're both soaked through. Let's get some warm cider in you."

Warm cider sounded like a miracle. They both turned toward the house, smoke from the chimney still visible in the distance. "What about Bredbeddle?" Percival asked.

"What about him?" Gawain replied.

When Percival and Llachlyn went to look for the stag, he was gone.

CHAPTER FOURTEEN

GALAHAD

IT WAS NOT often Anna du Lac, Galahad's mother, left her own apartments in Carelon, where she spent her days weaving and reading, but when she did it was always to the courtyard with the great apple trees. Though the rain fell that morning, staining the castle near red as blood at the top, the weather had cleared enough Galahad was able to meet with her and his brother Gareth.

They sat, the three together, on a quaint bench in the courtyard garden, while sparrows flitted from branch to ground, picking up the seeds his mother always scattered for them. The chill on the wind was refreshing as crisp leaves skittered across the cobbles and earth, speaking of the oncoming autumn.

Seeing Gareth put Galahad a bit more at ease. Of all his brothers, Gareth was the most comfortable to be around. He had a calm, easy way about him, able to navigate from topic to topic, person to person, with seemingly no effort. Gaheris was restless, often angry, and took little stock in conversation, even if he was among the faithful. Most often, Gaheris spent time with Sir Lanceloch—the twins' and Gawain's stepfather by marriage—rather than with Gareth.

Their mother was a cold woman, Galahad always thought, like her sister Elaine, who had raised him. Sometimes, when he sought Anna out, she would not see him. Other times, he found her so absorbed in her weaving he wondered if he had become a ghast. But at least that was how she treated everyone. She was a stranger to all, not just her youngest son, which gave Galahad a cold sense of comfort.

Gareth, on the other hand, made Galahad feel very visible. Important, almost. Though there existed a strange, underlying tension between them at times, especially when Lanceloch du Lac or Gawain came up in conversation.

"Do you know, Gareth, that your brother Galahad asked me to Mass this evening?" Anna asked her elder son.

Gareth leaned over to look at his brother. "Did he now?"

Galahad's cheeks flushed in embarrassment, but he squared his shoulders, anyway. He wished Gareth would not tease him about his faith. "God is welcoming to all. It would be good to have more of the family in attendance."

"Gaheris is a frequent attendee, as is your cousin Mordred," Anna said. She looked queenly, the way she sat so straight with her hands on her lap and her gaze forward. As she and the King aged, they bore more and more of a resemblance to one another: the fine bones, their long noses, their snowy blond hair.

"Yes, of course, and I am glad of it," Galahad said. "It is only I wish to bring you closer to the peace I feel in the church. It is a gift, that peace." It was an honest statement, and a pure desire, but neither his mother nor his brother appeared moved.

"I do not need the walls of a church to know my god," Gareth said, clapping his brother on the back. "In fact, the idea of having to sit with dozens of other worshipers sounds rather torturous to me. Especially if Gaheris is there. I hear enough of his sermons as it is."

"Oh, but it is not!" Galahad loved the church, every sweeping arc and high-placed window, every stained-glass pane, every glittering whorl upon the altars. It was divinity writ in art. "Brother, I assure you, were you to see the inside, even just once, you would understand."

"Indeed," said their mother. "The King and Queen have spared no expense to ensure it."

Galahad fell silent. The way she pitched her voice made him aware she did not wish to discuss the matter further. But oh, how he yearned to see them understand the joy he knew in Christ, the passion experienced in those moments of connection with God, and sweet Mary of Tears.

Anna and Gareth appeared to share a look between them, and it made Galahad feel both embarrassed and angry. If the King and Queen of the realm, and indeed the most famed knight in all the kingdom, knew of God and professed his words, why not his family? It reminded him of the way Percival and Llachlyn looked at one another when he spoke of miracles.

It would take a miracle, he decided, for God to turn their hearts. But the fault may be in him. Perhaps what he felt for his brother and mother was not quite love, yet. These past few months had been one awkward dance after another, Galahad reaching out again and again, only to be turned away. At least his father enjoyed speaking of their faith. At least Lanceloch would listen.

"Come, now, brother, I know what would cheer you up," Gareth said, standing. He drew his boot across the ground as if assessing the earth, and then held up his hands as if preparing for a fight.

"You want to fight me?" Galahad asked.

Gareth grinned, his eyes gleaming. "Indeed. Not with our swords or knives, but rather in the most honest way."

"Oh, Gareth," Anna protested. "Truly, this is most unnecessary."

"Not at all, Mother. In fact, I can't think of a better way to bring this lad into our fold. Gaheris and I practically spent the first half of our lives rolling around in the mud together."

Surprisingly, that elicited a laugh from their mother. "You are not mistaken about that."

Galahad's training was focused primarily on tournament weaponry: swords, maces, lances, shields. The idea his brother would prefer *fists* of all things was both preposterous and tantalizing.

"Gareth, he's half your age," Anna said, exasperation in her voice.

"He's still my brother," Gareth said, a wicked gleam in his

eye. "And brothers tussle. Gawain used to sit on Gaheris until he tired him out."

Galahad stood, brushing off his tunic. He'd be heading to the field soon, at any rate, so there was little harm in a quick bout of sparring. Besides, he wanted to be part of their brotherhood. He had the name to match, but not the experience. Perhaps this was his way in with Gareth.

Gareth stood nearly as tall as their brother Gawain, if Gaheris was to be believed. But where Gawain was a tower of muscle and bulk, Gareth was lean and elegant, agile. Galahad took every chance he had to watch his brothers fight in the tournament field during their drills, so he had some idea of his brothers' considerable prowess.

Though Galahad could not claim such height, he had a sturdier frame than Gareth and could use the weight to his advantage. He was also far spryer, having worked just as much on his reflexes as his attacks.

But Gareth had been to the front, killed men before. The very idea of killing anyone made Galahad feel ill. Hadn't the story gone that his own father had accidentally killed a fellow knight on the tournament field?

No matter. Fighting with fists would be safe enough.

"Very well." Galahad held out his hands in a defensive stance and watched Gareth.

His brother nodded, indicating they were ready to begin.

They began circling one another. Immediately, Galahad recognized the heat within him, the flare of Christ, come to life. It was a gift, he believed, recognized by his own Aunt Elaine when he was but a child. This blessing allowed him to fight with the strength heretofore unseen in Carelon.

Always victorious. Always pure. Always blessed. He had honed that flame into a weapon, into an engine of power.

Gareth lurched forward, chuckling, and Galahad easily dodged out of the way. In all truth, he was a bit insulted by the taunting attack. Had he not heard or seen what Galahad could do? Fighting was no game to him.

And that laugh. He did not like the laugh at all.

As they circled, Galahad took the measure of his brother. He was left-handed, a trait some said indicated demonic influence. No matter; Galahad could tell Gareth also favored his right foot. An old injury, he expected. Though seven years Gawain's junior, he still was old enough to be Galahad's own father. Age was not always a sign of an easy victory, but it did make a difference.

He needed to see how he punched, how he moved to avoid injury. So, Galahad went on the offensive, throwing the first punch toward Gareth.

Gareth twisted away, dust kicking up by his boots, spinning almost like a dancer. Then, using his momentum, he grabbed Galahad around the waist and dragged him down to the ground.

The impact took the wind from Galahad's lungs for a moment, but where it might shock another fighter, he always found it strangely comforting. For a moment he did not have to think about breath, only the way his body moved.

They rolled, Galahad twisting his legs around Gareth's. He tried to pin his brother's hand to the ground, but narrowly avoided a punch to the lower abdomen when it gave Gareth more leverage. God, he was so *long*. It was like trying to wrestle a giant serpent.

Gareth was still laughing.

Was he mocking Galahad? Was he mocking his faith?

"Come now, little brother, is that all you have in you?" Gareth asked, leaning forward and squeezing Galahad's neck.

He heard other tittering. Folk had gathered in the courtyard to watch them.

The distraction and roil of emotions cost Galahad. His brother managed to slap him on the cheek, making points of white light appear on his periphery.

That pain cracked Galahad open, spilling out all of his loneliness, shame, and sense of abandonment. This was how his family treated him when he came, at last, to Carelon? To pull him out in front of half the court, to *laugh at him*. Mocking his power was mocking God, and Galahad would not stand it.

Those glittering white stars turned crimson, and Galahad used his arm to twist back Gareth's elbow, catching it and locking it into place.

"Well done," Gareth said through clenched teeth.

"I'm not finished," Galahad said. His breath whistled hot in his own nostrils, blood rushing in his veins. It was the blessing, growing and expanding within him, Christ's flare.

"Good." Gareth twisted, corded muscle flexing around Galahad's grip.

The courtyard, the audience, their mother—all vanished, to be replaced by the clarity Christ's flare gave him. And had he imagined it, or did a shadow of fear slip across Gareth's features, then?

"Now, careful. Looks like you may have battle blood, too," Gareth said. "Don't let it overtake you."

"It's not battle blood," Galahad snarled in his brother's ear. "It's Christ's flare, His blessing to me."

Even in his compromised position, Gareth rolled his eyes. "Little brother, you mistake one gift for another. No use bringing Christ into this."

Galahad roared. In response, Gareth reared up, managing to get a knee between Galahad's legs. Distantly, Galahad heard his mother's voice, saying they ought to stop, they were attracting too much notice.

It mattered not. Today they would see the power of Christ's flare. They would understand the kind of power given to those who pledged their souls to the eternal life promised. They would not laugh again, least of all his brother.

Galahad grabbed Gareth's legs and crushing his chest with his own arms, flipped him over so he was now atop him. If he'd had a sword, it would have been pointed at his brother's neck. Instead, Galahad struck him on the side of the face and pushed down on his sternum with his knee. He was screaming, shouting, his throat raw as Gareth struggled beneath his grasp.

The world was red and white light, power and purity, Christ's flare and rage and—

He didn't realize he was choking Gareth until he saw his brother's face turning blue. Horror licked his spine, and he bucked as strong hands grabbed him.

Galahad's ears rang, he tasted blood in his mouth, and at the edge of his vision Gareth sat, choking and coughing, on the ground before his mother.

Struggling, Galahad kicked his legs to free himself from his captor, but another figure emerged from the red haze around him, followed by a voice he knew well.

"If that wasn't the daftest thing I've seen all week," Sir Palomydes said. He was pinching Galahad's ear now, like an irate nursemaid. It sent a clear, shooting pain down his neck and into his arm, anchoring him back in the present.

They dragged him through a narrow hallway off the courtyard and into a small, dark room. It smelled of old silk and dust, and it helped ground Galahad somewhat. His lungs were on fire.

The other man came into view. Sir Bedevere. If any knight in the King's employ was as important as Sir Lanceloch, it was this man. He was the King's closest advisor and tactician, and a veteran of more wars than nearly anyone at court.

Sir Palomydes, Galahad knew from the training fields. He'd been teaching Galahad double sword tactics as well as flexibility, and though he was from a land leagues and leagues away to the East, he had devoted his life to Arthur and Carelon.

"Care to explain yourself?" Sir Bedevere asked.

He was tall, his steel grey hair kept back in a neat queue, and his voice was frigid as a bare tomb.

"I—I'm sorry," Galahad stammered.

"You'll need to tell that to Sir Gareth when he's done vomiting three days of meals," Sir Bedevere said.

Galahad looked to Sir Palomydes for some kind of support but saw only disappointment. "He's my brother, and I—"

"He's not *just* your brother, Galahad," Sir Palomydes said. "He's a knight, as are you. We protect our own, and we must take swift and decisive action in these circumstances."

"It was his idea!" Sweat cooled on Galahad's skin, now, as he shivered in the aftermath of his power.

If Sir Bedevere looked angry before, he was positively livid now. "I doubt he intended for you to *choke him half to death*."

"You know better than this, boy," Sir Palomydes said. "I've been working with you for weeks, and I've never seen you behave in such a way."

Galahad tried to remember what had caused it, how God would have allowed such a thing. Was there aught demonic inside of Gareth? Had he known? Or was this a holy response to his brother's mocking tone when speaking of the Lord?

He couldn't say such thoughts aloud. They would not understand.

"I'm sorry. I take full blame," Galahad said, placing his hand on his chest to show his sincerity.

Sir Bedevere made a guttural noise of disgust. "Save that kind of fighting for the tournament field. Do not provoke Gareth again, or any of your brothers. Especially in front of your mother. She is in no condition to endure fratricide right before her eyes."

"Was it so bad? I didn't—I don't remember," Galahad said. He choked back tears, angry and inconvenient. What had come over him? "It was just a tussle. And then it wasn't."

"I'll expect you on the field an extra hour this evening. You and I are going to have some long discussions," Sir Palomydes said.

Sir Bedevere went to speak, but Sir Palomydes held out his hand to stop him. "Go, Bedevere. I believe him."

"Very well, Sir Palomydes," Galahad said. "I will go directly to the chapel and seek God's guidance on this matter. I do not wish to bring shame upon our brothers in arms, nor to my family. May God help me."

"Maybe get some rest before you do that," Sir Palomydes said, giving Galahad a squeeze on his shoulder. "You look like you could use it."

CHAPTER FIFTEEN

MORGEN

YVAIN AND I traversed the dense forest of Brocéliande in silence. The forest canopy grew dense, thickened with moss and intertwining branches, time standing still as if we moved through a forever dusk. Though no precipitation fell, I smelled the promise of it in the air, bright and clean and sharp.

I sensed, too, a spiraling feeling of unrest, which deepened as we traveled west.

The hair on the back of my neck and arms rose as the sound of bird wings caught my attention.

My crows had returned. Only a handful of them, their green eyes gleaming now and then, black beaks clacking as they swooped from tree to tree.

"Friends of yours?" Yvain asked, sparing a rare moment to turn and look at me.

I contemplated a moment before speaking, pulling myself over a fallen log behind Yvain. My feet, thankfully, were considerably better, though I worried what might happen once I removed the boots.

"I suppose they are," I said. "Do they bother you?"

Melic waited for me to catch up to Yvain. He was in the habit of doing that, tail flicking impatiently while he surveyed the closing distance. There were worse things in life than being protected by a lion.

"Intrusive crows are the least of my worries in this forest," he said.

"That sounds ominous," I said.

Yvain glanced at me over his shoulder. "Everything about this place is ominous."

"I was quite enjoying the view. Everything here is so alive."

Yvain's tone was patronizing and irritated. "It surprises me the most prized of Merlin's acolytes would not sense the dangers here."

"Were I not so bereft of my usual powers, I might. But as it stands, most of my energy and attention has been spent on putting one foot in front of the other whilst you press relentlessly forward with very little concern for my old bones."

He snorted. "Ah, yes, traversing the realm like the common folk," Yvain said, taking a moment to stretch against a tree. "It must be a remarkable strain upon Her Ladyship."

"If you think I travel through Carelon on palanquins, you are gravely mistaken."

My foot sank suddenly, my boot squelching with a great sucking sensation, and a putrid, musty smell rose up alongside it. I did not need magic to know that didn't bode well.

Quicker than I expected, Yvain was at my side. "Keep still."

"I'm more than capable of extricating myself from stinking mud."

"*Keep still.*"

I complied while he drew up beside me, his body going taut as a bowstring as his gaze swept the tangling brush around us. The cold mud seeped into my boots with impressive speed, slick liquid gathering between my toes. It took all my resolve not to make a face.

Rumbling, in the distance.

Yvain grabbed my knee and said, "Relax your leg."

"Are we in danger?" I asked.

Instead of replying, he leveled me with a look that stilled my tongue. Of course we were in danger. Every moment in Brocéliande was treacherous. Especially, I mused, for a man imprisoned within it. *Ah, Modrun. What did you do?*

Relaxing my leg, and leaning on Yvain's shoulder, I allowed his manipulation until, at last, my foot was free.

With no further comment, Yvain stood up and took a step back. "Watch for those. The ground gets soft out here; boggy even."

"I noticed," I said, shivering as I took a few cold, slippery steps forward.

"Don't let it happen again. We can't lose time."

WE WALKED UNTIL the sun began to set, and I wondered at our lack of progress. Though I myself had never visited Brocéliande, I did not imagine it would take so long to reach its center.

But then, time did not feel consistent within these borders, either. Nothing did. I wondered if Modrun had employed the power of Lyonesse, somehow, altering the flow of time and distance to her whims. I heard rumbling in the distance, often, like the echoes of an incoming storm, and expected a flash of lightning in reply. Yet we never saw rain, snow, or gale.

Given my guide's obvious distaste for discussion, I spent my time focusing inward, trying to find any whispers of my power. I recited prayers I knew, incantations I had been taught, thinking that in my practice I might kindle what was lost. Nothing happened. The only piece of me I could reach was my power as death's maiden, that keeper of the threshold between life and death. I felt the death of the forest all around me, but then what else was this place than the very crux of decay and rebirth?

My grief was palpable, but I could not imagine it had obliterated all else.

Even so, when we at last stopped by a small stream, Melic immediately splashed into the water like an exuberant puppy and I had to stifle a laugh.

Yvain kept his eyes on the treetops. My crows still followed.

"We will rest here for the night," Yvain said, not looking at me. "Then commence again in the morning."

Entirely at his mercy, I nodded and went to make for the water.

His arm shot out, blocking my way. "Drink from this," Yvain said, handing me the flask we'd been sharing. "That water is not to be trusted."

"Melic doesn't seem to mind," I said, taking the proffered water while I watched Melic lap up buckets of water with his immense tongue.

"Melic is made of this place. You are not."

Cryptic, as usual.

Despite myself, I shivered. My boots were still wet, and the temperature quickly descended as dusk fell upon us. Yvain, who noticed everything, pursed his lips and strode over to a small, flat area beside the water's edge. There, he cleared a space of detritus to reveal a ring of stones, charred from use.

Within a few minutes, Yvain had a roaring fire going, the heat so intense it made my eyes hot.

"Let's look at your feet," he said after we'd eaten dried fruit and nuts together in silence.

"I'm fine," I said, angling my legs away from him.

"No, you aren't."

Why did this man disagree with me on everything? "I am Morgen le Fay. I can mind my own feet!" I snapped.

"Just like you've minded your fingers?" He gestured to my hand, clutched before my chest in anger. The deep, blue-black color had spread to my palms, now.

Salvaging the tender, shredded vestiges of my pride, I consented to his request and removed my boots and socks.

The pain of my released feet left me breathless, the compression no longer disguising what lay beneath, and I fell back on my palms, gasping.

The foot within the drier boot merely burned, the skin swollen but otherwise unremarkable.

But the other foot, which had been in mud and moisture for the better part of the day, was a mess of angry red whorls, twisting out from the lacerations on my sole. My toenails were black as my fingernails, too.

"I suspect walking around in a wet boot didn't help matters," Yvain said quietly.

"If you knew that, why didn't we stop?" I demanded, trying to breathe through the pain. Anger helped.

"It wasn't safe," Yvain said simply.

"And *this* is safe?" I gestured to the eerie wood around us, branches creaking and my crows flitting above us from time to time.

"No. But it's saf*er*." He pulled out a small roll of leather from his pack, unwinding it to display a series of small implements: needles, tweezers, combs, all carved of bone.

I swallowed as he grabbed the tweezers.

"Yvain…" I cautioned.

"I'm going to need to remove what's in there."

My mouth went very dry, and I stood very still. "What?"

"You should look away," he said, leveling me with a serious look, dark brows knitted so a line formed between them.

"I've tended the dead, cured the sick, and interpreted the direst prophecies. I am no fainting maid. I hardly think I will—"

He met my gaze. "You have worms in your foot, Morgen. They're much bigger than you'd expect once you pull them out."

Parasites. My wounds had attracted them on the trek, and fueled by the forest's magic, they had taken root, quite literally, under my skin.

Nausea roiled within me, my world narrowing, my vision dimming.

Panicking, I went to pull my foot away, but Yvain grabbed my calf, his hand reaching around my entire ankle.

"Look. I have no desire to do this either, but if you're hobbled, you will slow us down."

"You seem unusually eager," I said.

Yvain's expression softened. "If Modrun lets you out, there's a chance she might let me out. Or at least open up the forest long enough for me to try."

I looked at my hands, at the puce and purple skin, wondering how a mother could do such a thing to her child.

He followed my gaze. "Do your hands hurt, as well?"

"They look as if they should. Do you think it's the same, my feet and my hands?"

"No," Yvain said.

"How do you know?"

"I just do. I'm the son of a witch and the longest-living inhabitant of Brocéliande outside of my mother." He nodded his chin to my fingers. "That is something you brought with you."

His words, spoken in that deep, even voice, distracted and disturbed me enough for him to pull out the first of the creatures from my foot. It resisted his grasp, moving deeper under my skin, but Yvain yanked impatiently, and my skin stretched and caught, as if barbed, then snapped back.

As the firelight illuminated the first writhing worm, twisting around in Yvain's tweezers and wrapping around his wrist, it screamed. And I, Morgen le Fay, famed sorceress and priestess prime, fainted, indeed, like a maid.

THE COALS BURNED low when I awoke, my foot throbbing and itchy but tolerable. I was under a second cloak, Yvain's, and far above me I saw tiny glimpses of the starry night sky, interspersed with the green-eyed crows' glittering stares.

Melic was curled behind me, his silky mane tickling the back of my neck, snoring softly.

I had not slept under the stars or trees for ages. Well over twenty years, in fact, back to the days when I'd traveled with Merlin. He had always preferred the shelter of a tent but I, wild and goddess-touched, wandered under the open sky and waited for the moon. It also gave me time to myself while the old bard slept, his hands no longer roaming and demanding.

Slowly sitting up, I recognized the source of my irritation: Yvain had wrapped my foot in yarrow sprigs. I smelled their sweet, dusty fragrance as I wiggled my toes.

Emerging from the darkness, Yvain threw down a bundle of wood and sat down across from me.

"Yvain... I—thank you," I stammered clumsily. My face heated with embarrassment, tempered with not a little shame. How had I come to this?

He nodded, the only indication I would get from him. "They're grotesque, but survivable."

"Encouraging," I said, drawing the cloak around my shoulders.

Yvain did not reply right away and Melic shivered, then nestled closer to me, accidentally nudging me toward the fire.

"Tomorrow will be easier," he said.

"Did you find me a palanquin?"

For a brief moment I thought I managed to make the man laugh, but when I looked again, he was just as surly and serious as ever, poking the fire with a stick to agitate the coals. "Go to sleep, Morgen," he said.

Exhaustion settled over me, heavier than Melic. I fell back asleep while the crows cackled overhead.

YVAIN WAS CORRECT. My feet were raw but sturdy, and once I was laced into my boots once again and had a meagre breakfast, I felt a faint glimmer of hope that perhaps we could reach Modrun, and I might be granted leave of the wood.

My guide wasted no time moving, after ensuring my feet were properly dressed, and with Melic beside me and the crows above, we went deeper into Brocéliande.

The forest floor dried as we left the water behind. I spied plenty of late autumn blooming plants, but noticed a conspicuous absence of fungi and fauna. Given the lush environment I expected birds, frogs, and even deer and rabbits.

Occasionally Yvain hummed to himself or asked after me in his brusque, straightforward manner, but we had no conversations of interest.

The vegetation grew so thick by the afternoon that Yvain had to hack through it to progress, using his long daggers like scythes. Had I my magic, I could have parted and quickened our progress, but empty as I was, I simply stood back and watched him.

I had just disentangled myself from a particularly enthusiastic clutch of vines when I realized we were at last at a clearing.

The wind rose up as we stepped forward, the sky streaked with long, blue clouds high above. I let the sun hit my face, watching the red glow behind my eyelids.

"I was beginning to wonder if the sun ever came out here," I said to Melic, who was again at my side.

I reached for his pelt just as he began growling, the reverberation sending a chill up my arm in warning.

More rumbling, closer this time. The trees across the glade shuddered, tops snapping as a misty form emerged. I smelled a charge in the air, a metallic burn, followed by a cry so loud it made my ears ring.

Beside me, Yvain unsheathed his sword. "Stay here," he said.

Wind whipped across the glade in every direction, ripping leaves from the trees and churning up columns of dirt and leaf mold.

And I gazed up, my eyes fixing on the two-stalked head, the glittering yellow scales, the fibrous and deteriorating wings.

A cockatrice. Bigger than a cottage, ranker than a bloated corpse. I had never seen one with my own eyes, only having sourced precious components a few times in my life for spells and incantations.

Immediately, I propelled myself forward. To do what? I did not know.

I made it only a few strides into the glade when Yvain turned around, teeth gritted and a look of rage on his face. He threw out his hand and immediately I was encased in a dome of glittering glass.

I gasped.

Yvain was a mage.

CHAPTER SIXTEEN

LLACHLYN

LLACHLYN RODE IN the middle of their small caravan upon a bay palfrey, trying to focus on the task at hand, but she could not properly wrest her thoughts away from what almost happened before the stag, and Gawain, interrupted them.

Aunt Vyvian's voice came to her again: *Romances and trysts are for the weak of mind and spirit. You, Llachlyn, come from the ancient line of Avillion. Fortify your spirit against such dalliances and you will be powerful beyond imagination. Your true love is metal and fire and flux.*

On their escape north, she and Percival spent days alone together, and never had he once touched her or even looked at her in such a way. Theirs was a deep friendship built on shared humor, a love of stories, and significant amounts of wine.

Part of her wanted the romance of it all, but there was too much jealousy in his attentions for Galahad. It was not that she wanted Percival—she just didn't want him and Galahad to have each other that way. She would be left alone. She could never compete with shining, perfect, handsome, virtuous Galahad. He was everything she was not.

Goddess. She did not want to have to be with them in the same room again.

So absorbed was she in these meandering, stomach-twisting thoughts, she failed to notice the direction they were traveling.

Llachlyn craned her neck around, eliciting a somewhat sheepish smile from Percival behind her.

"Are we traveling north?" Llachlyn asked.

Gawain, before her on a sturdy cob, nodded. "We are indeed."

Both Gawain and Hwyfar were arrayed in the lightest, most curious armor Llachlyn had ever beheld. It was a grey-green hue, etched with spirals and knot work, with nary a seam to be seen. She could not tell if it was hammered metal or made of hardened leather, and under their lush, moss green velvet cloaks and their red hair, the couple looked like a king and queen out of the oldest tales.

"Carelon is to the south," she reminded him.

Her cousin laughed, deeply and mirthfully. She felt the sound of it in her chest, warm and comforting.

"Yes, Llachlyn, I know where Carelon is," he said. "And we will head south tomorrow morning. There's one person we need to visit first."

"This is the first I'm hearing of it," Llachlyn said.

Hwyfar replied, her long braid swishing behind her, "You ought to listen more and quiet your thoughts."

"Easy to say, terribly difficult to do," Llachlyn said. "Who is this person?"

Gawain was quiet a moment, sharing a look with his wife over his shoulder. "They are rather difficult to describe. Let's just say they are an old friend, who has been known to help us in times of need."

A FEW HOURS later, the four travelers came to a half-ruined chapel, swallowed in lichen and vines, looking as if it had grown from the landscape itself.

Try as she might, Llachlyn could not quite absorb what she saw. The chapel was shaped as one might expect: an angular roof—what there was of it—and even a steeple. That was where it all ended, for the walls were either mottled and actively crumbling or else made out of vines. It was hard to tell if the vegetation was devouring the chapel, or if the chapel had grown from the vegetation.

Everything was green. The stairs, the walls, the thick tree trunks and even the stained glass in the rose window.

She looked sidelong at Percival, whose pupils were so wide his eyes appeared black, as if he'd gotten into a vial of belladonna.

Gawain and Hwyfar were, if anything, bordering on giddiness. The knight dismounted with a grunt, but then helped his wife down by grasping her by the waist and embracing her as her body slipped down his. Their eyes shone and they kissed, long and unbothered by their audience.

Llachlyn cleared her throat. "You seem to enjoy it here," she observed.

Hwyfar laughed, drawing her hand down her husband's face. "We were married here, more than ten years ago. It was a small affair, only a few in attendance, those we knew we could trust."

"And a lion," Gawain said, winking at Llachlyn.

She truly did not know if he was jesting or if it was true.

"This is a chapel, you said?" Percival asked. "It looks as if it might not be in use at the moment."

"Come, boy, get off that horse and let me introduce you both," Gawain said, waving them over. "Our friend is wise beyond the ways of our own world, and I thought it important that you speak to them."

Llachlyn dismounted first, avoiding Percival by a few more feet than might be considered appropriate. They both followed Gawain and Hwyfar up the rough stairs and toward the towering doors.

Gawain paused a moment, listening, then placed his hand upon the door. Immediately his armor began glowing, and Hwyfar's as well. Llachlyn noticed they both carried not just swords, but axes, too, which came alight now, both of them, with tongues of green fire and brilliant, gold filigree. Their eyes danced as they looked at one another, and just as Llachlyn opened her mouth to ask for some clarification, the large wooden doors swung open.

Magic. Real, elemental, living magic. She had seen charms and small spells from her mother and aunts, but not like this. Wonder bloomed in her chest, and she itched to understand what it was she saw.

Llachlyn could not remember passing through the doors. She only remembered walking, barefoot, onto soft moss in a forest clearing dappled with afternoon sunshine. It streamed into the small glade, which was shaped very like the interior of a chapel.

Neither Percival nor her cousin and his wife were anywhere near. She had just shifted across some unknowable distance, as her mother might have done, propelled by a magic force she had felt but could not manipulate.

She spun in a slow circle, trying to calm her racing thoughts, unsure if she had fallen into a dream or a curse. On her fifth turn around, Llachlyn flinched when she came face to face with a pair of ancient green eyes as large as plums.

The eyes, of course, belonged to a being, but her mind could not assemble the pieces of them together at first. They were green and massive, even larger than Gawain, and shaped both like a tree and a man. Though Llachlyn could see no chair, they sat with a large pike across their lap. Upon their head rested a crown made of spiraling icicles, each daubed with ruby cabochons. Their hair floated behind them, gently moving in an unseen breeze, the color of spring grass. Their skin, if it could be called that, was mossy and inviting, though mottled just like the walls of the chapel, aged verdigris.

"Llachlyn. Child of Morgen, daughter of fate, heir of the blood," the creature said. Green moths flew out from behind them as he spoke, flitting up to the sky in a twirling dance. Green-bodied beetles circled their feet. "Welcome to the Green Chapel."

"How do you know my name?" Llachlyn asked.

"The forest tells me," they said simply. "And you met Bredbeddle, and *he* told me."

Deciding the creature would not hurt her, at least initially, Llachlyn held her chin high and tried to look imperious the way

Hwyfar did. She did not want to show her fear. Many people mistook Llachlyn for a frightened creature, given how small she was; they did not know she was forged of steel. "Will you honor me with *your* name?"

The creature laughed and it sounded like a thousand leaves rustling at once while a babbling brook rushed over smooth rocks and down a waterfall. Something about that reminded Llachlyn of her Aunt Vyvian.

"Your cousin calls me the Green Knight. And that suffices."

"The Green Knight! The one he freed?" Llachlyn asked. The sunlight was so lovely on her skin, warmer and brighter than it had been in years. It reminded her of afternoons in Benwick when she and Galahad were children, chasing the butterflies, cornflowers rising around them in a blue-bobbing haze. "I thought you'd left this world."

"Gawain of Orkney keeps curious minds at bay with little lies. I am grateful."

She peered at their face again, lost in the shadowed green. "What are you?"

The Green Knight shifted, luminous eyes narrowing slightly. "That is a brave question to ask. Most often it is I who demand answers."

"I'm sorry. I didn't know there were rules."

The Green Knight laughed. "Fay child, indeed. What would you like to know?"

"Are you a god?"

"Perhaps I was, once. But my time is coming to an end, here. Your cousin and the princess helped me and, as such, have my protection. And advice, when they need it. They visit quite regularly."

"Gawain will need to tell me the whole story next time," Llachlyn said. "He clearly omitted some very important details."

"He is certain to tell you when he is ready," the Green Knight said. "But we are not here to speak of Gawain of Orkney."

"We're not?"

"No, little one. I sense great uncertainty in you."

"You wouldn't understand," Llachlyn replied softly.

The Green Knight chuckled, or as close to it as such a creature could manage. "I have lived longer than nearly every creature upon this earth. I have heard prophecies rise and fall, seen civilizations wither and dry up. So yes, I certainly do understand that your heart is troubled, more and more each passing day."

The Green Knight's eyes pierced through to her soul, looking deep and breaking her heart with their clarity. No one had ever looked at her that way, as if she was scoured of her body and stood as a naked spirit, the window to her very essence open to see.

"My father is the King," she said, her voice hardly a whisper. She had no reason to lie, not even the inclination. "And I suppose most people know, but they hate me for it."

"You are also from a long line of powerful women, yet you are but an ember of their magic. You have not been nurtured or trained, not shown the Sight or the Path. Why is that?"

"My mother has kept me away from court because she believes I may destroy Carelon. And Arthur along with it."

Llachlyn had never spoken the last words aloud. Oh, her friends knew her parentage, and she suspected half the court did as well. Without a doubt Queen Mawra, who had never brought a child to term with Arthur, held all kinds of hatred for her personally on the subject. But they did not know the whole truth of it.

The Green Knight nodded, but did not seem concerned. Their body moved, groaning in the effort as wood and sinew moved and reshaped. "Tell me the words of the prophecy, child."

"I didn't say it was a prophecy," Llachlyn said.

"Am I wrong?"

Llachlyn let her arms fall to her sides in defeat. "No."

"Then tell me."

She took a deep, steadying breath. "'The first born of Arthur will bring his end.'" There, she'd said it. "I am the first born of Arthur."

"Are you?"

"Of course I am. If I had a sibling, someone would have told me."

A slow, creaking smile moved the Green Knight's strange face. "Would they?"

"You ask a great many questions."

"Indulge me. It is usually the other way around."

She sighed. "My mother is a wise woman. A powerful woman. She both gave and interpreted prophecies for dozens of years. I do not think she would have told me something so grievous if it was not possible."

"All of those things are true, but Morgen le Fay is merely a mortal driven by fear, just as any parent is. And kings are known for sowing bastards like weeds."

"Are you saying I'm not Arthur's doom?" Llachlyn's eyes burned with tears, and her heart raced helplessly.

The Green Knight let out a long, earthy sigh, smelling of fresh tilled earth and fresh water. "That I did not say. Prophecies are a terrible business, and rarely do they mean what we think. It is why sorcerers like Merlin and Morgen learned to *interpret* them, to twist the language for clarity—and for their own gain. But Arthur has raised a son, Mordred, the son first in his heart. And he has a bastard, born years before you both. Gawain will tell you if you ask him."

A thrill of hope and fear intermingled inside Llachlyn, but she set her face into a mask of grim determination. "No matter my curse, I cannot do this alone. My mother is lost."

"Morgen le Fay is not lost. You will see her again. And I suspect she knows your fate is not yet set. There are many ways to kill a kingdom, many hands that twist the knives and pluck the eyes, and you alone should never hold such a burden."

Why had her mother allowed her to believe it? Llachlyn pressed at her eyes with the back of her hands, trying to breathe slowly and recount their few conversations on the topic. Morgen would not be moved beyond her insistence that it was safer for everyone if Llachlyn remained outside Carelon.

"But you have never truly been alone, have you?" The Green Knight leaned forward and pulled something out of the air beside Llachlyn.

She looked to her right, where a brilliant crimson thread trailed from her heart and up into the sky. The Green Knight raised their other hand and pulled at her left side: a golden thread, shimmering and far brighter than the red, trailing up and away again.

"What does that mean?" Llachlyn asked.

"I am not here to give you answers, Llachlyn, Daughter of Fate. Only you can find them. Strange and painful days lie ahead for you and your friends, your family—but also days full of wonder. You hold power in your hand, you must only decide how to shape it. Hope is a small thing, but it is the most powerful thing in the world."

The Green Knight began fading, a green mist rising around them both.

"Don't go!" Llachlyn cried, reaching out. Her hands met nothing. "What of the *graal*? Was our vision true?"

Laughter, deep and ancient, rattled through Llachlyn's mind. "You know what is true, but you must hold the answer and fashion it anew."

MOMENTS LATER, LLACHLYN stood again on the steps of the chapel, Hwyfar wrapping her in a warm, much needed embrace. She could not move, so frozen was she in her body from fear and revelation; her throat was sore from shouting. Had she been shouting at the Green Knight?

"Breathe with me, Llachlyn," Hwyfar said, her voice hypnotic and comforting.

"What did they do to her?" Percival's voice was high and shrill, but Llachlyn could not look at him.

"That is her business alone," Gawain said. His voice was weary, though hesitant. "We did not expect that to happen, Llachlyn. I must ask your forgiveness."

"Don't grovel until you're certain the situation requires it," Hwyfar said to her husband.

The princess brought Llachlyn over to a low bench outside the chapel, never letting her more than a handspan from her embrace. Llachlyn did not argue; she sensed a deep, welcome calm coming from the princess, along with the scent of honeysuckle and sweet rose.

Eventually, Llachlyn ceased her weeping, helped in no small way by Hwyfar's gentle humming and rocking. The men meandered, speaking lowly to one another, and she was glad for their distance in the moment.

"You do not need to tell me what burdens you so," Hwyfar said. "But know that I am here to bear it with you, whatever it may be."

Llachlyn shivered, pulling away from the princess, her eyes dry and her lips still trembling. No one had ever offered help to her like that; certainly none of the people who raised her. Sometimes Sir Hector was kind to her, indulgent even. But Lady Elaine always insisted Llachlyn manage her own troubles. It made Llachlyn's heart feel as warm as when Gawain laughed.

"Thank you." She took a deep breath again, measured, as Hwyfar clasped her hands.

"Very good, Llachlyn. You see? We can move through pain to peace and, sometimes, to joy after."

It was easier to speak now, the fear and shock becoming more distant. Llachlyn glanced over at where Percival and Gawain stood talking. "Did you each visit the Green Knight alone?"

"No," Hwyfar said. "The three of us were together."

Llachlyn felt shame grip her, hot and cold at the same time. Why was she always the one left out? "I should never have come here. You should have let me run away."

Hwyfar studied Llachlyn's face, her sharp features relaxing slightly. "Fate can be cruel, and even brutal at times, Llachlyn. But no one of us alone can claim to be the sole source of conflict." She sounded very like the Green Knight.

"You don't understand. You're powerful and beautiful and clever and I am not," Llachlyn insisted.

"Llachlyn, hear me," Hwyfar said. She took Llachlyn's chin in her hand and angled her face up, so she had to look into the princess's endless amber eyes. The ferocity there, the fury, was unmistakable. "Not all of the gods' gifts are loud, and all the better for those who wield them. Your line, and mine, have survived not because we proclaimed our power, but because we learned to wield it in the shadows. And that power is a choice. Who do you desire to be, Llachlyn le Fay?"

A stab of regret flared in Llachlyn's heart, wishing she had grown up with a woman like Hwyfar to guide her. Instead, every step of her life she had stood eclipsed by Galahad, for whom everything seemed effortless. Eventually, with constant chastising from Aunt Elaine and endless injuries and disappointments, she had just stopped trying. And her mother had been no help, always keeping her at a distance, reminding her of her shortcomings.

"I don't know," Llachlyn whispered. "Aside from what I learned of smithing from Vyvian, I have little to offer anyone, least of all myself."

Hwyfar seemed to contemplate this for a moment, her nostrils flaring as she warred with her silent thoughts. "Well. If your mother did not grant you the mysteries of the Isle, perhaps I can begin."

Going to argue, Llachlyn shut her mouth when Hwyfar held up her gloved hand. "I know Morgen had her reasons, but she is not here now, and she entrusted us with you. She would have known I'd not stand by and see you flounder."

"What if I become a danger?" Llachlyn asked.

Hwyfar's expression was wicked, her lips twisting into a devastating smirk. "Oh, darling. All women are dangerous. It all depends on how you shape your danger."

CHAPTER SEVENTEEN

HWYFAR

THE VISIT TO the Green Knight had not gone as anticipated, but then Hwyfar learned long ago that trying to predict the ancient being was a futile endeavor. Though she knew the Green Knight would not harm them, Hwyfar still felt a jolt of terror when she realized Llachlyn had not entered the chapel the same way as the rest.

"She is safe," the Green Knight said from their ornate chair in the center of the chapel, before anyone could utter a word.

Gawain was red-faced, furious. "I will hold you to that," he said. "A bit of warning would have been helpful."

The Green Knight stood to their full height, seeming to fill up the crumbling chapel from every corner, thousands of vines undulating in concert with their movements. Though Hwyfar never saw anyone else in the chapel, she always had the sense there were others watching, keeping the Green Knight company—an ancient court, just out of view.

"She is safe, son of Lot," repeated the Green Knight. "You forget I am in your debt as long as we all live. The Daughter of Fate carries burdens I cannot share, but requires acknowledgement in confidence."

Gawain stiffened. Of all his monikers, "Son of Lot" was his most loathed, even if true. Hwyfar watched as he balled his fists together and tried to form a coherent response.

Yet there was another moniker Hywfar found intriguing: *Daughter of Fate.* The words rippled through her mind, familiar and yet insubstantial. The Circle of Nine knew well of Llachlyn's potential, but after significant work, none had determined any glimmer of power in her. Fate, Hwyfar knew well, and such a title should not be taken lightly.

Hwyfar swept forward. Her husband was far less capable in diplomatic situations when he was already irate. "Green Knight, thank you for seeing us. We bring you one Percival, son of King Pellinore, who has lately seen visions, in addition to Llachlyn le Fay. They are friend, kin, and under our protection."

"Thank you, Hwyfar of Avillion, Daughter of Tregerna," the Green Knight said. They reached out and took a lock of her hair in their long sinuous vines, turning it over in their hands. "Time does not dim your light, nor does it quell your power. Keep to the Path, even when you have no guide."

Hywfar bowed, her hand upon her chest with relief. Indeed, since the Path fell, her own powers felt muted, unreliable. Lonely. Gawain did his best to comfort her, but he was not part of the Circle of Nine. He did not carry the same burdens, nor a kingdom in the balance as they did. Her mother was ailing, and soon, she would have to make her own choice about her inheritance in Lyonesse.

The Green Knight shifted, their whole body slithering in tendrils of verdigris, shivering in unison almost like waves upon a pond. "Come forward, Percival."

No moniker. That was strange.

Hywfar watched as Percival ambled forward, shoulders hunched and eyes wide. He was trembling.

The Green Knight leaned toward him, long vines rising behind them and stretching toward the lad. Hywfar recalled what that felt like and wondered if it was the same for the young man. Did he sense a thousand, gentle breezes? Smell the loam and ancient waters? See glimpses of the magics of the earth itself?

It was always the eyes, though, that brought Hywfar to the

precipice. The Green Knight's eyes were more fathomless than the night sky, dappled with glimmering threads of light, a world within a single creature. That Ymelda had managed to capture them still astounded her; even more so that she and Gawain had freed the Green Knight and vanquished the corrupted sorceress.

But then, she had held the *graal* spear. If not for that, neither Gawain nor the Green Knight would yet live.

Hwyfar's anxious thoughts calmed when she saw Percival relax and a smile spread across his face. Yes, there was that, too. When the Green Knight connected with you, all else in the world seemed inconsequential and distant, and joy complete. For a moment, at least.

"As this is your first visit to see me, Percival, you may ask me five questions. You can choose to ask them all now, or return again when the time requires it," the Green Knight said. "I am older than most creatures which walk upon the earth, and my power, though thin, spreads farther than you can measure."

Percival went to speak, and Hwyfar put a handle hand on his shoulder. The young man turned slowly, and she saw the telltale connection between him and the Green Knight: his dark eyes now shimmered green and gold, spiralling through each iris.

"Choose well, Percival," she cautioned. "Listen to your heart."

He nodded, slowly, as if he heard her words from a long distance away.

"Green Knight," Percival said. "Did my friends and I truly share a vision of the *graal*?"

CHAPTER EIGHTEEN

PERCIVAL

PERCIVAL'S MIND KINDLED in a green fire, lost in the Green Knight's gaze. All else fell away—the room, Gawain and Hwyfar. He stood, alone, mind to mind with this creature of magic and power.

So much was clear to him in ways they had never been before. All the smaller concerns of his life—his worries of his appearance or his bearing, his quibbles with his friends and his family—melted away as if through a mist. He wondered how he had ever let such things burden him in the first place.

"Green Knight," he said. "Did my friends and I truly share a vision of the *graal*?"

The chapel hall rumbled as the Green Knight let out a low, humming sound. Percival felt the reverberations all the way up into his teeth and his nose hairs. It made him want to sneeze.

"I am familiar with this *graal*," the Green Knight said. "And you have, indeed, seen a vision of the Shield of Joy. But I believe you knew that already. You ought not waste your questions on knowledge you yet have."

Percival let the weight of disappointment fall upon him. He had so many questions, but the Green Knight was correct: he had already known the answer to that.

Four questions remained.

"Is Galahad right in his belief that the *graal* comes from his god and not our own?" Percival asked.

The Green Knight's massive arms and legs quivered, the sound like a thousand dry beans in a basket. The small leaves along their crown flashed purple for a moment before dimming again.

"The *graal* belongs to no faith and all faiths. The *graal* was here before the gods and will remain after them. Its purpose is not to reveal its allegiances but to bestow miracles upon its wielders, or else be kept hidden. To relegate its power to one faith or another only diminishes its true purpose. You are that balance, Percival Lightbringer."

Lightbringer? Percival had to admit he quite liked that name. No one had ever given him such a moniker before, though he'd certainly coined his own now and again in daydreams.

The Green Knight spoke, as if he had heard Percival's own thoughts. "Know that one may only bring light where it is lacking. Light is not might, it is bare truth and illumination. The dark, itself, is not evil; and the light can be a scourge when it burns too brightly."

Your curiosity will be the end of you, his father King Pellinore often told him. *Just stop asking questions and follow along like everyone else.*

The warning in the Green Knight's words turned Percival's stomach. Unlike Galahad, Percival had no dreams of gallant fighting and great deeds of the sword. He had no driving desire to vanquish evil, mostly because he did not feel as if he had a clear idea of it. Galahad's constant need to ensure his actions were right was exhausting. What Percival wanted was joy, and to bring joy to others. There was nothing greater to him than making someone he loved smile, and no worse pain than watching them weep.

As a bastard, and one clearly unwanted, he'd striven to avoid notice whenever possible, but to also cleave to those who he knew truly cared. And, frankly, until he'd met Galahad and Llachlyn, there'd been few of them; none, if you discounted the animals.

Yet his two friends were opposite poles on a pendulum: a near priest of a Christian and the daughter of a famed witch. They loved and hated each other, and he was ever forced to provide the balance. Not that he was solely correct, but he could not believe either of them were wrong, either.

Galahad could see no center. The closer he drew to his faith the more he clung to an impossible duality that made his friendship and kinship with Llachlyn more impossible. Percival had thought it was a miracle that Galahad had let them go, but now he wondered if it was to the young knight's benefit after all. Without Percival advocating for Llachlyn, Galahad would live in his stark world of good and evil without question.

Percival, what if God sent this vision to test me? Galahad had asked him through the grate of their cell. Llachlyn was sleeping, he'd never have dared say such a thing around her. *What if it is a trial to see if my faith is pure? What if she is just my foil in all this?*

If the *graal* was not Galahad's, not a vision from his god, Percival was more at ease. Perhaps if he saw Galahad again, he would have the chance to explain that, if he would even believe it. If he did not accuse the Green Knight of being a demon. And that was not likely. Percival did not even know how to begin the tale of this part of their travels to anyone, let alone his pious friend.

"You may ask another question, unless you prefer to sit in your thoughts," the Green Knight said.

He most certainly did not.

"Do you know my mother's name?" Percival asked. "My father had a litter of bastards, but most of them were begat on local women or minor nobles, and they often visited. Whenever I asked him, he said I was a bastard's bastard."

"Pellinore is not your father, as well you have always suspected," the Green Knight said. A cold, brisk wind moved Percival's curls, his cloak suddenly flapping as if he were at the edge of a great cliff. And perhaps he was.

"I—well, I wouldn't say I *suspected*," Percival said, his voice cracking with emotion. "I suppose I hoped, as any child who grows up with a cruel father, that we were not blood. But I did not ask about my father."

"I do not think giving you your mother's name would serve you now. For she is not among the living."

Percival clutched his chest at the sudden pang of grief that grasped him. "Did she die a long time ago?" he asked.

"Yes. When you were very young." The Green Knight swayed slightly. "You look as your mother did."

"And my true father?" Was he some ill-begotten knave? No, Percival had to believe if he was raised among Pellinore's litter, given a noble's education and attentions, it was for a reason. Still. The shock was immense.

"He loved your mother in secret, before you were stolen away to serve the whims of Merlin the conjuror. But truths come to light. Ask the daughter of Lyonesse, for she is wise in such matters."

"Princess Hwyfar?"

"The same. She will answer you, if you ask. But you must be prepared for the answer. Now, you must go, Percival Lightbringer. May joy lead your heart to the truth it seeks."

The very air turned shimmering green, so bright it might have been the sun. Leaves flew across Percival's face, and he threw up his arms to protect himself. Then, with a rush of air, he felt Gawain's arms around him, and they staggered back as one.

Breathing heavily, picking leaves and detritus out of their hair, the three stood again on the steps of the chapel as if they had never gone in.

A wracking sob grabbed his attention. Percival turned to see Llachlyn crying in a way he had never seen before. Immediately, Hwyfar went to her and took her aside. Percival tried to follow but Gawain stood in his way. It was like an anthill trying to compete with a mountain.

"Come, Percival, let Hwyfar talk with her," Gawain said. "She's far better suited."

"Because she's a woman?" Percival asked.

"No, because she's a *sorceress*."

Princess. Sorceress. Dame. Percival wondered if it was difficult for Hwyfar to balance so many identities at once. But wasn't he doing the same now? He wasn't just a bastard, was he? He was a, what, a *foundling?*

Dusk turned the sky a deep lavender hue, the vines and plants now dark viridian. Gawain's own red hair looked muted and dark, his green eyes shadowed.

"Don't look over there, give her space," Gawain commanded. He put one of his big hands upon Percival's shoulder and guided him away.

"Did the Green Knight hurt her?" Percival asked.

"I should limit *you* to five questions," Gawain teased.

"I only asked three."

"Do you want to go back in and ask them more?"

Percival swallowed on a very dry throat. "No, sir."

"I'm sorry. I wasn't expecting such a show."

"What were you expecting, exactly?" Percival asked. His head was throbbing.

Gawain hesitated, glancing over at his wife. "I wanted you both to have a chance to speak with them, to test your mettle and to see if they knew aught of your plight. And perhaps offer you a bit of protection. Besides, we needed the Green Knight's knowledge, because the *graal* is beyond even Arthur and Morgen. And my wife there? She held a *graal*. Wielded it. And in doing so, helped free the Green Knight from a terrible curse. It has given her a long-standing gift, a kind of Sight, but it is not always reliable."

Percival had no trouble imagining Princess Hwyfar arrayed in armor, the light of the *graal* illuminating her face and hair.

"She held it…" Percival was astonished, his heart thumping unexpectedly with a mix of continued fear and excitement. "She wielded it! By heaven, that must have been quite the sight."

Gawain chuckled. "She did, and it was glorious. The spear, by the way. Though she had seen the cup, as well. They are hidden, now, and we do not know where."

"But no one has seen the shield. At least, not until our vision."

"No. Not in time out of mind. Ten years of work have given

no clarity on the subject. And Hwyfar and I have been, as you have seen, somewhat hindered from traveling."

Percival ran his hands nervously down his thighs, trying to order his rushing thoughts. "I believe the Green Knight may have told me I'm a foundling or some such. They did not call me son of Pellinore, even though the princess introduced me with the title."

"That is curious."

"They said the princess would know."

Gawain frowned, looking up at the sky, as if in supplication. "Hmm. Yes, my wife knows many things."

This day had made Percival weary indeed. "Would this Sight of hers be of assistance?"

"Do you want to know the truth, lad?" Gawain asked, kneading at his knee and wincing. "And would it make a difference?"

It was a good set of questions, Percival thought, from a man who appeared more brawn than brain. Perhaps Gawain was no philosopher, but he did have a quiet kind of cleverness Percival could appreciate. "I suppose I just want the truth."

"Truth remains the harshest teacher. We lie to ourselves and each other out of malice, but out of love, too. Revealing the truth, especially of one's birth, can be crueler than keeping it hidden. Just know you can never put truth back in the cauldron. And once you find it, it will cling to you for the rest of your life."

The words were indeed wise, and Percival sensed that Gawain knew of the pain of truth firsthand.

"When I am ready, I will ask her, I suppose," Percival said, as much resolve as he could muster in his voice.

"Then she will answer when it is time," Gawain replied.

Hwyfar and Llachlyn drew closer to them, and, without a word, the small group of travelers made ready to depart southward together. They would ride a few hours into the night and then stop, their minds and hearts full of strange and twisting vines.

CHAPTER NINETEEN

GALAHAD

PEOPLE SIMPLY *LIKED* Mordred Pendragon. Even though he did not pay his dues the way he ought. Even though he caused far more trouble than he should. Even though he had no knightly prowess to speak of and seemed to flagrantly thumb his nose at decorum. Perhaps it was *because* of all of those things, or because he was simply the heir apparent—or none of it at all. Either way, Galahad needed Mordred right now, and so he would have to lower himself, once again, to making the long walk and asking for help from his exhausting, self-aggrandizing, hypocritical cousin.

Aside from Galahad, only Mordred knew the inner workings of Carelon's passageways so well. And loath as he was to admit it, Galahad needed Mordred's help, especially after the fight and the extra work Sir Palomydes put him through. So, face still swollen and heart still bruised from his fight with Gareth, Galahad made his way through the narrow corridors between his quarters and Mordred's tower.

Of course, it used to be *Merlin's* tower, the twin to Morgen's. Once, when the two sorcerers were on good terms, it was said their parapets had shone with unholy light. In some ways, Galahad was quite relieved he did not have to witness such demonic power in his time. In other ways, he regretted living in a time where magic was so diminished.

The tunnel brought Galahad to the narrow stairs about

halfway up the tower, where it connected to the larger gallery heading toward the great hall.

Following the plush red carpet up the tower, Galahad could smell a heady mix of burning incense—something expensive and spicy he could not name. It was a scent he uniquely associated with his cousin and one that clung to his clothes whenever he left, but which made his eyes water.

"Come in," came Mordred's sweet, melodic voice, even before Galahad grasped the dragon-shaped knocker.

Galahad pushed open the door to Mordred's room, the sound of the prince's lute softly lulling him inside.

It was said when Arthur's first wife—and Mordred's mother— Gweynevere of Avillion, first came to Carelon, she brought with her the garish and bizarrely ornate decorative tastes of the Isle. Queen Mawra, who was the first queen's sister, called it amoral and antithetical to all Christendom to array one's rooms in such a manner.

Which was curious considering her nephew's room included the majority of the Avillionian furniture she'd tried to destroy, along with a multitude of gilded statues, paintings, velvet draperies, and more pillows and odd tables and chairs Galahad could count. Upon each visit, it appeared Mordred had amassed even more outlandish items from near and far.

Galahad's eyes adjusted to the strange light coming from behind dozens of stained-glass lanterns about the room. He tried to find a clear path toward where Mordred sat, legs over the arms of a massive gold and gem inlaid chair, wearing nothing but a loose velvet robe, strumming along without a care in the realm.

The prince was slightly older than Galahad and likely half his weight. Mordred was all fine bones and sweeping lines, with long fingers and eyelashes, a wide, lovely mouth, and curling, glossy, black hair that fell to his shoulders. He was very fond of hats, and today was no exception: he wore a wide-brimmed leather sort with an enormous plume. His deep brown eyes were always glittering with mischief or malice. Or both.

Mordred tilted his head up to meet Galahad's gaze with his own. "Cousin! To what do I owe this most esteemed visit?"

"Mordred," Galahad said. "I wanted to—"

"I know why you're here. I've told you; you don't need to ask. As far as I'm concerned, you could stay here all hours of the day and I'd not be bothered. Though you'd have to be shirtless, of course." Mordred's smile was all lightness, but the look in his eye was far from innocent.

"I—No, this time I've need of—"

"God!" Mordred leapt off his chair, throwing his lute to the floor, where it clanged once before settling in a voluptuous pair of pillows. "What happened to your face?"

Galahad reached up to feel his cheek. It *was* rather difficult to see out of that eye.

In a moment, Mordred was before him, hands gently prodding Galahad's face with the tenderness of a medic.

"Stop fussing," Galahad said, trying to twist away.

Mordred's small, delicate hands somehow evaded Galahad's attempts at stilling them. "That's not usually what you look like after tilting. Did you forget your helmet?"

"I wasn't wearing a helmet."

"I know you aren't terribly bright, Galahad, but you can't be *that* dim," Mordred said, finally relenting with a cluck of his tongue.

Galahad hated being around Mordred for this very reason. It was too easy to talk with him, to divulge his secrets. "I got in a bit of a scrape with Gareth."

"Your brother with decades more experience than you? The one who's roughly the size of an oak tree?" Mordred asked, rummaging around in the pillows, now. "How devastatingly clever of you."

"It didn't start that way—we were just trying to get to know one another. And I won, anyway. Mostly."

"I do not want to know." Mordred's expression was flat and unimpressed. But it brightened when he located a small, stoppered bottle, which he handed to Galahad. "There. Smear that over the wound. I'd offer, but it's clear you'd rather do everything yourself and suffer each step along the way. Such a self-injurious nature is clearly part of your du Lac inheritance."

"You store poultices in the pillows?" Galahad asked, looking into the yellow glass bottle and tipping it sideways. The bubbled, waxy contents did not move.

"I keep an extra cache of salve in easy reach just in case my evening's adventures result in chafing." Mordred gave a suggestive shake of his hips for emphasis. "I am a considerate lover."

Unlike Galahad, Mordred took the company of anyone and everyone and reveled in exhibitionism. More than once Galahad had come upon his cousin in arrangements with lovers he'd heretofore never imagined.

To make matters more confusing, Mordred was a proclaimed and devoted Christian. His baptism was hailed across the Realm as one of the most holy and blessed days in Arthur's reign. He attended Mass regularly and was known to debate scripture with the priests and cardinals who came to visit. Few had more knowledge of the Holy Word than he, outside the priesthood.

Which made things quite confusing for Galahad. As if he needed more confusion in his life.

"I came to ask for a draught to help me sleep," the young knight said to the prince, slipping the poultice into his satchel. "I have prayed to God for a calm spirit, but it is possible I have offended the Lord so thoroughly with my behavior earlier that he wishes me to be tormented."

Mordred twirled one of the long, golden chains on his neck around his pointer finger. "Well, if God wills that you find no sleep, should you question it?"

Galahad hadn't thought of that. "Mordred, I—"

"I jest, dear cousin, I jest. God is too busy to bother with you and your foibles, I assure you. Besides, you can always sin now and grovel later if you're feeling particularly penitent. That's generally my approach."

Mordred whirled sideways and pointed toward the right where an ornate stairway led to a shadowed alcove: the apothecary. "Shall we?"

"Thank you, Mordred," Galahad said.

"Of course. You're family."

Relief flooded Galahad as they climbed upward, knowing he was close to the kind of oblivion he needed.

Once at the top, Mordred took a key from his belt and unlocked a large door, which slid open. Behind it was a room best described as a cross between a library and a witch's hut. Shelves lined every wall and space, books interspersed with bottles and containers of every size and description. None of them were labeled, nor consistent in their placement. Only Mordred knew the shelves, and pity the soul who tried to decipher any semblance of order in the space.

Indeed, the prince was a strange, strange man. But alluring. And terribly useful, in circumstances like this.

Mordred gamboled from shelf to shelf, muttering and singing, pulling one bottle and then another, then returning them both as if they did not measure up to his scrutiny.

"How long do you want to sleep?" Mordred asked.

Forever. Galahad's face flushed with shame again, considering what had occurred with his brother. "I have to be up for training with Sir Bedevere tomorrow morning. And I don't want to miss matins."

Mordred snorted. "Oh, indeed. We must not miss *matins*." The prince had an irritating way of mimicking Galahad's voice just so. Before Galahad could reply, Mordred continued speaking. "Ah, yes. This should be enough for you to manage a few good hours of sleep without the sluggishness some of my more, ah, *involved* tinctures have. If you ever want to sleep for three days straight, I've got just the combination for you. You'll wake up hungry and willing to fuck anything within arm's reach, but it's well worth the escape."

The prince handed Galahad a small leather pouch tied in catgut.

Inside, wrapped in neat little bunches, were white dried flowers with stout green leaves. It smelled sweet, bright, and slightly dusty.

"Thank you," Galahad said. "What is the preparation?"

"Well, if you'd given me any forewarning, I could have put together an infusion for you in some wine, but given your endlessly demanding nature, you'll have to do with warm water. Take the contents of one of the tied bundles, steep for a quarter of an hour, and then drink. You may add it to wine after that if you wish."

"Easy enough," Galahad replied. "I don't suppose there are any strange effects I might encounter the next morning, though?"

Mordred gave an amused snort. "No, alas. Even though the best recipe for a sound sleep involves the release one can only achieve with the friction between two bodies. But I suppose you are still chained to your purity."

"I'm not *chained* to anything," Galahad said.

The look Mordred gave him was surprisingly mournful, his keen eyes piercing Galahad's very soul. Why did he have to look at him like that, as if he understood him? They could not be more different. The idea Mordred Pendragon knew anything about what it was like to be Galahad was preposterous.

"Of course you aren't," Mordred said, playfully slapping Galahad's cheek. "You are free and unencumbered. Just be certain to relieve your spear every now and again. Such denial can result in aggression and frustration. At least in my personal experience."

"My spear?" Once again, Galahad was utterly lost to Mordred's meandering language.

With a smooth, flamboyant gesture, Mordred indicated his loins.

Galahad's face flushed and he turned away, seeking his escape. He could not tolerate one more moment here with Mordred, especially given what had happened earlier. He'd been fighting with his fellow knight and brother; Mordred barely knew how to hold a sword that wasn't ceremonial.

"You don't need to be so crass, Mordred," Galahad said.

"Of course I don't. But it is delightful watching you blush. Speaking of spears and desires, I haven't seen your handsome curly-haired Percival about lately. Have you fallen out?"

Galahad really did want to strike Mordred now, but such behavior would certainly get him in even more trouble than he already was. The only person Galahad had ever told about his inclinations toward Percival was Mordred, and only because of a drunken evening together in the spring after a particularly bad row. And Mordred had seemed so different, then. Not a nuisance, but a true confidante. The next day, though, he had been back to his usual, insufferable self.

"I have to leave," Galahad said through gritted teeth.

"I'll be looking for payment," Mordred called out behind him.

"Give me a few days," Galahad said over his shoulder. He didn't want to look at Mordred one moment more.

Mordred had one of his own tinctures; he gulped it down and dabbed at the corner of his mouth with his sleeve. "You don't even know what the price is, Galahad. But fret not, oh angelic one, you will be back soon."

The sound of Mordred's laughter followed Galahad all the way back to his empty chambers.

CHAPTER TWENTY

MORGEN

IF I'D HAD any semblance of my powers, I'd have been able to shatter the dome Yvain put around me without so much as a thought. As far as sorcery went, it was not the most impressive structure—the glass was uneven, and not a uniform color—but it did its job keeping me inside and away from the cockatrice.

Futile as it was, I struck the glass with my fists. It was immovable. Had I an axe, perhaps with time I'd make a dent. But glass was earth magic, sand tempered with heat. It would remain here until Yvain decided otherwise.

And at the moment, his full attention remained on the cockatrice. Yvain was light on his feet, easily outmaneuvering the clumsy, furious attacks from both cockatrice heads. Some believed the cockatrice was a giant bird, but I could tell this close it was a giant lizard, perhaps akin to a dragon, with long, yellow beaks lined with dagger teeth.

Though a cockatrice could not turn a person to stone with its gaze as some tales said, it could paralyze its prey with the spurs behind its two legs or the spittle from its mouth. The result was a death-like stupor lasting days, sometimes a week. I had used the venom in some of my tinctures in more desperate times, though its cost was great both in acquisition and use.

The cockatrice roared and dipped, its wings shredding the trees and vegetation. Branches and leaves rained on Yvain, blinding him, and pattered against my glass dome. What in the name of the gods did he think he was going to do with that sword? The cockatrice certainly wasn't going to sit down and allow him to quietly disembowel it.

Then I realized Yvain was trying to *speak* with the cockatrice. Melic, poised for attack, also looked hesitant to engage in direct combat.

That was curious. I wondered if the dome was for my safety or his privacy. Or perhaps both.

Though the cockatrice was indeed impressive, I had no doubt it was unwell. Merlin had tended enough animals during our partnership that I'd gained considerable skill in their care, although I felt little kinship to them. Lizards shed their skin regularly, no matter their size, but the cockatrice's skin hung off its legs and chest in long mottled grey sheets. I spied redness where the skin pulled.

The wrongness made my skin prickle. Modrun would never have allowed such an ill creature to behave so in her wood. Brocéliande was no peaceful place, but it was not one of pestilence or suffering for its animals. It was, more than anything, a haven for those misunderstood and hunted.

Misunderstood or not, the beast showed no sign of calming despite Yvain's attempts.

Yvain changed tack. He rolled out of the reach of one of the cockatrice's claws—my heart was in my throat at how close he came to being gored—and then nocked an arrow. I was mesmerized at how fluidly he moved as he let loose his shot.

Alas, the arrow ricocheted off the cockatrice's scales. He'd have to be more precise if he meant to hobble the creature.

Easy for me to say. I hadn't swung a sword or shot an arrow in time out of mind. And even in my youth, I was never the most talented of my sisters in such skill. Elaine, now, *she* could rival the best of Arthur's bowmen if she'd cared to continue her work, and none was better among us than Margawse with the dagger.

No, I had always set myself apart with my magic. It had come to me as freely and naturally as breathing, and my mother was certain I would rise to greatness, even after all that befell her. I was a hope, she said, that the Pendragons could not take everything. Our magic, our power, our inheritance. But the longer I lived, the more of a burden that had felt, especially as I struggled to maintain the balance of politics and power in my own kingdom. I had never wished to be parted from my magic, but I did wish to be free of the responsibilities. Now, bereft of every spell and charm I knew, I was adrift.

I knelt down to feel the base of the dome where it met the forest floor. It was sealed tight, no obvious areas for me to pry. My work only yielded more black staining on my fingers, and new dirt beneath my fingernails.

An ear-splitting shriek grabbed my attention, and I looked up in time to see the cockatrice rear back, an arrow stuck in its flank.

Yvain stumbled as he tried to dodge, however, and was thrown back with a violent kick. He rolled and smacked straight into the glass dome, causing the whole structure to shudder and crackle into a thousand segments. It was not enough to break his spell, but certainly enough to weaken it.

"Yvain!" I cried, panic rising as he went completely still. My voice pierced my own ears, shrill and terrified. I wasn't aware I could make that kind of sound any longer. "Let me help you!"

As if I could! Why had my magic gone dormant? I had shaped a kingdom, moved Fate with my own hands, transformed myself and my abilities to mythic proportions. All that was gone.

Only death lingered. That last, silent gift. And I could not grant him that.

Folding inward into my own mind, I rooted around in the maw of death. It always appeared to me as a threshold, a great arch into the next world. I had helped countless souls through that archway, though I myself had never stepped foot in it. I was a midwife of souls, a guide from one land to another. Though inevitably, someday, I would pass through myself, I was but a guide.

I forced my inner gaze into the archway at the expanse upon the other side, steeling myself to gaze upon the unknown. Surely, I would see some answer, some glimmer of power.

Yet nothing appeared. I beheld only a grey, formless mist.

Pushing deeper, I finally saw pinpricks of green light—not through the threshold, but *above* it—and almost laughed. My crows. For who else waits for the living to cross to death? Who else has the unwanted work of giving our bodies back to the earth?

My eyes shot wide open, and breath rushed to my lungs as I gazed up through the crumbling dome and into the treetops.

Goddess be praised, my crows replied. I sensed their movement, each feathered frame and sleek, clacking beak, turning their attention toward me. My mind, my death magic, kindled inside of me; no, these could not be natural birds, they had to have come from beyond. I touched their minds, illuminating green wisps in my consciousness, and they had been waiting for me all along.

And instead of moving immediately, I did as Vyvian so often told me: I listened.

We are waiting.

Surprise, and no small amount of delight, blossomed in my chest. The crows were waiting for me, for my command. Never had I heard of such a gift, but I knew a sign when I saw one, and in this hour of desperation I would use whatever strength I had to guide them.

Yvain stirred, shaking off the worst of his dizziness, and didn't even bother to look at me as he charged forward again. His gait was surprisingly steady, given the bashing he'd just had. Though persistent and certainly capable, I could not see the possibility of him surviving this mad creature. I had to act.

Narrowing my focus, turning inward again to that dark archway, I breathed in that cold, unfamiliar power, and pushed it back out. It took a few tries, but soon I could sense the crows as surely as I could sense my own hair. I did not feel as they felt, but I understood how they connected to me: threads of green, glowing power—not unlike how Hwyfar described her *carioz* to me—

streamed out from my chest, through the glass, and skyward.

I allowed myself a breath of relief, but my hope was quickly dashed as Yvain slumped to one knee, driven down by a blow from the cockatrice's great wing, blood blossoming on the side of his face.

No time to dally. I pictured the crows not as singular creatures, but as a vast flock of consciousness, desiring to combine their abilities rather than command them individually. With so many years of experience as a sorceress, I knew it was best to approach any new spell work cautiously. Simplicity, I was taught, contributed to the elegance of magic—complexity might allow for more power, but it would take longer to control.

For a moment I thought failure was inevitable. The cockatrice roared up, claws jutting out as its fetid wings pounded the air. Yvain got to his feet, once again brandishing his sword, but he could barely hold it up, he shook so fiercely.

My heart stuttered.

Then came the crows.

There was nothing simple about these birds, no gentle command I could give. They descended in a black cloud and, like a giant hand, pushed the cockatrice back into the jagged tree trunks behind it. The cataclysmic sound of the cockatrice screeching and massive tree trunks snapping hurt even my ears, protected as I was by Yvain's dome. Leaf mold rose from the ground in more clouds, whipping about and obscuring my sight, a green and purple mist seeping from the ground like an enchanted fog.

I imagined the birds squeezing the cockatrice like a giant fist, snuffing out its breath. Delving deep, deeper into my center, I wracked my soul for power, harsh claws scratching at the edges of my own being. It hurt; goddess, it hurt. I tasted blood slipping down my throat, hot and salty and alarming. Magic always exacted a price, and new, untested magic was particularly demanding.

One of the cockatrice's heads twisted away, rolling into the forest, phosphorescent yellow blood oozing in its wake. That image stopped me, terrified me.

What had I become?

Fear cut short my power and I fell to my knees, breathless and weak. My vision swam, but I could still see the mist and dust clearing as the rain began falling in earnest.

The cockatrice was upon the ground, and Melic wrestled with its long, blue tongue, golden blood splattering in glittering arcs as it continued to scream.

Yvain ducked a ferocious slice from the cockatrice's venomous foreleg, just barely, and let out a bellow before running up its snout, past Melic, and sinking his sword directly into the monster's remaining head. The creature's wings flapped furiously, irregularly, a smell like old urine and rotting cabbage wafting over me.

The dome melted down around me and I staggered forward, my skin raw and humming with the power I'd wielded. Rain fell on my face, dampening my hair, cold and welcome.

"Yvain!" I called.

He had collapsed some strides away from the felled beast, but still I saw his chest rising and falling. Melic stood protectively, two great paws on either side of the knight.

Falling down beside him, I looked for any sign of injury. His eyes stared up into the sky, blinking now and again, but he did not seem to know I was beside him.

Terror grasping my throat, I pulled aside his tunic on his chest. He had some abrasions and scratches, but nothing that would cause this sort of reaction. With all the rain I expected to see blood streaming across the mud beneath his body, but none came.

"Yvain, look at me," I said.

Melic whined, high and sorrowful.

Just moments before, Yvain had been attacking the cockatrice like a warrior of songs. What had transpired? The dome had cracked and broken, allowing my escape—perhaps the effort of maintaining that spell and the exertion of battle had been too much for him. I could not heal him, could not reach him.

His blue stare continued uninterrupted, the irises so small and distant despite the darkening wood.

Without thinking, I put my hand on his cheek. Immediately, I recognized the pull of the Maw of Death, dragging me into my mind's eye.

And I saw Yvain standing at the threshold, and a hundred reflections of him besides. At first, I was confused, unable to decipher what it could mean. There were so many: some barely out of childhood, others arrayed in fine velvets, and more still in flashing armor. Over and over again, Yvain stood in the darkness before the archway, that great precipice of death, hesitating to take the next step.

Understanding dawned in me, and I knew: he had been here many times before. Just at the edge of death. Just near enough that one step would have taken him away.

And he had chosen life, time and again, but just barely.

He had not wanted to live.

I was yanked back to the present when Yvain grabbed my hand. He did not let go, but nor did he turn his face toward me. By then, my body quaked with exhaustion and fear. My eyelids were so heavy, my arms weak and my back, goddess!

Melic pushed his head forward, nudging me. Then he became more insistent, pushing my shoulders down so I was upon Yvain's chest. I tried, uselessly, to argue, knowing it was unwise to sleep beside the body of a dead beast in the darkening wood.

The lion was convincing, though, purring deep and long, so low the sound reverberated in my chest. I surrendered to the dark.

LIGHT DANCED ACROSS my eyelids, flickering and bright, and I smelled deep, green leaves and a brighter, almost citrus scent. My whole body tingled with warmth, wrapped and deliciously comfortable. I would not have been surprised to find I was merely back in my tower, fresh roses in a vase beside me, the fire low but still warm.

The fur beneath my fingers moved, however, followed by the insistent squeal of a stomach in need of food.

"Melic," I whispered.

The lion licked my cheek. I had curled up between his great paws, and the ridiculous animal had allowed it. Laughter nearly escaped me as I realized I was facing inward toward him, his great mane tickling my chin.

Slowly, I turned, expecting Yvain nearby. I did not find him. We were in a bower of blue-blooming vines and moss. Above us, the high sun flashed through the interlaced vegetation.

The bower rustled and Yvain crawled toward me, face pale but otherwise unharmed. Outwardly, at least.

Without a word, he tossed a small pouch at me.

I smelled the blackberries inside of it before I opened the bag. Out of season, entirely, and strange—but given we had killed a cockatrice, the presence of such food was the least of my concerns.

Yvain remained, watching me as I ate, organizing his pack and putting what I recognized as cockatrice ichor into it.

"You will need to transfer that to a wax-lined clay vessel before long," I said, gesturing to the stoppered bottle. "It will eat through the glass in a matter of days."

"You lied to me, Morgen," he said, voice cold and flat, ignoring my advice. "You acted as if you could do no magic. Like you were helpless and afraid. And I believed you."

"I was—I *am*."

"What you did there, that was not helpless. You—I'm not sure what you did, but it cracked open the sky."

Goddess, my chest ached. I was angry, of course, but I was also hurt. Strange, though, that I would care at all what this man thought of me. "I was helping you. And you never told me you were capable of spells."

"You never asked. The kind of magic you did—Morgen, I don't understand why you did it."

The words were hot on my tongue, forced out. "I thought you were going to die."

"You should have let me!" I had never heard him shout before, but I knew it was from hurt and not anger.

Ah, now I understood. He knew what I'd seen, his most private shame. His words chilled me, and I shivered back against Melic. For now, the lion had no intent to leave me.

"That would have gone against every vow I've taken," I said, bristling. "My position, my skill, even when limited, is dedicated to protecting the realm, and all those who live in it. Especially Arthur's knights."

"I am not one of Arthur's knights."

"Well, you *were*. And as such, you fall under my care."

"Bah." He swatted the air at me, as if that would dismiss me from his reality. "You are all the same."

Anger flared in my heart, defensive and sharp. Would that I could have burned down the bower to show him my fury.

Instead, though, I gathered my thoughts and calmed myself. I had dealt with far worse clashes, even within my own close family. Whatever transpired with Yvain, whatever death he sought, he had suffered at the hands of his mother, at the hands of magic-wielders, and was still trapped here.

"Ask me anything and I will answer you truthfully," I said. "If that will change your mind. Desperation awakened a power in me that I do not understand, but I can pledge to be honest with you, here and now."

"What?" Yvain's gaze snapped to my face, clearly taken aback.

"You do not trust me. And we have faced danger together, I doubt for the last time. Either sit with me and begin to build something true, or leave me to find Modrun on my own."

Giving him this choice tempted him, I could tell. I noted a haunted gleam in his eye, heretofore absent. Perhaps he feared me, now; perhaps his own ghosts lingered.

I did not want to lose faith in him. He could have easily left me alone, but he'd chosen not to. And he'd fed me, however grudgingly. Certainly, the thought crossed my mind that he had only done those things out of terror, having seen the aftermath of my magic. He would not be the first man who had done so.

"Fine," Yvain said, settling down across from me with a wince.

"Are you in pain?" I asked.

"I've been better. Strange as Brocéliande is, I am not in the habit of felling monstrous cockatrices regularly."

"You tried to speak to it," I observed, but he held out an obnoxious finger, silencing me.

"Truth first," he said.

Indeed. I had brought this upon myself. "Very well. I will answer your questions, in truth."

"How will I know you are not lying?" He tilted his head at me again, in that strange, almost animalistic way.

"I will swear by Iaia, my patron goddess, with whom I have sheltered and lived all the decades of my life. And I swear by this wood."

Yvain sniffed, then nodded. "Good enough for me, I suppose."

"I am relieved." I could not hide the hint of sarcasm in my voice.

He reached into his satchel and pulled out some nuts, chewing on them thoughtfully for a moment before asking his first question. A good tactic, that. Drawing out the moment so he could erode my own courage.

"Well?" I asked, impatience churning the berries in my stomach.

Yvain met my gaze, a challenge there. And, I suppose, I knew the question before he asked it. "Is it true you had a child by your brother Arthur?"

CHAPTER TWENTY-ONE

GAWAIN

WITH NO NEARBY village, Gawain insisted the small party stop by the ruins of an old temple by the banks of the River Hafran. He had been by this particular locale a few times on longer visits to Carelon over the years, and though it was beautiful, it was also very defensible. Perhaps the age of roving bandits was nearly over, but Gawain had been raised upon the battlefield and his training was etched into his thoughts as a result.

By the time they disembarked, Gawain's whole body was barking in pain. Their new companions did not know, of course, but when both Gawain and his wife wore their armor—crafted by the Green Knight themselves—as long as they were near one another, his pain eased considerably. Alas, not even blessed armor could completely mute the pain that riding wrung from his knees and hips. And he could not wear the armor at all times.

Knowing the limitations of his body was once Gawain's greatest shame, but now he approached the pain with a kind of welcome resolve. *If I am in pain, I am alive*, he often reminded himself. *And if I am alive, I am with her.*

Hwyfar approached him, and even in the dusk light he saw her worry.

"I'm fine," he said.

"You should have used your cane," his wife said softly.

The feeling of her hand on his was a welcome anchor,

especially as the cold settled in around them. Though they had plenty of blankets and would all sleep near the fire, he doubted he'd get much in the way of sleep.

"Aye, I should have," Gawain admitted, swallowing an unexpected lump in his throat. "Though I hoped I might not need it."

Voicing such a thing was no easy task, even to Hwyfar, even though they were beautifully comfortable with one another. Gawain hated how his own pride still got the best of him. His wounds and pains would only get worse with time, and though he had on occasional reprieve, soon the day would come where he would need his cane more often than not.

Hwyfar's sigh was soft as she smoothed back the hair on his sweaty brow. "We should arrive in Carelon tomorrow evening if we get enough of an early start in the morning. But, Gawain, if we need to stop an extra day, we can stay in Mathrafal."

Mathrafal was one of Arthur's many seats, won in a long and bloody battle by Uther Pendragon. It was not the kind of place Gawain wanted to visit, given his grandfather's many heinous war crimes. There were statues of the old king on every street corner and the last thing Gawain wanted was more reminders of how Uther's greed, lust, and warmongering had wrought this new age.

"I'd rather push forward and stay closer to Carelon if we can," Gawain said, taking a few, stiff steps toward where Percival and Llachlyn sat, supposedly to get a fire going but arguing more than working.

"You're being stubborn," Hwyfar said. She crossed her arms across her chest, and Gawain could not help but give her an appraising glance. How did she only get more lovely with each passing day? If it weren't for the young ones nearby, he'd certainly find the time to appreciate her more closely.

"Of course, I am. It's one of my most endearing qualities."

"At least take some of the tinctures I brought," Hwyfar said. Gawain hated the pleading note in her voice. Before he began to argue, she continued: "I know they make you feel drowsy, but perhaps they'll help you sleep."

He kissed her hard, surprising her enough she gasped against his mouth. "Fine. Make your tea if it will settle your mind."

"You forget I feel some of your pain," Hwyfar said, her voice slightly muffled against his chest.

"I never forget that," he said. How could he? That he could walk at all was due entirely to her magic, and their *carioz*. Thankfully, her pains did not increase over time as his did. "It isn't worse, is it?"

"No, not worse. But I get twinges when you've particularly pushed yourself. You cannot hide from me."

"Why would I ever want to?" He leaned his chin on the top of her head, smelling the honeyed fragrance of her and the light crispness of her sweat. If he closed his eyes, he could pretend they were still at Thistlewood, standing together in the orchard. "Besides, I'm very difficult to conceal."

"I love you, you oaf." Hwyfar chuckled, low and resonant.

"Eternally your oaf, princess."

IT TOOK SOME time to remove his armor, though Hwyfar was, of course, nearby to help. Without its support, Gawain was indeed glad he'd agreed to his wife's tinctures. He had once asked the Green Knight how the armor worked, how it could be forged in such a way to reinforce his body where it was weakest. He hadn't expected a straightforward answer, but he inquired anyway. The Green Knight said, "The armor does what it needs to do." Which was no help at all. Hwyfar told him it was rude to have asked in the first place and that one must not try to explain magic, especially those granted by godlike warriors of incomprehensible age.

The old temple gave them cover from the elements, and no need to erect tents. It was a small affair, abandoned generations before, with smooth limestone tiles, a sloped roof, and a wellspring in the center that provided fresh water. He appreciated the sturdiness of the structure, but also wondered at its old use. Had they burned offerings here? Or just incense? Were they followers of familiar gods, or those now lost to time?

The older Gawain got, the more he wrestled with such questions, weighing the passage of time and the changes that followed. Legacy, he supposed, was part of it. Arthur would not live forever, and the last time Gawain had seen his uncle, he'd been frail. Ailing. But Carelon was not only Arthur's. It was deeper than that. For all the scheming, murder, and betrayal, there had also been peace and prosperity.

Could Mordred be trusted with that future? Gawain barely knew the lad, but he did not seem well-suited to the role of king. It ought not bother him—Arthur himself had sent Gawain far from court these last years. Yet he was the eldest nephew. He still felt a lingering responsibility in the back of his mind he could never quite shake.

And this business with Percival. It nagged at Gawain. If, as he suspected, Gweyn was his mother, then what of Mordred? Was this all a ruse woven by Merlin, or were there other hands at work? Because Gawain knew Gweyn's secrets, even if she hadn't shared them with her sister Hwyfar.

"Are we not disturbing the old gods by lighting a fire in their temple?" Percival asked, coming to sit next to Gawain by the crackling flames, wresting away his attention.

Gawain had finally found a comfortable way to stretch out his leg as he sipped the minty, bitter concoction his wife had given him. "I think they're probably just glad of the company," he said thoughtfully.

The young man had a gentle curiousness about him that Gawain found annoyingly endearing. "Do you worship the old gods, Sir Gawain?"

"Just Gawain, please. We're not at court, yet." Gawain stretched his neck, rolled his shoulders. Sitting to relieve one pain inevitably led to another. He was getting too old for this sort of travel. "And no. I don't worship the gods. Never really did. I grew up in Orkney, in a crumbling castle by the sea, and my father—let's just say he beat any kind of faith out of me quite young. When I cried out, no gods, old *or* new, ever came to my rescue."

"I'm sorry." Percival's tone conveyed the deep kind of empathy one can only gain from a shared experience, his voice scarcely a whisper. "And yet how do you explain the Green Knight?"

"The Green Knight may yet be a god, but I do not worship them. I helped them, and they have helped me and my wife in immeasurable ways."

"Then it is not as the tales are told at court, that you beheaded the creature?"

"I did not behead anyone." Gawain glanced over where Hwyfar was arranging her pack, yet again. Settling her anxiety, he knew. "But my wife did. With my own sword, Galantyne, she separated the vile sorceress Ymelda's head from her shoulders. It was one of the most spectacular sights I ever beheld."

Percival whistled lowly, in admiration. "So your wife beheaded a monster, and you gained the friendship of a god."

"I suppose that's the closest word we have for such a thing. But I've a thought they are less a god and more an expression of magic as we know it, the last of a dying race."

"Like dragons and grifflets."

"Except real," Gawain said with a chuckle. "And you, lad? Were you brought up with religion?"

Percival poked at the fire with a smooth stick, his pale hair almost ghostly in the light. "King Pellinore is not a man of any faith, save that which might gain him favor. He converted some years ago, but has no real belief, just a desire to impress the right people. Which I think is abhorrent no matter who you worship. I went to Mass as one might expect, and though I find some of it intriguing, it has never settled with me. Galahad, of course, has tried to show me the path of righteousness, but he seems far too much in pain for it to be appealing to me. I do not think a loving god would require such self-hatred, which seems a common factor among many of the converted I know."

As Percival spoke, Gawain watched him more closely, looking

for answers. He beheld the lines of his eyes, the hue of his hair, and the way his nose turned up at the end. The way he said the word 'pain.'

Gweyn. *Tell me, Gawain. What brings you pain?*

It did not make sense to him, and he could not know for certain, but there was no doubt in his mind. Hadn't the Green Knight implied as much? Percival was a foundling. And Mordred and he had to have been an age.

Mordred looked nothing like either of his parents. To say nothing of his behavior.

"Faith is a complex thing," Gawain said, clearing his throat. "But one I prefer not to question in those I love. It is a personal choice, and that is something well known to me."

"My father—King Pellinore..." Percival had to clarify, "he told me my mother was a pious woman. So, I suppose, in my mind, I have ever seen her as a stalwart Christian. Even if who I am, and where I came from, was a lie. I do wish I had known her."

"All the more her loss," Gawain said, forcing the words out through a tight smile.

I have meddled in so many deceits, I have lost count, his mother had once told him. *From innocent babes to sitting kings.*

The Path was broken, but Gawain had his own ways of reaching his mother if he had to. Before they arrived in Carelon, Gawain needed to know the truth—Hwyfar needed the truth, too. If what he thought was true, then Percival was heir to Avillion and Lyonesse, and her most beloved sister's nephew. And Mordred was... no one.

Gawain's chest tightened with the implications of such thoughts.

"Pellinore ought to have treasured you," he said, the words slipping out before he could stop them. Damn the tincture.

Percival laughed ruefully, looking away from Gawain as if to hide his shame. "He treasured none of his bastards, least of all me. I was too talkative, too curious, too naïve—and not strong enough, not fast enough, not obedient enough."

Gawain swallowed the last of his tea, wiping his mouth and wincing at the grit and bitterness left behind. "All the more *his* loss. You're a good man, Percival. I can see that. You've taken good care of my cousin, in ways many men might not. I am indebted to you for that."

Percival's echoing smile was bashful, but a little sad, too. "That means a lot coming from you. I do not have the kind of brawn you and your brothers have, and I often worry that this world is not meant for people like me. Llachlyn has the heart of a knight, but a very small frame—I have the trappings of one, but no heart for it. Perhaps that is why we work so well."

And Galahad was both. The three were such a curious group.

Though far from a master of intrigue, Gawain guessed Percival, Galahad, and Llachlyn were far more than they appeared, together. Clearly more than they themselves even knew.

But three was a number of both balance and disharmony. It was difficult enough maintaining his relationship with the twins. First, it had been Gareth and he on the outs. Then, years later it was Gaheris. And Gaheris had never really been the same after he'd murdered their aunt Margawse, even if she had deserved it.

And, like it or not, the thought that his own youngest brother shared blood with Lanceloch du Lac made his skin crawl with disgust. Hwyfar insisted that Gawain learn to let go of his hatred, but try as he might, resentment was lodged so deeply it was like an old injury that wouldn't heal. And he knew that feeling well enough.

"Tell me about Galahad," Gawain said.

Percival's face relaxed into a thoughtful, almost sad expression, and he went very quiet. Given his propensity for loquaciousness, Gawain was surprised to elicit such a response.

Gawain clapped Percival on the shoulder, gently as he could. "You don't have to if you don't want to."

Percival let out a long, heavy sigh. "I met Galahad when I was fourteen. My father sent me to Benwick in the summers to try and train, because he said I was embarrassingly bad at everything I did. He thought that under the tutelage of Hector de Mares, Lanceloch's own brother, and alongside Galahad, I might flourish. Llachlyn was a surprise, given her mother, and we got on immediately. Quicker than Galahad and me. He was wary, at first, but then grew to appreciate having a lad his age about. Alas, it was very clear that, no matter how much I trained, I would never grow to accomplish much. There is nothing Galahad is incapable of doing. No weapon, no footwork, no formation he can't understand. It's uncanny. Even as a child I'm told he spent hours alone with his little carved stone soldiers and horses."

"I had a set like that once that belonged to King Arthur," Gawain said. "I wonder if they are the very same."

"I suppose you might have been like him, too, then, when you were young. Expectations for Galahad have always been immense, and yet he has always risen to them."

"I started out in such a way. But, as you can see, usefulness has its limits in Carelon."

"Well, given there are no such expectations of me, I suppose that's in my favor. Galahad makes up for it, though. All I've accomplished has been because I've been in the glow of his radiance."

"Do you resent him for that?" Gawain asked, trying to identify Percival's emotion and coming up empty. It was envy, perhaps, but also pity. And maybe even a little longing.

Percival chuckled. "Perhaps I should. But with Llachlyn there, with us together, it's always been so natural. Galahad is kind and even funny, sometimes. His faith has always been a part of who he is, but he never pressed us overmuch. We had many conversations on the matter. I admire his talent, but…"—he glanced at Llachlyn, who was still some distance away, tending to the horses—"but very often I feel pulled apart between the two of them, even though I know it's a ridiculous notion."

Was it, though? Gawain did not think so at all.

"I know very little of my brother Galahad, sadly. I was over twenty when he was born, and my mother had him sent to Gaul almost right away," Gawain said. "I hope to get the chance to know him a little better."

The young man shrugged. "I suppose we shall see where he stands once we're in Carelon. He saved us, after all. He didn't have to. I have to believe there is hope for him."

If Percival truly was Gweyn's son, it would mean they had to tread far more carefully than they thought. He would have to speak with his mother, first and foremost, if Morgen was nowhere to be found.

And there was a chance, the slightest chance, that Hwyfar might be able to help him.

CHAPTER TWENTY-TWO

HWYFAR

"WHY ARE YOU saying such things?" Hwyfar asked her husband. Her heart felt bruised by his words, her head swimming. "You can't just make accusations of such a grand scheme because someone reminds you of my dead sister."

No matter how much time passed since her younger sister's death, Hwyfar could not be rid of the knot of grief inside of her. Even though she had helped save Avillion, even though she had done everything right by her.

She could not deny the similarity, though, nor how her thoughts kept bending to her sister as they traveled.

"There are things my mother said once, that have left me questioning—well, everything. How much of our lives, how much of the stories we know, have been orchestrated."

"Clearly I made the tea too strong."

"Hwyfar, I'm serious."

"Gweyn would have told me," Hwyfar insisted. "If not in life, when she visited me after her death."

The entire course of Hwyfar's life had changed, over ten years ago, when Gweyn's spectre visited her with a challenge to protect the *graal* in Avillion. Once she had done so, Gweyn had never returned, though she had promised she'd held no ill will toward Hwyfar.

Still, the ache was unbearable.

"Tell me he doesn't look just like her," Gawain said, trying to keep his voice low.

It was so frigid Hwyfar's teeth chattered. All she wanted to do was to have her husband shut his mouth and let her curl up next to him and go to sleep. They had enough difficulties going on between them right now. As if going to Carelon wasn't terrible enough on its own.

"I cannot imagine how such a ruse could have been carried out under our *very noses*," she grumbled.

"Eighteen years ago, you and I were very different people, my love. I was lost in my own anger and drink, and you were—"

"Do not call me the Whore of Carelon, or I will bite you," Hwyfar snapped.

"As tempting as that is, I was going to say, you were at the height of your own vices. You yourself said Gweyn was distant from you. She desperately wanted an heir, and we both know they struggled, intimately. I do not think it surprising she would have taken matters into her own hands. Perhaps even with the King's blessing."

They were all tired, and Gawain certainly more than he let on. Hwyfar was beginning to think perhaps she ought to insist more strongly on better lodging tomorrow and a slower pace. The fact he was unraveling this thread *now* made her seriously doubt its validity.

Gawain pulled her closer, the heat of his body settling into her bones in the most pleasant way. How he was always so warm, she could not say. Even on the coldest nights, she could turn and nuzzle up to him and feel his radiance.

"You presume much," Hwyfar said.

Gawain kissed her forehead. "I know. But you did not speak with her on these matters. I did."

She wasn't there, is what he meant. And he was right. "What are you saying, Gawain?"

He went quiet, his muscles tensing. Even in ten years together, she and Gawain had not shared every last part of their past.

Indeed, their new life focused so much on their present that spooling back memories of Carelon seemed a kind of betrayal.

"I know Gweyn did not get pregnant by Arthur," Gawain said at last, his voice strained and low. "At least, not the first time. Before Mordred, she had a pregnancy that ended in loss. Early."

"What?" Hwyfar had to pull away to study her husband's face.

"In the beginning, he would—" Gawain struggled to get the words out. "Arthur visited very infrequently, and when he did, they did not often do… what was required."

"Surely he would know," Hwyfar said. She was an expert on such matters, after all, given her very long, diverse list of lovers at Carelon. She knew well how to get to, and how to avoid, childbed. "There are *steps*."

Gawain gave a low laugh and squeezed her hip. "I'm well aware of that. Gweyn told me Arthur would visit so drunk he would swoon in bed with her. The first thing he would ask in the morning was confirmation they had done what needed doing."

"Gweyn was no liar."

"No, but Arthur was desperate for an heir. All eyes in court were upon her. It burdened her greatly and she *wanted* a child, with all her being." Gawain stroked Hwyfar's arm calmly, soothingly. They had thought, once, that a child might bless their own marriage. Fate did not move that way, however. "So, she sought another option."

"If you tell me it was you, I shall annul our marriage straight away," Hwyfar said, even though she knew that was not the case. She loved her husband enough, understood him enough, that if he'd done such a thing, he'd have told her ages ago.

"Gods, no. No, of course not."

"You would have been a good candidate. You are closest to Arthur by blood."

"Mmm. And when a little lad with bright green eyes and vivid red hair, tall as a giant, showed up, every single person would know. No, it had to be more subtle."

"Gweyn was so pious, though. I cannot imagine…"

"It was not until after Mordred's birth that she began to truly cling to the Christian faith, and Avillion is not so prudish about such matters. And even so, she did not want to disappoint Arthur. She kept trying for more children, worried that Mordred would not thrive. He was a small child, difficult and fussy."

Hwyfar rubbed at her face. The Pendragons could not do anything by halves, even when it came to the most important heir of the whole kingdom.

Gawain swallowed. "She had a lover, Hwyfar. He's a good man, and they loved one another. In another life, Gweyn and he could have lived together in gladness."

"Who?" Hwyfar had to know, though she was never one for such petty gossip. "Who did she love?"

"Do you remember Gweyn's funeral?"

"I was *exceptionally* drunk."

"If you had turned your eyes to the knights, all standing in a ring around her bower, you would have seen one with eyes red and weeping beneath his visor."

"You're being poetic and it's annoying."

"It was Lanval."

Hwyfar knew Lanval well enough, and he was, indeed, poetic in every sense. Handsome, friendly, much beloved, even if he'd come from minor means. He adored song and poetry and would often recite long sagas after meals. She could see why Gweyn would have loved him.

"The other pregnancies?" Hwyfar asked. Gweyn had tried to get pregnant, again and again, even when she had been advised against it—Arthur wanted more children, in case Mordred was killed.

"I do not know for certain, but she kept trying even when the medics said not to—and moreover, Arthur kept pressing. Her fear became his paranoia," Gawain said. "She became sicker with each one. And then…"

No, Hwyfar could not think of that. She could not allow her mind to wind down such dark caves of regret and guilt.

"But what of Mordred?" Hwyfar asked.

"That's why I need to try and speak to my mother. You've said my blood would make the spell work."

Hwyfar's whole body was unusually sensitive since the Path had fallen. Everything was too loud, too rough, too bright. She had headaches and toothaches whenever she tried to access the Path, that bright and comfortable guide that helped fortify the three kinds of magic she possessed.

She was alone. Adrift. But there were other spells, other ways.

Hwyfar's doubts swirled—in herself, in their capabilities, in their futures. Weeks ago, such a ritual would have been simple. Gawain and his mother were tied by blood, and he and Hwyfar by their *carioz*. Now, she was not so certain that the rules of magic itself hadn't shifted.

The Path was her guide, her comfort. Her power was there, inside of her, and that had not changed. She just felt as if her own world had shifted irreparably.

"You doubt yourself," Gawain said.

"Indeed. Would you go into a fight without your armor?"

"I have. Thankfully, I had a princess come save me."

THEY WAITED UNTIL Percival and Llachlyn were asleep before they made any attempts to contact Lady Anna. Hwyfar was anxious, but her husband maintained a surprisingly cool, calm presence as they held hands over the small well at the center of the temple. Hwyfar did not know what to make of Gawain's surprisingly astute theories about Percival and Mordred, but she was fearful of the answers. They had lived so far removed from Carelon, and to be thrust into its deepest secrets made her angry and sorrowful.

Still, they agreed Gawain would travel. Hwyfar could likely not maintain the connection as strongly, as they did not share blood in the same way. She would keep Gawain safe while he spoke with his mother. If it was even possible.

It made sense to use what remained of the well, as waters were holy in Avillion and beyond. If there was any remaining power in this ancient place, Hwyfar would need to harness it. The traveling had already left her exhausted, and magic always took more.

Yet when Hwyfar drew up to the well and put her hands into the cold water, all doubt fled. Here was connection, a conduit, and it soothed her soul right away, smoothing away her discomfort and hesitation.

"You think it will work?" Gawain asked.

"Close your eyes. I want you to imagine your mother's rooms. As clearly as you can. Every detail, down to the carvings on the hearth and the scratches on the door," Hwyfar said. "We may not have long, so I need you to focus all your will upon that place, and I will send you as far as I can."

Gawain did as she commanded.

CHAPTER TWENTY-THREE

ANNA

LADY ANNA DU Lac stirred in her sleep, a heavy, uncomfortable sensation flitting down her legs and into her feet. Bedevere slept soundly beside her and did not rouse when she crept from the bed to the hearth on the other side of the spacious room.

She listened, taking her spindle from the basket where she kept it, trying to shake the sense of foreboding cloaked around her still. If she had dreamed, she could not recall it in images, only in the deep, lingering shudder of fear and dread. Something waiting. Something calling to her. Something she should have heeded, but had not.

When the hearth sputtered to life, she was more relieved than surprised, feeling the rush of magic into the room. Finally, Morgen brought tidings. At last, she would have answers.

Except it was not the form of Morgen le Fay emerging from the flames at all, but her son, Gawain.

Anna started, dropping her spindle and rising from her chair, her heart beating rapidly in her slight chest.

"Gawain—" His name came out strangled as she beheld a fiery version of him, tall as ever, his hair truly like flames on top of his head and his broad shoulders smoking. He strode from the hearth to the carpet, glancing down his body, then around the room. She could see through him, barely, to where Bedevere still slumbered.

172

Gawain did not speak right away, but turned in a circle, as little embers trailed in his wake.

Even in this incorporeal form, he limped. Anna held back the desire to help him, knowing how fragile such spells were, and swallowed her tears.

If she loved anyone, anything in the entire realm, it was her eldest son Gawain. So much of her heart, she knew, had burned away decades before, when she had conspired and entrapped Merlin. For a few years she wondered if ever she might feel whole again. At times, she did not know why she continued living.

Then, in darkness, came the truth: her son Gawain. She'd loved him enough to help him leave Carelon, to live a life with the wife he'd been forbidden. And she'd protected that secret with utmost care, knowing every day for him was a gift. Perhaps she would never reach her other sons in the way she hoped, but what small power and influence she had left, she had bent to Gawain's protection.

"Mother," Gawain said, his voice barely a whisper through the magic. "This is strange."

"Magic is strange, but you have not always fared well in its application."

"I know. Hwyfar is here, she is helping."

"That gives me great comfort."

"Yes, my wife is clever and powerful," Gawain spoke the words with more warmth than the roaring fire, and Anna knew Hwyfar must be nearby. "But I fear we may not have much time."

"Of course. Are you safe?"

"For now," Gawain said. "Hwyfar and I are headed toward Carelon—we will arrive in a day or two."

"It would be safer for you to stay far away; I wish you would not come here where the priests clog the halls, and Morgen has gone from us without warning."

"I know," he said softly. Gawain scratched at his beard; the motion was made strange by the smoky translucence of his body, yet it was familiar, comforting. "I would love nothing more than to remain in Thistlewood, but Carelon has come calling. My cousin Llachlyn, and Galahad's squire, arrived with quite the tale."

Percival. The child she had taken; Gweyn's son. The one Merlin had given to King Pellinore and whom Galahad could not stop speaking of.

"Gods above," Anna muttered. "The castle is in an uproar. Galahad is beside himself without his friends."

"Before I bring them, I need to understand something, Mother. You said you had done terrible things, and I have not asked. But you said to me once that there were babes involved, infants. And looking at Percival, we cannot help but wonder... We loved Gweyn so much..."

Anna looked down at her hands, so thin and fragile, and did not need to hear the question. If she closed her eyes, she could still see the face of that babe, his hair pale as sunshine and his lips pursed; she could feel the weight of him in her arms as she passed him along and placed the child who would be Mordred in Gweyn's embrace.

The price of Merlin's death was taking Gweynevere's blood-born son and giving her another, a task she had done at Morgen's behest, and been told never to ask questions. It was part of a greater plan. A destiny Merlin himself orchestrated, in a most curious irony. "He is all of her that is left in this world," Anna said. Tears coursed down her cheeks and into her mouth, bitter and strange. She could not remember the last time she'd wept. "I wish I could explain myself in a way that does not make me a monster, but I am afraid I cannot."

"Why? Why did you do this?" Gawain demanded, confusion and anger making his voice low, dangerous. She remembered that tone, in the years of his own drunken tantrums, and did not wish to revisit it again. "What could you possibly gain?"

"I did what I had to do." Goddess, she was so tired these days. Her whole body felt too light, listless, as if she were fading away. Would she take this suffering to her grave?

"You still think me too dull-witted to understand. After everything."

"I paid the price. I am still paying the price, perhaps," Anna said. "And I love you, Gawain. I have sacrificed much for your secrecy, for your marriage. You know what I am."

"A witch? A sorceress? Aye, so my wife tells me. But you—you tell me nothing. What did you need so badly that you would know this secret?" Gawain demanded.

She began trembling, then. The weight of twenty years of guilt and secrecy set her whole body afire. Gawain had never been a clever man, but it seemed where Gweyn was involved, he saw more than she suspected.

Bedevere could not hear, could not know. Anna glanced toward him, marking the steady rise and fall of his breath. Now and again, he had seen her powers manifest, but this treachery would undo their fragile comfort, their love so hard fought.

"Gawain. There are circumstances you cannot understand."

"Tell me." His anger made his glowing chest simmer like coals, his eyes bright.

"I needed access to Vyvian when she was chained to the lake. To do that, I needed a favor. To get that favor, from Morgen, required this—a switch in Gweyn's room, the night she went to childbed. I was the perfect mark. Gweyn trusted me, loved me."

He made a sound of disgust. "You and your damned shadows."

"Merlin believed Arthur could not raise Gweyn's child—even if he was not the father—and I deluded myself into thinking it was for the greater good. I do not mean to excuse myself, but I had so few options."

Gawain went very still, the magic around the edges of his body flickering. They would not have much time. "What could you have done that the price of these children's futures were worth the cost?"

Anna pressed at her eyes, hot tears stinging her cheeks. "When I am gone, Morgen will tell you. But for now, yes. Percival is Gweyn's child."

"Lanval was the father, aye?"

"Yes. Though I did not know that until later," Anna said softly. "I don't know if that makes any of this worse or better."

That was most of the truth. The rest, she could not bear. Gawain would not understand. *Could* not. She could at least divest herself of this treachery, even if that was not the entire tale. For Mordred, the Prince of Carelon and all of Braetan, was the other changeling child, and he was a son of Orkney, begat by her useless, drunkard, monster of a husband on her maid, Anette. That rape had been the very last crack in her reserve, the moment she'd decided Lot of Orkney would die. He had always been convinced his son would inherit the crown, but never like this.

As if hearing her thoughts, Gawain said with a scoff, "I would ask after the prince's parentage, but I am too afraid of your answers. And I have a feeling you would not answer me."

"Not now. Not yet…"

The tannic scent of magic intensified; the spell was almost over.

"We will arrive in two days' time," Gawain said, his legs no longer visible, just branches of smoke trailing into the fire. "You and I must discuss these matters, and I will do all I can to keep the young ones safe."

"If you go to Carelon, you will be embroiled in the same political mire you left so gladly. Think of your wife, your life among the orchards and hills of Thistlewood. You have peace and joy like none of us have ever held…"

"And pain, Mother. There is no escaping it. And I will not cower in Thistlewood while Carelon falls to the hands of a tyrannical queen bent on her vision of *purity* no matter the cost. I will not let your husband scrape and simper behind her, lies multiplying in the dark," Gawain said, his voice echoing like sizzling embers. "There is a time in a man's life when inaction is cowardice. I will not leave this world knowing I could have done more for… for her."

He meant Gweyn. Anna had not known of their bond, had not even been at court to see—and it had taken years to build enough trust with Gawain for him to tell her. But she had loved

Gweyn, as did so many who knew her. Though she was long dead, the youngest daughter of Leodegraunce still held a most powerful spell upon their past, present, and future.

Anna's guilt kept her quiet, knowing she deserved every bit of her son's derision. What she and her sister Morgen had kept from their own kin could fill more books than Merlin's library, and she believed it was to keep them safe.

Yet the cost was not insignificant. Losing Vyvian and then Morgen in such quick succession had left her feeling utterly abandoned. Her powers were once great, but now less so. Their presence had given her such a sense of safety, of belonging. Was this the cost of her vengeance? The shattering of her relationship with her eldest and most beloved son, after twenty years of repair?

As Anna watched the embers of Gawain's apparition fade back into the crackling fire, she wondered what she had traded for his protection, and how long it could last. She had lived so much of her life in the shadows, but they could not protect her forever.

"Anna?"

Bedevere stirred, thick coverlets rustling in the dark.

"Anna, come back to bed," he said, his voice low and full of sleep. "Is aught burning?"

She wiped tears from her face and meandered back to the bed where her lover awaited her. In the dark, the white streaks on either side of his beard and at his temples were bright enough to nearly glow. In all this time he had managed to only become more handsome to her, dearer.

"Shh, love. Just a stray ember," Anna said. She slid into bed beside him, feeling the steady warmth and solidity of his body next to hers.

"I was dreaming of Orkney," he said, his voice already drifting off to sleep. "Of making love to you in the moonlight."

Anna smoothed Bedevere's brow, waiting for his breath to even out before she turned away from him and fell into dark dreams.

CHAPTER TWENTY-FOUR

LLACHLYN

EVEN AFTER HWYFAR and Gawain returned from the other side of the temple, where they had asked for privacy in a way she most certainly did not want to interrupt, sleep escaped her. No matter how many times she marked the stars above, or moved upon the bedroll, or repeated lines of poetry, she could not rest.

She could see patterns in her mind, shapes she might twist into rings, or chains, or torcs. Her whole mind blazed with possibilities. When she got to Carelon, she would make a matching pair of rings for Hwyfar and Gawain, in thanks for their help and their love. For that's what it was, somehow. Llachlyn had never felt so loved, so safe before. It would not last, but her gifts—if they were accepted—might.

The Green Knight had given her hope, and it bloomed in her chest like the first few sips of wine. Not for the last time, she wished she could write to her aunt Vyvian, wished she could glean just a little more wisdom from her. What would she have thought of this adventure? Had she seen it come to pass already?

Greatness is in your hands, Llachlyn. Greatness and the power to shape the very earth itself. She wrote those words so often, and for so long Llachlyn had not been able to believe even a whisper of it.

"Lass, if you keep up that racket with your sighing, you'll wake the old gods," Gawain said from beside her.

She had thought him sleeping. He'd half fallen into his bed

roll when he'd returned from speaking with the princess. "I'm sorry, cousin."

With a groan he sat up, craning his neck. "No need. You've had a long day."

Llachlyn sat up, bringing her knees under her chin as she stared into the low fire. She loved the sensation of heat on her face, making even her eyes feel hot. "The Green Knight told me I have a half-brother. And that you knew him."

"Llachlyn, I…"

"Everyone already knows Arthur is my father," Llachlyn said with a sigh. It felt good to say it aloud, though. To dispel the fear. "You will not shock me. I have lived with this all my life—the one secret my mother did not keep from me."

Gawain cleared his throat. "I learned, nigh on ten years ago, that King Arthur fathered a bastard named Loholt the Bold. He would be more than thirty now."

Llachlyn's heart thumped, a swaying sensation in her stomach. "So, Arthur had a child. Before he was wed to Gweynevere."

"Indeed, though he is not the first king to do such a thing. Loholt is my cousin, and your half-brother. He's got our eyes." Gawain's voice cracked slightly, from sleep or emotion or both.

"I've never been close with my brother, for obvious reasons," Llachlyn said.

"You are not close with Mordred?" Gawain asked, more than a little uncomfortable with the question.

Close? Was anyone *close* to Mordred Pendragon? Perhaps Llachlyn and her half-brother had managed a few pleasant conversations as adults, and they did grow up close to one another for the first few years of their lives. She had a few good memories of him, of their gamboling down the halls and pranking the knights on their rounds.

For all that, there was a wall between them. She did not know if he knew the truth about her, calling her *cousin* and never *sister*. He was well-connected, though, and gods knew people at court gossiped. Leaving court for Benwick was a relief, if she was honest with herself, because she had lived under the shadow of both Galahad and Mordred since her birth.

"Mordred is very much, well, *Mordred*," Llachlyn said after a moment's consideration. "He lives by his own rules, entirely, ensconced in Merlin's old tower, concocting potions and sleeping with half the keep, and then professing his faith at Mass. He's always been the one who shone, while I remained hidden, distant."

Gawain looked into the low fire, his gaze far away, contemplating. "Whatever you do, Llachlyn, whatever your fate, you have a choice in shaping it. It's in your blood, but more importantly it's in your spirit. I've seen it."

That sounded so much like Aunt Vyvian it made Llachlyn's skin shiver.

"I can't even make the most basic charms," Llachlyn pointed out. "Hwyfar tried for two whole hours this morning, and even she seemed surprised. I have no predilection for magic at all."

"You need practice, but only if you want. Hwyfar wants to teach you so you can protect yourself against whatever we might encounter. There are other ways you might be able to do so without powers," Gawain pointed out.

"I'm small. I can't see well. No archery for me, no combat. I suppose it may be time to start learning how to run and hide," Llachlyn said with a sigh. "I'm not strong enough to hammer weapons or armor—I only make trinkets."

"One must never judge the power of a thing by its size," Gawain pointed out. "I have seen a *graal* before. It was a simple spear, plain to the eye. And the cup, so says my wife, would hold no more than a handful of water."

"My fate is not so noble, I do not think," she replied, after a moment. "Even if I am small."

"Well, Fate is fickle. According to my mother, and yours, I was destined to die on the battlefield the day I fought Loholt. It was not a prophecy—not the kind read by the priestesses in Avillion—but a kind of pathway they sensed."

"How did you change it?"

He glanced across the fire where Hwyfar lay, her breathing even, her red braids down over her shoulders and pooling on the ground. "My wife. My Hwyfar. Together, we chose another option, though the price was high."

"I don't suppose you could lend her to me a while?" Llachlyn asked with a laugh. "It seems to me the Crown Princess of Lyonesse is a most worthy ally."

"You will find those who do the same for you. In fact, I suspect you may have already."

"I suppose," she said softly, worrying at a thread at the cuff of her tunic, and glancing toward where Percival snored.

"There is no supposing about it, lass. You're part of this family. And I will protect you, no matter the cost. It takes time for us to find out who we really are, to have our mettle tested. And you have time yet."

As THEY PREPARED to depart the next morning, Llachlyn watched as Gawain had to try three times to get back on his horse. Though her cousin was indeed frustrated, he still took his time and pushed through his pain and was kind to the princess as she helped steady him. He was certainly different from Galahad, in that way, who crumbled quickly under any frustration. Perhaps that was the cost of being good at so many things: when you could not, the blow was all the harder.

Hwyfar looked exhausted, dark half-moons under her eyes and her hair more disheveled than Llachlyn had ever seen. She was guilty thinking of what the princess was giving up to help keep her and Percival safe.

"You're quiet, Mallow," Percival said from behind her. He, on the other hand, looked refreshed. Given all his snoring, Llachlyn supposed he'd been the only one to get a full night's sleep.

"It was a long night," Llachlyn said.

Percival nodded. "I don't think either of us will see Carelon the same way when we return."

"That's what bothers me," Llachlyn said. To be honest, it was one of many things that bothered her. "I am glad of this protection, but without my mother at court, and with Galahad so very torn between his faith and his duty—do you think it would be better if I just went to Cornwall? To Tintagel?"

Though he squared his shoulders and gave Llachlyn a very pointed look, she could see her words had bothered him. Mostly because he didn't reply right away.

"My mother could be there," Llachlyn insisted. "It's where my grandfather lived, where—well, where everything went wrong, didn't it? Where Merlin disguised Uther, and my grandmother was taken against her will, and Arthur begat and…"

"You've had the dreams again," he said softly.

Llachlyn did not want to admit it, for dreams had plagued her all her life. And Percival did not mean the dream they had shared, but the dream she'd had since she was a child. Once, drunk and melancholy, she had told Percival all about the young man in her dreams who asked her questions about the end of all things.

The dreams were almost always the same: She would stand on the highest parapet at Tintagel, looking across the night sky. Below her, two great beasts were fighting, snarling and roaring, the echoes reverberating against the stone. Above her, two moons rose: one blue and another blood red. Always, she would gaze up above the moons, and then, when she could smell blood from the fighting animals, two great stars tumbled from the heavens, and all turned to fire.

She would become aware, then, of a pair of deep brown eyes in a kind face. Man or woman, she could not tell. They would ask her questions, none of which she'd have the answer to. Then, she would ask the figure: "Who comes after Arthur?"

At those words, the world would end.

Aunt Vyvian had believed her dreams were proof of her power, dormant though it may be, a kind of Sight perhaps lost to the ages. *Dreams are powerful, Llachlyn. Do not discredit them, especially the sort that return time and again.*

"It was just the once, last night. And I woke myself up before the end," Llachlyn said. "But yes. The same dream. It's been over a year since it happened."

Percival's cheeks were pink from the cold, and he gave her a kind, knowing smile. "Sometimes dreams are just stories we tell ourselves while we sleep. You are not your prophecy or your nightmares. And you have me."

"If I decide to leave for Tintagel, will you come with me?"

Percival's eyes betrayed his sorrow and, perhaps, his fear, too. "I will ride with you until the stars burn down, Mallow. You know that."

She did know that. But she also knew that in her dream, she was alone. And she suspected, no matter how hard she might try, Fate would have other plans for her. Because in Carelon, Percival and Galahad would have one another again, and she could not follow them.

CHAPTER TWENTY-FIVE

MORGEN

YVAIN'S QUESTION PIERCED me as deep as an arrow. This whole time I believed, however foolishly, he'd seen me aside from the gossip at court and the whispers that had followed me all my life. First, as Merlin's trollop—never taken for my own abilities and only respected because of my proximity to him—and then for that fateful night with Arthur so long ago.

My sister Margawse was no longer numbered among the living, yet she had ensured my secret went far and wide before her downfall, still. Hers was a magic corrupted long ago, her soul tarnished with hate and fear. I had trusted her, in my terror and the aftermath of what had transpired between Arthur and me, but to my detriment. Yes, I understood what made her so, what poisoned her, for I had fought against the same tide my whole life: how could I protect Arthur, Carelon, as the child of a woman raped and deceived, not just by Uther but by Merlin, as well?

Merlin had made me believe his plans were greater than my mother's pain, at least for a short while. Margawse never believed it and fell deeper and deeper into her power until it left her nothing but hatred and loathing. And when I would not fight against the Pendragons for fear of breaking peace, she whispered my secret in shadowed corridors until all knew. Until I could no longer keep Llachlyn at court, until I sent her away—until I had to tell her the truth.

None of these realities made the confession to Yvain any easier. How deceived I was in thinking him different from the rest.

"I told you I would give you truth," I said to Yvain, a knot of deep regret and sorrow opening up inside me. "I will grant it, as you have asked, as I do not go back upon my word, no matter what folk say."

His angry expression became more guarded. "Perhaps I chose ill."

"You chose the path most do," I said. "You wish to see my shame, my weakness, I suppose."

"No—I only—"

I leaned forward, lowering my voice. "You will be gravely disappointed, I'm afraid."

"I seek no salacious details or gossip," Yvain said. "I merely wish to separate the woman from the myth. Should I place my trust in you, as you so desire, I think I am owed that."

I laughed, bitter and brusque. "Owed? You are owed nothing, son of Modrun. You are not granted secrets or explanation simply by virtue of your greater strength and stature as a man, though this appears a concept widely forgotten today. Perhaps I cannot blame you in that."

"Perhaps not," Yvain said, voice low. He would not look me in the eye any longer.

I did not like to speak of Merlin, or even think of him. Since his death, I had taken many of my memories and confined them to the deepest chambers of my mind, tying them down with root and vine so they would not find the light of day.

But I was no longer capable of fending for myself. I needed Yvain. So, I began untangling those memories, beginning with my mother, Uther Pendragon, and Merlin.

"I was scarcely more than five when my mother was raped by Uther Pendragon and then taken from my father. The deceit was orchestrated by Merlin. Now, of course, the story is told in breathless wonder, how Uther was so struck by my mother's great beauty he convinced Merlin to change his visage to look

185

like Gorlois her husband and my father. That tale softens the blow of the truth, for who would have followed Uther so, knowing he'd worn no such guise?"

Yvain's eyes widened for a moment as the realization settled upon him. "Morgen…"

I held up my hand, palm out, to keep him from speaking further. This tale required a distance from emotion, or else I would be lost to it. "You see, Yvain, my parents loved one another, and that was their greatest weakness. Igraine was a joyful, vibrant woman, a priestess of Avillion who left a peaceful life of introspection and connection to her magic for a man she loved. When Uther saw her beauty, and the way she looked upon my father, and he upon her, his jealousy overtook him. He wanted what he believed he was *owed*."

Once, tears might have punctuated my tale. Goddess knew I had cried for years, cried rivers of sorrow as I watched my mother fade, waste away, and die. Worse even, I had witnessed as the brutal violence she'd suffered had changed into a charming tale. Dull, dim-witted Igraine, so easily deceived by the grand enchanter's spells, easily opening herself up to a man who merely looked like her beloved husband. As if she could have been tricked, even by an enchantment! Igraine was of Avillion, a priestess and a scholar, talented and kind and full of joy. Our family was her greatest love, and Uther and Merlin had cut us all down without thought, as easily as a sickle reaping wheat in the autumn.

"Uther, newly crowned King, came with his entourage to Tintagel, where we welcomed him with song and dancing. I was but a wisp of a child, and yet I remember well all the bright tabards and horses draped with silks and ringing with shining bells. Never had we been given such a great honor, and my parents had such hope for the future of Braetan.

"The final day of their visit, the afternoon before the great feast celebrating the peace accords between Cornwall and Carelon, Merlin led Gorlois to the forest, secretly, to hunt the Glatisant. The old conjuror claimed he had seen it on his entry to Tintagel, and that if Gorlois were to slay the beast, he would be held in highest esteem. Uther would bestow greatness upon him and his line. We were not a wealthy country, but such a boon would ensure longevity and safety. In those days, Braetan was scarcely more than a hope between kingdoms, not as it is today. My father was a shrewd man, a seasoned fighter, and he trusted Merlin. Besides, he had three daughters to think of.

"My father was killed in the forest by the white boar Trwyth, for Merlin knew he would be there. While my father bled to death, his bones torn from his body by blood-red tusks, Uther sent my mother a false letter in my father's hand to take her from the celebrations, and raped her in Gorlois's bed. And so Arthur was conceived. We feasted that evening, unaware that my missing father was dead, that my mother had been ravished—Merlin assured us they were merely waylaid. In the morning, our scouts found my father's broken body, and both Merlin and Uther were gone, along with our summons to Carelon. My mother was given no choice. If she denied the tale, her reputation—*our* reputation—would be ruined. So, for our sakes, she allowed the story, allowed Uther back into her bed, played the game, and it ate her up inside like a canker." I paused, watching Yvain's tense expression. "It is not the tale you heard, I am certain, but perhaps you begin to understand."

"You apprenticed under Merlin," Yvain said, clearly trying to understand my motivations. "You—you became his lover."

"I was a child, Yvain, and we had no means to fight the power of Uther Pendragon and Merlin. I had shown remarkable aptitude in magical prowess, the only weapon I could bend to my will. You see me—I am a slight woman even now."

"Yet you are a daughter of Avillion, of great power."

"We should have been. Instead of sending me to Avillion, and Margawse along with me, Uther demanded we be kept together in the tower opposite Merlin's own, and where the enchanter taught us the ways of his power. We visited the Isle, of course, for long seasons, but we were not given the same education as others. I saw later it was Merlin's way of keeping us under his eye, as we knew the truth of his treachery, his complicity in murder. And for Uther to keep us from our mother's inheritance, who he'd always feared.

"Margawse quickly bored of Merlin's tedious instruction, but I flourished. By fourteen, I was his lover—not by desire, but out of self-preservation. Once Arthur was born, and the future of Braetan all but assured, Merlin became far more of a politician than a sorcerer. I assisted him in all these endeavors, moving through court as both a lady and as an informant. I carried secrets and I worked wonders. My powers bolstered his own, you see, and he bent me to his will.

"Merlin was not, as commonly believed, a prophet himself. Rather, he was a sorcerer and an interpreter of prophecies. For truly, the priestesses of Avillion spin so many prophecies it is difficult to know which to seize upon. One could more easily recognize a single snowflake in a blizzard than decipher all the possible futures of the Isle. Still, Merlin had a way of bending Fate to his will. He trained me in this power, but we, like Vyvian, did not always agree on the interpretation of such prophecies. As he aged, he became increasingly obsessed with objects of power meant to give him—and, he claimed, Avillion—more strength in the days to come. He also insisted I would give him a child, powerful and necessary for the future of Carelon."

Melic snorted as if in reply, breaking the deep, uncomfortable tension. I reached out to rub behind his soft, round ears, measuring my next words.

"He told me it was my fate, that my prophecy spoke of the child I would bear, one that would usher in a new age. When I balked, he claimed I had two choices: bear his child—who would usher in a generation of plenty—or carry my half-brother Arthur's, one who could bring the very end of our age.

"I rebuked him, believing such a fate impossible. For I had seen Merlin, growing old and infirm, and did not think his power ran so deep. I was tired, distracted, hurt and angry at

Merlin's dismissal, when I found myself in Arthur's quarters years later. It was as if the whole realm held its breath…"

"You don't need to tell the rest," said Yvain. He reached out to touch my arm, but then pulled back.

"You asked for my truth, so I give it to you, Yvain." I leaned forward, my voice barely a whisper, daring him to look me in the face. "Perhaps Arthur and I were dosed with some strange tonic, or Merlin cast a spell upon us. I do not know, though I suspect it was Merlin's vengeance upon me, forcing me into a sin greater than all the rest, and leaving me with the reminder of it. Still, I would have chosen it time and again. Not for love, but for the knowledge that I did not bring Merlin's vision to fruition. I believe he sought the *graal*, and he would have manipulated our child into a fate worse than my daughter's, given that power. I carried her, and nearly lost her, even though I knew she had the potential to destroy Arthur's line."

"That is a burden neither you nor the child should have to bear," he said.

"I removed myself from my daughter's upbringing, sending her to Benwick to be with my sister Elaine and her stepson, Sir Hector de Mares, when I felt court was no longer safe for her. Her childhood alongside her cousin Galahad was uneventful, but happy. I visit her as often as I can, and find she is headstrong and curious, though small and terribly near-sighted, as many children are who are born too early. She has never shown any prowess for magic, though I know well enough that can be deceiving, but it does give me some measure of relief."

"May I ask the words of the prophecy you speak of?"

"'The first born of Arthur will bring his end.' Merlin believed a child between us would negate the prophecy. It was not so, nor is it clear of whom the prophecy speaks. Llachlyn was the first known to Arthur; Loholt, the first in age; Mordred the first in his heart. It could be any one of them, or all of them."

Yvain's face wrinkled in distaste. "Prophecies. I do not envy your role, Morgen."

"Llachlyn knows of the prophecy—I did not want her finding out from someone else. She does not know of my choice, that Merlin's curse pushed me toward her conception, and her likely part in Arthur's downfall. But though Merlin was vanquished, I have reason to believe his power may be poisoning Carelon now."

We both fell silent, the bower rustling in a surprisingly warm breeze. My whole body ached, my ribs sore and my hips digging into the hard ground. It was not often I felt every year of my age, but after telling the story to Yvain and enduring what we had with the cockatrice, I noted them now with hard clarity.

"And you knew my father," Yvain said.

Coel was his true name, though Uriens was what he was crowned. Even now, my heart ached to think of him. "Yes. I knew your father." Loved him, though I did not say it. "Merlin sent me to Rheged, to glean information from your father, not long after Arthur was married. I did not expect to find such a kindred soul in King Uriens, nor that he would propose to me. I spent months at court with your brothers and sister, when they were but little toddling things. I saw a happy life for myself there, but for Merlin's command I returned."

"I have spent precious little time with my father—a bastard is rarely a gift," Yvain said, catching himself and wincing. "And my mother has no love for Merlin, either. As you saw, she has given me some of her knowledge and power. But I cannot pretend to know what you have endured."

"You have endured your own trials, Yvain."

He stilled, dropping his hands to his lap. "I have."

"Now you know my truth, every mote of it. Our tales are strangely tied—I nearly married your father, and your mother has been a friend to me these long years. So, tell me: Why does Modrun keep you here?"

His gaze met mine, piercing and steady. "Because I cannot die in Brocéliande, and though I have tried time and again, she will not grant me that peace."

The truth and shadow of Yvain's statement cut to the very

heart of me. Never had I contemplated such a terrible end for myself, but I had known many who had. My own mother, one could certainly argue, had taken her own life by simply fading away, refusing food and drink and company, until the goddess took her. I only regret it took her so long, for her anguish was truly beyond bearing.

Yvain's sorrow was a palpable thing, tinged with anger and hurt.

"I have long suspected your mother is not well, but I did not know she'd trapped you here," I said, gently as I could.

"Madness is a familial trait, and the last year or so she has fallen into a wicked, feverish state. I remain far from her, not for my own safety, but to keep myself from losing the fight against madness again." He gestured to himself, then rubbed his chest, just above his heart. "What you see is not always so. Many a time I have been lost in the wood, most often since the forest was breached by the agents of Ys and I nearly lost my life."

I had heard of those events, some ten years before. Hwyfar and Gawain were among those attacked, and their escape led to their meeting and, ultimately, their union. I knew Yvain had attended their wedding, and Modrun with them, but never would have guessed at his long suffering.

"There is no shame in that, Yvain. Many have become lost in the woods," I said softly.

Yvain looked at his hands, leather gloves creaking as he flexed them. "I was conceived in love, but my mother did not want me raised in Rheged—my father was not yet king, then. She fled, and in doing so put herself into great danger. On her journey to Avillion, where she sought escape, she was set upon by a demon of a man who took her by force after giving her rest in his manor. My mother fought so hard it broke her when she did not succeed. For all her power, it was not enough. Brocéliande gave her succor when others would not—but she never again returned to live among us. And when I nearly died, it broke her further."

I knew parts of the story, but Modrun never spoke of her life before the wood. We all knew that what had happened had reshaped her mind and body, and though she had many days of lucidity and control, it was only the power of Brocéliande that kept her hale.

"Men have a habit of taking what they want," I said, "and do not consider the outcomes, beyond satisfying their desires. Though I do not always agree with my brother, I am yet glad he has given more protection to those like Igraine, so they cannot move so easily through the world. He knows, after what we endured with our mother, that one can kill more than a body with violence. One can kill a soul with it, too. And that deserves punishment."

"Would that I could kill the man who broke her," Yvain said.

"Perhaps once your mother allows you passage," I said.

Standing, Yvain brushed off his thighs, our strange conversation finally coming to a close. "The man is already dead. I cannot kill him twice."

CHAPTER TWENTY-SIX

HWYFAR

THE FIRST TIME Hwyfar of Avillion, eldest daughter of King Leodegraunce, had passed through the gates of Carelon, she had been scarcely sixteen. Carried upon a grand palanquin, flanked by dozens of priestesses, a shimmering royal guard, and streaming banners of gold, chartreuse, and turquoise, she had been veiled and quiet and terrified, counting down the heartbeats until her fate as Queen of Braetan was sealed. She had been haunted by recent events, her body sundered from her magic, but prepared to make the sacrifice for her future.

It was never to be. For King Arthur, when presented with his new bride, had seen her younger sister, Gweynevere, and demanded her as his wife instead. *She* had been scarcely *thirteen*, pale and lovely and petite, far from the towering, sharp-featured Hwyfar.

Now, as she rode beside her husband, Hwyfar passed again through the gates veiled. This was to blunt the shock of her identity, one they must present to Arthur first alone, but it did not deter her splendor. In matching armor to her husband, an embroidered green cape flowing from her shoulders and over the back of her horse like a verdant waterfall, she shone like royalty of old.

This time, the parapets and crenellations were mostly void of attendants. There were no great crowds, no garlands of flowers. It seemed unusually quiet for such a bustling city.

Through the great portcullis they went, crossing under the

great barbican and to the final roadway to the keep itself. Looking up at the pink exterior of Carelon Castle, Hwyfar thought it smaller than she remembered. Yes, it was grand and sprawling, tier upon tier of smooth stone and magnificent high towers, but it was no longer as imposing as it had once seemed.

Still, it held great memories of sadness. Of Gweyn. Of Merlin. Of the woman she once was. But new concerns, as well. Percival, Gawain had confirmed, was indeed who they'd suspected: Gweyn's true son. But not Arthur's. And Mordred? She did not want to find out. Holding such secrets inside of her was exhausting, and she wondered, as she often had these past years, how Morgen managed such grace and strength with all her knowledge.

"The first time I passed through these gates," she said to her husband, who rode beside her, "I thought I was going to lose myself, certain that even to gain a crown as Queen, I would cease to be Hwyfar."

"I suppose I can understand that," Gawain said, slowing their pace even more. "And now?"

If Hwyfar had been the sort of woman to weep often, she might have shed a tear. Instead, however, her anger—at the situation, at Arthur, at Mawra—burned away all vestige of sorrow and left behind a roiling fury.

"I have never been more myself. Yet, for all of this, I do not feel we have an ally in my sister, or in the King. To say nothing of his famed captain. We will be separated, you know. Our guests have twisted our fates to the wheel, and we cannot go back."

Gawain gazed up at the highest tower, the very same where Merlin once cast his sharp eyes across the whole of Braetan. Hwyfar wondered what he remembered of the old conjuror. It seemed a lifetime ago that he had haunted the corridors.

When he turned back to his wife, his eyes shone with tears. "I will always wish we had more time," he said. "I would have lived a thousand years with you in Thistlewood."

"And I would have regretted every day knowing we could have stopped whatever malfeasance has come to Carelon," Hwyfar said.

The inner courtyard was muted, but for the distant sounds of sparring and the general hubbub of those going about their work. They dismounted, and were greeted by a handful of young squires Percival seemed to know. The young lads offered them both shy smiles, the eldest of the group clearly enamored of Gawain, already asking questions about the Green Knight. Hwyfar found she did not mind being written out of the story, for it protected her. Still, she found it amusing to see just how her husband's legend had grown.

A scuffling sound drew Hwyfar's attention to one of the arched doorways to her right. She readjusted her veil as Sir Cai emerged, his hitched gait more pronounced than ever. He looked, as always, like a wrinkled, peeled apple, scowling with his brow and half his balding pate.

He had been one of Hwyfar's most vocal critics, and she had no wish to make herself known yet. Given he had become a Christian now, she doubted that situation would have improved.

"Sir Gawain, Dame Ragnell," said Sir Cai, not even a remnant of warmth in his rumbling voice. "You're half a day behind schedule."

"Cai." Gawain patted the seneschal on his shoulder. "You're lucky we're not still upon the road. We had half a mind to linger longer and bring you back some casks of wine, but alas, we pushed on as we could. All due to my most inconvenient body. Surely you can understand one's limitations in such a way."

Sir Cai pursed his lips, and Hwyfar did not miss him taking note of Gawain's cane. Then he seemed to recognize their companions all at once. "These two wretches! We've been looking for them."

"They are under my explicit protection. Do you question that?" Gawain asked the seneschal.

Hwyfar watched as her husband transformed before her eyes. In their decade of marriage, they had never had cause to be at court together. Now, his gait changed, and his voice grew exacting and deep and resonant. People turned to look at him, drawn by his presence.

Even Cai looked cowed. "No—I suppose I cannot."

"Then, you will take me directly to the King. And inform my brothers of our arrival."

"I will surely tell Sirs Gaheris and Gareth, Sir Gawain, but the King is occupied at present. And perhaps your wife and guests might prefer time to recover from the road," said the seneschal.

"They're not simply my guests. Lady Llachlyn is my *cousin*, Cai," Gawain said.

"It is difficult to keep up with your rambling family tree," Sir Cai said, clearly nonplussed. "I have many responsibilities here at court, you know, and I'd prefer not to be later than I ought for my next appointment. Mass is soon."

It was by sheer will that Hwyfar kept from making a noise of disdain.

"We don't need a guide. Just let me know where we're staying, and I shall make myself comfortable," Gawain said.

THE CORRIDOR WAS familiar to them both, having been the way to Gweyn's apartments. It seemed Queen Mawra no longer used them, and had, instead, built an expansive wing of the castle overlooking the chapel.

Hwyfar was so tired from the journey that she had scarcely noted the direction they walked, only stopping when the flooring changed to the worn blue and yellow tiles Gweyn had installed during her short tenure as Queen. Once, each tile had been studded with a delicate rendering of an apple blossom, but now only vague, ghostly outlines remained as the glaze had worn away.

The gentle squeeze of Gawain's hand on her shoulder gave her comfort, wordless commiseration.

The other remnants of Gweyn were nowhere to be found, the entire apartment and its six rooms swept of Avillionian influences and replaced with heavy, oak-carved furniture and comfortable, rather somber velvets and brocades. One stained-glass window overlooked the courtyard below, but there was precious little sunlight due to the new chapel's obstruction.

There was some mournful poetry in that, Hwyfar thought.

"These are the best rooms the castle has to offer," Llachlyn mused, re-emerging from her room. "The King tried to give them to Mother once the Queen left, so they could renovate her tower, but she refused, of course."

"Well, Gawain is Arthur's closest kin, save for Mordred. He deserves a place of honor. These were my sister Gweyn's rooms once," Hwyfar said, starting to untie her long braid. She had refused attendants for now. "I am not surprised Mawra had her own apartments built. She always had the most exacting tastes. And Gweyn was, among us, the most ostentatious with decoration. Still, this room holds many memories for me." She found a tangle in the braid and took up a comb to tease it out. She would have to look somewhat presentable, even if they planned to hold this ruse for a little while longer.

Llachlyn hesitated and then offered. "I can help with that, if you like. I'm not the most dexterous, but I am good at getting the knots out."

Hwyfar nodded, handing the ivory carved comb to Llachlyn. From the other rooms, she could hear Gawain humming to himself and Percival walking around, commenting on the workmanship of various pieces of furniture and the provenance of certain paintings. Her own magic was present, but dormant, like a cat sleeping by the flame; after the spell that sent Gawain to Carelon, she was still regaining her strength.

Yet, the momentary normalcy of the scene before her gave her a sense of comfort.

This arrangement felt not like traveling companions, but like a family.

She supposed they were. Percival... her *nephew*. Now, it seemed the most obvious thing in the world. How she ever could have thought otherwise. But the ramifications of this knowledge was no small thing, and she did not know what bringing it to light would do.

An impatient knock upon the door sent Hwyfar to her feet,

and Llachlyn dropped the ivory comb with a soft gasp. They had left explicit instructions to be left alone.

With a speed that surprised her, Gawain swept into the room and went down the hallway to the main door, out of earshot and view. Hwyfar's heart pounded in her chest, a strange, unwelcome fear twisting through her gut.

Percival meandered back into the room, looking around like a curious bird. Somehow, even in fine clothes, he looked gawky and out of place. And still that endeared him more to Hwyfar, and she wondered how she had ever missed her sister's influence in his face. Standing here, in this room, there could be no doubt. What would he say? When would he ask? She both welcomed and dreaded the moment.

The door shut, hinges shaking, and then Gawain returned, his face pale with shock, making way for the two figures behind him: Sir Bedevere, tall and proud, and the King himself, Arthur Pendragon.

They all fell to their knees.

When she looked up, the King was before her, resplendent in his robes. Her expression must have belied her emotions, for he spoke first to her.

"Please, princess, quell your concern," King Arthur said, hands out in gentle placation. He was thin, wan, his hair almost white. Ten years had fallen on him like an unexpected storm, eroding away his boyish features and leaving behind a sorrowful man looking far more than his fifty years. "I carry no ill intent this day, and indeed, welcome you as my sister to Carelon at last. As I ought to have done a long time ago—eh, Gawain, my boy?"

Hwyfar could not breathe properly. King Arthur had never spoken to her in such a kind, sweet, playful way. And his eyes were filled with a deep, bone-aching sadness that made Hwyfar feel the weight of all his years of rule, all the choices he had made, and all the terrible decisions yet to come.

The world—their world—shifted once again, and she felt the threads of Fate tighten around her.

CHAPTER TWENTY-SEVEN

GAWAIN

TEN YEARS OF uncomfortable separation be damned, Gawain couldn't very well deny the King entry. He wasn't just Arthur's guest, but his eldest nephew. And his uncle looked so terribly withered, as if all the color had been leeched out of him since they'd last met. Gone was the strong, lean set of his shoulders, the arrogant tilt to his chin, the surety in his steps.

Arthur was ill, and the knowledge of it shattered a part of Gawain's heart. Bedevere caught Gawain's expression, his lips set grimly, and nodded almost imperceptibly.

"Please, sit, Your Majesty," Gawain said. "We've only just arrived, or we would have prepared." Prepared for what? No number of comfortable chairs or teas or tinctures would help Arthur, not in his state.

A pit of guilt opened wide in Gawain's chest, watching how Bedevere had to help Arthur take a seat comfortably. Though he was well aware of his own failing body, Gawain never considered the toll on Arthur, who had always seemed lively and strong. Had there been signs before? Arthur had always been the first to point out Gawain's own shortcomings, after all. He had never imagined sickness would fall so fast upon the High King.

Percival and Llachlyn stood, frozen, hands clasped, eyes wide, the squire's gaze flitting from face to face.

Hwyfar stood tall and furious, every muscle taut and prepared to flee, or fight. The latter, most likely. Only Bedevere might have a chance against her, Gawain reasoned. After all that riding and no real sleep to speak of, he'd be useless.

"Thank you, Bedevere," Arthur said, as his commander arranged a wool coverlet across his lap. He gave an apologetic smile. "Now, Gawain. Is there aught you wish to tell me?"

"I am Hwyfar's husband," Gawain said, simply. "And she is my wife."

Gawain reached over and took Hwyfar's hand, and before the High King of Braetan, he kissed her fingers tenderly.

He had expected anger or betrayal. Years, they had avoided this, knowing their union had flown in the face of their sovereign's wishes. Treasonous, truly.

King Arthur did not look angry at their declaration of union. He did not look particularly surprised, either. Tired, yes, and burdened, but his shoulders were relaxed, and his eyes were bright and soft about the edges.

Bedevere had the gall to even look a little bored. "Yes, Gawain. That is fairly obvious," he said.

"Obvious?" Gawain asked.

"You think me blind to your ruse, Gawain?" Arthur had a playfulness in his voice that reminded him, momentarily, of Merlin.

"No, Your Majesty. Of course not," Gawain said, words thick in his throat. Hwyfar squeezed his hand, her fingers strong but still cold against his skin.

"And you, Princess Hwyfar?" Arthur turned his attention to Gawain's wife.

She did not reply so quickly, but eventually said, "No, Your Majesty."

Arthur glanced at Bedevere, who remained placid. "I suppose I am not the sagest of kings, and at times you must see my reasoning as simple and my decisions without discernment. But you forget I have known you since before you knew yourself, Gawain. Bedevere and I rode to Orkney a year after you were born. Even then, you were sizable. And squalling. My poor sister Anna, she was the only one who could quell your shrieks, until I discovered how you enjoyed riding along my back and being tossed into the air."

"How long have you known?" Gawain asked, dreading the answer even if the release of a long-held lie lay within his grasp.

Arthur leaned back, folding his hands upon his stomach and smiling. He was enjoying this. "Known which part? That you two had fallen in love, or that you married without my blessing or consent?"

Bedevere let out a little chuckle.

"A while now. In Avillion," Arthur said. "After you bested Loholt. I could tell by the way you looked at one another that you had fallen deeply, irreparably in love."

Hwyfar's expression remained cold, her eyes unwavering from the King's countenance. "Then why did you try to hold me to my oath?"

Arthur replied, "Oh, I had no plans to allow the marriage, at first. Love like yours is, at best, a political inconvenience. The implications of allowing such a union, especially with the fragility of the situation with your father, King Leodegraunce, were potentially disastrous."

"What swayed you?" Hwyfar asked.

"A few things." Arthur closed his eyes and took a deep, steadying breath. Not out of nerves, but trying to push down the pain. Gawain knew that feeling well. "Mostly because I was tired of all the machinations, all the constant arrangements and betrothals. You had already given so much for the realm, Gawain, and you clearly had no ambition for the crown, or you would have claimed your father's title yourself."

"You know the line of Orkney will die with me," Gawain said, looking at Bedevere now, keeping the old commander's gaze. For indeed, though he did not consider his brothers any less for their sire, they could never claim the title of Orkney by blood. It was, perhaps, the second worst kept secret in all of Carelon.

"You know," Arthur said, stroking his beard. "It's a funny thing. Before your mother's most remarkable surrender of the

Orkney crown, I had lost all faith Orkney would ever bow. Lot used to write me letters, claiming that one of his sons would be King, that an augur had told him. Merlin took no stock in such ramblings, of course, and your father was very fond of drink, but I always found it remarkable that you and your mother gave it away so freely. You were not tempted by the power at all."

"I was not," Gawain said, meaning it. "Perhaps it was petty of me, but my father was not a good man, sire. You were always..." He swallowed, pushing back on mounting emotion. Hwyfar gave him a kind, loving, steadying look, and it soothed him. "You were always there for me. When it mattered."

In turn, Arthur's eyes shone with pride, and he nodded courteously before clearing his throat. "As for you, Princess Hwyfar." The King turned his gaze. "Your mother and father, Queen Tregerna and King Leodegraunce, are alive and well and thriving, thanks to you. My spies also tell me that your mother plans to defect soon to her brother Meliadus, with your consent."

"I have helped Lyonesse as I have been able," Hwyfar said, her voice steady, standing as queenly as any woman ever had within the walls of this castle. "But Meliadus saw the country through twenty years of their regency and is much beloved. My desires these days are far simpler."

Gawain was still trying to reconcile this conversation with the last decade of his marriage. "I do not understand why you would give us ten years living apart in secrecy, Your Majesty."

"You were miserable, my boy, when I saw you last," Arthur said gently, expression pained as he looked upon Gawain. "Bedevere and I discussed at length what the ramifications might be, and we felt it best to keep as much distance as possible."

"Save your spies," Hwyfar intoned.

Arthur did not indulge her temper. "I was happy to play to the ruse as long as you both needed, given how much you walked away from to live a life together. And, I suppose, I still am a romantic man, for all my failings in love. It seemed a great sin to me to come in the way of such a connection. Especially for you."

Tears stung Gawain's eyes as he tried to reorganize his thoughts. The agony and anxiety of the last ten years had been naught but penance, orchestrated at Arthur's hands. But for all the strain, theirs had been a deep, miraculous love, stronger and more certain than any he had ever known.

"Your mother does not know we know," Bedevere added, wincing slightly. "It was important she did not feel threatened by the knowledge, given her fragile state. We know she worked with Morgen to ensure your inheritance in the North."

Gawain was unsure they had any idea just how involved Anna du Lac had been in the whole scheme. At least, he supposed, there was some comfort in knowing that. Though, given Bedevere's proximity to his mother, there was a chance it was not the entire truth.

"Surely there are other concerns at present beyond our own marriage," Hwyfar said, ice still in her voice. "Else you would not have gone to the trouble of such a dramatic entrance, sire."

Arthur seemed to consider her words a moment before leaning back in his chair, steepling his fingers. "I suppose some remember those early days, princess, when you roosted and gamboled like a wild goddess of old, but time makes us all forgetful. Besides, your nephew Mordred has inherited quite a lusty and notorious streak of his own, certainly from your side of the family, and I daresay his antics keep tongues wagging and rumors flying every day."

"I believe she means in terms of heirs," Gawain clarified.

"Oh, of course," Arthur said, looking only slightly chagrined. "Well, you have not had children so far, and I do not think you intend to do so. I know, it is a personal observation, and I would apologize if it wasn't my purpose to know.

"Unless I am mistaken?" he asked when neither Gawain nor Hwyfar replied. "I do not believe you have a family beyond your bond."

"Not unless you count these rascals," Gawain said, turning to where Llachlyn and Percival stood. "They are the cause of our return."

"It is a brave thing to sacrifice your privacy for their safety," Bedevere observed. "But I would expect no less of you, Gawain."

"We tried to convince them otherwise, my lord," Llachlyn said quickly, nearly tripping on her own feet as she stepped forward. "But they insisted we returned."

At Llachlyn's voice, Arthur's expression did change. Surprise, worry, hesitation. Part of him wanted to intercede, but Gawain knew well the anxieties children of complicated fathers felt, and he also did not want to speak over her. She had chosen to address Arthur herself, which showed remarkable bravery.

"Approach me, child. Let me look at you," Arthur said.

Everyone fell silent. Bedevere sat up straighter. Hwyfar held tightly to Gawain's hand, and he breathed deep and even, wondering just how complicated his family could get. It seemed their legacy was not finished exposing secrets.

"I know my wife behaved abhorrently to you both," said the King, inclining his head to Percival. "There are complications at court that are well beyond the three of you, and I do wish you could have felt comfortable enough to speak with me, or with Bedevere or Cai or Palomydes, before resorting to your Northern adventures. But you are now under not just Sir Gawain's and Princess Hwyfar's protection, but mine as well."

The room fell completely silent after the King's most remarkable vow. He held Llachlyn's gaze a little longer, and she and Percival muttered overwhelmed thanks.

Gawain was prepared for Arthur to say more, but there came a great blasting of horns from the courtyard—a warning, a clarion call, followed by the sound of guards forming and moving—loud enough to shake the windowpanes.

Gawain did not know the meaning of the horns, but Bedevere did.

"By Christ," said Bedevere, rushing to the door. "We must get the King situated in his rooms—Gawain, if you can manage it, I think you should come along with me. We will continue our discussions after we solve this other matter."

CHAPTER TWENTY-EIGHT

GALAHAD

MERCILESS LIGHT FILLED Galahad's bedroom as a hulking figure dashed about, pulling back drapes. Galahad's head pounded, his throat dry as sand, and his face still ached from Gareth's fight. Whatever Mordred had given him to help him sleep didn't seem to work at all, so he'd turned to wine, regretfully.

He had been dreaming before the rude interruption. Percival had returned. And they were comfortable again. Comfortable in that way that made him feel seen and complete and—no, best not to think about that. The priests were most clear on that matter. What had transpired between him and Percival ought never happen again.

"Get up, Galahad."

For a brief moment, Galahad thought the man storming about his bedroom was Gareth, returned to finish the job, and rightfully so. Where was Pip, his servant? Why hadn't he prevented this impending murder?

Pulling the thick fur coverlet up under his chin, Galahad sat up and got a better look at his visitor.

It *was* his brother. But it was the other twin.

Gaheris.

Fairer and slightly stouter than Gareth, Gaheris had a perpetually stoic expression that verged on stern. Today was no exception. He looked positively livid, the skin around his nose pale with the effort of keeping his breathing steady, the pewter cross he wore around his neck slipping across his smooth woolen tunic with his impatient movements.

"Gaheris. What is happening?" Galahad inquired. "Is aught amiss?"

"Christ, your face looks terrible," Gaheris said as a band of light hit upon Galahad's face.

"I know," Galahad said, touching his cheek and wincing at the tender flesh.

Gaheris let out a low, frustrated sound. "Gareth is no better, but at least he has a sense of humor about it. The same cannot be said of Sir Lanceloch."

"My father is upset?"

"Incensed, more like. He's challenged Gareth in the ring, before the whole court, and I'm not certain either one of them will survive it," Gaheris replied, punctuating each word by throwing a pillow from the bed to the floor.

Galahad swallowed back nausea, and it mingled with the heat of shame. His father challenged his brother on account of their scuffle? In front of *everyone*? They would all think Galahad had put him up to it—they would look at him and think him weak and childish. By Christ! He wanted to jump out the window.

"What are we going to do?" Galahad asked.

"Pray to God we do not lose a brother this day." Gaheris fumbled in the great wardrobe for some of Galahad's tunics, and threw one at him with the same aggression as he had the pillows. "Get dressed. They've already begun."

HALFWAY TO THE tilting fields, Galahad still arranging his belt, they came up on Mordred. The chap was still wearing his sleeping robes—deep crimson velvet tumbling to his feet embellished with golden fringe and viridian beads that clacked as he walked. He somehow managed to look more put together than Galahad, and regal at that.

"Oh, there hasn't been a proper brawl in—well, at least a

day," Mordred said, clapping Galahad on the shoulder. "The whole castle is up in arms. Isn't it spectacular?"

"Greetings, Prince Mordred," Gaheris said, flatly. "Come along, Galahad, we must make haste."

"Yes. Haste, haste, everything in haste," Mordred mocked in Gaheris's low, grumbling voice. "If you are indeed in a rush, then it's quite a blessing you've found me. For no one gets a crowd moving like I do. Crown prince and all."

Mordred's sleepy, charming smile did nothing to ameliorate Gaheris's mood. Especially considering he was correct. No one was more wary of Mordred and his behavior than Gaheris, who only barely managed to bank his revulsion in public.

"Does the King know what is going on?" Galahad asked his cousin.

"He's occupied, of course, which is likely for the best. I hardly think he'd ever approve," said Mordred, directing them both down the winding stair as people parted for them. At least half of them went down on their knees, or bowed their heads, as the prince navigated with the kind of grace and aplomb only one of such an upbringing could manage. "But then, Father rarely attends these kinds of spectacles. And I should know. Usually I'm the cause."

A cool breeze set their cloaks and hair moving as they went down through the eastern gate and toward the tilting fields. Galahad could already hear swords ringing against one another, but not with the practiced cadence of sparring. This was an angry, clanging sound, brutal and unpredictable, and it made his jaw clench as if he could feel the reverberations himself. He balled his hands into fists, trying to find a semblance of Christ's peace inside of himself, but only coming up with pain and shame and guilt.

Then he saw them, two figures glinting in the guttering green of the tilting field, swords and helmets glinting in the morning light: His brother and his father, faced off against one another. Because of him.

Never in his life had Galahad beheld his father in combat. As anyone raised in the realm, he had heard the stories, of course, and given his father's strength and poise he had no doubt of his prowess. Galahad assumed his own talents came from the du Lac line—he could not attribute them to his mother, after all.

Yet seeing Sir Lanceloch squared off against his brother Gareth in the sparring ring made Galahad's whole body heat with shame, despite his marvelous form and astounding footwork. It didn't matter.

This was not his father's fight. The two men had no reason to combat one another, and if anyone was in the right it was Gareth.

Galahad wanted to turn into a pillar of ash and blow away in the wind to avoid what came next.

"We need to stop them," Galahad said, hearing the high-pitched panic in his own voice. "I can go there. I can—I can stop them, I can explain—"

Gaheris snorted. "I would not recommend that, little brother. I know Gareth, and once he's roused in the blood, he's damned near impossible to stop."

"Sir Lanceloch will *kill* him," Galahad said, his hands shaking now.

"Oh, do not fret, cousin," Mordred said, dismissively waving his hand. "Sir Lanceloch is not the shining pinnacle of brawn he once was. Look at Sir Gareth! He is younger, and faster. Oh, this shall be quite the event."

"It doesn't matter. Gareth was just trying—he was trying to be brotherly, and *I* was the one who lost control," Galahad insisted. "Is there not anyone who can just stop this?"

No one answered Galahad, and instead, the crowd built all around them, with close to three dozen people gathering, mostly knights in attendance. All around him, Galahad spied a flurry of excitement and movement, and they all knew—They all knew why this was happening. Christ, he wanted to die.

The horn blared again from the parapet; three short blasts intended to clear the sparring ring. Which, everyone knew, would have the precise opposite reaction, only drawing more attention.

Staggering toward the ring, Sir Palomydes intercepted Galahad just before he stepped on the field—to do what, exactly, he didn't know. But clearly no one else had the presence of mind to prevent this farce, so by God Galahad was going to at least try.

"Let them be, Galahad," Sir Palomydes said. His expression was stormier than he'd ever seen it, jaw set and brows down.

"But this is about *me*," Galahad said. "This is my fault."

Sir Palomydes leveled Galahad with a warning look. "You might very well have precipitated this incident, but I promise, it isn't about you."

Mordred was grinning like a toddler before a platter of sweets. "Oh, my dear Galahad, you are woefully unaware of the blood feuds in your own family. Though I suppose it is a bit confusing when it's one half versus the other."

"My mother and father?" Galahad asked.

"Your *brothers* and your father," Mordred corrected. "Or do you not know the tale of how Sir Lanceloch bested Sir Gawain before the entire court in the tilting ring? Almost killed him. Christ, I wish I'd been there to see it."

Sir Palomydes shook his head at the scene unfolding before them. "It was a brutal day. Made only worse when Sir Lanceloch was betrothed to your mother, Sir Galahad. Which made him stepfather to the Orkneys."

"It's got naught to do with blood," Gaheris said, snappishly. "Gareth should never have agreed to Lanceloch's challenge in the first place."

"Half the court is related to us at this point, cousin," Mordred replied. "And I hardly think this is the most dishonorable thing to happen to us. By God's grace, if Gareth is in the right, then he will triumph over Lanceloch."

"By God, or Fate, or perhaps, the passing of the breeze," added another voice.

Galahad turned to his left where a young lady of the court stood, her glossy black hair tied with ribbons amid one of the longest braids he had ever seen. It fell well past her ample waist.

Her eyes were warm brown, fringed with dark lashes, and her cheeks peppered with freckles. She wore a dress patterned with delicate knotted embroidery, the floss so lifelike he thought, for a moment, she was encircled in rope.

"My lady," Galahad said, bowing as courtesy required, Gaheris following suit.

Mordred held out his hand and the lady kissed his signet ring. Then he announced, "This is the Lady Linette, younger sister of Lady Lyonora, daughters of Lord Aimar of Letavia—newly arrived at court, but not in my heart."

Lady Linette laughed, and it was a merry sound. "The prince only means we have known one another since we were children, for my father is well known through Braetan and beyond as a most excellent breeder of horses. Sir Cai brought the prince to visit us nearly every spring to examine the new foals and fillies."

"Oh, my darling, that was not all I examined," Mordred said, eyes devouring her form.

Galahad, unfortunately, had experienced Mordred's behavior around young women and men at court, but was surprised to see not even a blush upon Linette's cheek. Indeed, there was a spark of challenge in her eyes.

"Yes, but you did require use of a stool to adequately assess our herd," Lady Linette teased. She was significantly taller than Mordred, and she met him jape for jape.

Galahad wished he had the tongue for such wit. Every time he thought he had a good turn of phrase he'd end up getting the words out wrong. Percival was quick-witted and Llachlyn was clever in a thousand other ways. He was just a brute.

Which is how he got into this catastrophe in the first place. Christ, he wished he were back in bed. Or buried somewhere.

"Did you hear the official challenge?" Gaheris asked Lady Linette. "I noticed you were here before us."

Lady Linette's smirk held a wolfish glint to it. "Why, Sir Gaheris, you think I am so quick to stand witness to violence?"

"Of course not." Gaheris glowered, unmoved by her charms.

"I only hoped you would enlighten us, nothing unbecoming of your status."

The young lady wrinkled her nose at Gaheris and threw her hands up. "Gentle knight, you think too much of me. I am positively not below running toward danger and good gossip. For what other power do I hold as a woman if not that?" Lady Linette gave Galahad a knowing grin. "I will extend charity to you for Galahad's sake."

"My sake?" Galahad asked, taken aback as she edged closer to him. She smelled like sweat and crushed rosemary, and it was intoxicating and distracting.

"Well, given your brother and father are occupied in such a frightful display, I would think you have considerable concern. As to the charge: Sir Lanceloch challenged Sir Gareth directly for assaulting a knight of the realm, unprovoked, and stirring dissent in the ranks against him, their chief commander."

"How dramatic," Mordred said, feigning shock.

Galahad's face flushed so hot he thought he might faint. His whole body felt distant from him, separate from his thoughts. Would he float away if he could not tether his soul? Was God punishing him for freeing Llachlyn and Percival?

He should have been at prayers this morning, not passed out under his mountainous blankets sleeping off whatever was in Mordred's draught and the three goblets of wine he'd had. How could he be so undisciplined? If he had been awake, perhaps he'd have seen his father at prayers and had a chance to mitigate this absolute nightmare of a situation.

Until now, Gareth and Lanceloch had been circling one another, sizing each other up. They had come together a few times, swords flying, but it was clearly the kind of fight that might take its time, or so Galahad thought.

Mordred rubbed his hands together as they heard Gareth shout. "Ah, now the show truly begins."

Gareth went on the offensive, showing far more quickness on his feet than Galahad thought possible given his size. Hadn't

Lanceloch trained Gareth himself? It was hard to remember. That could be an advantage, or a disadvantage. He wasn't certain which.

On the tilting field, when in sanctioned combat for competition's sake, one would choose their weapons strategically, often going against another with pike or lance while their opponent chose sword and shield or longsword. Here, both men used near identical swords and shields, likely from the recently passed Lady Vyvian du Lac, whose arms were works of art and peerless in construction.

Lanceloch was dexterous for his age, but he took the first serious blow, anyway, as Gareth parried to the left and elbowed him in the face. The clang of steel upon Lanceloch's visor rang, and the captain fell backward, nearly stumbling.

Immediately, Gareth pressed his advantage, slapping Lanceloch's back with the flat of his sword. It almost worked to bring Lanceloch to his knees, but not quite. The captain twisted sideways, recovering in a crouch, and steadied himself with his shield—then he sprang up again.

"Enough of this," Gareth said, voice muffled but still loud enough for those close enough to hear. "Stand down, Sir Lanceloch. For the good of the realm and the stability of the Table Round."

Lanceloch was unmoved, despite Gareth's words. He shook his head like a bull flinging away flies. The crowd began cheering him on.

Gareth took a most elegant pose, eyes glinting beneath his helmet, his shield—emblazoned with the Pendragon crest, nonetheless—flashing in the sunlight. His armor was not pristine in the way Lanceloch's was, its surface scratched and worn from years of use. Nor was it as modern, half of it in chain and half in plate.

And yet, Galahad could not help but think Gareth looked more like a knight than Lanceloch did. He carried himself in a more guarded way, yes, but he looked comfortable.

When Lanceloch's assault came next, the sound of their colliding shields rang across the field. Lanceloch's handwork was a wonder, maneuvering his sword with such lightness it seemed unearthly. The sword arced and swiped, and though Gareth made to block, it was Lanceloch's elegant riposte that was his downfall.

Gareth staggered backward as Lanceloch's sword slipped in between his greaves and cuisse, just by his knee.

The crowd gasped as Gareth fell to his other knee, crying out in agony, his chin striking the top of his shield with a terrible crack that reverberated against the castle walls. Lanceloch's sword came away with a smear of blood on it.

Galahad lurched forward in shock and fear, stopped only by the combined efforts of both Sir Palomydes and his brother Gaheris.

"Let God judge them," Gaheris whispered angrily. "There is naught to be done about it now."

Galahad tried to shake off his brother's hands. "He's your brother, too! How can you leave it to God so easily?"

"Faith, little brother," Gaheris said, voice surprisingly gentle. "Let it free you from the burden of grief and fear."

Galahad wanted to believe that, wanted to feel assured of God's justice, but the idea of watching his brother be killed by his own father was too much for him to bear.

Lanceloch kicked forward, splitting Gareth's shield down the middle and Galahad let out an animalistic growl, the sound swallowed up in the roar of the crowd.

"I will take you from this field if you cannot contain yourself, Sir Galahad," Sir Palomydes warned. "I know this is difficult to bear, but it is the way of Carelon."

The cold tone in Sir Palomydes's voice was enough to quiet Galahad.

He watched in agony just as Lanceloch barreled into Gareth, the sound of their armor and swords so loud it was like the earth groaning, or someone bending the very iron of the portcullis. Like the maw of hell.

Concede! God, please, Gareth!

Galahad was not certain who he was trying to reach, God or his brother. There was no honor in dying or losing before half the court. There was no honor in *any* of this. Why would God allow such a thing to happen? Why did the King not stop it?

Again, Lanceloch's sword came down, the pommel smashing into Gareth's face. The visor snapped off, flipping over itself before coming to a standstill in a patch of mud. Gareth's handsome face was streaked with blood, hair plastered to his head with sweat, but there remained a ferocity in his expression that gave Galahad a sliver of hope.

Not that he wanted his father hurt. Of course not. He only wanted God to show his favor in this situation, for Galahad knew in his heart of hearts the entire matter was his fault, and due to an overreaction on Lanceloch's part.

He was not a child, and he did not need his father protecting him, honor or not.

It looked like Gareth might be raising his hand to concede, but instead he hooked his feet around Lanceloch's and twisted. Gareth, being much taller, managed to flip Lanceloch over to his side, forcing him to throw his shield or else risk falling onto it.

The whole crowd fell silent. Linette let out a cry, grabbing Gaheris by the arm.

Lanceloch crashed to the ground, his sword falling out of his grasp.

For a blessed moment, Galahad thought it was over.

Alas, God had other plans. As Gareth righted himself, Lanceloch rolled, found his sword, and was back upon his feet again.

Gareth's face, now bare to see, held a quiet kind of rage. He did not try to replace his helmet, nor did he immediately go upon the offensive—his knee was likely bleeding, filling up his greave and boot, and the side of his face was slick and red.

"I'll not continue in this madness all day, Sir Lanceloch," Gareth said. "I am your humble servant, and your brother in arms. Though you have, undoubtedly, challenged me in error, I will lay down my arms in peace should you agree to cease."

It was a pretty speech, but Lanceloch seemed incapable of hearing. Silent, he continued his assault with unceasing power, his attacks so precise and deadly it was a miracle Gareth could hold out.

"Lance, please," begged Gareth, between ragged breaths.

Galahad watched his brother's mouth, knowing the words there, though they were spoken softly.

Concede!

Though he did not know his father well, Galahad knew hope of concession was scant if not impossible, now. Sir Lanceloch was a legend made man, and he would never compromise his reputation. Gareth was flagging, stumbling, tripping over his own feet.

"This is wretched," Lady Linette said, dabbing her eyes with a small kerchief, green woven with gold. Gone was her bright countenance, replaced by true fear. "I cannot bear to look."

Even Mordred looked pale as milk as he said, "Is there no one to pull rank, with my father away? Where is Bedevere? I enjoy a tussle now and again, but this is unbecoming."

Lady Linette called out, "Sir Gareth! Have faith!"

Seemingly bolstered by Lady Linette's words, Galahad watched as Gareth redoubled his efforts, mastery flowing into his attacks at last.

For the first time since their combat began, Galahad truly saw how much Gareth had learned from Lanceloch. He seemed to preternaturally predict Lanceloch's moves, cutting him off repeatedly while the captain tired himself out. Indeed, Lanceloch still looked impressive, his skill abundantly clear. However, Galahad knew he could not continue in such a way. Gareth was ten years Lanceloch's junior and had considerably more time in the field—no matter how talented he was, Lanceloch du Lac was inexperienced.

Though Gareth staggered and Lanceloch took full advantage of his injuries, Galahad was not surprised when his brother managed to disarm Lanceloch after he feinted. He'd been planning it, somehow, measuring Lanceloch's responses down to the heartbeat, and the motion was almost comical in its simplicity and effectiveness.

"Concede, Sir Lanceloch, and we can return—"

Gareth did not finish for Lanceloch rushed into him, hands going for his head, brutally ripping his helmet away fully. He shouted in surprise, falling backward, as Lanceloch punched and twisted, near crazed.

What madness, indeed?

God, protect them. Give my father the courage to admit his defeat. Give Gareth the discernment to put aside his anger and take no life today.

But Gareth remained calm, and took Lanceloch by the neck, hooking his arm around, and then had the advantage, placing himself bodily over the captain, pinning him down.

The crowd erupted in celebration, but Lanceloch flailed, legs kicking and hands grasping at Gareth's forearms, which held him down steadily. He looked like a caged animal.

"Sir Gareth!"

"Our champion!"

"Concede!" the crowd cried in halting shouts.

Linette hiccupped sobs while Prince Mordred comforted her, her courage gone in the face of such abhorrent violence.

But Lanceloch would not concede.

Just as Sir Palomydes was going to rush in and separate the two, a figure appeared on the opposite side of the field, the crowd parting around him, and a hush fell across the field.

He was immense, this knight, accoutered in strange green armor, his red hair slightly grey at the temples but still vivid in contrast. He strode forward with the assistance of a blackwood cane, yet did so with poise and purpose. And Christ and his Mother, the expression on the man's face was fury and fire so great Galahad was almost afraid on behalf of *both* combatants.

Whispers rose around him, but it was only when Palomydes shouted, "Gawain, thank Christ!" did Galahad understand.

So that was what he looked like. Galahad realized it was his eldest brother, Sir Gawain, returned from the North where he lived with his reclusive wife, Dame Ragnell. There was no sign of her, but Gawain's presence itself was large enough to draw every eye to him.

He had come. Just at their moment of greatest need.

Lanceloch still struggled, snarling, Gareth barely keeping him subdued, as Gawain drew up next to them both. He raised his cane up like a wizard's staff and threw it down into the soft ground by Lanceloch's head. It shuddered and stuck.

Gawain leaned down and spoke so quietly, no one could hear. At last, Lanceloch settled, head turning away.

Crows called to one another on the parapets, and then Sir Gawain lifted one of his great arms as he rose.

"He concedes!" Sir Gawain exclaimed, his great, deep voice booming across the field with finality.

CHAPTER TWENTY-NINE

PERCIVAL

PERCIVAL DID NOT know what to make of their strange return to court. He had never met the King, had never even seen him save at a distance. The man he beheld was so different from the one stamped into coins and woven into tapestries; he could not quite reconcile the two. Was that what King Arthur truly looked like? An ailing old man? Still, knowing they had the King's protection from the Queen was a welcome relief, even if it raised some concerns about their relationship.

Perhaps Arthur was not as kingly as Percival had hoped, but Sir Gawain certainly made up for it. He had walked across the tilting field with more regal presence, limp be damned, than anyone he had ever seen. Every eye turned toward Sir Gawain—no small feat considering what had happened. Percival felt as if he were watching the man for the first time, as if he had walked across some invisible border and shifted the power of Carelon irrevocably.

Seeing Sir Gawain among his knights, the people of court, and the way they reacted to him, made his heart thud with a kind of wonderful awe. He was so loved, admired, even after years of being away. There was relief on their faces where there had been agony just moments before.

Sir Lanceloch had been bested by Sir Gareth. Gods and saints, what a strange thing to behold! Not even an hour after returning to court.

Somewhere along the way Percival had lost Llachlyn. One moment during the din she had been right at his side and then, without warning, she had slipped away. Now he felt terribly awkward, belonging to no family here, and standing to the side, searching...

The fight over, he followed the crowd into the castle proper, trying to catch a glimpse of Llachlyn.

Then there was Galahad, standing across the hall from Percival, and his heart leapt. The poor fellow looked sunken-eyed with purple bruising about his cheek, as if he'd been the one fighting. Though there were a handful of knights around him, he remained by himself with his hands crossed before him.

Percival reined in the urge to run toward his friend. It would not be proper, given he was a simple squire of limited talents and Galahad was, well, Galahad. They had only been gone a few weeks and yet Percival knew his friend had grown and changed somehow in their absence.

Shoving his way through the throng, Percival made steady progress toward Galahad. Their eyes met, still strides away, and the expression on Galahad's face was deep, soul-stirring relief.

They reached across, hands closing the distance, just as Sir Palomydes broke in between them.

"Percival, by heaven. We've been worried sick," their old training commander said.

"We found Sir Gawain," Percival said, staring across at Galahad.

"All the way north?" Sir Palomydes asked.

"Christ, Percival," Galahad said. "I never thought you'd actually do it."

"You underestimate Llachlyn," Percival replied, finding unexpected tears in his eyes, wishing she was near. He sorely wished Sir Palomydes was not present. "I have her to thank for just about everything."

"Did you find the Lady Morgen?" Sir Palomydes asked.

"No, alas. Of her there was no sign. But there is so much to tell," Percival said.

"Galahad! There you are. Your father is looking for you!" Sir Gaheris made haste toward the three men, his face pale and hair clumped to his forehead with sweat.

Percival watched as Galahad froze. Every inch of his honed body went still as a deer in the woods; strange to see a man of such strength behaving like prey. Galahad worked his mouth, but no words came out.

Seeing Lanceloch? After *that*?

"I'll bring Sir Galahad along presently," Percival said, inclining his head. "If you don't mind, Sir Gaheris. I think my friend needs a moment to catch his breath. Perhaps after evening prayers?"

Sir Gaheris put his hand on Galahad's shoulder. "Would we could delay, but he has asked to be taken to the Joyous Guard and plans to leave within the hour."

"Of course," Galahad said, too quietly for Percival's liking.

"He's in the main stables with Sir Lionel," Sir Gaheris said. "You can make your way there."

"I'll walk with you," Percival said to Galahad.

He was expecting a fight. With Galahad, violence and obstinance was his first language. Except this time, Percival startled as Galahad grasped him about the arm, squeezing tight. His pale grey eyes held a desperate kind of pain in them, and Percival did not know what to say or do.

They walked together, out the eastern gateway and through the garden. Shriveled toadflax littered the edges of the pathway as they walked, while sea campion still bloomed enthusiastically in low-lying clusters; Percival noted lingering purple knapweed blooms awaiting the first frost.

They came to the low gatehouse, not far from the stables, and just as Percival was getting ready to ask a question—he had at least thirty—Galahad turned and grabbed him by the shoulders and slipped through a large iron door into one of the small arsenals.

Percival let out a strangled cry as his friend pushed the door shut with his foot and then shoved him up against the stone wall.

Galahad's face was just a whisper from Percival's, tears

streaming down his cheeks, breathing labored and ragged.

"Don't *ever* leave me again," Galahad said, voice so strained it almost sounded like a sob.

Percival's heart leapt in his chest; his mouth was very dry as he watched the young knight's eyes shining in the dim light. "Galahad—*you* let us escape."

"I did not expect it to work—did not expect you to truly leave," he said. "Christ, Percival. I thought I would go mad without you."

The press of Galahad's body against his own was a strange, yet welcome contrast. Galahad, so honed and strong, whilst Percival remained lanky and delicate. It did not bother him in the way it might for some, as he rarely had delusions of knighthood. Percival was still taller than Galahad, and so was looking slightly down on him.

"We came back as soon as we could," Percival said, his hand going to Galahad's shoulder and squeezing gently. He was still in his sleeping tunic and smelled of lavender sprigs and sweet silk, his lashes dark with tears, cheeks flushed. He was so beautiful it broke Percival's heart a little every time he drank in the sight.

It was not the first time the two had come this close, but it was certainly the most intense. Since their third summer together, they had balanced a curious tension between them. Long had Percival admired Galahad's form, and favored his way of speaking, his passion, and his stubbornness. And it was clear Galahad felt the same way, yet he would not allow himself to reach out and touch his desires, believing them an affront to his God.

"Did you love her, while you were gone?" Galahad asked, looking away.

"Love her?"

"Llachlyn. You spent days together. Surely you—"

"Galahad."

The young knight snapped his attention up to Percival, as if his command were powerful enough to beguile him.

"You and she have always had a spark between you, a place I couldn't go. A place full of laughter and understanding and freedom. A place… without me. I know I shouldn't care. The priests say it is an unwelcome, unmanly thing," Galahad continued.

"Your jealousy, or your attraction?" Percival used his other hand to gently stroke Galahad's cheek, feeling the rough resistance of his morning stubble against the pad of his thumb.

Galahad swallowed, his lips trembling, as he leaned into Percival's touch. His answered whisper was harsh: "Both."

Never had Percival felt so powerful. They had spoken of this, before, together—what it would mean to share the pleasures of their bodies with one another. For Percival, such pleasure given without the strictures of fixed affections was best—he did not think about the future, really, and did not question the reactions of his body, whether they were for Galahad or for anyone else. His own acceptance of his nature, dual as it might be, gave him far more freedom and control in the situation, strength that Galahad could only dream of.

"Llachlyn is like a sister to us both," Percival said. "And she—well, I don't think such things like romance are part of her, really. She has told me as such."

"So you did not—in all that time…?"

"Was that truly what you feared?" Percival asked, now stroking Galahad's tender lower lip, flushing as the young knight drew a tremulous breath in response.

When Galahad grabbed him by the neck and pulled him down for a kiss, Percival could not help but smile. Galahad tasted salty from his tears, a little bitter, too, and though he was inexperienced he made up for it with enthusiasm. Percival's heart soared, his whole chest expanding with unbridled joy.

"I missed you," Galahad whispered, pulling away to speak against Percival's cheek.

"I noticed," Percival replied with a chuckle. "I've only been back a few hours and—"

Galahad silenced Percival with more kisses, this time more insistent. Without words, Percival showed Galahad what to do—how to angle his head, when to press and when to pull back.

When Percival delicately dragged his tongue along the edge of Galahad's mouth he was rewarded with a low, plaintive moan.

Every inch of Percival's body tingled in response. It was abundantly clear they both knew the pull of pleasure, the need rising between them. And it was delightful and freeing and welcome. And Christ, and the goddess, and anyone else who might have listened, it was finally happening.

Though he wished otherwise, Percival pulled away to run his hand through Galahad's rosy blond hair and said, "Alas, I cannot delay you forever. Though I am glad of this closeness, what I'd like to show you is far better suited atop sumptuous bed linens than a rank armory."

The look of pure desire in Galahad's countenance was enough to give Percival pause at his own words. If only Galahad could fly free from the burdens of his family and his religion!

"You deserve far finer things, it is true," said the knight.

Agony, pure agony. The last thing Percival wanted to do was stop what they had at long last begun. "I do want you, Galahad. Please do not mistake my curiosity for disapproval, but this is a rather unusual beginning to our reunion. Am I right in thinking you might have influenced this very strange contest upon the field?"

Galahad dropped his head, shoulders rounding. "My brother Gareth and I had a tussle. When Father found out, he accused Gareth of sowing dissent among the knights. He never even spoke to me, for if he had he would have known I was at fault. If Gawain hadn't showed up, I don't know what would have happened."

Percival did not agree with Sir Lanceloch's behavior, yet he did marvel at the idea a father would go to such lengths to protect his son. "I believe, however mistaken, your father meant to preserve your reputation."

"My father *shamed* me," said Galahad, righting his tunic and slowly, painfully, pulling away from where he had trapped Percival so well. "He thought he was helping, but now he has broken his reputation further, and mine along with it. I swear, Percy, the moment you left the whole castle went mad."

"You are only shamed if you allow it," Percival said, grabbing Galahad's hand and bringing his fingers to his mouth. "No one is allowed to claim your shame but you."

"I do not wish to see him. My father, I mean. I don't care what he has to say."

"You will regret it if you don't," said Percival. He was quite pleased with himself at the moment, given everything. "And I won't be far if you need me."

Galahad's features, carved like the statues of old, softened. "You really are here."

"I really am."

"Wait for me?"

"Always."

CHAPTER THIRTY

MORGEN

WHEN WE LEFT the bower, the forest had changed. Twilight came earlier than my own reckoning, and along with it the loamy breath of decay and mushrooms. My feet no longer ached as they had before—given both Yvain's salve and his most sturdy boots—but weariness settled in my soul.

I unburdened myself of truths to Yvain, shared with him the story as I knew it. Vyvian was fond of telling me such moments of vulnerability might relieve me of my own melancholy, given my propensity to withhold and ignore deeper emotions.

Except I did not feel unburdened. If anything, I felt more melancholic, the memories of those days now pushing up through the surface of my present like persistent and unwanted vetch in the garden.

Even the story I told Yvain was spun with care, omitting the parts I could not find within myself to tell him. Stories of my first love, Lord Aimar, and how Merlin had conspired with Arthur to marry him to a beautiful, fabulously wealthy woman from Elge. They had two daughters together, not long after.

And stories of Yvain's own father, King Uriens, and a life I might have loved had I not been entangled by the fate of Arthur's Braetan.

I could not tell him how Merlin flaunted other women before me while he insisted I remain his alone, or how he took me to his bed whether or not I desired it, and how I became ill from so many abortive herbs when I feared he might have gotten me with child. Nor did I tell him how I had helped my own sister poison her husband, and then given her the keys to Merlin's undoing.

No, I had not murdered Merlin with my own hands. After my fate had entwined irrevocably with Arthur's, Merlin had abandoned me, stripped me of my titles, and refused to even look at me in the face. He had tried to shame me, tried desperately to ruin me, but I had proven difficult to break. I do not think he had understood how early in my life I had been broken, and how I had used those jagged pieces to protect myself at all costs.

I did not believe all of Arthur's dreams, but I did not blame him for what his father did to my mother. I did not blame him for what had come between us. Arthur was, forever, the center of the wheel of the realm, the lonely middle from which all the stories flowed. Like me, he would never openly gamble his stature for love, no matter how much he desired it. Like me, he was a prisoner of fate, and I always kept a measure of pity for him in that respect.

We walked in silence toward the center of the wood where the Ivin Yew stood, a solitary evergreen of immense size stretching out like a great bank of shadowy fog. Here, it was said, the entirety of Brocéliande had grown from a single red berry, dropped by a swan as she escaped an ogre a thousand years before.

It smelled of death, and what I could see from the approach of the tree did not bode well at all. The scaly bark striated and twisted, like straining tendons on the neck of a dying man. No birds sang, and even my crows dared not approach. Indeed, I had not seen or felt them since our fight against the cockatrice.

Melic's ears twitched as we drew closer, but when the figure of Modrun appeared to us, he ran to her feet in bounding joy.

Yvain was far more cautious. "I have never seen her so diminished," he said quietly. "This does not bode well."

I narrowed my eyes to get a better look at Modrun. We had both aged, and that was expected. But where I remained relatively sprightly, Modrun's body was a ruin of hunger and pain. One of her eyes was gone and, unlike the last time we had seen one another, she wore no scarf or patch. The void of her eye socket was like the very maw of death itself, and I had a sudden fear I might see teeth emerge from it. She wore no clothing save threadbare rags tied about her loins. All that remained of her body was skin drawn tight over angular bones where she had once been round and comely.

It smelled of the magic of Ys. Overwhelmingly so. Spicy and citrusy, making my nose tingle as I inhaled.

"Yvain, there you are," Modrun said, looking toward us from where she sat on the ground beneath the yew. "Have you seen my eye?"

Her son set his jaw and walked forward, drawing down to a squat as he had once with me. "Mother, I have brought a friend."

Modrun turned to me. "Morgen le Fay is no friend. She is a husk, a shell, a broken vessel. When she closes her eyes at night it is to the sounds of creaking bones and shuffling mice and the biting, biting, biting of death."

Her words fell like daggers in my heart, and I tried to steady my voice. "Modrun, the wood brought me here, and Yvain found me. He has been very kind."

"Between your legs already, then?" Modrun asked, her tongue reaching out to lick at her chapped lips, the split wounds looking like the segments of a dead worm. "Merlin will be so jealous."

"Nothing of the sort," I said shortly. "But my time here is ended. I would ask of you a boon, so I may leave and help my family—and the Circle of Nine."

Modrun's whole body trembled as she let out a strangled, howling noise, and Yvain gave me a warning look. I had spoken the wrong words, somehow.

"I watched you slaughter my cockatrice, Morgen. I saw you split the maw of death and twist out its tongue as blood ran down your lips, and you *smiled*," Modrun said, her voice singsong. I noticed, for the first time, that small, pale mushrooms were growing on her legs and arms, as if death had already claimed her.

Yvain put his hand in mine, and I nearly startled at the intimate touch. He squeezed gently, encouraging. To my own surprise, I squeezed back.

"Mother, you cannot keep Morgen here forever," he said. I had never heard his voice so soft, so loving, and yet so full of pain.

"She is here to take you from me," Modrun whined, crawling over to Yvain, and pulling on his boots with her claw-like fingers. "I should kill her."

"Modrun, I will not have you speak of me in such improper terms. You and I have endured years together, walking the Path as equals," I said, my temper flaring at last. "A great threat has befallen Carelon, and I am without my greatest powers. It is your mercy I seek in this—I must return, and soon."

"Always with the doom of men! Always with the prophecies and the moon and the wolves and Morgen le Fay pulling out the innards of fate!" Modrun screamed.

My world twisted and flipped, lungs burning, as I let go of Yvain's hand and fell to the cold ground, knocked back with an invisible, all-encompassing power.

I barely had time to shout as Modrun lunged for me, her hands going to my throat so quickly I was immediately robbed of breath. Behind me, I heard Yvain scramble as she tumbled to the ground, then a blinding yellow light exploded from between us, and I heard no more.

Indeed, I saw no more. The wood collapsed into darkness, or else I was blinded entirely. My ears rang as I reached up to pry Modrun's cold fingers from my throat, but as I touched her, reality again twisted into something new as my death magic flared to life.

I was again at Death's Gate, at the maw, and this time, Modrun stood with me.

She was not as I had just beheld her, but instead as I remembered her on our first meeting: a sturdy woman with long chestnut curls and clever eyes, dressed in homespun linen with leaves in her hair.

Her expression was relieved when she saw me and beheld where we stood, but then it turned to deep, utter sorrow.

"Morgen," she said, her voice gentle as a wind through barley, but free of madness. "I did not expect you to come so soon. So, Vyvian is gone, then."

I recognized the prickling pressure of a crow on my shoulder, then heard the telltale rustle of feathers. It seems they had found me again.

"Indeed. And strange tidings are upon us. Modrun—the forest is not well. Yet I have the sense you are aware." Tears blurred my vision as the threads of fate came together and resolved in my mind. Death yawned wide.

This was why I had come to the wood. To help Modrun cross the threshold, to give her peace, to guide her to the next realm that awaits us all.

She reached up to touch her face, finding both of her eyes in place of the one she had lost. "You must do this, as I am now a danger to you, and to Yvain. My dear, sweet boy."

Modrun's body began to fade, looking more like a reflection in a pool than a woman standing before me. "I wish we had more time, Modrun. I should have come to you sooner."

"The schemes of men keep the most powerful among us busy with politics and funerals and the ever-shuffling of deeds and papers and proclamations. I understand. I am sorry. I felt when Vyvian left us, and I fear she held some fragment of my own sanity, wound up in the Path."

"You believe she protected you."

After a moment's look of distraction, her eyes glazing in thought or the pull of the gate, she watched me again. "Vyvian was Merlin's foil, and a protector of us all. As a priestess of Avillion, and a being of great power, she should have outlived him. Likely she thought we had more time, as she ought to have told you her secrets to maintaining the Path, to keeping balance."

"Merlin's foil?"

"The Path was not just a method of connection; it was also protection. Vyvian's power helped establish the Path, to intermingle our collective magics, and to protect the *graal* relics.

She began the work of reviving it when she was at the Lake, and it was a great gift she and your sister Anna gave us. But something has happened with her death—that protection is missing, and our doom accelerates." Modrun looked through the gate and then took a step closer, only stopping herself when I asked after her again. "It cannot be rebuilt."

"After her burial, my magic fled," I said. I did not want to beg her, but I knew our time was limited. Her words gave me no comfort.

"It is not Vyvian's fault you turned your back on your duty, Morgen."

"I needed time to grieve, that is all. Am I not allowed?"

"Not all of us are afforded grief. I am so tired."

"Please, Modrun. I need to know how to get it back."

"You seek the wrong answers," Modrun said, sighing almost impatiently.

She had already brought me down a pathway I had not intended. "What of Merlin? I felt his power."

"The Path kept him bound," Modrun said, reaching out for my hand. "The man may be gone, but his magic is not. You helped your sister weave a bower, but it woke what slept beneath Carelon, and what is left of Merlin and Nimue with it."

"What will happen if that power escapes?" I asked, although I knew the answer. I had warned my sister that her magic would exact a price. But I suppose I had also deluded myself into thinking him gone forever, not wishing to face the truth that I had contributed to such corrupt, powerful magics.

"This age will end." Modrun took my hand though I did not remember giving it to her. I needed to guide her through, but my heart ached like a wounded bird in a thatch of briars. "Carelon will crumble. But you knew that already."

"Then you see now why I must return to Carelon—I must warn them, I must help them."

"Why must it always be you, Morgen?"

I did not have an answer, but tears prickled my eyes. "It doesn't matter."

"You are weak and confused and ailing." She gestured to my blighted fingers. "You resist your gifts, and they fester."

"I have done no such thing. Death is all that remains in me now."

"It will kill you if you do not let it in."

Her look of exasperation had me feeling like a scolded child. "I will fight it."

"The wood protected you, but once you leave the illness will spread."

"I am a healer. I will manage."

"Very well." Modrun gazed toward the abyss. "I will send you home, first. Then perhaps you will be strong enough. There is more for you to do before you reclaim Carelon."

The draw of the threshold overtook me, and Modrun breathed in relief as her body began to diminish. She held up her hands, turning them as they evaporated, pulled inexorably toward the end, and I could feel her gratitude, her grace, passing to me.

"My son... I will no longer be able to protect him," she said to me. "Tell Yvain I have always loved him in my way, and that I only meant to keep him safe. But I have long lived among the trees, and time is easily lost to me. And madness and grief are easily turned to weapons."

"He carries within him a great, lingering sorrow," I said.

"I know. His sorrow is his sword, but his line may yet bring you hope. Both of you. Do not forget all the faces you have worn, Morgen—especially the ones you let slip."

I could not argue that I had worn masks, so many of them. At times, I wondered who I truly was, beneath all those trappings. "I'm sorry, Modrun. I wish I could have brought you peace sooner."

"Time is a great wheel, and it always turns again." That made no sense to me, but neither did half of what she said. I knew better than to ask again for clarification. "The fate of Rheged is bound to yours, Morgen, as it always has been. Do not make the same mistake you made once. Take with you my gift, and may it serve you well."

The Maw of Death opened wide, the gate flickering to life.

The steel grey stonework kindled the same blue as a blooming comfrey. She was ready to go.

I did not know what awaited her, for I could never see what lingered on the other side, but I had one remaining gift: to lead her across the threshold.

Her magic flared to life, bright and clear—the knowledge of the earth, its depth, its connections. I gasped as my awareness expanded as deep as the roots of the yew, then quieted. Her power, passed on to me, or at least some measure of it, soothing and beautiful and redolent of Ys.

Just as her transparent foot crossed that gate, she turned to me and said: "You underestimated Merlin's grasp, Morgen. Do not do it again. He does not lie here beyond."

WHEN I OPENED my eyes again, I was cradling Modrun's corpse in my arms as Yvain stared at me in shock. My initial thought was to explain myself, but just as I opened my mouth, Modrun's body simply evaporated into a mist and blew away faster than I could hold. Spores, I realized. Her body changed and was reborn as her beloved mushrooms.

Yvain dropped his head, weeping freely, as the whole wood itself shivered. Indeed, it was as if a shroud had pulled away, the wood breathing for the first time in an age, and sunlight filtered in between the branches of the enormous yew tree and dappled our faces.

Would that I were a gentle woman, I might have held Yvain in his grief. But though I knew little of him, I also did not think him the kind of man who required it. He had been alone for nearly a decade, and the greatest kindness I could offer him was to simply sit beside him.

The wood felt lighter, freer, cool breezes and sweet smells upon each new leaf. My crows were absent, gone perhaps to ferry Modrun's soul deeper into the beyond, but I knew they would return. I gazed down at my hands, the blackened fingertips no longer so terrifying to me; perhaps the bruising was mitigated some in its progress.

Someday I would cross that shadowy threshold, my soul no longer clinging to the burden of my body. It did not frighten me to die, only what I might leave behind. Only the spells and the connections left unfinished, the knowledge still within books and minds and in the tracery of nature's song.

"I must leave now, Yvain," I said at last, turning my face to the gentle breeze. I could smell winter on the air, the promise of fresh snow and the dormant, resting time to come. Some find the cold months full of despair, but I have always considered them the most hopeful. Every seed and root awaits the spring; that even they must rest is inspiring for those of us incapable of stilling our own feet.

Yvain drew up beside me. "Where will you go?"

In our quiet mourning I had considered Modrun's words. If there was a place where I began, that I knew as home, it was only one place: Cornwall. And more specifically, the castle where I was born. She had picked her words carefully, though she had still spoken in riddles. I expected no less from her.

"Tintagel," I said. "Or what is left of it."

Melic pushed at the back of my knees, almost knocking me over. "The beast will miss you," Yvain said.

"And I, him."

Yvain's countenance was softer, unburdened subtly in grief. "Thank you, Morgen. I would not have been able to face her alone."

"She loved you to the end. I know it does not erase what she did, or how she twisted that love. But her last thoughts were for you."

She had claimed our fates were intertwined, but I could not believe such a thing, not when the pull of departure weighed so heavily upon me. It would be good to put miles between me and Brocéliande, to gather my thoughts.

Yvain turned to me, and his eyes shone, dewy with tears. Gently, he touched the long end of my pale, white braid, gently and reverently. It was a bold action, but one I felt he deserved. I had saved him; now he would have to save himself.

"I hope you find peace, Morgen, along with the parts of your power you have lost. Just don't go traipsing about without shoes again."

"Where will you go?" I asked him.

"To Rheged. To find my father and my brothers and sister. I cannot abide Carelon just yet, though I must when the time is right. I must beg the King's forgiveness for my absence. So, perhaps we will find one another again."

I could not withhold the smile I gave him, and I reached to my tiptoes to kiss his brow as he stooped down. "Find your rest, Yvain, and joy in your freedom. Thank you for all you have done for me, even though I was a great interruption to your life. I am glad we had the chance to know one another."

He let go of my braid almost reluctantly, but said nothing.

I turned to see the wood open a path before me, yew and alder and beech leaning away to show me where I might place my feet. Modrun's gift reverberated in my chest, and I welcomed the connection.

I ruffled Melic's mane and scratched behind his ear. Then I began my journey toward the sea, to find myself a ship to Cornwall.

WITHIN A FEW hours I found my way out of Brocéliande and to one of the uneven paths toward Withiel and the high seat of Avillion, where I would then turn westward and north to Tintagel. I could arrive by evening, find Skourr Ahès—my ally and fellow sister in the Circle of Nine, who had long been at my father's old keep—but the thought did not settle me in the way it should. Old ghosts lived in Cornwall, many of which were best left to the mud.

I found my way to the small village of Lantyrnog, knowing in the morning I might find passage on a ship to Cornwall. It was a sleepy hamlet, barely more than a small cluster of buildings on the river, and I was glad no one recognized me. I kept my hands hidden, trying not to draw notice as I exchanged a gold ring for a night's sleep and a bath. The innkeeper gave me an extra shift and cloak, promising to launder mine by morning. The reverent way she looked at my clothes indicated she had at least some idea of my status.

My hands ached as I tossed fitfully in my small bed, restless to no longer be under the sky. How curious to have spent so many of the last years beneath the cover of Carelon's roof and yet now, after scarcely a few days in Brocéliande, to feel the loss of open sky while I slept.

I dreamed of Merlin's face in the mirror, and heard Modrun's warnings over and over again. Brocéliande had protected me, from whatever pestilence was festering within me, and indeed, now that I was back out of the wilderness, I felt the reek of illness.

I woke to a fever, my body drenched in cold sweat, lights dancing before my eyes, my hands burning as if I had been pierced with thousands of glass shards.

I cried out for help before descending into madness.

Three days I spent, tossing and turning in my sheets, half mad with fever. Speaking was nearly impossible, but the innkeeper and her wife took care of me without question. I only vaguely recalled their tender care as I flitted in and out of strange dreams too fragmented to ever remember.

Though I have had many portentous visions in my sleep in my life, these were nothing but the mindless meandering of illness racking my body. I was at the mercy of my own fragility, too far gone to even consider what was wrong with me. I recalled other hands, other faces, but could not decipher them from my hallucinations. I cried out for my crows, but if they had followed me from the wood, I could not see or feel them.

On the third day, I woke to the sound of morning birds singing outside the window. My whole body felt boiled in the skin, joints and muscles screaming in agony. The most potent aspects of my power still remained out of touch, so I had to find peace by wrapping myself in furs and sitting in the chair by the fire, like some old grandmother. I suppose, given my age, I could very well have been one.

That was when I noticed the bruised purple markings on my fingers and arms were all but gone. What remained was naught but faint impressions, yellowing on the edges.

I had been unable to help myself, forced to rely on the kindness and skill of complete strangers. Perhaps I ought to have felt shame. In my younger days I certainly would have seen it as a personal failing. How could a storied healer have neglected her own care so thoroughly?

Except I found a strange peace knowing there were those among the common folk capable of the healing arts, kind enough to have come to my aid. This was no simple illness, and I certainly had not helped in the least. My powers were as they had been, naught but the Maw of Death and an emptiness where my vast magics once rested.

Once the worst of the chill and pain subsided, I tidied myself as best as I was able and meandered downstairs. The floorboards creaked in my wake and the comforting sounds of low conversation greeted me, along with the scent of sweet, honeyed bread. Braids of Una, I realized, which I had not eaten in an age. They were a specialty of Avillion, once reserved for the priestesses alone and now widely regarded as wonderful breakfast fare across the entire isle. My stomach's resounding growl was a good sign of my slow and steady healing.

The innkeeper stood with her arm around her wife, both their faces bright with laughter. They kissed briefly as a little lad of about three chased a black cat across the rushes, its tiny tin bell tinkling brightly. By the window, I noticed an older man standing, arms across his chest, looking through the wavering glass with an intensity I could only describe as longing.

All three adults turned to me as I alighted upon the bottom stairs.

And, embarrassingly, the two women bowed. In Carelon, my presence was far from unusual, and I was not accustomed to such decorum. I had never enjoyed it, not like my sisters Elaine and Margawse.

"Lady Morgen," the innkeeper said, her hand pressed to her forehead. "Thank the goddess you are well."

"My thanks go to you and your wife," I said, even though my voice was ragged and worn. "I am not certain I would have survived without your care."

The innkeeper's wife wiped a tear from her face. "I wish I could say we were particularly skilled, my lady, but in truth we merely tried to keep you as comfortable as possible. 'Twas a fearful illness that took you, and we prepared for the worst."

The innkeeper disagreed. "My wife is a talented woman, make no mistake, Lady Morgen. She is too humble for her own good."

"Either way, I am indebted to you," I said, beckoning them both to stand. "Do tell me your names, at least."

The little boy let out an immense burp, frightening the cat. My heart ached at the quaintness of their little scene.

"I am Argantel," said the innkeeper. "This is my wife Rozenn. We live here in Lantyrnog, and have for the last two decades served as the proprietors of this inn. Rozenn is also a midwife."

"I, too, have served as a midwife," I said. "It is goddess-given work."

"Yes, I agree. But our guests here also helped immensely," said Rozenn, gesturing to the man by the window.

I doubted he was of Lantyrnog—not only were his clothes of a finer make than even mine, but he had all the bearing of a person quite out of his element. That, and both women kept glancing his way as I spoke, in an anxious but anticipatory way.

"We are all glad of your recovery, Lady Morgen," the man said to me, his voice low and resonant. As he stood by the window, I could not quite make out his features, as the bright morning light obscured his face in shadow. "Briefly, I feared I had come too late, and we would never speak again."

Again?

As he approached me, I understood. Courtly, composed, elegant. I had kissed those lips once, gasped at the trace of his fingers down my spine, lost myself in the passion between us.

Just one year of my life, buried so deep I wondered if my heart had simply grown around it.

And of course, he had the same eyes as his son, Yvain.

"King Uriens," I said, but did not bow. "What brings you here?"

For all his decorum, however, I noticed how close he was to crying. He reached out to take my hand and I, reluctantly, gave it.

"Yvain brought me here, Lady Morgen. And you helped free him, so I am now in your great debt."

CHAPTER THIRTY-ONE

LLACHLYN

LLACHLYN TOLD HERSELF she wasn't running away. She was, after all, not leaving Carelon proper. And certainly, she may not have been going in the same direction as everyone else, but she could not resist the pull toward her Aunt Vyvian's old smithy. With Vyvian gone and dead, she supposed it would have made most sense to visit the mausoleum, but Llachlyn didn't *feel* as if Vyvian would be there. What remained of her was mingled with the flux and ash.

Before they had fled the castle, Llachlyn had never summoned enough bravery to visit the forge. She couldn't say what kept her away other than the realization that Vyvian was truly gone, and her last letters would remain unanswered forever.

When Vyvian was alive, finding her way into the smithy had been almost impossible. Llachlyn had only had the chance to do so a handful of times, when she and her mother visited court for unusual circumstances, but the memories were so vivid. Vyvian was always so kind to her, and not kind in the way many relatives were simply because of their blood ties. She took time to show her how to handle different metals, how to read the flames, and pushed her to try new approaches to her craft. She remembered watching their hands together, one old and wrinkled and one freckled and plump, and wished they had not been so far apart in age. Even then, as a child, Llachlyn knew her time with Vyvian

239

was limited. But the smithy was *their* place, full of their secrets, and a world Llachlyn understood without complication.

Perhaps it was that comfort she sought. Llachlyn had only heard stories of her grandmother Igraine, and few of those, but Vyvian was Igraine's sister and one of the most powerful women in the realm. In her heart, Llachlyn had supposed they were surrogates for one another—Vyvian never had children of her own, after all. They'd written back and forth to one another for a decade, bonding over their love of smithing and the language of metals.

It was not until Llachlyn was well inside the quaint little smithy and saw Vyvian's own handwriting upon a slate that she began to cry.

Someone had come in and taken all the finished weapons out of the room, leaving behind only the ones Vyvian had been working on. The forge was cold as death, the embers long since reduced to pale grey lumps, edges ragged as if kissed by frost. Her parchment notes were scattered about the floor, even more disorganized than they had been in life.

The forge was devoid of life. Worse than the mausoleum; at least the dead waited in the burial grounds for company. Here, Vyvian would never return.

Anger, hot and sudden, blazed in Llachlyn as the weight of betrayal fell upon her. They had come here and taken Vyvian's weapons, her livelihood, her value. They had not known her, they had carelessly left all the parts of her that were truly her own: her writings, her clothing, her whimsical little moldings and forged animals. Left it in shambles.

Well, that would not do.

There was still enough wood, damp though some of it was, to start the forge going again. That was the first step.

Then came the cleaning. Not everything left behind was worth keeping, but it was somehow all the more profane to leave the detritus and litter about the room when Vyvian was gone. Half the bottles Vyvian had used for her own poultices were gone, as well as the additives for her flux and other recipes, but plenty remained to keep Llachlyn occupied a while as she ordered them by name.

By the time the sun began its descent into the chilly evening, she could see the floor again, and all Vyvian's notes lay together in neat piles. Llachlyn was sweaty and hungry, but she was more clear-headed than she had been in a long time.

When the door clattered open, however, she started like a frightened deer in the wood. It was a good thing she'd been stoking the fire, for she had a very hot, very pointy, poker in hand to defend herself.

"How did you get in here?" The question, tinged with deep irritation, was courtesy of Prince Mordred, who was cloaked in fur and velvet, looking both most royal and sincerely annoyed.

"I walked in," Llachlyn said, lowering the poker. Not even she was so hotheaded as to forget herself. She fell into a curtsey. "Your Highness."

Mordred walked over to her, boots scuffling across the smooth, clean floor, and then held out his hand. "Rise," he said.

She kissed his ring, taking his rough, warm hand in hers, and then looked up just as recognition dawned on his face.

"Llachlyn," he said. "I thought you were gone."

"I was. But I'm back. Percival and I, I mean."

Mordred narrowed his dark eyes, calculating. "That would explain today's most curious proceedings. I thought I saw that slip of a boy wandering around Sir Gawain's heels, but the crowd was so enthusiastic even I could not get to them. That also explains where Galahad went off to."

"What do you mean by that?" Llachlyn asked.

Mordred looked as if he were about to speak, but thought better of it. Which was strange. The prince almost never thought twice about what he said, especially around people like her.

"I'm surprised you found your way here," he said, walking toward the forge and peeking in with an appraising nod. "It took me two weeks to figure out the lock mechanism after your mother sealed it."

"Lock mechanism?"

The prince laughed. "It was spelled. But I suppose as the daughter of Morgen le Fay, you have access to all sorts of wondrous methods I could only dream of. I must bumble along through Merlin's old remnants, and half of what he left behind is impossible either to read or to manage on my own."

"I just opened the door," Llachlyn said, glancing down at her hands, now. They were covered in soot. "Vyvian showed me how to do it, ages ago."

Mordred might have been impressed. "Were you close to our aunt?"

Llachlyn spoke to almost no one of their friendship. It was too precious. Except now that Vyvian was gone, what was she holding onto?

"She was my friend. My correspondent. She kept me apprised of things at court, but mostly just…" It was hard to put into words. "Mostly she was just there for me. She always replied, even though her duties were great."

"You're blessed. She either ignored me or called me—what was it?—oh yes, a 'disgrace to the very crown I wore upon my bloated head, and a mistake of cataclysmic proportions.'" He was grinning when he said it, as if recalling words of kindness. "In retribution, I called her a dusty old crone with cobwebs between her legs, and then she whacked me in the back of my knees with her cane."

Llachlyn almost laughed, if not for the pang of jealousy. She'd never have spoken to Vyvian in such a way, of course, but the idea of living such a casual, comfortable life together in the same castle… It did not feel fair. Mordred was certainly not as talented as Galahad, but she could not help but feel a similar pull of inadequacy.

Perhaps detecting the change of tone, Mordred said more gently, "It was a beautiful funeral. Your mother forbade a Mass, even though du Lac tried his best. Ultimately, the priests refused, given that Lady Vyvian was staunchly un-Christian."

"I wanted to be there," Llachlyn said. "A storm blew us off course, and by the time we got back…"

"And I hear you ran afoul of the Queen after scarcely stepping foot off the ship," Mordred said, going over to the forge. He took off his long cloak and set it aside, then shirked off his tabard. At last, he rolled up his sleeves. "Something about masquerading as a page?"

"I was convincing," Llachlyn said, a sweet thrill of excitement making her almost laugh.

Mordred stoked the fire, moving about the forge with a comfortable familiarity she could only wish for. "You most certainly were not. If you'd come to me first, I'd have given you far better pointers on the matter—and a far better wardrobe. I had no idea she had imprisoned you, of course, as I was far too occupied with…" He grunted, hefting a long length of iron from the wall and putting it up on the well-worn anvil. "Well, I won't get into tawdry details. Some things are best kept from one another. Especially from my—ah, from my family."

Family, indeed.

Sister, more like.

Though, even at this meagre distance, Llachlyn could see nothing of herself in Mordred's features. Nor anything of Gawain or of Hwyfar's family, or even Arthur. Mordred was certainly a handsome man, but his bearing and expressions were so entirely his own it was difficult to believe he had come from Pendragons and Avillion priestesses.

"Thank you, Prince Mordred," Llachlyn said. Timidly, she made her way over to him, surprised to see how muscular his forearms were and how deft his fingers. "You're a smith, as well?"

The firelight caught in his eyes, dancing like writhing nymphs under the moon. "I was an apprentice to the greatest smith of this age. And she asked, if the time came, for me to show you what I know."

Llachlyn forgot how to breathe. "Vyvian? But I thought you and she…"

"Oh, we mostly hated each other. Except when we didn't. Given Galahad never came to court, she made me her next experiment. I'd be glad to share what I know, so long as you tell no one."

That was curious. "Why not?"

Prince Mordred looked thoughtful again, then glanced away, measuring the heft of the hammer in his hands. "I am a prince, and I keep very little of myself away from the prying eyes and begging hands of court. I am the minstrel, the libertine, the potions-maker, the spoiled prince—except here. Here, I am just Mordred. And I bend iron and steel. I'm particularly fond of making helms."

"Prince—"

"Just Mordred. While we're here." It was a command, yet delivered with a soft, almost pleading note. It struck Llachlyn's heart.

"Of course. Just Mordred."

CHAPTER THIRTY-TWO

HWYFAR

PULLING AWAY FROM the narrow window with a deep sigh, Hwyfar thanked every deity she could think of for helping her husband remain calm. At least, calm enough on the outside. When they'd all realized Sir Lanceloch had challenged Gareth, panic had spread through the room, and she had feared their plan would spiral out of control.

It was Gawain who'd brought a measured, thoughtful solution: he would walk upon the green himself, as soon as he could get there. He was both Gareth's eldest brother and Lanceloch's stepson, only outranking him slightly by virtue of his relationship to Arthur directly. Given that no one had seen Gawain in years, the effect—especially as he was still in his armor—would be impressive, and a good distraction from Lanceloch's boorish behavior.

What *was* the man thinking?

Hwyfar's unease did not let go of its thorns, however. She, Percival, and Llachlyn had followed Bedevere to a small chamber overlooking the green, and, with a handful of other members of the court and staff, watched the proceedings. Hwyfar was not yet ready to proclaim herself to court and did not wish to join her husband so soon.

When Hwyfar turned back to where Llachlyn had been standing when they'd entered the room, the young woman was gone. The throng of onlookers were too busy chattering to one another to even take notice—some were laughing, other brushing tears from their cheeks. Percival went to find her.

She knew Llachlyn was not a child, nor did she need minding. Hwyfar was not concerned with her behavior or potential breaches of decorum. What did worry her, however, was Llachlyn's tendency to run from conflict altogether. To hide her feelings and emotions until they spilled over. Since they'd begun training together, it was a daily troubling thought: what if Llachlyn was simply preventing herself from using her power, erecting walls between her magic and all else? And if she had no power at all, what then? She doubted herself enough as it was.

Hwyfar was not Llachlyn's mother, and yet she sensed the answers to their troubles were in Morgen's disappearance. She must have left clues behind—there must be answers that others, without powers equal to Morgen's own, could glean. So she would look, she would listen. And, perhaps, Llachlyn would do the same.

Calmly, drawing her hood up to conceal her features, Hwyfar used the cover of the busy halls to make her way towards Morgen's tower; Gawain would no doubt be occupied for hours, after that particular show.

When she'd lived at court, Hwyfar had rarely visited the towers. Now, she had learned, Merlin's old tower was occupied by Prince Mordred.

Morgen's tower faced east, the spiraling stair dark and shadowed even in midday.

Unsurprisingly, there was a guard at its base, but one without a helmet and with a flushed, red face.

"Sir Sygremors," Hwyfar said by way of greeting. She knew the knight well, having met him toward the end of her tenure at court when he'd arrived from Dacia, on his father's orders. He'd been scarcely sixteen then, and though he retained the same shaggy brows and curious brown eyes, the intervening years had shaped him into a warrior: taller, stronger, and more rugged.

The knight turned his attention to Hwyfar, inclining his head. "Madame."

"Technically, the title is 'Your Highness,' but I shall allow you the error as it has been nigh on a decade since we last saw one another," she said, gently removing her hood.

Sir Sygremors' eyes widened. "Princess Hwyfar," he said. "I had no idea you were due back at court. And what with everything gone on this day already. Did you know Sir Gawain has returned as well?"

Hwyfar almost laughed at the absurdity. Indeed, Arthur might not have been fooled by their ruse, but it appeared the rest of the knights were not so astute.

"I had heard," she said smoothly. She was still travel worn and tired, but it was almost shockingly easy to slip again into the sweet-tongued woman of her past. "I watched the proceedings, and am glad, indeed, the day did not end in bloodshed."

"If you're looking for your sister, Her Majesty the Queen, she has long since gone to the Chapel of the Weeping Lady," Sir Sygremors said, a little haltingly.

The Chapel of the Weeping Lady, indeed. The last person Hwyfar wanted to see was Queen Mawra. "I thank you, Sir Sygremors, but I am not yet seeking my sister. I understand her devotion is deep and I would be loath to interrupt her prayers. I am looking after a young woman with short brown hair and vivid green eyes. She'd have been wearing a green cape, the edges embroidered with gold floss."

Sir Sygremors frowned as if trying to draw a clearer idea of Hwyfar's description in his head. "Alas, I'm afraid I have not seen a woman of such a description."

"More is the pity. Would you mind if I take a look, then?" Hwyfar asked.

The knight scowled now, looking over his shoulder. "I would not recommend going up there, princess. I am far from the sort of man who might concern himself with such dark tidings, but I am told that since Lady Morgen's disappearance, the rooms are unsafe."

"I am quite capable of taking care of myself," Hwyfar said, straightening her back to indicate just how much taller she was than Sir Sygremors. "And I won't be long. I suspect my friend might have vanished up the stair during all the commotion."

"The Queen has forbidden anyone from entering," Sir Sygremors said, though his voice wavered. "She says the ground is unclean."

Hwyfar bit back on a scathing reply, mostly involving what her sister could do with herself should she be in possession of a hot poker. Instead, she smiled demurely. Loyal though Sygremors might be, she was well aware Queen Mawra was *feared* but not *loved*. Before the destruction of the Path, Hwyfar had spent many evenings in Lyonesse, poring over reports from Carelon and those still loyal to Queen Tregerna and her uncle Meliadus. Queen Mawra was supported by the growing Christian priesthood; they paid her well in gold and attention, helping to build her favorite chapel and singing her praises across the continent.

But her ladies in waiting were loyal to Tregerna, at least aside from Lady Clarine and Lady Iblis—both were ex-priestesses of Avillion who had converted with the same level of zeal and mercilessness as Mawra, eschewing the goddess and using Hwyfar's own behaviors at court as an example of the corrupting power of faith outside the Christian Church.

Hwyfar had a feeling her knights could be trusted, especially since she was known to impose the strictest of regimens, including lengthy periods of fasting, oaths of purity, and the wearing of hair shirts.

"And what do you think, Sir Sygremors?" Hwyfar asked.

"Your Highness?" Though Sir Sygremors might have been from noble stock himself, it was clear he had not been asked his opinion in an exceedingly long time.

"Do you think that Lady Morgen, most powerful sorceress of the realm and dearest sister to Arthur, King of Braetan, would ever have allowed for her beloved tower to fall into a state of uncleanliness?"

He looked askance at Hwyfar, then shook his head. "I suppose not, Your Highness."

"And do you suspect that Arthur, King of all Braetan, would

ever have kept Morgen le Fay near should she herself pose any risk to the realm, be it corrupted magics or murderous intent?"

Sir Sygremors sighed. "To say otherwise would be little short of treason," he said.

A feeling of satisfaction bloomed in Hwyfar's chest. Indeed, she ought not to have worried about her courtly skills at Carelon. The intervening years negotiating the dance of politics in Lyonesse had only honed her abilities.

Once, she might have used seduction to convince Sir Sygremors to help her. She was not ashamed of what she had once done to maintain what power she needed those first years at court—to the contrary, it had served her well. Still, there was a sense of accomplishment knowing she did not have to employ such tactics. Nor did she want to.

"I promise you, Sir Sygremors, I will be scarcely more than a shadow. And I will speak a word to no one." She paused, adopting a solemn tone. "I would not ask were it not of utmost need."

In the end, Sir Sygremors simply stepped aside, averting his eyes as if Hwyfar were, indeed, no more than a shadow. She herself had never learned the art of pulling shadows, a gift Gawain's mother Anna commanded with expert ability, but she imagined the result was similar. Most of Hwyfar's life at court had been in pursuit of the opposite: garnering as much attention as possible.

She scaled the twisting staircases, feeling the weight of her armor and exhaustion weighing on her with every step. Though there were a number of rooms on various floors—some she had visited on her own years ago in search of certain herbs and tinctures Morgen might provide—it was to the top she went. There, she knew, housed the greatest of all the mirrors on the Path, the oldest and the most prized.

Llachlyn would have known that, too.

And for a brief moment as Hwyfar crested the final flight, sidestepping a broken old lantern, she thought she beheld Morgen standing before the mirror. It was hard to tell through the sudden oppressive *wrongness* in the air. Hope flared in her chest.

But no, it was not Morgen.

Indeed, there was a pale-haired figure before the great mirror. But the mirror itself was spiderwebbed with thousands of cracks, the edges tarnished in blood-red and purple blooms of rot. The lingering scent was acrid, heady, with a deep, lingering musk that threatened to choke Hwyfar altogether.

Her vision spun, her own magic distant and slippery when she reached out for it.

"I am so glad you came," said the figure at the mirror.

Lady Anna du Lac, once Queen of Orkney, sister to Arthur and Hwyfar's mother-in-law, turned her haunted eyes toward her.

"I sought Llachlyn," Hwyfar said, trying to walk deeper into the room, her legs and body resisting the constant oppressive power. "I see she is not here."

"No," Anna said, turning slowly. She strode toward Hwyfar and stretched out her hand. "I believe you will find her in Vyvian's smithy, but I suspect giving her some space might be prudent, as well."

Upon taking Anna's bony hand, Hwyfar relaxed. Breathing came easier and the constant drumming in her heart dissipated. Her head, however, began aching in earnest, a heavy, constant pressure between her brows.

"Did you see the confrontation on the field?" Hwyfar asked.

Anna nodded, her eyes unfocused. "I knew Gawain would be there."

Hwyfar's magic prickled, a shivering sensation gliding down her back. "My lady Anna, you do not seem well."

The longer Hwyfar gazed at her mother-in-law, the more she noticed the deep shadows beneath her eyes and the pallor of her skin.

Anna did not let go of Hwyfar's hand, her grip almost desperate. "I had not come here since Morgen went away," she said. Her voice was soft, ragged, as if from screaming. "I was afraid. She has always been my guide, through all of what I'd done—and I did not know what I might find here. But something compelled me today."

"I, too, felt the call," Hwyfar said softly, trying to keep the worry from her face.

"So much of Vyvian's work was holding us together, and we had no idea. Holding things back from the dark."

"Whatever it is, we will face it together," whispered Hwyfar, shivering in the cold.

"I just did not expect to see *her*, Hwyfar."

Dread twisted deep in Hwyfar's chest, a warning. Hwyfar followed Anna closer to the shattered mirror. The air grew colder, wisps of it eddying around her fingers and biting at her nose. And terror, the scent of blood and fear, clung to every breath Hwyfar took.

"Look, Hwyfar." Anna's voice was cold, now, toneless and void of emotion. "And see the terror we two have wrought."

But when Hwyfar beheld the mirror, she saw naught but a roiling, dense fog where the Path had once been.

"My lady, I see but a dark and misty land," Hwyfar said gently, knowing magic revealed itself to many in different ways. "Though I do feel the power within, without a doubt."

Anna shivered, and Hwyfar put her arms around her narrow shoulders. "It must have been my dream. I—I have not been well, Hwyfar. I feel Nimue; I hear her sometimes. I thought I beheld her in the mirror just now."

"Let me take you to rest, Lady du Lac," Hwyfar said. "Let us leave this foul place for now."

"Perhaps she has gone below," Anna whispered, clutching Hwyfar's sleeve. "If I ask, would you take me there?"

"First we will get you some food and some sleep," Hwyfar said, trying to keep her voice calm and soothing. It was not her strongest skill, she had to admit. But Lady du Lac seemed balanced on the precipice of madness and magic, and Hwyfar had no choice but to help her from tumbling down.

CHAPTER THIRTY-THREE

GAWAIN

HE HAD BEEN here before, it seemed, standing in this very room with his closest of kin, their long-suffering troubles at last bled out upon the floor. But then, it had been his mother doing the talking and he being scorned; then, he had been a child in the mind still, tempestuous and enslaved to drink and anger and self-loathing.

Now, Gawain stood in the center of his mother's parlor the day after his arrival back to Carelon, with his three brothers—Gareth, Gaheris, and Galahad—and accepted the burden of peacemaking upon his shoulders. He wished his wife were here, that his own *mother* was here. But they were both occupied elsewhere, and these conversations could not wait. Not when their honor was at stake.

Gawain could not allow his hatred of Lanceloch to cloud this moment. Except it was monstrously difficult given the man's utter cowardly behavior.

"This was far from the reunion I imagined for us," Gareth said, leaning back on his chair and wincing as his stitches pulled. The ones at his side were vicious, and Gawain knew from experience just how long they would take to heal, even with the attention of the best healers in the realm. For all his vigor and power, Gareth still looked ashen, and Gawain suspected his brother had not slept a wink the previous evening.

Gaheris was the picture of health—eyes bright, cheeks pink—but he still held the sourest expression. "You could have said no," he told his twin. "And we'd have had a much less eventful summoning."

"It doesn't matter how we got here, only that we *are* here," Gawain said pointedly. "We are brothers. All of us. Blood ties us together more than any other bonds."

"Says the man who hasn't been at court for ten years and secretly married the one woman he was forbidden to," Gaheris said. "Had you even met Galahad before today?"

Gawain pushed down the twisting anger summoned so skillfully by Gaheris. He would not rise to the bait. He was the head of the family, and he could not let his temper get the better of him.

"I was at Galahad's baptism," Gawain said. "And I visited Benwick more than once when he was a child. But you are right, Gaheris. I should begin this discussion with an apology to you all for not being forthcoming about my marriage to Princess Hwyfar."

"You're married to Princess Hwyfar?" Galahad looked absolutely stunned and Gawain chastised himself inwardly for, once again, forgetting all the details between his brothers.

"Yes, Galahad. Dame Ragnell is Princess Hwyfar. No one knew," Gawain said.

"I knew," Gareth said, smug smile on his bruised face. "And Palomydes knew."

"Palomydes knew?" Gaheris's face went crimson as he stood and turned on his eldest brother. "You told the Saracen and not me?"

"I'll not have that word uttered in this space again," Gawain said, meeting Gaheris toe-to-toe. "We had a great many more difficulties between us all when we went to Avillion ten years ago which required a level of trust and care."

"And I was not trustworthy, or caring enough?" Gaheris seethed.

"My wife's life was at stake. I only let Palomydes and Gareth know because—"

"Because he wasn't certain he would live through it," Gareth finished. "Really, Gaheris, you're so busy polishing du Lac's boots these days, you can't possibly find it surprising Gawain would want to keep things closer to his chest?"

"I'm his *brother*," Gaheris said.

Gawain waved his hand dismissively at Gaheris, not wanting to get distracted again. Trying to keep these men focused was more difficult than corralling chickens. Even if Gaheris had a point. Once, they'd been the closest, and Gawain would have gone to him first. But the years were long between them, and they were both changed men.

"That's not why we're here today," Gawain said, anchoring himself in his breath. "At least, not entirely. We need to come together, as brothers, Orkney and Pendragon both."

Half-brothers. But brothers, nonetheless. Looking at Galahad it was so easy to see their mother's blood. He had the golden curls and the long, proud nose, but lacked Uther's powerful gait and height. Still, Galahad looked so young beside his brothers, so untested. There was no doubt about his skill, but he was like a perfect sword tested only in the sparring field. Even with those bruises healing on his face—nothing compared to what poor Gareth looked like—he seemed unearthly in his innocence and beauty.

It was hard to see his father's face in Galahad's countenance, at least. That helped. Because in the moment, Gawain was quite certain if he *did* see Lanceloch du Lac, he'd have punched him squarely between the eyes. Hwyfar begged him to let go of his resentment toward Lanceloch, but every time he was close to doing so, he'd have another reason to detest him. None more than today, it seemed. Although he had to admit, he *had* gotten him to stop; perhaps the victory was not Gawain's entirely, but it was close enough.

"We don't owe this to ourselves," Gawain continued, taking a seat again with a grunt. His whole body was crying out for a relief he was hours away from. "We owe it to our mother."

"Christ knows we put her through enough the last few days," Gaheris said, finally finding common ground with Gawain.

"The last few *years*," Gareth corrected. "Four sons. No daughters. Endless fighting."

Galahad shifted uneasily in his chair, eyes wide and so innocent. "I fear I have made a terrible impression on you all and brought shame to her. And the King."

"No more than any of us have done before," Gareth said. "Don't give yourself all the credit, little brother."

Galahad looked shocked at the humor—and kindness—in Gareth's tone. "But—my father—he challenged you in front of the entire court, Sir Gareth. Because of what *I* did. Because I couldn't control myself when you were just trying to be brotherly."

"The Pendragon temper is a potent thing," Gawain said, knowing better than perhaps all of them. "And we are all familiar with it, Galahad. It was almost my ruin, once. Gareth and I didn't talk for almost two years. And now I can't get him to shut up."

Galahad relaxed perceptibly, a glimmer of relief on his face. But then he shook his head, shuddering as if at a sudden memory. "I feel like a stranger to you all. Like I don't belong. Like you shouldn't even welcome me here."

"You stayed," Gaheris said, reaching over to clap his younger brother on the shoulder. "You stayed here when you could have gone to the Joyous Guard."

"Because I don't feel welcome there, either," Galahad said, anger in his voice now, but so close to breaking, to weeping. "My father begged me to come, told me I was a danger to myself here, that you all—that you all would work against me." He swallowed hard. "But I couldn't even look at him. He shamed me twice, and he is behaving like a coward to run from court after that. Our captain! It's a disgrace is what it is."

They all fell silent, and Gawain tried to consider how to speak without anger, without his shared shame. When he had seen Lanceloch out upon the field, behaving in such a maddening way, every inch of him had wanted to respond in violence. It was as if his body remembered his own humiliation upon the field, their roles reversed: Gawain unable to concede and Lanceloch unable to stop his attack.

Part of him still thought he ought to have let Gareth finish

Lanceloch off. It would be a weight off his and his mother's shoulders, to be certain.

Hwyfar would be furious, though, and he had already made enough of a mire of their lives of late. There were so many other paths to peace besides force, and Gawain knew it well enough. Especially where his family were concerned.

"Sir Lanceloch behaved as any knight does when they believe a grievous insult has befallen them," Gawain said, trying not to catch Gareth's eye. "The way of the sword, of combat, is a sacred old tradition, and many skirmishes have been fought in such a way. I do not think he was right in his belief but, gods, I've learned that one cannot change another's mind by sheer will alone."

"We Christians believe God himself helps guide the hands of the victor," Gaheris said. "And in that, Gareth was judged truly."

"*Gareth* doesn't hold quarter with your God, Gaheris," Gareth said with a sneer. "So your logic is unsound—and at present, irritating."

Gaheris glared at his twin brother, but then sighed and batted the air. "It is not the time for ecumenical discussions. But I have faith you will see, in time. As for the matter at hand, Galahad— you are our brother, no matter what. I hope you know that whatever Sir Lanceloch said to you of our aims is untrue. For the sake of our mother, of our proximity to King Arthur, you are protected here."

"I wish none of this had happened," Galahad said miserably. "I cannot begin to understand what my father's aims were."

"Perhaps he feels shame now," Gawain offered. "Give him time, lad."

"Does he often go to the Joyous Guard?" Galahad asked.

"Indeed," Gareth said. "Especially in the heat of summer and the cold of winters. In a few weeks he will return, and all will be forgotten."

"The *Graal* Quest begins then," Gaheris said, a curious light in his eyes Gawain most certainly did not know how to interpret.

"We shall need him, Galahad, to help seize the implements of power for Christ—aside from his most egregious recent behavior, his faith is an anchor for all of us at court."

Gawain sneered, thinking of Lanceloch and Mawra's frequent trysts. He could almost hear his wife's chastising words: *you show your every thought on your face; practice being more mysterious now and again.*

So he relaxed, squared his shoulders, and leaned back in his chair. "Whatever befalls the kingdom in the seasons to come, we must be united as one. To support one another, the realm, and King Arthur. We are his nephews. We have a unique circumstance few others understand."

"Family is powerful, Gawain, but ours is also fickle," said Gareth. "I cannot help but wonder if Vyvian's death and Morgen's disappearance are causing distress."

"Perhaps it was simply God's way of clearing the path toward the *graal*," Gaheris offered, not unkindly, but not appropriately either.

"Gaheris." Gareth looked disgusted at his brother's implication. "Our aunts are not the antithesis to your holy crusade."

"You didn't see what Margawse had become in the end," Gaheris snapped. "You would think different if you had stared evil down its glowing red maw, as I had."

Gods, Gaheris would never truly recover from murdering his own aunt. *Their* aunt. And Gawain had been too drunk and angry to even know what was happening at the time, how Nimue had captivated Gaheris's imagination and… gods. *Gods.* Margawse had become a monster, it was true, but she had not always been so. The sisters of Arthur all suffered in immeasurable ways, and although it did not excuse Margawse's abhorrent behavior and corruption to the most profane of magics, it did explain.

"Lady Morgen is a good woman. Wise and mysterious, yes, but not—She does not work to thwart God's plan," Galahad said softly. "I have had the chance to meet her, and though it is frustrating she does not heed the word of God—"

Gawain snorted; he could not help it. "Galahad, remember not all of us feel as strongly as you, nor ascribe to a deeper faith."

"Of course. My apologies. I only mean to say she is not evil, not that I can tell. She is strange and distant, but so is my foster sister—our cousin, Llachlyn. Perhaps the women of our family are simply spun of another thread. I suspect they possess knowledge we shall never know."

The boy had no idea.

"Indeed. And their loyalties remain akin to ours: to the vision of Arthur's Braetan. We have not fought with the Ascomanni or the Sachsens for many years, but peace is a dangerous dance. We, above all, as Orkneys and Pendragons, must stand by the King as a single force," Gawain reiterated. "He needs us now as he never has before."

Gaheris folded his arms and shook his head at Gawain. "Convenient that you come now, when all is so bleak, rather than a decade since."

There was no point in following Gaheris down these dark alleyways of blame. So Gawain did what his heart told him to do, rather than argue. He stood and went to his brother Gaheris and embraced him truly and kindly, firmly and without pretense. Gaheris stiffened, and then relented, squeezing back. When Gawain pulled away, Gaheris's eyes shone with tears.

"I cannot change the past, brother," Gawain said, holding Gaheris out at arm's length. He looked so lost. "But I can pledge to be here with you, now."

Gareth looked toward the window, just as a crow alighted on the sill, clicking its beak. "The King is not well and has not been well for some time. We cannot afford to add to any gossip, to fuel court naysayers, in such a time as this."

"And what of the Queen?" Galahad asked.

They all turned to him, surprised. Galahad appeared quite simple, a young man of brawn, passion, and religious zeal, but he had an unpredictable streak, too. A curiosity that Gawain found both familiar and a relief.

"What of her?" Gaheris asked, tone more than a little accusatory. Galahad licked his lips, nervous. "She has not left her chapel since the altercation," he said. "And—well, I suspect some of you know by now what transpired between the Queen and Llachlyn."

"I do not," Gaheris said, and Gareth nodded his agreement.

"From what I know," Gawain said, trying to measure his words as carefully as possible, not knowing where everyone's loyalties lay, "there was a misunderstanding between the Queen and Llachlyn. As a result, the Queen tried to make an example of Llachlyn and their friend young Percival, which did not go to plan."

"I let them out of the cells they'd been put in," Galahad said, the words rushing out faster than he could keep them in. "I only worry—"

"The Queen will find her way back, but the King has offered Galahad, Percival, and Llachlyn his protection," Gawain said, though he did not believe a word of it. Whatever was transpiring between her and Lanceloch was a long time in the making, and he did not like to think what its ultimate conclusion might entail. If Arthur knew of his and Hwyfar's love, certainly he was not blind to the trysts of his first knight and queen.

"Now your wife is here, perhaps there is hope," Gareth offered. "We could use her power and her wisdom—and I suspect her sister will be much soothed to see her."

If only that were the case. Gawain had not seen his wife in over a day, now, and they were due to discuss exactly the situation shortly. If Hwyfar's words did not work on Mawra, then he was going to have to step in, and he was loath to do so. Madness was a family trait, Hwyfar was fond of saying, and given her sister's behavior of late, she was growing more concerned for her well-being. It was difficult enough to have a King in the throes of illness and age, yet another to have a Queen lost to religious ravings and anger and spite.

"Perhaps," Gawain said. "But for now, I hope we are all agreed. All four of us. We work together. We support our uncle. We remain firm."

"I think we ought to lead the *graal* quest," Gaheris offered. "I could ask the King if we can start sooner than planned. I suspect it would be a welcome distraction from du Lac's behavior."

Gawain did not want to consider it, not even for a moment. His wife—his mother, his aunts—they all knew the price of the *graal* and its anchor to their own power and ways. Gaheris meant to capture it for the Christian priests, to sway the balance of power. It would mean the end for Avillion, for beings like the Green Knight and the few others who still remained, who were shaped, at least in some way, by their power.

But he could not very well disagree with the King himself, not after just lecturing his brothers about unity.

Still, Gawain could agree outwardly, but it did not mean he had to be entirely on their side, did he? He could be, as Hwyfar always said, *political*.

"I will speak to my uncle after dinner this evening," Gawain said, standing with a grunt and clapping his hands together. "We are all expected, and Mother will be there. It is the first time we shall all be together under one roof in time out of mind."

"The last time, Galahad was still in his changing linens," Gaheris teased lightly.

Galahad even laughed.

Perhaps there was hope for them, even if it seemed an unlikely, fragile thing.

AFTER HOBBLING HIS way toward the apartments Arthur set aside for them, Gawain had to pause a moment before entering. He knew Hwyfar was within; though their *carioz* had never grown again to the strength it once had, he always sensed her when she was near, a pull, a song, a strength when he needed it most.

Guilt crawled up and down the corridors of his mind, greater with every hour he remained with Hwyfar in Carelon. She had come willingly, had even been the catalyst for their return, but he could not help but feel as if it was *she* who had all to lose now, not he. The night before was their first apart in four years, and the ache of sleeping alone in the royal silks and furs of the chamber's bed made him contemplate their inevitable separation across the threshold of death.

Their ten quiet years together felt like a dream. Stolen. Frittered away like plundered treasure. It would end. Their tale would end. But he could not believe their love would end.

Gawain was not surprised when she opened the door before he even knocked, looking up at him with tired, but beguiling, eyes.

"Are you going to wait out there forever?" Hwyfar asked him.

"Not when I know you await me within," he said, taking her by her waist and kissing her fiercely. Ah, gods, but he loved the way she softened for him, how her breath changed when his skin met hers. There was great comfort in such a familiar response.

Breathless, Hwyfar pulled away to put her hands on either side of his face. The gesture always made his heart beat a little faster, the way her tenderness was conveyed in such a simple motion. *I see you, I love you, I am here.*

She helped him inside, not speaking of the way he limped, but allowing him to lean on her. He was glad of her sturdiness, and not just for how comely it made her. Physically, she could support him when exhaustion took over. And it happened so much more often these days. He'd hoped the journey would not impact him so, but he could scarcely get up and down from a chair without his cane, and he wondered if it would remain so.

The room was dimly lit, as it faced north, and the windows did little for illumination given the chapel obscured what once had been a rather lovely sweeping view of the hillsides. It smelled of spicy incense and sweet silk, and the lingering fruit and honey fragrance of his wife. He wanted nothing more than to bury himself in her, slide deep inside her, and live within the scent and feel of her. But he was so tired.

One of their servants brought him some warm tea, and Hwyfar helped him get situated by the fire. She was quieter than usual, he thought, but he knew she had news to share—even more concerning than his, to be sure, given the contents of her last letter.

Carelon had taken away her joy yet again. He had delighted in being able to make her smile, to watch the years of struggle and judgement fall from her shoulders. Less than two days at court, and he saw just how heavy the burden was upon her already, and it hurt.

"You can stop brooding, Gawain, I'm here," Hwyfar said, sitting down across from him. Her long, deep red hair was still damp at the ends, and she was in a fur-trimmed robe of green quilted silk. "I have not fled."

"I know, my love. I know," he said. "I'm glad to see you, is all. Glad for a moment's quiet and gazing upon a face not belonging to one of my brothers."

"It has been a very long few days," she said. She was fidgeting with the end of her long hair, wrapping it around her knuckles and then letting it spring back. Nervous. Not a habit Gawain typically saw in his wife.

"Your letter, it hinted at dark tidings indeed. Do you wish to speak of it now?" Gawain prompted.

She hesitated, eyes going far off for a moment. "I do," Hwyfar said softly. "I spoke to Lady Anna."

"My mother?" Gawain shivered as a prickle of guilt rose. He ought to have gone to see her, but everything with his brothers was so fraught he could not imagine seeing her before that was settled. So many difficult years between them had been because of his impulses and lack of preparation. "Gods, I should have gone to her. I should have written to her."

"She understands your circumstance, Gawain. Perhaps more than anyone. There is no need to fret so."

"Is she well?"

"None of us are well, Gawain," she replied with a sigh. "I was looking for Llachlyn, and I found your mother up in Morgen's tower. There is much for us to unravel, but the circumstances around the Path's breaking are deeper and stranger than we imagined, and without Vyvian and Morgen, I feel powerless to stop it."

"You are more powerful and more capable than anyone I have ever met, Hwyfar. Do not tell me now you have lost your courage," he said softly.

"How did ten years go by so fast?" she asked. "I feel like we are strapped to the rocks, and the tide is rising, and I cannot stop it. The *graal*, my sister, the priests, our secrets all upturned. I do not know what to do."

"Breathe, Hwyfar. As Gweyn always told us," Gawain said. "We must be strong for those who will come after us. We must make the difficult decisions, even though it breaks us to do it. We had our joy, our peace. Now, I fear, it is an age of pain."

"I am selfish and terrible, and wish for nothing more than to take you from this place and go back home," Hwyfar said, her voice breaking as tears bloomed in her amber eyes.

Gawain reached for her, and she crumpled to the carpet before him, putting her head in his lap. Her pain was tangible to him, a writhing, aching fire in his chest. His wife was not without her sorrows, but she rarely showed them so bare, even to him.

"You are not selfish. You are human. And if you are terrible, then I am worse, for if you were to ask it of me, I would take you from here without question."

"War will find us. No matter where we go."

"Aye."

"I will not run if you do not falter," she whispered.

"I know, my love. And that is the bravest of all. Come, let us weep now, for tomorrow... tomorrow we must be brave," Gawain said.

As she wept, the wool of his tunic warmed from her tears. He ran his hands through her damp, tangled hair, and when she wordlessly handed him her comb, he began the long work of teasing the knots away. Some might have thought the task womanly, but he had always loved the challenge and intimacy of it.

The simple act soothed him as it soothed her, and when she'd finished weeping, her long red tresses were smartly plaited and out of her face, showing just how sharp and beautiful her features were.

He never tired of the sight, even when her eyes were red and puffy, and her lips swollen.

"I love you," he told her. "Until the stars go out."

Gently, she sat upon his lap and laid her head on his shoulder. He could endure the pain knowing, at least in this moment as the world swirled like a gyre of uncertainty, they had one another.

"Until the stars go out," she replied, voice thick with emotion and a little hoarse from sorrow.

And for the moment, it was enough.

CHAPTER THIRTY-FOUR

MORGEN

IN THE QUIET autumn morning, I sat across a weathered old table in the inn at Lantyrnog with King Uriens of Rheged, sipping mint tea and picking at thick oat cakes studded with currants and walnuts. It was a quaint scene, if not for the presence of its players: for in what strange bard's tale would we two meet again, in a place like this, after what I had just endured?

Time had been kind to Uriens—Coel, as he preferred when we were alone. His rugged, handsome features had only intensified with age. Unlike my brother, he retained much of his vigor, as well. When he was not hunting, he was often off on excursions and long walks in Rheged, fond of mapmaking and surveying when time allowed him. He'd had druidic tendencies when I'd known him and had trained with Merlin for some time in his youth.

"I trust Yvain is in good hands, now," I said, when the silence between us had stretched to the point of breaking.

"He is free. Long I had fought to pierce his mother's brambles, knowing he must suffer within. I have set him on a ship to Rheged with his brothers Rhiwallon and Rhun, where they will help him heal in whatever way he needs," Uriens said. "At home. Where he belongs."

I welcomed a deep sense of relief. I knew Yvain was fragile in his mind and knew even better that there was rarely a cure for such things entirely. But his isolation and removal from his family for so long could not have helped matters.

"I owe Yvain my life," I said. "I am not the powerful sorceress I once was. When I found myself in Brocéliande, I was as helpful as a newborn deer against a dragon."

"From his descriptions, your power still remains impressive," Uriens said, smiling as he sipped his own tea with both hands.

I was not certain how much I should share with Uriens. Over twenty years stretched between us, and though he had been among the better men of my acquaintance, I had been so often burned by ambition and power I was hesitant to open up. Even if my heart yearned to reach out.

Somehow, looking across the table at the man who might once have been my husband and seeing the look of calm understanding in his eyes made me feel even more alone.

"Surely you must make haste back to Rheged, my lord," I said. "For its king to stray this far is quite unusual."

Uriens laughed, low and mirthful. I had not realized how much I'd missed the sound. "My daughter, Princess Morfydd, is my heir, and far better suited to the duty than I have ever been. You know better than almost anyone else I am not built for castle life."

Princess Morfydd was scarcely talking when I last saw her, a riot of bright brown curls and freckles. She was the youngest of the four children between King Uriens and Queen Blasine. I'd never known Blasine, myself, but she was a cousin of Merlin's who had died shortly after Princess Morfydd was born. Merlin had sent me to Caer-Ligualid to assist in tutoring the children and aid in the country's dealings. And, of course, to ultimately bring King Uriens to the larger alliance under Pendragon rule.

When Merlin discovered Uriens had asked for my hand in marriage, he recalled me to Carelon immediately. Yes, I had taken the Oath of Passage as a priestess and sorceress, but such antiquated concepts were well out of fashion, especially for a King's sister. Such a declaration was more of a political commentary than a conviction. Vyvian once told me the Oath of

Passage was meant to protect young, royal priestesses from early marriages, the kind my sister Anna had endured. But even then, I was not young. To say nothing of my tenuous connections to Avillion. Merlin had made me a new kind of sorceress, for good and ill. I was certainly not celibate.

As with most laws enacted to help women, the Oath of Passage was used against us, or at least, rendered potent only when men in power deemed it necessary.

First and foremost, I was Arthur's sister, and Merlin's own paramour. I do not know if Merlin called me back because of jealousy or political anxiety, but I was forced to leave Uriens, and his clever, curious children.

Yvain had never known them. Uriens and Modrun had fallen in love briefly and intensely in their youth, and she had not told him about Yvain for many years. I knew the way Uriens loved his own children and could only imagine the pain he had felt, knowing Yvain was separated from them while Modrun grew mad and powerful.

"He found you quickly, Yvain," I said, trying to catalogue the days lost to me. "Were you near when the spell broke?"

"No, but we had favorable winds, and I was already at sea, set for Cornwall. I felt the breaking of the spell, felt the winds shift and a pull here." He pressed at his chest with his strong fist, rings glittering. "We pushed the ships, but arrived not long after, and Yvain met us at the cove just north of here. You'd fallen ill by then—he'd followed you, out of concern."

I wished I could thank Yvain directly, but I was glad of his decision. "He followed me, truly?"

"Well, Melic did most of the following," said Uriens with a laugh. "That beast is cleverer than many men I know, and suspiciously long-lived. I suppose it is good he was granted some gifts of the wood, when so much of his time there was cursed."

"Time is a circle, Vyvian used to say," I replied, drawing one on the table with my thumb. "Balance. Neither good nor ill, but simply a cycle. Luck or curse, it is our interpretation."

"I was trying to remember the last time I saw you," Uriens

said, brows wrinkling. "It must have been a tournament. Was it truly twenty years ago, when Lanceloch du Lac first appeared at Carelon?"

"It must have been," I replied. "Merlin yet lived."

His deep brown eyes, warm as hazelnuts, narrowed slightly. "And now Merlin no longer lives, does he still direct your steps?"

We had argued, more than once, on this very subject, for decades, through letters. Until I had finally stopped writing, burning all his incoming correspondence. I had been far too tired to consider revisiting that particular part of my past and had known Uriens was stubborn in such matters.

No one had ever wanted to marry me, let alone a king, with such surety.

"As grateful as I am for all Yvain did for me, I cannot dally longer."

"We are not dallying. We are establishing our story."

"*We* are not doing anything."

He grinned, teeth flashing. "Oh, but we are. You have saved my son, reunited him with his family, and restored a piece of me I never thought possible."

"Then ought you not be with him?"

King Uriens leaned back, looking at me with a mixture of disappointment and mischief I was not at all pleased to see, not least because it was charming and disarming and I had no time for such distraction. "Would you refuse me?"

"I do not need help."

"That is not what I asked. Never would I stoop to such an assumption," he replied, quicker than ever. "However, you have not allowed me to finish my tale. The only way I convinced Yvain and his lion to leave and go to Rheged was to pledge my oath to your protection, personally."

Anger flared in me, bright and sharp, and I wished, not for the first time in my life, that I had a man's temper. I could have drawn my sword, I could have smacked him across the face— even better, I could have simply stormed out.

Except I froze, staring unbelievingly at the king before me.

He leaned forward, clasping his hands together. "I have never stopped loving you, Morgen. And after hearing what you did in the wood, I remembered why I never found satisfaction in another lover. You are headstrong and clever, powerful and beautiful, but above all you are fearless."

No one had ever called me *fearless*. Indeed, some days my entire life was run by fear. I lived terrified of Uther Pendragon, terrified of Merlin, terrified of my own power. But the masks I wore were indeed ferocious, though they were more fragile than anyone knew.

"I did as duty dictated, no more," I said, finally finding my feet and standing up. My traitorous body swayed in the simple exertion, and before I could argue, Uriens was up, his arm supporting me lest I tumble over like a maiden with sunstroke.

"You nearly died, Morgen, and put up a fight doing it. The innkeeper and her wife had to force their help upon you."

I did not recall, but I could not argue. It did sound like something I would do.

Uriens continued. "Whatever you plan to do next, unwise as it is to undertake any adventure, will surely be your undoing if you go alone. I have sturdy horses, tack, money, supplies—everything we could need."

Turning my head away like a petulant child, I tried to ignore him. Except the fool was right. Even I was not so deluded in thinking my body was prepared for any kind of real adventure.

Besides, I needed his presence, his arms around me, lulling me into a state of calm and warmth. He smelled so familiar, so comfortable.

"You don't even know where I'm going," I finally said.

"To Cornwall. To Tintagel," he answered simply. "Which is where I was headed in the first place. Fate, it seems, was drawing me yet again."

Yvain must have heard everything, and shared what he knew before departing.

"This is not a quest to reclaim your missed youth, King Uriens."

"You know I hate that name."

"It is your *crowned* name. And I do not have time to argue semantics with you."

"Well, you'll have plenty of time to say nothing on the journey to Cornwall. I promise, I won't say anything unless you command it."

KING URIENS—COEL—did not *say* anything as we began our trek to the small ship that would take us both across the Narrow Sea—but he did sing. At first, I bristled, anticipating annoyance. I was no singer, no blessed bird of song, and I always resented it a bit. So much else came easily to me, how strange that the matching of notes was so foreign?

Coel's voice was both low and bright, and frustratingly beautiful. Just when I began to tire of one song, he switched to another melody, and I was lost in the shifting notes and tales within. I'm certain there were good stories there, those of Rheged and Carelon and beyond, but I found listening to the words detracted from the music.

By the time I saw the sliver of the sea at the horizon open up to a great bay, I had lost track of just how many songs Coel had sung and was lost in my own thoughts.

His fleet spread across the waters, small vessels bobbing on the salty sea. They bore his colors, and his sigil: silver and black, with nine crows above and below a setting sun. I wondered about my own birds, still absent from my sight. What would they do once I crossed the Narrow Sea?

Then, I realized with a start, I missed the damned creatures.

Coel slowed his horse and waited for me to join him on a sturdy cob.

"This is an impressive fleet for an old king," I said to him.

He leaned, resting his forearms on his black roan's neck. "An old king. And what does that make you?"

"An ancient crone with very little patience. How long do you expect the journey to take?" I asked.

"We should arrive at dawn to the coast, but then it will take until dusk to reach Tintagel. I'm afraid even an old king's ship is hardly suited for the likes of the renowned Morgen le Fay, but we have a small, usable cabin that should serve well enough to rest in, should you need it."

I did. But I balked at the idea of any kind of special treatment. "I can sleep on deck with no trouble. I would like to see the stars again."

Coel did not argue with me, but I knew the discussion was not over.

I did not expect to see, however, Skourr Ahès, the chief priestess of Avillion, coming toward us on her own horse. She had stopped wearing the glamor over her disfigurement years ago, along with the veil many priestesses had adopted; her simple beauty remained intact. Like many who dabbled in the magic of the Three, she was of an indistinguishable age. I put her around Hwyfar's years, but she could have been older or younger. Certainly, Ahès possessed a wise spirit far beyond her years.

It had been too long since I saw her, face to face, and I did not miss the look of utter joy on her expression as she beheld me, though she looked weary.

"Morgen," said the priestess, touching her forehead in thanks to the goddess.

Tears filled my eyes; a dread I did not know I had been clinging to rose from my shoulders. Part of me had wondered if my other sisters, those in the Circle of Nine, had experienced painful fissures in their magical connections as well, but I recognized the strength and wisdom of Iaia so keenly in Ahès, I could scarcely believe it. I felt both a stab of jealousy and a whisper of relief.

"I'm glad you got my missive," Coel said to Skourr Ahès. "It is good to see you, cousin."

"Cousin?" I asked, reaching across to grasp my friend's hand, half to assure myself she was still alive.

Again, her power shimmered across my skin, and I breathed in deep, gratefully, though the magic did not answer me back. The connection between us was a living, breathing thing, and I wanted to bask in it.

"You recall, I am a disinherited princess of Ys," Skourr Ahès said, nodding to Coel. "My mother, and King Uriens', were half-sisters—and I was raised by King Marqus's own brother, Prince Meliadus. We thought it best to show a united front in Cornwall, given the state of things."

I was confused, sifting through my brain for the confounded genealogies of our houses. I was missing something. Some*one*, no doubt.

"I have not told her yet," Coel said, a little sheepishly.

Ahès frowned. "Morgen le Fay is forged of iron. Why ever did you not tell her?"

Coel chuckled. "She told me not to speak to her on the journey. So I sang. I did try to give her clues in the songs, but I do not think she was paying much attention."

"Please cease with your antics," I demanded. "And tell me, now, what madness we will find in Cornwall."

Ahès was who answered, gently and not without a little hesitation. "In your absence, King Marqus has taken up residence at Tintagel. It seems this past spring, Sir Tristan ran off with the Princess Isolde—but alas, Marqus found her again, and has kept her at Tintagel, threatening death to Sir Tristan and all who aid and abet him."

"Again?" I asked. This was well-trod history between them all.

"Again," Coel said.

"Tintagel is mine," I said, knowing full well King Marqus outranked me in the matter. With no living Duke of Cornwall, I would be its inheritor—though Marqus was still king in name. "I will challenge him for it, if I must—you understand, Modrun insisted I go there."

Ahès shook her head, shivering into her cloak. "There is not much reasoning with King Marqus these days, I am afraid. But with King Uriens and me to help you, perhaps we have a chance. Tintagel is not the fortress you remember, it pains me to say."

The bitter tang of jealousy coated my tongue as I stewed on the idea. I wished, not for the first time, I was gifted like Princess Hwyfar by visits from the deceased, so I could divine my next steps through their portents. Alone, adrift, without my magic, I had to depend on reason and avoid emotions. Exhaustion made me susceptible to feelings, and it did not bode well at all.

Coel insisted I take the small cabin upon the stern, typically reserved for him, while he slept with the rest of the crew above deck. I considered arguing, but having slept outside and in drafty, cold cabins, I welcomed the idea of the snug little room. And my recent illness had left me physically and mentally drained.

It was quaint and minimal, though I noticed a number of Coel's own personal effects as I blearily made my way across to the narrow cot. Books, mostly, small and well-worn, as well as scrolls and bits of metal and decorative crystals all neatly affixed to their shelves. And, unsurprisingly, a harp.

When I awoke, I had no memory of actually falling asleep. I remembered the familiar sensation of the boat slipping out into the waters, and an unlocking deep inside of me as I accepted my freedom from Brocéliande. And grief for Modrun. So often, in my life, grief came to sit with me, and though I did not cry, I let the aching waves of it lull me to my dreams, apparently.

I smelled roasting fish as I opened the cabin door, and took in the chilly, but comfortable, deck. Sailors danced and laughed, a little cluster of musicians playing in the corner, as moonlight cast the whole world in bright blue, punctuated by sea green glass lanterns aboard. They were cut to reflect light in whimsical shapes: twisting vines, sharp-petaled flowers, and spiraling waves. The view was not extravagant, and the sailors were hard-faced people used to difficult lives upon the merciless sea.

But in that moment, they chose joy.

"Something tells me you haven't danced much in the last twenty years," Coel said. He had drawn up beside me and draped me in a warm, quilted velvet cloak trimmed with beautiful silver floss. A king's mantle.

I wiped tears from my eyes, face still heavy with sleep. The truth was, I could not recall the last time I'd danced. Not even at court. I was so removed from everyone, from everything, both by my choices and my rank. The idea of dancing so freely, under the stars, moving from partner to partner without the risk of raising political scandal...

Like music, I would not consider myself good at dancing, not when I had seen women at court like Hwyfar of Avillion or Linette of Litavia, both blessed with such a comfort in their own bodies; watching them was like seeing a great painter create a fresco—save it lasted only the duration of the song. I always loved how dancing in such a way lingered only as long as it was performed, so clear and perfect in the experience, yet vanished when complete.

"We danced. Once," Coel continued when I did not answer. "I am not certain if you recall, but I do. It was not for long. And I think you might not have known you were even dancing with me."

"We never danced," I said. "I would have known."

He chuckled warmly, hearkening back to days when I'd harbored the hope of love in my heart. "It was before I was announced. I knew you were coming, and I wanted a better, closer look at you. I wore a mask of white peacock feathers."

"How terribly banal."

"They were rather fetching, I thought. Studded with silver beads and green glass."

I did remember, now. We had danced a local *carole*, the words utterly lost on me in the dialect of Rheged. "I am not a very good dancer," I admitted.

"You didn't step on my toes, and you kept to the circle well. But you could have danced like a drunken troll, and I would not have noticed. You wore a long, scarlet gown with a wide sash—popular in Carelon at the time—and you had a simple silver circlet upon your brow, your hair like a waterfall of midnight. How the ladies whispered."

The music and Coel's words were conspiring to melt my cold, hardened heart. I could have none of it.

"Much has changed since those days. My hair is far from midnight and more like the morning frost."

"Well, seeing you made me happy. It always has. It still does. And the white—it is beautiful." I could tell he wanted to touch my hair, but he did not.

"I do not think King Marqus will be happy to see me," I said, moving ever so slightly away from Coel.

"Oh, he'll be livid. He believes you dead, as many do, apparently."

I looked directly at him, then. "Dead?"

"Well, given how long you were gone."

"I was gone a handful of days. I am not so old as to raise concern to an entire realm with an unexplained visit to Avillion."

"You were gone for a month."

"A month?" Fear seized me as my mind made calculations. No matter how I tried, I could not produce enough time to make such a difference. "Goddess, the wood takes so much."

Coel nodded, but there was concern in his gaze. "I have not yet sent word to Carelon, but will do so immediately if you wish. I know there are people worried for you, still mourning Vyvian's death and wondering if our power is truly leaving the world now. Though I had every hope, and bit of faith, you were alive, I still know you well enough you must have had your reasons."

Damn the man. Most men—and kings more than most— would have run immediately to Arthur. Coel gave me a choice. He always had. Even when I was too cowardly to make the right one.

"Not yet," I whispered, wishing again his fears were unfounded. If the gods had left me, who was next? Modrun was gone. Aside from Ahès, there were few of the next generation with enough power to hold against the coming tide of Christian priests—and whatever awaited me in Carelon in the depths.

The very fabric of power was torn. And not by the priests I so loathed, but by the man who had taught me the art of sorcery himself: Merlin. Meanwhile, the priests sought the very items of power we needed to preserve our ways.

I needed my power before I returned to Carelon.

Perhaps it was better, for a time, if they did not know where I was. Even Llachlyn, though the thought hurt me deeply. If she had made it to Carelon without my protection, by now the Queen's henchmen and simpering clergy likely surrounded her. She was in danger enough as it was. And stubborn, too. I had a measure of peace knowing, at least, Galahad would protect her. But if he were to defect to his father's side or fall under the influence of Father Scurfa and his ilk, Galahad could turn against his cousin.

Deep despair fell upon me.

Coel did not ask me, nor did he press for more detail. He did not leave my side for the next hour, leaving only once to bring me back some warm, spiced cider.

I WAS NEAR sleeping again, nestled in furs in the cabin, when I heard a soft knock upon the door. Reluctantly, I arose and found Skourr Ahès there, looking expectant and a little apologetic. I welcomed her in with little fanfare, and we sat beside one another on the little cot.

She smelled of salt and cider, her dark hair down over one shoulder, as she peered out the window above the cot.

"I want to help you," she said softly. "You seem changed. Hesitant. Your power is not as it once was."

I took her hand, clasping it tight enough her rings clinked against one another. There was no point in denying it. "The goddess has left me, and though I believe Modrun gave me strength, I am still much diminished," I said. "I think if I am to find her again, I must do it alone."

The priestess turned to examine me, as if I had just said the most unintelligible babble she'd ever heard. "Morgen le Fay.

How curious I would be the one to tell you: nothing can separate us from the goddess. You were kindled to life by her spark, given the air from her breath, touched with power beyond the reckoning of most men."

"I cannot feel her," I said, placing my free hand on my chest, feeling the rise of my collar bones beneath my fingers. "After Vyvian died, I felt the connection slipping from me. I went to the tower, to my mirror, to seek answers and—I ended up in Brocéliande with no power other than... Well, it is not Iaia's power. It is death itself, I think."

Ahès listened, nodding. And then she said words that shook me to my marrow: "What if Iaia is only quiet because this new voice is so much louder?"

A new voice. Death. The Maw. There were many goddesses, it is true, who had commanded power over death. I had never been an acolyte of any goddess save Iaia, and in my panic over what I'd lost I did not consider the possibility. Death and I had a long correspondence, it was true, but I had never believed I could commune with Her directly.

"But I have always been a midwife of death," I said.

"Death is triune, and one remains a greater mystery than the others, often identified by her crows."

"Nemayne," I whispered. The goddess of death.

Ahès squeezed my hand. "Or one of her sisters. Or all three. I have often wondered, in my long hours of pondering this strange time of religious turmoil, if our Three—Nemayne, Badb, and Machea—were not the inspiration for the Trinity of the new Christian priests. Together, it seems to me, they are greater than apart. Would it be so strange, given the trials of recent days, they would bless you—greatest and most powerful among us—with their full power now, in our hour of greatest need?"

Deep inside my body, my magic shifted in response to her words. It made my heart flutter, my teeth ache. I scolded myself for missing the possibility I was not cursed at all, and tears stung my eyes yet again.

"My grief over losing Vyvian was so great, Ahès. But it was trapped inside me, somehow, like a violent storm inside a phial. I went to the tower to seek answers, and the crows found me. I begged for answers, and the Three sent me to Brocèliande. There, I found healing and helped Modrun walk across the threshold to Death."

"You have brought others across before," Ahès said. "How was this time different?"

I thought of what it had felt like to touch Yvain, to sense his madness and darkness and despair. And, too, the sense I'd had when I'd freed him. When he had reached out to me.

"I spoke with her. We stood, together, upon the threshold, and she was free of the shackles of her mind and her pain."

"Which is why we are going to Cornwall?"

I nodded, shivering as realization took me. "I will be stronger when I leave there," I said. "Modrun told me as much."

"Yes, you will," Ahès said gently. "I will make certain of it."

CHAPTER THIRTY-FIVE

THE FEAST OF HALLOWMAS

ARTHUR STARED AT the flagon of spiced wine before him, watching the oil—from the cloves, Merlin had once told him—spread and shimmer in the lantern light. He quite enjoyed Hallowmas, mostly for food and music, and because it reminded him of his childhood before he became Arthur Pendragon, High King of Braetan. In Lundenwic, where Sir Ector's expansive manor lay, the celebration was full of dancing, merriment, and visitors from all over the world. Lundenwic was a crossroads of trade—and so full of life!

Hadn't Carelon been that way once?

So swiftly, Arthur's mood shifted into a loamy abyss. The wormy place.

Where was Cai? Oh, there. Ushering in the next lord and lady someone-or-other Arthur could not recall. Were they even old enough to be a lord and lady? The fellow barely had a beard. Were the courtiers always so young, or was he just getting old?

Christ, his back hurt. The wine was a bit sour, too, so it wasn't helping things as much as usual. He should see what Morgen was up to and maybe...

Wait. No. She was gone. Dead? No. Surely, he would know. I Ic'd rooted out a few old druids still living inside the walls of Carelon, mostly down in the city, and they'd assured him they knew of no portents against her. He'd written to King Leodegraunce and even Queen Tregerna to see if she had somehow landed on their shores. It just wasn't like her leaving without notice.

Especially when Llachlyn was at court.

God, she was the fierce little image of her mother, but even sharper. Defiant, clever, tempestuous. He would almost not believe the child was his, if not for her eyes. Pendragon green. That, and she had his ears, poor thing.

If only Merlin was here. He would know exactly what to do. Arthur didn't have to agree with him, of course—which was part of the fun of having a sorcerer. To be honest, Arthur had almost always agreed with Merlin. It was just easier. He had so many decisions to make every day as ruler, having Merlin—so wise and talented and powerful—take the responsibility on his own shoulders was such an immense relief.

Lady Vyvian wasn't so easy. She liked to make Arthur work for the answers, and it was tiring. And Mawra was always complaining that Arthur wasn't forthright enough. Now, she was even mad at him for reasons he couldn't parse. *He* hadn't sent Lance away. *He* hadn't made him behave in such a strange way.

Lance.

He should be among them now. *This* was his place. Here in Carelon, here at the feasts and festival. For years, when the dark grasp of fear clutched his chest, Arthur could always look down the table and see Lance there—their eyes would always meet. And he would believe in love.

"My lord," Queen Mawra said, her voice clipped and impatient.

Arthur started. His wife must have been talking, and he had missed what she had said. It happened more and more these days, especially as his thoughts meandered toward the shadows. "Yes, my Queen," he replied.

"You've been asked to bless the feast," Mawra said, her voice softening only out of politeness before so many others.

Father Scurfa leaned forward, his ice-pale eyes narrowing with disdain. Arthur wondered why the Church would ever want such an unpleasant man as their representative in Carelon.

Merlin would have hated him.

Christ, Arthur missed Merlin.

Christ, he missed Morgen.

At least Gawain was here. At least he could look upon his nephews and his son and feel the possibility of a future. If only it didn't all *hurt* so much.

PALOMYDES PUSHED AROUND the boar on his plate, trying to focus on anything else other than Sir Agravaine's prattling nonsense. The man had been away from court for five years until last summer, living with a group of monks in Ireland. He had been self-serving, spoiled, and violent before, and now he was pedantic, zealous, and officious. Strangely enough, Palomydes would have taken the old version of him without a second thought.

He did not need any more sermons.

"I told you, Agravaine," Palomydes said, watching the King, now. He should be ready to make his speech at any moment. "I've already pledged my sword to Christ and to the King. I've no need of further preaching."

Agravaine leaned back in his chair, his bland expression looking even more like porridge with currants in it than usual. "You just do not seem too different to me. One could look upon you and still see a Sar—"

Palomydes interrupted Agravaine by raising his hand before he uttered the slur. "God lives among my people, too, you know. The stories are not so different. I still worship the same God, I only have a new understanding of the tale. Christ compels me to be a better man every day. Besides, you cannot know the heart of a man by his face or his bearing. I have learned our Christ lived in the heart of Canaan, not far from my people. Does it not indicate he might have looked a bit like me? I doubt he dressed in clothes like you favor, or anyone at court, for that matter."

Opening and closing his mouth like a startled fish, Agravaine reached for a small loaf of bread. "I don't know about such claims. You would have to speak to Father Scurfa about these matters. I am but a mere layman."

Far from it. "You are the king's family," Palomydes reminded him. "What you believe matters."

"Not to my cousins," Agravaine said, scowling toward where Sir Gawain sat beside his brother, Gaheris. "Do you suppose Gawain might——?"

"Whatever you're going to say, don't."

It had never stopped Agravaine before, and it certainly did not stop him now. "It's only I worry for his soul."

"The only person who needs to worry about Gawain's soul is Gawain."

"But his wife…"

"Is Crown Princess of Lyonesse, beautiful and brilliant, and personal savior of my life at least more than once."

"She is a *witch*."

It took a massive power of will, honed from years upon battlefields and in diplomatic situations, for Palomydes to stay his hand and not rain violence down upon Agravaine. Though he did allow himself a brief moment of very detailed imagining.

The King was standing—slowly and with the Queen's assistance—to give his speech. The crowd began a polite applause, just so Palomydes's threat could reach Agravaine's pebble brain before he said anything.

"She is a sovereign. She is a light. She is more intelligent and thoughtful and loyal than you ever will be. If I even hear so much as a whispered word against her—firsthand or otherwise—so help me, Agravaine, I will split you from lip to navel without fear of reprisal from God or His army of angels."

The smattering of applause erupted into cheers as Arthur began to speak.

GARETH OUGHT TO have been listening to his uncle's speech. It had been months—perhaps even more than a year—since the

King had been well enough to address the court in such a way. And he did look stronger, with a light in his eye. Or perhaps it was just the bright red of his tunic and the way his hair parted. Gareth knew, living behind the curtain of royalty and pageantry at Carelon, that one's image was often carefully curated. Unlike many of the ladies of court, Arthur had servants and tailors at his disposal should he need to look better than he felt.

It was nigh impossible for Gareth of Orkney to concentrate on anything, not even the very present pain of his bruises and stitches, when Lady Linette was nearby. And, thanks to the great goddess of Fate herself, Gareth was sitting directly across from her. Tonight, she wore blue silk embroidered with white flowers, their petals like stars—in the center of each was a little twist of silver thread, like water had fallen into the center. The sides of her gown were open, showing a daring view to the delicate material beneath, which blossomed again at the edges of her long sleeves.

But, ah, gods, it was the way her body lived inside the dress that gave him cause to squirm in his chair. The sweep of her shoulders, the swell of her breasts, the pull of the cloth on her arms as she moved. Then, to her brow, high and fair below the tall, brocade-wrapped conical hat she wore. Her own hair was mostly covered, save for two long braids, so deep brown they were almost black.

The tiny strings of pearls were his undoing, really, because once he realized they twisted into her braid, all Gareth could think about was carefully, measuredly, unwinding them in his hands. All he wanted to do was feel her dark hair sliding down his palms, then across his chest, then...

"...we give thanks to God for the miracles we have encountered in these days," Arthur was saying. "For great, wondrous happenings have given us hope, even in times of confusion and darkness."

Gareth could only see the gentle curve of Linette's cheek now, as she turned to watch the King more closely. Her lips parted in concentration, and Gareth had to take a large swig of wine in order to keep himself from further embarrassment.

He had never told her. And why not? He had pursued plenty of women before and enjoyed their bodies and their passions together. Of course, he wanted the same from Linette, but he also yearned for another connection, beyond fleeting trysts. He'd never felt that way about a woman before.

They were *working* together—she was working for him. Linette was the Queen's handmaiden, and Gareth's primary informant. In the last few days alone, with all the gossip and strange happenings, Linette had somehow risen even higher up in the Queen's esteem. Which put them both at risk. Gareth, like many other knights at court, suspected the Queen of plotting some sort of coup involving Mordred, or Lanceloch, or both. Gareth did not wish to bring any accusations to Arthur until he was certain of their treachery, but getting Linette's attention was going to be far more difficult, now, given the Queen's constant attention.

He missed their evening meetings. The way her nose wrinkled when she concentrated, trying to remember details, when he prodded her for more. The way she smelled—like fresh rain and roses—and the heat of her body when she walked next to him.

"And it is with great gladness in my heart I welcome, once again, to Carelon, my nephew, Sir Gawain of Orkney and his wife, Crown Princess Hwyfar of Lyonesse."

Well, that got Gareth's attention. *That* had not been the plan. As he watched his brother and sister-in-law enter the grand hall, dressed in matching green brocade, he had to force his expression to neutrality. Indeed, the entire feasting party rose to their feet—some even wept.

Though his oldest brother limped and steadied himself with a blackened wood cane, he looked every bit of him kingly. Certainly, he was not as fit as he once was, and his face showed the lines of his age—but with Hwyfar at his side, who possessed an otherworldly beauty and poise—they were together a near perfect representation of Carelon's hope. Not the pale, cold pair Arthur and Mawra made, sitting in uncomfortable distaste beside one another.

For the moment, however, the Queen's expression gave nothing away. Just placid, supportive blankness. No matter how much powder and paint they had put upon her, she still looked terrible. No doubt, with her lover absent, she was far less protected than usual. And now the House of Orkney was rising again, well. That was a losing bet.

Once Gawain and Hwyfar took their seats—Gawain taking the very chair Lanceloch frequented—food and song began in equal measure. A good tactic, given the whispering was already beginning.

It also meant Linette finally turned around and Gareth could see her face again. Someone placed a bowl of pale green soup before him, but all Gareth wanted was to gaze at Linette's perfect face a little longer. And linger on her lips. Especially her lips.

THERE SHOULD HAVE been seventy-seven guests, but now there were just seventy-four. Three missing.

Cai tapped out the count one more time from his place at the very end of the immense, horseshoe-shaped feasting table. It was his job to ensure all the right people were in attendance, and for some reason he had lost track of three of them.

His first inclination was to look for Mordred, because the prince generally did what he wanted regardless of propriety. That included shirking off any royal duties assigned to him and vanishing at parties. And God above, he could get away with it, too. But no, Mordred sat—bored and slumped—on the Queen's left.

Next, Cai looked for Galahad, Percival, and Llachlyn. That trio was back, regretfully, and if they were missing it was an easy answer to this puzzling question.

Galahad sat beside his brother Gaheris, however, and Percival and Llachlyn across from one another a few seats from Sir Bedevere. Neither of them looked even remotely pleased to be invited to such a glorious event. Not surprising. They were coddled, spoiled, thankless *children*. Cai would never have taken such an opportunity as this for granted. Indeed, when he had been invited to tend to High King Pendragon at their age, he and Arthur had bowed and scraped and kept silent, not lounged around sullen and pouting.

Christ Jesus, but Gawain looked like Uther Pendragon, though, at this distance. Cai didn't want to keep looking over at where the eldest of the Orkneys sat with his wife—something he did not wish to think about too deeply at the moment—but he couldn't stop himself. He had been in this very room, once, in the presence of King Uther, and was moved in a way he had almost forgotten. A man of presence, that's what Sir Gawain was.

"Bors!"

Cai hissed the command, and the hirsute knight came to a stop by him.

"Yes, steward," Bors replied, white teeth flashing in his greying beard.

Cai never could tell if Bors was being flippant or just friendly. It seemed impossible one could be so pleasant all the time, and people were so rarely nice to Cai.

"We're down three," Cai said, pointing to the guest list. "Find me the missing offenders."

Bors snorted, then clapped Cai on the shoulder. Not hard enough to cause any pain—Christ knew Cai's whole body was wracked with it—but enough to jostle him a bit. "You know some people don't show up to feasts, Cai. Or they might have had to go out to take a piss."

"The King's invitation is not to be ignored. Besides, I counted seventy-and-seven earlier, and now we're down to seventy-three. The second course hasn't even been set yet."

"Well, given the events of the last few days I'd not be surprised to see folks decide to stay where things are a little less exciting. This new generation isn't used to such dramatics, you know."

"I don't like it."

"You don't like anything, my friend. You don't even like me."

That was true. "I like Arthur."

"He's your foster brother, and the King of the entire realm, so I should hope so."

It was true. Cai didn't like most people, but he took his job very seriously. How could he explain to Bors that attendance didn't just reflect the King's reputation, but his as well? When Cai had proven too ill for fighting, arranging events such as these became his own stronghold, his place of power and control.

But even that would not last.

"Hwyfar of Lyonesse," Bors said when Cai did not reply, wistful and awestruck. He must have noticed him staring again. "Somehow, she's even more beautiful than I remembered. Taller, too."

"Given her reputation, I'd never imagined she'd marry, let alone show her face at court," Cai said sourly, even though his insides twisted with the words. "Do you suppose they've been wed this whole time?"

Bors shrugged. "What does it matter? The King has declared them as his own. Clearly Gawain is happy. And have you seen the way Hwyfar looks at him? She might have had a reputation once, but now he is the only lover in her whole world."

At that, Cai's heart quivered. He had thought, after ten years of not seeing her, he might feel otherwise. But it was inescapable. He would forever pine after Hwyfar, whilst proclaiming the worst of her. Because unreflecting love, for him, was a slow, unrelenting poison.

QUEEN MAWRA RECITED the Penitent's Prayer once more in her mind, focusing on the words pertaining to suffering and the sins of the body.

If she said it, and truly meant it, would God send Lanceloch back to her?

Arthur reached out to take her hand and she flinched. He looked at her, his sad blue eyes full of pain, and went to take a sip of his wine instead.

She hated how weak he was. How little he fought—for her, for anyone. He knew what she and Lanceloch were to one another, just as she knew what he and Lanceloch had once been. They punished each other by sinning with their bodies, holding Lanceloch up between them like a shield in battle.

Didn't he mark how thin she had become? The bruises? The silences stretching between them? Did he not care? Theirs had never been a lusty union, but it had been one built upon friendship and care, once. Arthur had trusted her, relied on her, brought her into matters of state and faith.

Lanceloch should still be here. Why had he fled from her? Why had he even bothered to fight Gareth in the first place—and why had he lost?

Mawra glanced over at Gareth, his face still bruised but a lopsided, charming smile on his face as he told a story to his brother Gaheris on the other side of him. Galahad was just a few seats over, but looking at him would require looking past Gawain, and Mawra wanted to put a knife in his eye.

How dare Arthur allow Gawain to sit in Lanceloch's seat? That angry oaf leaves for ten years, and Arthur welcomes him back like a war hero—as if he had anything to do with the current peace? What a farce. Godless, reckless, stupid Gawain!

Was God punishing her? Was *Arthur* punishing her?

She deserved it. Try as she might, she could not release her sins. She could not even regret them—not for all the penance, the pain, the prayer. For when she lay beneath Lanceloch and he moved inside her—oh, Mary, Mother of God—only then was she happy. And it made her wicked.

There is a light in your eyes you only show for me.

And now Hwyfar was here. Welcomed. Celebrated. Lauded. The whore. The harlot.

"Your Majesty?"

It was Lady Linette, perched before her with a crystal goblet of wine.

"What is it?" Queen Mawra snapped.

288

Mordred turned toward them at her tone, and she offered him a placating smile.

"My dear mother," said the prince, "is aught amiss?"

She hated so many people, but she could never find it in herself to truly hate Mordred. After all, she had practically raised him as her own after Gweyn's death, and she felt some measure of pride in his faith and his manners. Most of the time. There was great room for improvement, but he had many years ahead of him.

"No, no," Queen Mawra said, flapping her hand at Mordred. "I am merely tired."

Lady Linette bowed her head. "Of course. I only came to see if you needed me. We are coming to the meat course, and you asked that I seek you out."

She did? She hadn't recalled. But then, the last few days were a haze of pain and sorrow. In some ways, Mawra wished she was still in her gyre of emotion and suffering. She deserved it.

"Mordred will see to me," Queen Mawra said, summoning as much warmth as she could into her voice. "Please, enjoy your evening, Lady Linette, and forget your charge for a few hours."

Queen Mawra had seen the way Sir Gareth was looking at Lady Linette. Especially as he drank more. That was an orchestration on her part. She had no desire to injure the fellow, for Lance had already done enough. But there was more to the tale than she could immediately see.

It was likely that Lady Linette was allied with someone outside her circle, and if that was the case then Mawra needed her as close as possible. But she also needed a reminder of exactly who was in charge. Linette was already promised to another, and well she knew it.

For certainly, she had only one purpose now: to ensure Mordred's ascension to the throne and eliminate any other possible threats to his rule.

* * *

AGRAVAINE MISSED MONASTIC life in more ways than he would have ever admitted to himself. Most especially because there was no dancing among the brotherhood. He had always despised dancing, and though he wanted to enjoy himself at Hallowmas this year, despite the Queen's insistence it was rooted wholly in the Faith, he saw hints of the pagan past everywhere. In the food, in the clothing, in the choice of music.

Well, it wouldn't be long. Soon, he and his faithful knights would have the *graal* in their hands, and with it, the power to vanquish the demons of their past. Did it matter that, in his mind, those demons wore his mother's face? Father Castius had insisted it was just his spirit's way of making sense of the evil he'd endured as a young man at the hands of his mother, Margawse of Cornwall.

Soon, he would be married to his betrothed. Soon he would have children of his own, and he would raise them to fear God and praise Christ above all. They would be free from the corruption he had endured.

Speaking of his betrothed, it was time she paid more attention to him.

"Lady Linette." Agravaine came up behind her at the table, placing his hands upon her shoulders. Her dress was unseemly; he would have to correct that afterwards. To say nothing of her corpulence. Had she no restraint? "You have not come to me as I asked."

Gareth, who sat across from Agravaine's intended, snapped his head up. "Lady Linette and I were in the middle of a conversation, cousin."

To his pleasure, Linette paled and looked away, prompting a confused expression from Gareth. Ah, so the fellow didn't know *everything*.

"Ah, well, my betrothed and I are due a walk outside," Agravaine said, pushing back one of her escaped curls from her cap. She tried not to recoil—he could see her effort—but it did not work. It should have bothered him, but it did not.

She did not have to find him attractive to perform her wifely duties when the time came. And perhaps better for it, for she would approach him without lust. Such sins were particularly unbecoming in women.

"Betrothed?" Gareth nearly choked the words out.

Good. Let him gag.

"You hadn't heard?" Agravaine slipped his hand possessively down Linette's arm, feeling his arousal grow as she shuddered. "By personal blessing of the Queen and Father Scurfa. Now Morgen le Fay, in all likelihood, is dead, the dukedom of Cornwall falls to me. And Lady Linette was an ideal match. She will make a good mother and a pleasing wife."

When Agravaine took Linette by the arm, she did not resist. Not in a room so full as this.

"Perhaps we might dance, Sir Agravaine?" Linette asked, a sudden energy in her voice. Perhaps she was trying to save face in front of the handsome young Orkney.

"You jest, my dear. Such carousing is only for the heathens."

No one was more surprised than Elaine of Corbenic when Sir Gawain approached her for the Hawk's Reel dance. She had not seen him in over fifteen years. When she saw him enter the hall with his wife—Hwyfar of Lyonesse, of all people—she suddenly remembered just how much they had once cared for each other. And how carelessly she had been cast aside.

It took Elaine a moment to stand, given how late in her pregnancy she was. Her husband, Sir Lovel, was far from court at present, managing diplomatic discussions on the King's request. Theirs was a pleasant marriage, if a little dull. She was taken care of, and lived not far from her father's castle and visited him often. Many women at court had suffered far more in their marital arrangements.

Sir Gawain gave her a sympathetic smile, his bright green eyes gleaming. She had always thought him handsome, even though he was broody and bull-headed—but seeing him now, smiling and kind and attentive, made her heart do strange things.

"I, too, am not so quick on my feet these days," Sir Gawain said. "We can keep to the edges of the dance and leave the younger folk to their flounces."

When they were in position, he bowed to her and they began, hands clasped, both taking hitching and waddling steps toward one another.

"You look well, my lord," Elaine said, gesturing to his most impressive finery. "Time away from court has served you kindly."

"I am blessed with the best of wives," he said, and she did not miss his longing stare toward where Hwyfar of Lyonesse sat in conversation with Prince Mordred. "And good country air. I see you are in good health, as well?"

She laughed. "Are we so old now we discuss our health and the weather?"

Gawain's answering chuckle was delightful, boisterous and unreserved. "You are right, of course. I only wanted to apologize to you, in person, for my behavior so many years ago. I should not have been such a brute, nor should I have abandoned you without word."

Elaine, in her younger years, would have blushed and demurred. No longer, though. She had endured too much. "We were both being manipulated, my lord. You were wise to heed your mother's advice—I assume it was her advice."

He nodded, walking her in a slow circle as the dance continued. "It was. And I presume you are referring to my aunt Margawse and her sway over us both?"

"Indeed. I was coerced into distracting you—she and my father had an understanding." Those words were painful, but necessary. "But I made the mistake of loving you, anyway."

Gawain's eyes widened in surprise, and part of Elaine was proud of herself for engendering such a reaction from one of the greatest and most powerful knights of the realm.

"You loved a man I could have been," he said, taking her hand

and kissing it gently, as if in benediction. "I am glad, for both of us, we did not remain so, for your future would have been bleak, indeed."

"You have found your match," Elaine said, looking back at Princess Hwyfar. It was hard to credit she was the Queen's sister, their bearing was so different. "God has blessed you."

"And you," Gawain said, glancing at the swell of her belly.

"Indeed, He has."

If only, this time, the child would live long enough to draw breath.

MORDRED COULD HARDLY believe he had the luck to be sitting next to Princess Hwyfar herself. If he was honest—which he rarely was—he had half thought she was a myth. Could a woman have truly lived as she had, among the knights, carousing and fucking and stirring up trouble, right under the noses of her own sisters?

He'd always recognized a kinship to her. Aside from being her nephew, of course. Because he, too, seemed propelled by an insatiable desire for more in life. More beyond the propriety of his position and his status—a hunger. A need.

Not to mention she was marvelously beautiful. In the way she moved, spoke, and interacted—Christ, just the way she *sat* was beautiful. Mordred had never seen anyone look so absurdly regal.

And she kept striking up conversation with him.

"I must admit, being next to you is a bit of an experience," Mordred admitted as the dancers took to the floor. Even Gawain was dancing.

"An experience?" Princess Hwyfar raised a dark red eyebrow at him and then picked at one corner of the cheese spread before her.

Mordred laughed—nervous, not pleasingly, then swallowed. "You are a bit of a legend around these parts."

"Am I?" There was a note of caution in her tone.

"I mean that in the sincerest way possible. I am an appreciator of pleasure and indulgence myself. Of course, not officially." He glanced at where the Queen had been just moments before. "I have a number of reputations, I suppose you could say."

"Shame. I only had one."

"And it was splendid."

Her grin widened, sensuous lips tightening over her teeth. "It was, I suppose, a kind of power. And, for a time, it was a great balm to my troubled soul."

Mordred cleared his throat, unsure how to remain tactful in his next line of questioning. "But for all the joy of gamboling and licentiousness, you found satisfaction in monogamy?" He gestured to where Gawain danced at the edge of the circle, keeping up surprisingly well given his size and injury.

Hwyfar did not answer right away. Instead, she watched her husband with a look of intensity that moved Mordred to his very heart. As she gazed at Gawain, he looked up to see her, too, and Mordred could swear he felt the snap of their connection like lightning. He had never seen two people look at one another in such a manner—certainly no one had ever beheld *him* so.

It suddenly occurred to him that there was far more in life than carnal love, pleasurable though it might be.

"Satisfaction, yes. It was not difficult to walk away from the life you so admire, Mordred; I eventually would have destroyed myself had I continued on that road. I see no sin in pleasure or in the seeking of it, but when one goes to the well again and again and gains no comfort, no love, no rest, it becomes a kind of poison. And for some, I suppose such a fate is manageable. For me, eventually, it was not. When Gawain and I found one another, we were broken. Together, we began to mend."

"How poetic. But surely, as a woman of appetites, you must miss part of the old life."

She turned her amber gaze upon him and shrugged. "If I did, I know my husband would not prevent me from seeking out such comforts. Our connection is more than our physical connection, and I have long desired the company of men and women. To speak truly, I had thought I *would* ache more for it—but our lives are so full of one another, and such small joys, I find myself only pondering it in passing."

Truly remarkable, on all counts. "My father and the Queen despise one another," he said, lowering his voice. "It's difficult to imagine a marriage without the bitterness of mutual loathing."

"Fate blessed us. But we also chose our fate. Together. Men of court may have a little more say in their marriages, but overall, most do not. We marry for love only at great risk."

"And you risked it."

Hwyfar looked down at her hands, turning them in the candlelight so they glimmered: hammered gold, rubies, pearls—a veritable treasure of wealth. Yet her nails were short, the cuticles rough, and her hand freckled from long hours in the sun. "There is always risk. Even in not taking it. Ultimately, we fought for each other. The King was not pleased, but he was not unaware. In the end, we had ten years away from court together. And that is a gift I will never be able to truly repay." She sounded sad enough that Mordred had to swallow an unexpected emotion.

Ten years. At his age it seemed such a long stretch of time. "And yet you came back. How long will you stay?"

For the first time in their conversation, the princess looked weary. She closed her eyes and breathed in slowly. "As long as we must."

Given the Queen had left the feast early and had gone out of her way to avoid Hwyfar altogether, the princess decided to take matters into her own hands. Thus, after informing her husband of her plans, Hwyfar found her way to the Queen's apartments by the chapel and wandered through the halls until someone caught sight of her.

Sir Aglovale was unimpressed by Hwyfar's presence. "The Queen has asked for no interruptions."

Hwyfar held her chin up and squared her shoulders, speaking as calmly as she could. "I am the Queen's sister, Sir Aglovale.

Princess Hwyfar of Lyonesse. I seek an audience with her after ten long years away from court."

"I'm sorry, Your Highness," Sir Aglovale said, not without derision. "My orders are my own."

Hwyfar was seriously considering either leaving—for she was truly terrified of what her sister might say or do when they finally saw one another again—or casting some sort of spell to frighten the knight, when a comely young woman opened the door of the Queen's chamber.

"The Queen is unwell," she said, voice low. "I do not think—"

"Bring my sister to me, Linette."

Queen Mawra's voice was still loud enough to carry, but it rasped as if she had screamed for hours on end. Hwyfar felt her own magic recoil at that sound, as if it held powers in and of itself.

"With haste, Your Majesty," Sir Aglovale said, gesturing for Hwyfar to walk forward.

Linette nodded to him, and helped Hwyfar navigate the cold, stark apartments. Indeed, Hwyfar noticed they were hewn of the very same stone as the chapel, nearly bereft of all ornament save for a crucifix and a tapestry depicting Christ upon St. Mary's lap, his body limp and pale in death.

It smelled of myrrh and vinegar, and Hwyfar steeled herself for what was to come.

Queen Mawra sat upright in her bed, itself carved of pale wood and draped with scarlet. Her face was sallow and stretched, her eyes bright with feverish intensity. Goddess, she was so small, Hwyfar realized, as small as Llachlyn and thinner besides. It was hard to imagine their parents—both tall and broad and powerful—had much of a hand in her creation. Well, if not for the fact that her face was nearly a twin to Tregerna's.

Hwyfar knelt at the foot of the bed, but only as long as courtesy would require. She could smell blood in the air, though there was no sign of it from what she could see.

When she stood, Queen Mawra was staring at her imperiously. "Sister."

"Queen Mawra," Hwyfar said.

Linette made a motion to leave, but the Queen held up a hand in command. "I did not dismiss you, Linette."

"Yes, Your Majesty," Linette said, and bowed her head, keeping still.

"Linette, this is my eldest sister, Hwyfar, come all the way from the North, where she has been tupping my husband's beloved Sir Gawain. Finally found a prick you couldn't live without, sister?"

If the words were meant as an insult, they did nothing to rile Hwyfar. She felt oddly calm, almost relieved. "I am well married and bedded regularly, indeed. But I will not live in shame for my life before Gawain. The King has given us his blessing, and I wanted to share the happy news with you."

"God will judge you. I have no doubt," Queen Mawra said, turning her face away as if just looking at Hwyfar was unbearable. "You mean to usurp the crown. You will not have it."

Hwyfar wanted to laugh. Of all the things in the world she desired, the crown was at the very bottom of the list. "I had hoped we could speak plainly, you and I. I had hoped to speak to Sir Lanceloch, as well, but he has fled to the Joyous Guard, it seems, after his tussle upon the tilting field."

That, at least, appeared to get a rise out of the Queen, who bared her teeth. But then she called Linette over. "Linette, get me the unguent again."

Linette scampered to the side of the bed and drew out a small packet, complete with a sponge and a clay bowl filled with a waxy poultice. As if it were the most unremarkable thing in the world, Mawra lifted up her shift, displaying her emaciated, horrifically injured back to Hwyfar.

Hwyfar's blood ran cold. There were welts all along the Queen's back, some bruised so deeply they were black.

"You may try and shame me, Hwyfar, but I am cleansed every night, body and soul. Made new. I am as a virgin, bathed in Christ's forgiveness," the Queen said, letting out a moan as Linette gently treated the wounds. "While you live in sin."

"I am not here to speak of sin, but of family." Hwyfar had to root herself to the ground again, not to get lost in her sister's madness and bitterness. "Lady Vyvian is dead. Lady Morgen is missing. Lady Llachlyn, thereby, is under my charge and protection."

"Lady Llachlyn?" Mawra scoffed. "What care have I for that useless slip of a girl?"

"One might even claim her title higher than Lady," Hwyfar warned, stepping forward and pushing out her own magic, her presence and power. "As daughter of Morgen le Fay and my niece by marriage, she is mine to claim. If you ever come near her, or threaten her, you will have far more to worry about than your God's judgement. No excoriation will rid you of my fury. And that goes twice for the boy."

"Ah, the witch is perturbed," Queen Mawra hissed through her pain as more of the vinegary salve was spread over her back. "Which boy? I lose track these days."

"Percival of Pellam."

The Queen took a deep, shuddering breath, closing her eyes, lids trembling. Silence fell between them all, and for a long moment, Hwyfar was certain this was the end of their conversation. They could never mend their relationship, but Mawra and Gweyn had found God together, and surely, they had shared in some of their secrets. Surely, they had loved one another.

"He has his mother's eyes," the Queen said softly, tracing the scarlet silk blanket before her.

A momentary flash of hope ignited in her chest. She seized the moment. "I understand the pain and price of love, sister, and how wholly out of control it can seem."

"Do not speak your treasonous lies to me, Hwyfar," replied the Queen, but there was not so much venom in it. "And do not threaten me with gossip and lies."

Hwyfar had too long avoided her sister, had kept far away, reasoning that she was unreachable. But she had to try. This last time. "Sometimes, I've found, *treason* is simply another word for *truth*. I have no desire to threaten you, sister. Goddess knows you are torturing yourself enough. I just—You are not the first to love without—"

"Linette, show the princess out," Queen Mawra said, her body shuddering with pain and rage.

Linette, who was weeping fat tears by now, started and rose, dropping the unguent to the ground, where it shattered.

"Stupid girl!" Queen Mawra shouted, but there were tears in her voice. "Get out!"

CHAPTER THIRTY-SIX

GALAHAD

HE'D HAD TOO much to drink, and Galahad scolded himself for it. Now that he was back in his rooms, alone, he sank into melancholy. He looked like such a jester in his ridiculous cloak and tunic. Why had he agreed to wear the du Lac colors in the first place? No wonder people looked at him as if he were a traitor. He thought he was doing the right thing, but once again—again!—he was the idiot.

Even worse, he had tried to find Percival again. To do what, he couldn't say—but it was all building and building, and he just couldn't take it any longer. That kiss had seared its way into his heart, and he could do nothing but think on that sweetness, that promise of more, that need he always felt when Percival was near.

He knew it was wrong. At least, that is what the priests said; Galahad was never much one for the scriptures. His faith was much more of a feeling, a closeness he knew when he was in the chapel or outside. The idea God's power could be contained inside a scroll or painted in a book seemed so very strange to him.

And Llachlyn was avoiding him. All evening, through the entire feast, every time he had managed to get close enough to speak to her, she'd twisted away. Then, at some point, she'd snuck out altogether. He wanted to tell her how lovely she looked, and how glad he was to see her, but she was still clearly upset with him.

God! He missed her.

A shuffling sound at the edge of the room caught his attention, and he fumbled for his sword. He had thrown it in the corner in a drunken fit.

"It's just me, Galahad. Please do not murder me this night."

Percival.

Galahad's heart made a most curious gallop, and he swung around to see the tall squire dusting cobwebs from his hair. He had taken the tunnel that happened to emerge to the left of the thick tapestry depicting a lion hunting a unicorn. Percival looked rather roguish, standing there, pale hair stark against the deep red background, littered with thousands of little flowers.

"Oh." Galahad folded his arms before him to still his shaking hands. The fug of wine still lingered in his head, obliterating all sense.

"Not the rousing welcome I was expecting," Percival said with a laugh. He took a few steps forward, feet silent upon the thick carpets. Tilting his head, he laughed. "Are you still drunk?"

Galahad couldn't have denied it if he'd wanted. "Mostly."

"I barely had time to drink tonight, but I suppose I wasn't up there on the dais for everyone to gawk at, gleaming in my father's armor."

That made Galahad grimace. Why was he crying? When he went to speak, he found he could not.

Then, Percival was there, hands upon his shoulders, gazing down into his face with pleading concern. "Oh, I'm sorry— Galahad, that was awful of me. I didn't mean to tease."

"I feel the whole castle crumbling," Galahad finally managed, drunken panic fueling his emotions. "I feel us crumbling. The King dying. My father leaving. Looking at Sir Gareth with his bruised face all night… I don't belong here, Percival. I've barely been here a season, and I've brought utter ruin upon Carelon."

Percival pulled a red kerchief from his tunic and dabbed at Galahad's cheeks, gentle and attentive. "Well, given Llachlyn and I arrived at precisely the same moment, I wouldn't give you *all* the credit."

Galahad had to laugh, even a little. "Now I can't stop drinking or crying or being angry."

With a sultry smirk, Percival asked, "Well, it hasn't all been so terrible, has it? Some rising passions are worth the suffering."

He was getting closer, and Galahad reached up to stay his hand. "I don't know what to think about it."

"Maybe don't think about it. Maybe just let the moment take you," Percival offered.

"But the priests... They say such a thing is a sin in the eyes of God."

"You've said as much before." Percival rolled his eyes slightly as he spoke. "If it truly concerns you, then I do not wish to be a wedge between you and your faith."

"Do you truly not believe?" Galahad still slurred his words, and he was glad for Percival's arm—he clung fiercely to him.

"I cannot deny there are facets of the Christian faith which speak to me—but neither can I ignore things I have seen and experienced outside of it. I haven't even had time to tell you what I saw in the North, Galahad."

"But you are not a heathen."

"I am not. I don't feel the need to ascribe to any faith. But I will also respect yours."

"No—Percival..."

"We've shared visions, you and I. And tender embraces. I know you desire me, and I think I have made it quite clear I would have you without a moment's hesitation. But I will not be your cross to bear." He was getting angry now, and it made him look so handsome: the color high on his cheeks, his dark eyes full of simmering fury and searching Galahad's face.

His head pounded, and he wished he had not imbibed so enthusiastically. This moment would feel so much clearer. He'd know the right words, the right actions. But with the floor moving beneath his feet like that, he couldn't right his own thoughts.

"I would never want to place you in such a situation," Galahad said, reaching for Percival's face. The squire's skin was so soft against his thumb, yielding and then sharp against his jaw. Percival's lips parted at that action, sending sparks down Galahad's belly.

"I would not let you," said Percival, resolute and unflinching to Galahad's affections. "You might not want to, but you would, and damn my heart, I would probably let you. Because, Christ, Galahad, I do want *you*."

Percival, always so pleasant and kind, nearly growled the last. Galahad shivered at his admission, blood rushing to his loins in response. Never would he have guessed he wanted to be possessed by this young man in such a way—but he did, desperately. To submit. To relinquish power. To concede without struggle. For once in his short life, he did not want to fight. And it was thrilling.

"And I—I desire the same," Galahad managed to say, though the words were stilted and certainly not as convincing as they had been in his head.

Percival took a deep breath, eyes searching Galahad's face. "And after you are sated—what would you think, looking at me across the hall? Would you feel shame, or joy?"

The questions hurt, raining down upon Galahad as surely as blows from a mace: brutal, resounding, impossible to ignore. Percival's lips were so close to his own, his body angled with desire and anticipation. If he would just stop talking, this would all be so much easier.

Galahad was a terrible liar. He had none of the guile his fellows had. Gazing up into Percival's eyes made it even harder. The squire's intensity came in brief moments, usually, mostly around his favorite scholarly subjects. Now, however, all of that turned toward Galahad directly and he was bare, vulnerable.

He broke away from their near embrace, mostly to avoid being the victim of Percival's gaze.

Percival sighed behind him. "I suspected as much."

"I didn't say—" Galahad tried.

"You didn't have to."

"I don't understand why you're putting such pressure upon me," Galahad said, anger hot and sudden, making his face burn.

"We've both established our mutual attraction and affection. I've never—this is all new to me. I didn't plan to feel this way, to respond to you like this. But from the first time we met, I just—I ached to be with you."

Percival's reply was measured, calm, even in the face of Galahad's temper. "It's got nothing to do with your experience, and everything to do with who you are as a person—your beliefs, your morals, your heart. I told you; I will not be your secret shame."

"Why not?"

It wasn't quite what Galahad meant to say, and he cringed, expecting Percival's mood to darken.

Instead, Percival just shook his head, sighed and walked toward the door.

"Because, sweeting, I deserve more than that," he said.

The words were simple and decisive, cutting straight to Galahad's heart. The endearment made it sting all the worse.

"I'll try and be better," Galahad said, closing the space between them.

"I will not come between you and your faith. Not unless you are willing to fight for me, too."

Galahad went to try and convince Percival otherwise, summoning up the last of his drunken courage to kiss him, to hold him, to beg him. But just as he reached Percival, the room began shaking.

No, it was not his drunkenness. The tapestries trembled, and a roaring, moaning, creaking sound shuddered through the room.

Fear as deep as he had ever known shot through him, and Galahad scampered away, throwing himself down upon the ground and covering his head. Was God wreaking his vengeance upon him for even contemplating this sin? The walls shook again, dust raining down from his ceiling, as the timbers groaned. In the distance, he heard a horrible cracking sound, like a mountain breaking apart.

Throughout the castle, Galahad heard shouts and clattering below, thumping above. Were they all going to die?

At last, the shaking ceased, and Galahad looked up to see Percival. He hadn't moved. Well, his head was tilted up as if listening, and he had shifted his weight to his other foot—but otherwise, the horrific shaking hadn't bothered him at all.

For a brief moment, Galahad wondered if he had imagined it. Had madness taken root so deep inside him?

"Well, *that* was strange," Percival said at last.

"Strange?" Galahad's voice squeaked in reply. "The whole castle could have tumbled and killed us all."

Percival put a hand on the bare wall by the door, then slapped it like one might a horse. "Buildings settle. And sometimes the earth moves. I've read about it—accounts from over the sea."

"How do you remain so calm?"

When Percival laughed, Galahad could scarcely believe it. Laughing! When God might be raining down his curses!

"I'm not afraid to die, Galahad. And should it happen all of Carelon falls upon me, I do not wish to face it with eyes averted."

CHAPTER THIRTY-SEVEN

HWYFAR

"YOU CAN GET off me now, my love," Hwyfar said, her heart still thundering in her chest. "We both yet live."

They had retired to their rooms after the Hallowmas feast concluded, slipping naked beneath the furs and silks of their bed and slowly, purposefully, enjoying the rhythm of their bodies in the quiet and the dark. It was gentle lovemaking, sweet and unhurried, and they both fell asleep warm and sated and at peace. Never had they done such a thing beneath the roof of Carelon; never would they have dreamed it. And yet, they'd both lived half their lives in this very castle, unaware that a love of their magnitude awaited.

Hwyfar had just begun to drift off to sleep, when the room started shaking. Gawain had rolled atop her, and for a moment Hwyfar thought he was waking her again for another bout of passion.

But then, bits of stone dust began falling into his hair and on the bed, and she heard cries of alarm through the castle grounds.

Goddess, was this the fall of Carelon? Hwyfar knew the portents were ill, but she did not imagine the literal crumbling of the castle. Holding tight to Gawain, feeling his strength in her body, she stilled her breath and dug deep into her power, to make them safe.

Three great shudders followed, and then the entire castle went still. Now, though, it was like a hive awakened. The sound of footsteps above and shouting below punctuated the darkness.

"Gods above," Gawain said, his massive body relaxing. He let his head fall into the crook of her neck and breathed deeply. "I thought it was the end."

"Well, how very like you to have me on my back for your last moment upon this earth," Hwyfar said coyly. She reveled in the sound of his gentle chuckle against her skin, the warmth of his breath. He kissed her neck, and her muscles loosened with his welcome comfort.

She let go the magical net supporting them, the effort making her breathless. As ever, they had protected one another without question.

Slowly, groaning in pain, Gawain rolled off Hwyfar and staggered to the door. One of the servants was already there, lantern in hand, checking they were well. A moment after, Gawain was sitting beside her again, his face illuminated in golden light from the candelabrum.

"What a bleak day," Gawain said at last, rubbing at the bridge of his nose. "I am woefully unprepared for such excitement. It has been one unforeseen adventure after another since we arrived."

"You should go to the King," Hwyfar said, though it pained her to do so. He would be even more frightened than they, likely ready to cleave to his priests' explanations. "He needs you."

"I was thinking much the same. But Hwyfar—what *was* that?"

Strange tidings, once again. "Something I cannot explain. I should seek out your mother. She was only at the feast for a brief time, and I expect this will disturb her greatly."

"You are courageous to seek her out in this kind of mood," Gawain said, reaching across the bed to get his thick fur gown. "But I agree it's best."

"And if I can, I will look for our wards." This is what they had taken to calling the three youths. "Someone must look after them, after all."

* * *

THE WHOLE KEEP was in a thither, people flooding to the chapel to pray, dropping candles in their hurry. Hwyfar moved against the crowd, shrouded as best she could, searching for faces she might trust with the right questions. Goddess, she loathed this kind of skullduggery. The pulse of her armor beneath her cloak was a constant reminder of her purpose, her strength.

But earthquake was so much worse than she had considered. Their apartments were far from the center of the catastrophe, but much of the rest of the castle was in shambles. The devastation was difficult to absorb, but even with meagre lighting the damage was terrible. Carelon had begun to crumble, far more literally than she had ever imagined.

Someone was wailing as a priest stood over them, trying to convince them to walk. A few people had visible injuries, but from what Hwyfar saw, no one was in mortal peril. Some of the more even-headed knights were trying to keep the peace as panicked servants flitted to and fro carrying clean linens or moving detritus.

At last, she spied Palomydes and Bors, ushering people through the causeway between Merlin's Tower—well, Mordred's now— and Llachlyn behind them, hands pressed to the wall. Her face was pale as milk, and her eyes swollen as if from crying.

"Llachlyn—Sir Palomydes, Bors," Hwyfar said, sweeping up next to them.

Palomydes wiped a hand over his brow, and it came away with some blood. "Princess. I'm glad to see you're unharmed. What is the news from Sir Gawain?"

"Off to be with the King," Hwyfar said, surprised when Llachlyn took her arm with a fierce grip. "I came to find word of Lady Anna's whereabouts."

"I tried to go after her," Bors said, miserably, "but she'd have none of it."

"After her?" Hwyfar asked, a sense of foreboding slithering up her spine. "Were her quarters so badly damaged?"

"No. The worst of it was in the prince's tower—the prince

is…" Bors shook his head. "Not in a good way. That tower could not sustain the force of the earthquake."

Goddess, no; not now. Not with all they knew, all they understood. Losing the heir would surely mean the end of Carelon, of their lives, of their future. She could see Mordred's handsome, curious face watching her with awe in their conversation just hours before, and she had wanted to know him better. Indeed, she had wondered if she could help him grow into the sort of man who might rule one day, work as an advisor. The thought had been surprising, even to her, and yet it made sense. Hadn't Morgen and Vyvian been preparing her for this all along?

"I will pray for him, to any deity that will listen," Hwyfar said, "that he should heal swiftly and fully."

"In the clamor, Lady Anna went to the dungeons," Palomydes said. "She went alone. Bedevere is with the King, and she slipped away like a creature of mist. I tried to go after her, but you see we are quite occupied at the moment."

How insufferable Mawra must be at this moment. Hwyfar was glad to be far, far from her. No doubt, she knew it as a sign from God for her own transgressions. Or the transgressions of others at court. Or proof of her powerful faith. Though, if Mordred was in mortal peril, even Mawra would struggle to twist that to her benefit.

"Aunt Anna looked afraid," Llachlyn said. "I saw her, for a moment, and then… then I didn't."

Hwyfar squeezed Llachlyn's hand. She would not be in danger. Not even in this time of panic.

"Then to the dungeons we will go," Hwyfar said, making to move as quickly as possible.

"We?" Bors asked.

"Llachlyn?" Hwyfar asked. "You are more than welcome to accompany me, to see to the King's sister's safety."

"Of course. I'm staying with you," Llachlyn said.

Bors and Palomydes exchanged looks. Most of the residents were through now, and they would certainly all need to convene for more specific instructions soon. Hwyfar knew enough how such matters worked.

"I'll escort them," Bors said at last. He was a big man, broad of chest and face, with a black beard and lively eyes. Gawain had only ever had praise for the man, even in the face of long campaigns and difficulties among the ranks. He never stirred rancor among his fellow knights, and often came to the defense of those less fortunate than him.

Hwyfar was quite certain she could protect herself, but she would not turn down help. Especially if they needed assistance clearing out detritus.

THE DUNGEONS WERE strange, labyrinthine, and built to confuse. Some turns led to safety, while others meant to trap and torture the unwary.

Bors seemed to know an inordinate amount on the subject.

"Of course, Uther built the dungeons," he said as he shook his lantern, which had been damp to begin with and was now guttering alarmingly. "In his day, punishment was meted out with little regard to the law. Being accused of treason against the King was as good as proof."

"It's rank," said Llachlyn, who had tied a scarf around her mouth.

"That's on account of the cabbage," said Bors.

"Cabbage?" Hwyfar asked. Indeed, she had experienced many a foul cabbage in her years farming at Thistlewood, but the sulfuric stench far exceeded her recollection.

Bors pushed open a door, examining the hinges, which were broken—pale flakes of wood gleamed where it had been forced open. It was not the first sign of life they had seen.

"Cabbage," repeated Bors. "There was a surplus this autumn, and through some clerical error, they ended up here. There was no place to put it, out of sight, save the dungeons."

"The stench is foul. It's intense even for cabbage," Hwyfar observed.

That was when they felt it: another vibration, long and strange. Like the sustained purr of a cat—but a cat so large it made the walls tremble.

When it passed, they all looked at one another in fear and shock.

"That was not the same as before," Llachlyn said, her eyes wide, panicked. "It sounded almost animal."

The smell did not improve as they descended, following the trail of disturbed ground and the occasional relocated beam or crate. The walls looked excavated by hand, with no sign of brickwork or scaffolding to support them.

A cry in the distance—a woman's wail—was enough to make them all go faster. The temperature dropped and the smell intensified.

At the bottom of a short flight of rough stairs, before a high archway, Anna du Lac—once Anna Pendragon—lay in a crumpled heap. Blood flowed from her nose, streaking the side of her pale face. Her lantern guttered behind her, and she held fast to something in one hand.

Hwyfar sent out her magic as a shield, hoping to sense more in the darkness beyond her. She could not yet see, but sensed a great, yawning cavern ahead, far deeper and greater than she ever would have suspected.

Then her magic, unprovoked, lit a bright green flame to illuminate all she saw before her, filling the massive room with light.

Then she fell to her knees by Anna's side.

Roots. Roots, everywhere. They reached from the high ceiling, across the battered ground, thick as trees themselves, riddled with white blossoming cankers. All were covered in strange, red hairs reflecting Hwyfar's flame. The entire foundation of the castle must have been encircled in these roots—no wonder it was shaking.

She had seen plant magic before, but this was corrupt and wrong, more like parasitic veins than any kind of natural growth. It reeked of the magic of Ys, and other powers she could not recognize immediately, foreign and oppressive.

"Anna," Hwyfar whispered, feeling for the woman's heartbeat

as she turned away from the hideous sight before her. It was there, strong and sure, but she did not respond to her name.

"Bors, come help. We need to get her back above," Hwyfar commanded. The knight did not even hesitate a moment, nor did he question her use of magic.

"What is this blight?" Bors asked.

"Is the castle safe?" Llachlyn asked.

Hwyfar's gut lurched at the thought. They would need to go somewhere else, away from danger. There was no explanation for Bors, and no comfort she could give Llachlyn.

"Bors. Show us to the first fork. If we go left, there is an exit to the green, where the great tree still stands. We will go to the armory first, and if the knights have secured the castle, we will bring her there. If not, then I know of a place."

She would have to return, and soon. That same uncanny prickling warned her. Though they had come and gone years before her own powers bloomed, there was no doubt whose magic was here, and what had drawn Anna down to the depths.

Merlin.

Nimue.

For hadn't they been captured in a tree? And the tree yet lived. And, perhaps, as the mirror had shown them, this was what Vyvian had been holding back all these years.

Hwyfar went to steady Anna's hand as Bors picked her up, and as she did two small, flat objects fell from the woman's hand to the ground.

Kneeling down, Hwyfar picked them up and turned them over in her own dimming light. Serpent's scales, large as the dried pods of a lunaria plant—one white and one red.

In the armory, Hwyfar fell against the cold stone to breathe, steadying herself. Lady Anna was well-situated, and Llachlyn was tending to her with sweet consideration.

Hwyfar's whole body felt bruised. Her magic had not

responded that way in time out of mind, and she needed far more sleep than she had been granted.

She was so out of her depth, entirely lost to her power, alone in this place, untrained and unmoored. How could she have ever thought coming back here was going to help matters? They were all in danger, and if the court wasn't going to tear itself to shreds of its own accord, the whole castle was going to come down upon them.

Vyvian. Modrun. Morgen. Anna. One by one, they were falling away, and she could do nothing to stop the tide. Merlin's magic had left an impression on her skin, and she recognized the wrongness of it on her now.

If wishing could have brought back Morgen, Hwyfar's plea to the goddess would have conjured her immediately.

"Breathe," came Gawain's voice, rushing over her with calm, solid welcome. "I'm right here."

And he was. She fell into his arms, face hot but tearless, breathing in the scent of him and reveling in the solidity of his body.

"Your mother…" Hwyfar tried.

"I know. I spoke with Bors. You looked as if you needed a moment to yourself," he said gently, pressing his brow to hers.

She hesitated to ask. "The King?"

Gawain took a long, measured breath. "I got waylaid on the way to his quarters, but I hear he's with Mordred in the chapel. I have not been in to see them yet—I wanted you to come with me. I did not think I could manage it alone."

"To the chapel?" Goddess, it had been a long enough day as it was without having to parade herself before the priests.

"I'll be there with you, and you arrayed as a warrior; they would be fools to spurn you," Gawain said. "Arthur is very troubled, from what I hear. Bedevere told me Arthur himself carried Mordred from the rubble—bore him on his back—until rescue came. They're calling it a miracle."

"Oh, the Christians will love that image," Hwyfar said. "Like St. Christopher, I suspect."

"He loves his son," Gawain said. "We can often do things greater than ourselves when we love completely."

"And what of the Queen? Has she been accounted for?"

"She has not left her room and is refusing all guests save Father Scurfa. Her chamber is far from the worst of it, so I suppose she's safe enough." He paused, looking over her shoulder and then gently leading her away from those gathered behind them.

Hwyfar was strangely relieved to hear her sister was safe. She did not enjoy the intermingled love and hate she held for her, and even summoning up a mote of pity was difficult. But the idea of having to see Mawra beneath the rubble, or sprawled out as Lady Anna had been, unsettled her.

"You smell like spoiled eggs," Gawain said, taking a lock of her hair in his fingers.

"Where we found your mother…"

"Bors said Mother was in the dungeons—well, below them."

"Indeed. And it reeked. There were roots everywhere. It had an evil feel to it, Gawain. Take every joy we felt together with the Green Knight, that connection and understanding and wonder, and find its utter opposite. That was what it felt like."

"What was she doing there?"

Hwyfar had not let go of the scales, and she held them out to Gawain. The edge of each was chipped slightly, as if it had clung onto some skin or flesh before being taken off.

"The tree—where Nimue trapped Merlin," Hwyfar said slowly. "It has grown up under the castle. That would explain some of the movement—I think this is what Vyvian was keeping at bay, a danger she did not share with us. I would think the worst is over, except that these were in your mother's hands."

Gawain took the white scale and turned it over, face scrunched in concentration. "What is it?"

"They look like scales to me."

"What kind of creature would have scales so large?"

"Only one I can think of," Hwyfar said.

CHAPTER THIRTY-EIGHT

GAWAIN

GAWAIN WAS NOT well. He was not well at all.

Firstly, he had lied to his wife. Secondly, he had fallen deep into the throes of his war-mind, and barely escaped.

There had been nothing amiss as he first departed toward the King's wing. In fact, though his heart still beat fast, and his body was rebelling against the sudden activity, he was emboldened, as if he had a purpose. Arthur needed him. The court needed him. With Lanceloch gone, he had a reason to help. He would escort the King to safety, meet up with Bedevere and Cai, and figure out what was going on. Years of tactical warfare had given him an edge during these moments, and he could be strong for them all.

He had made it down one flight of stairs before he saw a young girl, one of the serving maids, crushed up against the side of the wall where an iron candelabrum had fallen over her. No. Not over her—*through* her. Blood covered the ground, reflecting like black pools in the light, and the low, gurgling sound she made sent a thrill of horror down Gawain's arms and into his chest.

Then came the stench as her body voided itself in fear and death, and with it the memory of battlefields long ago: hot corpses rotting in the sun, the sound of swords whispering through flesh to stop the needless suffering...

Gawain had not even noticed that he'd ended it for her. He stood, hands shaking, tears falling down his face, gasping for air, a dagger still in his hands. There were wounds one could not come back from, he knew that—of course he did. But this girl had had a life, had a family. The only reason she was dead was because she had been walking down the corridor, doing her job. She couldn't have been older than Llachlyn.

He fell to the floor, body shaking, unable to feel his hands or his face. There had only ever been this corridor, this dead body, this pool of blood. There had never been joy or laughter or warmth. All was dust.

Gawain was dust.

Food for worms.

Drowning in blood.

Breathe, Gawain.

An apparition, a wisp of recollection: a slip of a girl with golden hair and eyes like deep cool pools of water. Her hands, so small, taking his, as she traced little stars on the inside of his palm.

Gweyn. Before the world had broken her. Gweyn, his dearest friend, the one who saw past his bluster and rage. Gweyn, who had brought him and Hwyfar together, somehow, even after she had crossed over to death.

What brings you peace?

Hwyfar. She needed him. No, *he* needed *her*.

He could not say how long he sat there in the dark, watching the girl's blood slowly congeal, but the sound of distant bells helped him shake off the worst of his woe. Gawain's hands no longer shook, and it seemed no one had seen him—he was utterly alone with the girl's corpse.

"I will send someone for you, little dove," Gawain managed to choke out.

The journey toward the King's quarters took far longer than it should have, and not just due to the state of the castle. Gawain fought panic every step of the way, and pain on top of that. He welcomed the pain, though, for it grounded him in the material world, and helped him push away from his mind's broken tricks.

What brings you pain, Gawain?

He threw off his blood-stained fur and listened to the progressively quieter castle. Good, most of the people had found their way out. He tried not to think of his own cowardice, falling apart as he had, in contrast. There were hundreds of souls in need of helping and he couldn't even make his way out of his own wing of the castle to find them.

It was hard to judge how much time had passed, but far more than would be seemly for him to show up now with the King.

Slowly, but with determination, Gawain made his way down to the courtyard, where the last of the knights remained.

Sygremors was there, and Bors beside. Lanval. Lucan. Palomydes.

Palomydes took one look at Gawain and was beside him, checking for injuries, even though they both knew what ailed him was not an affliction of the body. The knight began singing, low and sweet, in the comforting way that had brought Gawain back from the brink dozens of times before.

Gods, he was grateful for his friend.

The panic subsided, and Gawain could breathe once again.

"Have you seen my brothers?" Gawain asked Palomydes.

"Aye, I have. Galahad I saw with his squire, not long ago, both on horseback. Gareth is at the armory and Gaheris is in the chapel with the King and... the prince."

"Is the prince dead?" Dread threatened to choke Gawain again, but Palomydes' grip tightened on his arm, rooting him to the earth.

"Severely injured, according to the report. As is the King," replied the knight, woefully. His dark eyes were wet in the firelight from the lit lanterns, and morning was still a way off. "The King retrieved Mordred from the rubble himself. Bedevere and I barely got to them in time before the second story collapsed. The prince's tower took the brunt of the damage."

"Any word of my wife?" Gawain asked, his mind frantically categorizing everyone he loved and could lose. "My mother?"

"We found your mother deep below the dungeons," said Bors, coming up to join in the conversation. His big, white teeth flashed in the dark as he grimaced. "The princess and I were able to deliver her to the armory, and Llachlyn with us."

Good. They were all safe for now. Not well, but safe.

"Gawain…"

He'd started moving toward the armory without a second thought. He had to find his wife. He had to hold her.

"I'm fine," Gawain said to Bors. "When Bedevere gives the assessment of the structure, send troops inside to clear away the detritus and see to the dead. Get Cai to number and name the dead—find what priests you can, to see to the survivors."

He could hear his own voice, as if coming from a distance. Had he not given the same commands countless times before, upon battlefields and battlements across the realm? How was he now doing the same, inside his own castle? War had found him, yet again. Though today he did not know his enemy.

Now, AFTER BEING blessedly reunited with his wife, with a scarlet cloak from the armory wrapped around his shoulders, Gawain prepared to meet the King and the injured prince. With Hwyfar by his side, peace was possible.

The chapel was dark even during the day, and with hundreds of yellow candles flickering low, filling the air with a thick, murky fog, it felt like a crypt.

Dozens of people—mostly lords and ladies, their families, and some of the most prized castle staff—crouched together in groups by the statues and paintings along the sides. There were a number of smaller chapels built into the northern end of the nave, and this is where Cai led them.

Gawain did not miss the looks of judgement and, in some cases, disgust, as he and his wife made their progress. Perhaps the younger folk did not remember Hwyfar's reputation, but these priests certainly did. They were the most religious, most affluent, and most connected. Hwyfar, no doubt, was a cautionary tale to them.

If she noticed, or cared, she did not so much as flinch. Hwyfar stood, firelight glinting off of her copper hair and flashing across the spun gold of her long, brocaded night robe, which she had tied over her armor. She did not bear all the trappings of royalty, yet held herself with more poise than any of her sisters had ever managed.

She squeezed his hand as they crossed under a pointed arch to the Lily Chapel, dedicated to Christ's mother.

Inside, the prince lay on a small altar, draped in an outlandish embroidered chasuble now serving as a blood-stained blanket. His pale, handsome face was still and unmoving, half of his black hair plastered against his brow with blood.

He looked like someone, but Gawain could not arrange the features to make sense. It was there, lurking in Gawain's mind, but the connection stayed out of reach.

The King leaned up against the altar, his eyes closed, draped with a long, velvet blanket. He was still in his night chemise, blood smeared all over it, with hastily tied boots upon his feet. There was even blood smeared in his white beard.

Father Olwein, one of the priests Gawain found remotely tolerable, gently roused the King.

"Gawain," Arthur gasped, trying to get to his feet.

Gawain was there, catching his uncle without so much as a thought. His body was so light, the bones so fragile, and Gawain's heart thumped in alarm.

"Uncle," Gawain said, letting the King rest his head upon his chest. "We came as soon as we heard."

"What grim days these be," Father Olwein said, shaking his head. He was younger than most of the priests, perhaps in his thirtieth year, and bald as a plucked chicken.

"Tell us what befell the prince, Father Olwein," Hwyfar said.

The priest seemed surprised at being addressed, perhaps supposing he might erupt into flames at the Princess of Lyonesse's attention. She stared him down, hands on her hips, and waited.

"The princess is a healer," Arthur said, his voice strangely clear as he pulled away from Gawain. "Let her examine Mordred."

"Sire, if God chooses to grant Mordred life, so it will be. We have no need of pagan interference," Father Olwein said, as kindly as he could.

"Pagan interference, as you called it, is what delivered this crown, and pays your tithes," Arthur snapped. His eyes were wide, his brows down, and there was no mistaking the command in his voice.

Bobbing his head, the priest stood out of the way.

"It is strange how your priests seem to revere Merlin, yet still fear and misunderstand the women of the Isles," Hwyfar observed coolly, striding over to Mordred. "But I suppose the old man is not here to directly defend himself, and so we are better targets. Men are always remembered in death with the sheen of reverence, while women seem to only diminish, reduced to patient mothers, crones, or whores."

Gawain's unease grew, seeing the flicker of concern on Hwyfar's face as she lifted the chasuble. He caught her eye, seeing real fear in her expression, but she remained calm.

"Father Olwein," Hwyfar said, "what is your assessment of the prince's condition?"

The priest made the sign of the cross, hastily, as if Hwyfar's mere question somehow compromised his faith. Cretin.

"A beam fell upon him, across his head and chest. There is a considerable amount of bruising across his ribs, but I do not think any bones are broken," said Father Olwein.

"Has he at any point been conscious?" Gawain asked.

"On and off, then he wasn't," King Arthur replied. "We were able to get him some tinctures to ease the pain."

Hwyfar was no longer listening, Gawain could tell. She rarely used her powers around others, and healing was by no means her strongest inclination. No matter, though, she changed when she drifted into the current of power: her eyes dimmed, her skin seemed to glow slightly, and her movements became uncanny in their precision. Gawain wondered if she saw the world differently when she was part of her magic—she had said as much, of course, but could not describe it to him in language that made sense. She said it was like trying to explain the feeling of one's own thoughts.

Gently, she ran her hands over the prince's body. She closed her eyes and pursed her lips, though he knew she was certainly saying some kind of refrain in her mind. Focusing on the goddess often helped her, given how unpredictable her own powers were. She was a rare woman, able to blend three types of magic: healing, movement through space, and connection. Each came from one of three islands: Avillion, Lyonesse, and Ys. Along with their connection to the Green Knight, his wife was indeed one of the most powerful in generations.

Yet it was a dangerous time for powerful women. If it had ever been safe; he could not say.

Mordred shuddered as tiny, scarlet dewdrop-sized spheres fell from Hwyfar's outstretched hands and sank into his chest. She coughed in response, and Gawain went to her immediately.

Their connection, their *carioz*, thrashed in pain.

"Do not stretch yourself too far, my love," Gawain whispered to her. He knew well the price healing could take on its wielder.

She ignored him, and instead looked over to King Arthur, who gazed at her in wonder.

"I can help stabilize him, but there are herbs, medicines, which would help him if I could access them—there might be some in Morgen's tower, or elsewhere... Most are fairly simple, but it would put my mind at ease to fortify his body as much as possible."

"Someone would have to risk the journey," King Arthur said. "Perhaps we ought to send knights?"

"We will go."

They all turned to see Percival in the doorway, having somehow managed to slip into the room along with Galahad, Llachlyn watching them with a mixture of relief and wariness. They were covered in dust, looking like ghostly versions of themselves, but resolute, too. For the first time since meeting him, Gawain sensed the mettle of a warrior in Percival. He stood with his hands across his chest, eyes blazing with a kind of resolve impossible to overlook.

CHAPTER THIRTY-NINE

PERCIVAL

PERCIVAL FELL TO his knees, Galahad and Llachlyn following suit, knowing his interruption had been a breach of decorum. He had seen what Hwyfar had done and was, honestly, quite surprised Father Olwein hadn't tried to burn her at the stake right there.

He supposed if it were for anyone else but the crown prince, his reaction might have been different.

In the last hour, he and Galahad had worked with the other knights, rescuing at least eight people from the rubble. Only a few were unaccounted for, and they had decided to take a rest.

Then, they'd come upon Llachlyn. After tearfully reuniting and apologizing to each other—mostly to Galahad on Llachlyn's part—she told them what had happened to Prince Mordred, and Galahad insisted they go looking for him to see what they might do to help. The fellow was absolutely beside himself with worry about his cousin, especially after hearing how Arthur himself had dragged him out of the fallen tower.

"My young ones," King Arthur said, gently and without judgement. "You offer great courage in this time of need, but were I to accept your offer it would put you at great risk."

"With your pardon, Your Majesty," said Percival, taking a hesitant step forward after standing up, "we have just escaped great peril. And we have ways of getting into the castle, or at least through parts of it, that others may not know of."

To Percival's surprise Arthur looked almost amused at this, then turned his attention to Gawain. Both nodded to one another. He realized how daft he was thinking King Arthur, who had lived in the castle since just before his beard came in, would have missed something like hidden passageways.

"There is also the matter of what lies beneath the castle," Hwyfar said, frowning. "As I'm certain Llachlyn told you."

"Yes," Galahad said, all bravado. "We are prepared to fight whatever needs vanquishing."

Percival almost chuckled.

"I do not think it wise to storm to the under dungeon presently, Sir Galahad," King Arthur said. "At least, not until we have some more answers. For now, though, focus on Prince Mordred's life."

IT WAS DIFFICULT to breathe, Percival realized, as he picked his way through the rubble of what had once been Merlin's tower. Two whole floors had fallen, and in the dreary morning light, he caught brief glimpses of the opulence once enjoyed by the prince. A broken bauble here, a scrap of cloth there, the shattered body of a lute.

Mists shrouded the castle, dampening their hair and making the space difficult to navigate. Llachlyn took the lead, being the smallest of them all, but it was Galahad who knew where to look.

Llachlyn was most disapproving. "You're telling me, Galahad, that you've been going to the prince for tinctures. You, of all people."

Galahad looked pale but striking as he straightened atop a heap of rubble—what once might have been a richly tiled cupboard. Then he made a face like he'd smelled a foul egg. "Me of all people? I suppose as a du Lac, I must simply shoulder every single burden I'm given without so much as a complaint?"

"That's not what I meant," Llachlyn retorted, pulling aside some mangled wood.

Percival leaned over to help her. It had been a ladder once, he thought. "I think she means you typically eschew such assistance in lieu of prayer."

"You weren't stuck here for weeks alone, without you two. Playing through everything that happened, over and over again," Galahad said, catching his balance as one of the boards tilted underneath him. "Prayer can only take a man so far before he begins to unravel."

"Either way, I suppose we must be glad you did, otherwise we'd have no chance of finding anything," Llachlyn said, looking up to the remainder of the higher story. She pointed to a small outcropping where the floor once held, and an archway was still intact. "You want me to climb up there?"

Galahad nodded. "It looks like his entire potions alcove was spared in the earthquake. It was a sort of ante room, off the side of that floor. There should be all sorts of bottles in there. We can grab everything we can manage, and hope Princess Hwyfar recognizes the contents."

"I can recognize things very well, thank you," Llachlyn said, hands on her hips. "One's understanding of herbs has naught to do with one's magical prowess."

Percival was not terribly fond of the idea of Llachlyn going up there all by herself. Her eyesight wasn't terribly good, and her coordination even worse.

"I'll go up first," he volunteered, watching how she hesitated. "I've got a few inches on you both, anyway."

"You?" Llachlyn asked. "I've seen you trip and fall trying to mount a horse."

That was true. But also, not the point. Percival was seized by a very irrational desire to impress Galahad, even though he was quite cross with him and would prefer to avoid any conversation on the subject of what happened before the castle tried to collapse in on itself.

"Exactly," Percival said simply, managing to pick his way to the wall where he could, indeed, reach the exposed beam. It wouldn't be hard to get to the outcropping, so long as someone could hold him up. "I've been tossed around enough to know how to recover."

"Percival…" Galahad nearly whined his name. "It isn't safe."

"Not this again," Percival said.

"Not what again?" Llachlyn asked.

"Galahad thinks the earthquake was due to his own personal failings, and I think now he's afraid we're going to wake it again."

"I didn't say that," Galahad argued.

"It was strongly implied," Percival said, forcing himself to look away from Galahad and toward his next challenge. "And while I do think Sir Galahad is very important, I also do not believe God is so concerned with the matters of his life he would go to such lengths to rebuke him."

Llachlyn was just beside him now, and she looked up at him. She was clever. He had no doubt she had noticed the strained air between them. "I told you both, it's a presence in the under dungeon. It was like what we saw at the Green Chapel, Percival, but—*wrong*."

At the comparison, Percival shivered. He tried not to think about that day very often, because speaking with the creature had unveiled some considerable complications to his life he'd prefer not to have to detangle yet.

"I really ought to be the one to go," Llachlyn said when he did not reply.

"You *both* have impressive pedigrees," Percival insisted, testing his boot against a crevice. It was firm enough. "If anything happens to you, there are high-standing nobles of the most import to the realm who will morn you. If I die, it will simply be another of Pellinore's supposed bastards lost to time and fate. No title. No lands. No holdings. No great deeds, even! Just remembered as a fellow who had a habit of befriending people far more important than he."

It was perhaps an unkind assessment, but it was no less true. Strangely, Percival didn't care. He did not need to be great.

Never, in all his life, had he entertained deeds of valor and renown. Yes, he had accomplished what was expected of him, and he wasn't the worst squire. But the idea of ascending to such heights as Galahad reached made him feel ill.

The Green Knight had indicated he was more, of course, but he was still a bastard. It did not matter, truly, who his father and mother were, because Percival was his own person. He always had been. And in the face of danger, and near death, he wasn't about to risk his friends' lives.

Percival wanted truly little save the favor of his friends, and he loved no two people more than the ones with him now. Even if their relationships were fraught—they were bound to be.

"You are important," Llachlyn said.

For a moment Percival thought he saw tears glistening in her eyes, but then they were gone.

"I didn't say I wasn't important," Percival said, heaving himself up on the wall. He scrambled for footing, but then was able to get himself quite well situated. It really wasn't that high a climb. "I just said you were *more* important."

That settled, Galahad helped Percival get to the next foothold, and then he was on his own. He didn't dare look down, as he was not terribly fond of heights, but also knew he might lose his resolve if he saw the two of them again.

Just as he was about to reach the outcropping, he lost his footing, and only barely regained his balance to pull himself up again. Below he heard shouts, and he called down, his voice shaking, to assure them he had not perished.

The breeze blew his hair, making his skin erupt into prickles as his sweat cooled. Breathing deep, lips dry and bleeding from gnawing, he slowly stood. Thankfully, the boards across the floor were mostly unharmed, and indeed, he could see the little threshold Galahad described.

And yes, there were hundreds of little bottles up on shelves on the other side—though many of them had fallen loose, their contents muddied and spilled at his feet.

It was not that, however, that took his attention. For when the castle had shaken, it had knocked loose another wonder, revealing an inner wall somehow bricked over, likely during the construction of Merlin's tower.

"Llachlyn—Galahad…" Their names tasted like fire in his throat. "You must come up here—you must see what I'm seeing."

CHAPTER FORTY

MORGEN

To BEHOLD TINTAGEL in such a state smote me to my heart. I did not think I'd cared, even as I'd braced myself for the inevitable changes in the landscape. At my age, change was not unusual. I had delivered children who now had children of their own, or who had died as men upon the battlefield. Carelon had grown from a sturdy castle to the greatest city in the realm, and I remembered every brick.

This, though, was not simply change—this was more insidious. Purposeful deterioration, willing neglect. The scent of spoiled crops greeted us first, and then the clouds of flies, so thick upon the horizon I thought at first it must be smoke. Though I spied some tenants and farms, most were abandoned. Those left occupied were in such a state of disrepair I did not want to think how they lived inside them.

"My father would never have stood for such shameful disrepair," I told Coel as we rode, side by side, down the mud-slick road leading to the castle.

Tintagel rose in the distance, black stone covered in dead vines, punctuated by plumes of smoke. We marked many wagon wheel tracks, and indications of both horse and man walking, as well as their cast-offs. It was a large host, and I had no doubt King Marqus was here.

"Much as I would like to blame King Marqus for all of this, it looks as if the land was let go long before his visit," Coel said.

"Sir Cador was not the most present liege, so wrapped up in overthrowing King Leodegraunce and allying with Prince Ryence. And it has been ten years since anyone claimed the land—for fear of your retribution, I think," said Ahés.

I clenched my teeth in anger—at myself, more than anyone. I ought to have visited more, I ought to have insisted to Arthur that I, like so many of his court, had a place to retire to when the clamor of daily life grew unbearable. But I did not. I remained, as ever, stalwart and immovable and dedicated to Carelon, and the Circle of Nine, and Arthur, and...

It would not do to come to King Marqus in fury, for he was skeptical of women at best and murderous at worst, and known for his frequent bouts of jealousy and violence. Even our own few conversations over the years had been strained.

As we approached the castle, and I took in the utter devastation of the landscape, I had to bite down on the inside of my mouth to keep from weeping. My mother had lived here, had loved here, had been deceived and raped and ruined here. I had begun here; Arthur, too. Merlin's treachery cemented within these very walls. How was I to hold it all in?

The wood to the north now crowded so close to the castle, it looked as if it might devour it whole. I almost wish it had. Better to be destroyed by nature than endure this half-life.

At the gatehouse we were met by a pair of suspicious-eyed knights. Thankfully, they recognized both King Urien's chains—which he had donned at my insistence—and Ahés. They did not ask my name, nor did I offer it. Doubtless, after my travails, I looked like a crone half in the grave, and not the sorceress sister of the High King of Braetan.

Horns blew perfunctorily, and unseen hands pulled up the portcullis, the squeaking and grinding resonating through me in a most unpleasant way. A groom took our horses, and I was reminded of Penryn, the kindly ostler who'd taught me how to ride a pony in this very stable yard. I hadn't thought of him in years. Had Uther killed him, along with everyone else in the household? I had never asked. I couldn't bear the answers.

How many secrets had I buried in my pain? How much was interred by grief?

The king's presence in Tintagel should have called for some measure of decorum, but it could not have been farther from the truth. Before us, the sickening scene played out, and we were all but ignored. Against my better judgement, I clasped Coel's hand to steady me. He gave me a look of understanding, and squeezed my fingers back.

The court had been hunting, but instead of bringing the spoils to the barns or kitchens, their quarry had been gutted and left to drain all down the long entryway to the great hall. Boars, hares, deer, and hundreds of smaller creatures strewn about, bloodying the once white and blue tiled floor. The stench was horrific, to say nothing of the noise of the flies.

The path through my beloved Tintagel ran red with blood, and my heart stuttered with the weight of this omen.

Ahès choked down a retch, and I stroked her back while she gathered herself.

Feet slick with mud and blood, we at last made our way to the great hall. My heart pounded, my vision prickled, and it was too much to absorb all the details at once.

The great hall had been a place of joy, and even though I'd been a small child, I still remembered the brightness, the silken banners streaming from the vaulted ceiling, the great tapestries of the unicorn hunt stretching the length of the long walls. I had learned to walk in this hall, had been chased by my sister Elaine, had sorted flowers and seeds upon the dark wooden floors. I had been happy, my magic awakening in my body, my family whole.

Now, all was a cruel mockery.

King Marqus sat in my father's chair, picking at his teeth. He was striking, Marqus, with black hair gone only slightly frosted at the brow and keen blue eyes, a powerful body honed by years of sparring and hunting. His raiment was fair, his jewels golden and polished. But he ruled from a throne above a mass of decaying wreckage.

Perhaps there had been a fire, or a flood. Or both. What remained of the furniture was unrecognizable, save for a few benches upon which sat King Marqus's retinue. Perhaps twenty men, all wearing his colors of black stripes on silver, glanced up from their conversations as we entered.

One more figure sat by the great hearth. She was a small creature, but sturdy in her build, with long legs for running and strong shoulders, draped from head to toe in fine, golden fur. Sadness clung to her, though, like a heavy mantle, and magic, too. I had no doubt, even without seeing her face, this was Queen Isolde.

King Marqus looked up at our approach. A slow, predatory smile spread across his face, teeth white and glinting.

"Morgen le Fay," he said, his voice rising high and clear. All the murmuring, eating, and whispering came to an abrupt halt.

I did not fail to notice the lack of formal announcement for a king, a high priestess, and the sister to the High King. However, we were terribly outnumbered, and goddesses' breath, I regretted listening to Modrun. I had assumed she meant for me to come to Cornwall, to Tintagel, to find answers to my own past—to learn how to combat this snare Merlin had laid before his death.

Instead, I was in a snare, well and truly caught. This man was mad, the presence around him so evil I felt it on my skin.

Still, I calmed my mind. I was no novice, and I had stared down worse before and walked away with my life.

I fell into a curtsey, as low and elegant as I could muster in such a state. "Your Grace," I said to King Marqus, never letting my gaze fall from his face, challenging him to look away.

King Marqus stood, brushing off the velvet tunic he wore, as if he'd just realized he had guests and might want to make a good impression. "And who else do we bring here? An old king and a fading priestess who was once a princess. An odd gathering."

Coel inclined his head but did not bow. "It has been years

since we've had reason to cross paths, Your Majesty, but I thank you for your courtesy in welcoming us."

"King Uriens of Rheged. So very far from home," King Marqus observed, standing beside me, but turning to give Coel his entire attention. "Strange, I hear your ships came from off Avillion—near Brocéliande, to be exact—which is curious, as I did not think any ships were permitted there, by the witch within."

"Modrun is dead," I said, bowing my head to show my grief and respect, though I knew Marqus would not. "And I have King Uriens, and his son, Prince Yvain, to thank for my life."

"Strange, that. *You* were supposed to be dead," King Marqus said. He poked a sharp finger at me, and I realized he was quite drunk. "The great Morgen le Fay, they told me, vanished after the death of poor old Vyvian du Lac, with no sign. Everyone was quite distraught, but then they went on, as they tend to do."

We had discussed our answer to this question, but I was still bothered at how quickly—and bitterly—King Marqus began this line of questioning.

"There are matters beyond the kenning of kings," I said to him. "As you ought to know. And times where, though I would wish it otherwise, I must separate myself even from the realm of my brother, the High King. I will soon send word, as the realm is in peril. But for now, I was directed here."

King Marqus grinned again, now stroking his beard thoughtfully. "To my favorite new castle. Which is rather marvelous. Isn't it marvelous, Isolde?"

Isolde, still at the hearth, turned around slowly. Even in this fetid place, her beauty shone with an otherworldly splendor. But so, too, did her sorrow. Her face was carved from marble, her eyes wide-set and clever, her lips full and bowed, her skin smooth and her hair dark as a raven's wing. But, goddess, she was as sorrowful as if she had drunk from the Cup itself, her whole body curved like a tear in grief and separation. How long would this infernal war rage between Marqus and his nephew?

For a moment, as she caught my eye, I saw defiance in her. I could swear I felt it. One of her gloved hands clenched, and then she turned around again to look into the flames.

"We have just finished a hunt this morning," King Marqus said, clapping his hands together, the sound echoing around the hall. "You might have noticed our unconventional decor. But there is just so much ripe for the picking. And I find it keeps unwanted visitors at bay."

"As king, you may do as you please," I said.

King Marqus laughed, cold and brief. "The woods are overrun with creatures, so I have done a favor to the place. But I have other aims, as well. You see, it is rumored the Questing Beast, the Glatisant, roams these lands. What better way to lure her here than to provide fresh prey?"

"Clever, Your Majesty," Ahès said. "Long have men sought the Glatisant."

Did he know it was the same lie Merlin told my father? Did the castle itself recall? I felt time folding in on itself, strange and doubling, a wheel—an end.

The king looked around the room with bleary, unfocused eyes, then wiped at the side of his face. "I'm afraid Tintagel isn't what it used to be, but we can have a few rooms set aside for you if you wish to rest. Tonight, we shall dine together by the fire outside, as we used to do in times of old."

Nothing about this felt right. I did not want to break bread with this brutal king, nor stay in the company of his evil-eyed soldiers. I wanted to sneak poison into his flagon.

I noticed Coel stiffening by my side, but Ahès was the one to reply.

"Our gratitude, Your Majesty. It has been a long journey for us all, and we look forward to sharing our story with you."

SOME HOURS LATER, I awoke from an all too brief rest.

At least, this far from the carnage of the great hall, the stench was gone. Granted, it smelled like old wine casks and the rinds of moldering cheese, but I had clearly supplanted someone else in the room, for it was clean and felt lived-in.

Someone was knocking on my door.

I was relieved to find Coel standing there, holding a small platter of dried fruit and hazelnuts, my stomach twisting in hunger and my heart dancing treacherously.

"I'm certain you're hungry by now," he said, handing the platter to me with an imploring look. "I must apologize, there was twice as much when I received the platter, but I could not help myself."

He also produced a small flask of wine, which I took most enthusiastically. It was thick, sweet, and spiced, but I managed to drink half of it swiftly, welcoming the hot sting. Perhaps it would clear my head. Or dull it. I could not decide which I wanted more.

I ushered him into the room and closed the door behind him, steeling myself for a conversation with him that was well overdue. Here was as good of a place as any, I supposed.

"I have the sweeping apartment next door," Coel said, taking another dried plum and gnawing on it. It was easy to forget he was a king, sometimes, especially when he ate like an enthusiastic bairn hardly past their full teething. "It has a window. Though the vines have grown over it. Your view is unimpeded, which I would count as a mark of esteem from our host."

"The priestesses used to stay here, the ones who taught my sisters and me. Friends my mother brought from Avillion," I said, surprised at the memory. I had not thought of them in ages. I glanced around, finding a sense of comfort. "In fact, in this very room, my mentor, Valda, slept and prayed and reflected. We would spin together, sometimes, here. Though the wheel is long gone, along with most of the furniture."

"Valda. I had an Aunt Valda. She used to beat me every time I stole from the larder at her house. Which was often, as she always had the best sweets."

It was not so difficult to imagine Coel as a child doing just that, especially given how he licked at his fingers.

"This Valda was from Avillion. She had taught my mother and was as close to a nursemaid as we had, save she began our foundations in magic. We had a druid, too, named Jowan, but I suspect they are long dead…"

Coel sighed, drawing his hand over the thick sill of the single window in the room and then wiping the dust from his fingers. Which was difficult, given he had just eaten honeyed dates. "I wanted to see how you were faring. It cannot be easy to face this place alone."

"I am more than capable of managing my emotions—and even the ghosts of my past," I said to him. "You do not need to mind me like a lost lamb."

As if sensing my thoughts, he sat down on the cot and held out his hands to me as if in supplication. "I know you don't trust me, Morgen, but I do wish you would try. Have I ever given you reason otherwise?"

I had not wanted to entertain this conversation, yet I'd stumbled directly into it. "No, but I have learned, in my long life, that one must only wait for a man's treachery, as it almost always rises to the surface."

"You stopped writing me."

"I did."

"I did not stop writing you."

I had directed the messengers from Rheged to burn all correspondence from Coel to me, ages ago. He was nothing but kind, reflective, poetic, and sweet in his correspondence, never stooping to insipid love poetry or doggerel, but instead reflecting on the seasons, the plants and animals, the flow of magic in his world. He only complimented me when the pain of our separation grew too much for him to bear. Still, he was as good a man as I could have ever asked for, and that was the tragedy of it. His missives reminded me of how trapped I truly was, and it was far easier imagining freedom when I could not so well taste the shape of his life in Rheged.

Sighing, resigned to this conversation, I finished my wine and squared my shoulders. "If anyone is to be distrusted, or scolded, it is me. I walked from you."

"Aye, you did," he said, though without reproach or anger in his voice. Merely an observation.

"And I understand you owe me a debt for helping Yvain, but I relieve you of it here and now. We are embroiled in dangers far more than even I had suspected, and it is not your fight to pursue. Especially not here, with a diabolical tyrant such as Marqus."

Coel leaned back on the cot, splaying his hands behind him, as if to get a better look at me. "So, your reason for dismissing me, a king and knight of the realm both battle-hardy and attentive, is because you are in *more* danger than you'd initially thought?"

"Yes."

"I do not think it is the soundest logic, Morgen."

"Perhaps not."

"Then can we perhaps agree to friendship?"

"I do not have friends," I said.

"Why do you feel you must take everything on your own shoulders alone? You must be exhausted from pushing everyone in your life from you. And miserable!"

I flinched. "I am not miserable. You presume too much, King Uriens."

Oh, but I *was* miserable. And I had been miserable for so long, I had forgotten what hope felt like. What love and friendship could do to nourish a person's soul. I was hollowed out by grief and the weight of Carelon's future, my choices, and Arthur's dreams. I knew it could not hold, but then, no one had ever asked me to lay down my burdens, either, or offered to carry them for me.

"It's the truth." Coel was unflinching, anger in the set of his jaw, now. "I don't think you're used to people speaking so straightforwardly with you. But I am a king, and I may do so if I please."

"I would rather we not speak of these things. Not here. It is vexing, and I am tired."

"I vex you because I tell you the truth. Because I know, twenty years ago, you wanted to marry me. You *loved* me. You never said it plainly, and goddess knows I never expected a romance of passion and impulse, but you fled to the captivity of Merlin and Arthur and away from what it would mean to give your heart, even a part of it, because you could not be a wife *and* a sorceress. And I understood. Because I have had to push people to the edges of my life, too. As a king—and a reluctant one at that—I have spent my days sizing up every single person who walks into my castle. I have had to learn to suspect everyone, even my own children, of subterfuge. But there have always been those special few who I have held to, who I have allowed myself to love and trust. And you were one of them."

This was becoming overwhelming, and I was afraid of the consequences of the discussion. "This is hardly the place," I said, desperate to change the subject, my face hot with unexpressed emotion.

"Don't act as if you haven't carried this place within you since the moment your mother was betrayed," Coel said, his eyes flashing. "Which is what happens when children are broken, and they are never allowed to put together the pieces again. You have spent your whole life doing your best to keep yourself and your family safe—"

"Coel—"

"No, please. Morgen, let me finish." From another man the command would have been unheeded, but there were tears in his eyes and his tone was gentle, almost pleading.

I stilled myself. I was cornered, my whole body ready for flight—but where could I go? Into the carnage downstairs? The idea of finding more of this castle in ruin, more of my childhood defaced and defamed, was too much to bear.

"Very well," I said.

I sat down next to him on the cot, unable to manage my own weight any longer. Cautiously, Coel held out his hand to mine, palm up. I took it, not because I wanted to but because I needed it. Goddess, my whole soul cried out for touch.

Gently, he stroked his thumb over the side of my hand. I didn't have to look at him directly, but I sensed him, every mote of him, beside me, strength and magic and calm. He was trying to fight for me.

No one had ever done that for me before.

When he spoke again, his voice was gentler, but still firm. "I can only begin to know the kind of burdens you have shouldered, Morgen, the secrets you have locked away, the power and the politics you've entrenched yourself in. You were misused as a child—Merlin took advantage of you, and no one was near to defend your honor because you were an asset. No, your *power* was an asset. That shatters a person, down to their very soul, to be seen day in and day out as a pawn. Everyone sees you as untouchable, and you have certainly earned it: I, like them, am in awe of your talents, your beauty, your wisdom. But don't you see? You did not deserve to live so isolated. You did not deserve to live only to survive. And now, more than ever, you must ask for help. Or we will not survive this."

My tears pattered upon my gown, blooming in ragged shapes on the grey wool. I told Coel, once, of my childhood, and of Merlin's behavior toward me. He had been so incensed; he was half-mad with ideas for killing the old conjuror himself. And it was not long after that conversation he had proposed, and I had left.

"I do not see what use it is to bring up the devils of my past when so much is amiss in the realm now," I said, softly as I could. "I do not have time for my own vengeance." Not when my sister Anna had done it first.

"If you do not allow yourself rest, all this will fester inside of you, and I cannot bear to see that happen. Because when Vyvian died, she took the last remnant of your mother with her. And now, here you are, in Tintagel, the very place your life fell apart, and you are expected, once again, to be Morgen le Fay—not Morgen of Cornwall, daughter of Igraine and Gorlois. The terrified little girl who watched her life fall apart before her eyes.

Who capitulated to a monstrous king to save her family and her sisters, but bargained away her own freedom."

"I have done terrible things," I said. "Perhaps with noble aims in the beginning, or out of self-preservation, but I am ashamed of what I have done to maintain Arthur's peace since then. A stroke of a pen here, a whisper there, a spell no one could detect. You would not love me if you knew what I was capable of."

He squeezed my hand tighter, and I could feel the power of it in the center of my being. "I'm not asking for anything other than who you are, right now. For a moment, let yourself grieve— for Vyvian, for your mother, for yourself. I can endure it."

No one had ever seen me like Coel—King Uriens of Rheged— had. Even I, in my age and set ways, could not deny our connection.

Every word he spoke was truth. He might as well have pierced me full of arrows for the pain I felt of it, in that release.

When I finished weeping, I pulled away from Coel and marked the handsome lines of his face, the soft waves of his pewter hair, and did indeed feel a lightness inside me. I did not think I would ever truly heal from what was done to me, nor would I forgive myself for all the machinations I'd been privy to, but allowing this moment of connection was a welcome reprieve.

"Thank you," I said to him. "For sitting with me. Would you mind if we just… stayed here a while?" It was as vulnerable a question as I had ever asked.

Coel relaxed and he let out a long, satisfied sigh. "As long as you need."

And it occurred to me that no one in my recent memory had done such a miraculous thing: to wait for me, to give me space. I was always and forever on someone else's time, at their behest, on their behalf—I did not even own my own time. But here, in the ruin of my childhood home, Coel gave it to me.

"Ahès told me," I said after a moment, "it's possible I was blessed so deeply by the Three my other powers feel dormant now, in comparison."

For a moment, a shadow crossed his expression, as if my

words had troubled him. But then he smiled. "She is wise in ways I will never dream of. And I know you still possess mighty power. You just do not need to shoulder it alone."

I squeezed his hand, bringing his fingers to my lips to kiss them gently, and settled my head on his shoulder to rest my burning eyes.

SOMETIME LATER WE were summoned outside for the feast. I was loath to leave, and even less happy to endure the cold, but I knew not to leave this deplorable tyrant waiting. King Marqus played these games well, and I could not yet sense the particulars of his schemes; until I did, I was at his mercy.

They led us down an old corridor I did not directly recall, descending three flights of stairs, until we reached the long solarium my mother had installed. The large glass panes, a marvel of the age, were long since gone, and now all that remained were the jagged edges of stone and trace work. It looked not unlike the carcass of some strange, ancient being.

King Marqus had employed his men to drag out furniture to the now open-air solarium and clustered it around a large bonfire, which cast long, ghostly shadows on the walls and over the bare ground. There were other fires farther back, over which makeshift spits turned, covering everything with the heavy smell of meat and char.

"Ah, Lady Morgen," King Marqus said, striding up to me and Coel. Ahès was sitting by herself some way away, staring into the cup in her hands, but she did turn her head slightly at his presence. "Perhaps you can help me with a bit of a mystery."

I offered my most deferent expression. "Of course, Your Majesty."

"We were having a dispute over the use of this ruin," he said, gesturing to the broken walls. "One of my advisors said it must have been some kind of temple to one of the ancient goddesses. Another posited a garden. As someone who grew up here, I thought you might be able to enlighten us."

I would not give him this memory, this satisfaction. Already this day I had laid my soul bare—but it was of my own accord. King Marqus had grown wicked with age, and I had no doubt he knew precisely what this room was and what it meant.

The long galley had been hung with plants in the summer and lit with low fires in the winter. My mother had built it to entertain artists, musicians, and writers. Here, the greatest minds of Cornwall came together to tell tales and regale one another. It had also served as an overflow for the library next door. It had been the greatest library outside of Carelon, and people had come from miles around to study and learn. I could always find someone intriguing in the solarium when the library was open to visitors, but I preferred those days when it was closed, when I would find my mother alone, her face raised to the sky, her hands outstretched, welcoming the sun.

"I regret to disappoint you, Your Grace," I said. "I was but a child of five summers when I left Tintagel, and have precious few memories, save for chasing my eldest sister Elaine down the hallways and stealing bread from the kitchens."

King Marqus pursed his lips and then shrugged. "Well, I suppose we shall remain in the dark," he said at last. "Though it doesn't matter much now, does it? I don't suspect the place will last another winter."

I glanced down at the tiles, lit by firelight, noting how the metallic-glazed squares still shimmered. As a child, I had placed rocks on those designs, pretended they were fantastic beasts or flocks of birds, lost in the whorls and colors.

"Perhaps not," I said. "But time is the killer of us all, King Marqus. Though some monuments to our greatness remain longer than others, none of us shall escape the relentless hand of death."

He laughed, short and bitter. "You remind me of Merlin, the way you speak. He always had an adage to share. Perhaps you are right, but though time marches forward for all of us, I think it is the fault of short-sighted men who do not seize power when Fate brings it upon them. That, I suppose, is where kings came from in the first place. Those willing to do what is uncomfortable rather than sit and grow fat in complacent servitude."

Coel, beside me, could not contain his snort. "You have a high opinion of kings, then. For it seems to me, in our age, kings are made more often by the schemes of others rather than seizing anything themselves."

King Marqus rolled his shoulder, clearly unimpressed. "Be as it might, I am a king who does not spurn the opportunities granted to me. And tonight, with your arrival, Lady Morgen, we have a unique opportunity."

This did not surprise me. I bowed my head in a deference I did not feel. "I have suspected you had something you wished to say to me, Your Majesty, since the moment I arrived."

The men around the bonfires had hungry looks in their eyes—wary, still, but far more like a group of revelers about to be entertained by a bard than a mob of second-rate guards and knights awaiting their liege's command. Despite his bloviating, I did not think his soldiers showed much discipline or conviction.

King Marqus nodded, pressing the tips of his fingers together. "I am lately converted, you know, to the Christian faith, alongside my wife, the Queen Isolde. The gods, alas, have long since abandoned me, and I have put this Christ to the test. On my way here, I prayed most fervently that I would find an answer to my deepest frustration. My constant puzzlement."

"I will do all I can to assist you, as you are protected by the peace of Arthur of Braetan, King of the Realm, and I am his humble servant, no matter which god you worship," I said, giving him the most diplomatic answer I could muster.

"Of course, all by now know my plight," he said, striding over to where Isolde sat with a neglected lyre on her lap. He took her by the chin, gently, but with a direct power that made my skin crawl. She did not meet his eye. "My pretty, precious wife has long been the bedfellow of my treacherous nephew, Tristan of Cornwall. Long have I wondered how, in all the realm, a woman such as Isolde would find that petulant, inconstant boy more desirable than me. Me, a blessed and blooded king, strong of body and mind, who never, until now, struggled to convince a cunt to my bed."

I knew well to let the man speak, understanding where the blame would fall no matter his logic. But I was not afraid. Instead, as I looked down at the tiles, awareness sank into me. This was the place of my birth, my birthright. How easy it was to forget, in my grief and sorrow, that I drew my first breath among these stones, and the caul and blood of my birth lay here, nurturing the hazel trees and the gorse bushes. Yes, we were but a few, the three of us, but we were not without power. Ahès commanded the strength of both Avillion and Ys, and though I was much diminished in my abilities, I had risen up against a cockatrice not long ago. Coel, though past his days of glory, was yet fit and focused, and a more than passing druid and healer.

"Indeed," Coel said, catching my subtle expression: *Let us wait*. "The legend of your virility has reached far to the North."

King Marqus pulled out his sword then, catching the attention of every eye. He did not flourish his weapon, or point it with purpose or threat, but he did not need to. It was a fine weapon, perhaps made by Vyvian or one of her few apprentices, carved with twisting inscriptions down the blade and inlaid with garnets at the hilt.

Coel went very still, and Ahès, who had risen to join me, put her hand on my elbow.

Unasked for, her power flooded into me, warm, tinged with the scent of burnt lavender and salt spray. I had to hold back a gasp at the rush of her magic running through me. Tears sprang to my eyes, but I blinked them back, desperate to keep hidden this gift. I did not know she could transfer her power in this way: a gift of Ys, thought long-lost.

I would need it. And soon.

The edge of the wood moaned in the wind, a tree limb snapping in the distance, as I gave a silent prayer of thanks to Iaia.

"Long I have pondered this problem, Morgen," King Marqus said, now staring into the long edge of his blade. "And after much discussion among witnesses, and conversations with my wife, at last I have learned the truth."

"I am glad to hear of it," I said calmly. "Truth is a grand gift, indeed."

"Perhaps for me, now I can rest in my knowing. But not for everyone. You see, now I know that both Isolde and Tristan drank of a love potion upon the ship returning from Eire, when my nephew was meant to simply return my bride to me. He did this to spite me, not because he loved Isolde, but because he wished to take my lands, and Cornwall itself. To usurp my power."

Love potions did not exist. I made many tinctures, and occasionally potions did provide some fortitude or healing properties. But the idea that anyone, even someone of Merlin's ilk, could convince any two hearts they belonged to one another, was madness. It would have saved him immense trouble had he been capable of such enchantments.

Besides, Tristan was many things, but ambitious he was not. Anyone who knew him would laugh at the king's logic—he was impetuous, inconstant, and flippant by turns, but Tristan's love for Isolde, which I had witnessed, was beyond all his shortcomings.

Marqus continued: "But how would such a powerful potion find its way to a useless little brat such as Tristan? Ah, you see, through more discourse, I arrived at a name... Morgen le Fay, known sorceress and consort of Merlin, who provided tonics and potions at a most terrible price. And a cousin to Tristan."

Discourse, indeed. He meant torture.

"I admit, of course, to helping those in need with the application of tonics and tinctures," I said calmly, keeping my hands out before me in a gesture of peace, even though Ahès' power had lit my blood afire. "But I have never exacted a price, nor concocted anything capable of bringing people together in love when love did not already kindle between them."

King Marqus laughed through his nose, that sword rising, now. "There is no use in denying it, Lady Morgen. Perhaps you did not ask a price, but you are, and always have been, a secret-keeper. And who better to tease secrets from than Prince Tristan, poised to overturn his uncle—he knew exactly what he was doing. Do you deny you sold him potions?"

I took a deep, measured breath. "I did not *sell* Tristan any potions. I did give him a selection of tonics meant to assist with long travel, as he is prone to the sickness of the waves, as was his father before him."

Judging by the gasps in the collected entourage, such a confession was damning enough.

"I see God has answered my prayer this day, then, by delivering you into my hands," King Marqus said, the sword's point glinting in the red-flamed fire, reflecting in his eyes. "Christ compels me, then, to exact my vengeance upon you."

Most likely he would let his men kill me, but given the madness and what I now recognized as drunkenness in his eyes, I could not rule out death by his hand. I supposed there were worse ways to cross the threshold than being felled by a king.

"You touch her, Marqus, and I promise you will not live to see another sunrise," Coel growled, his Northern vowels deepening. "She will turn your bones to ash."

Men encircled us, the reek of drink and onions and meat mingling with sweat and dried blood. The smell of burning flesh, left untended in the fires, filled my nostrils and made my stomach churn. I did not often use my powers to bring death, and murdering King Marqus before half his court would pose a significant strain on my own diplomatic sway, if I were ever to reach Carelon again, but I knew it was possible. Here, at Tintagel, where my magic was singing again.

To my surprise, King Marqus signaled his men to put down their swords. There was some grumbling at this, but they complied.

"Very well," King Marqus said, sheathing his own sword rather inelegantly. "Then prove to me God has not anointed me in this task, Lady Morgen. Show me the power the old gods gave you, those demons of the dark."

I did not want to perform for him, did not want to command pretty lights and dancing figures. If I were to demonstrate the power given to me, it would not be in beauty or in ease: it would be in terror.

For I was Morgen le Fay, Daughter of Gorlois, Duke of Cornwall, and Igraine of Avillion, forged in the fires of their love. I knew the bones of this land, the blood of *my* land. Its story was in my marrow, in my veins.

I did not need to rely on illusion, or commanding fire. No, King Marqus had shared his fears with me already. They were littered on the pathway to the castle, bleeding out in the halls. And all the while he had talked, so intent on his own deeds and power, he had not minded the edge of the fire.

Men kill what they most fear. They hunt and maim and brag, celebrating their victories as if they were truly earned.

But I commanded death, and death moved my steps. "May the gods have mercy on you," I said, and closed my eyes and held out my arms as if in supplication.

I could feel their attention upon me, their gazes like beams of cold light upon my skin, and I twisted that to my benefit, pulling those cords of energy to me, feeding them back to Ahès, who knitted them together and spun a deeper spell than any of them could detect.

The priestess gave and gave, opening herself wide to me. While I commanded her power, I also found my way through her own illusions and charms. She had hidden it from me, cleverly, so I would agree to this communion.

Ahès was *dying*. She was already there, half upon the threshold, and I had not seen through it. Clever woman. I never would have consented, had I known what pestilence grew inside of her, weakening her, eating her from the inside out. My heart stuttered; I nearly faltered.

I'm sorry, sister, her voice whispered to me, faint and small.

When our foe is vanquished, you will carry me over the threshold. As you were meant to do, daughter of death.

No matter my guilt, or the tears now running down my face, our connection had grown too strong. I could not have stopped what we were building even if I wanted to, so fiercely did the priestess give.

"You see?" King Marqus said triumphantly when nothing happened. "This witch who claims blood with the King is naught but a deceiver! To rid the world of her will do the High King a favor. No doubt, when she dies upon our swords here, he will wake from a dream of lies."

The men cheered, and some snarled, but I did not open my eyes. I remained as I was. King Marqus was a maggot of a man, but to strike a woman as I was, advanced in my years and helpless in his eyes, would be a grave fault.

Perhaps I should have been afraid. Except, indeed, Modrun's own power and guidance had opened up inside of me: Tintagel itself reminded me; Ahès guided me; Coel had broken me open.

"Sire…"

A voice from out toward the edges of the fire, the words swallowed up by a slight argument elsewhere.

"The Glatisant!"

"Could it be?"

"To arms!"

I did not fear death, nor the remnants of Her visit. My power, new and familiar at the same time, sang the song of death and lulled it to move. Perhaps it was with the same strength that kept the firmament in the skies, or that moved the sun and moon, I know not. But in the moment, as I prepared for death myself, I knew with perfect clarity who I was and what I could do.

Those carcasses, left to rot by the arrogance of man, could not seek justice alone. But I could help them.

With Ahès's power and my own, I wove those beings together. Hoof and claw, tooth and horn, fur and feather, I plucked their eyes and their ears and made a great creature of indescribable power and terror, tall as a tree and twice as wide, while Marqus continued his blustering.

The creature we wove together was all of them and none, and it lumbered, leaking and shambling, toward the fire and King Marqus himself.

I did not look to see its shape, but turned to Coel's waiting arms to anchor me, as the shrieks began. His presence was cool as a stream, steady and unrelenting.

Exhaustion took me such as I have never known, as I pressed the beast onward, keeping my focus, controlling its unpredictable form. I knitted together every fissure in its body, the places where nature pushed against magic, with the strength of my friends to fuel me.

I drew from below, from the roots of Tintagel, where I felt the blood of my father deep in the earth, heard the cries of my anguished mother, and felt the wind change at my command: We would give them their beast!

Some of the men tried to fight it, but most were too afraid. The closer they got, the more it reeked. Arrows did naught but sink into its already decaying hide, and their swords merely opened new mouths with claws and eyes and teeth.

King Marqus was already recoiling, falling back to his more seasoned warriors—I felt the thread of him tighten and vibrate, though I did not open my eyes. He would run, he would take the coward's route, and we would be victorious.

A CRY PIERCED the night, inhuman and not of my own making. I had heard such a sound before, and realized in my pride I had overlooked the possibility that King Marqus could have been right about something:

The Questing Beast. The Glatisant.

His lure had worked after all, the piles of festering meat. And now, as King Marqus and his men fled, and my power waned, all that stood between me and the beast was Coel.

I opened my eyes as the Glatisant barreled into the midst of the gathering, her long, snakelike neck glimmering black and purple. Her head, arrow-shaped and larger than a horse's, was wreathed in green flames. She stood taller than three men, and certainly larger than my own fell beast, her powerful forelimbs tipped with sharp claws and her strange back feet wide and cloven. Her long tail was feathered and armored, like some strange lizard, and when she cried out the edges of my vision prickled.

Furious, the Glatisant bit the head off a soldier as he fled, shaking it back and forth so blood sprayed down upon us.

Coel made to rush forward, but I prevented him. "No—it is too dangerous. Let Ahès and me try."

The King of Rheged frowned at me, fear and fury in his expression. "This beast is beyond us all, Morgen."

"We can fight it," Ahès rasped, grabbing my hand. "Take all of my power, Morgen. All of it. Leave nothing to me; I give it to you freely."

Coel looked between us, drawing his sword, confused.

I did not want this gift, but it was hers to give. My magic pulled it from her, surely as if it were sweet honey from the comb, my darker gifts readying to take her across the threshold. There was no fighting the Glatisant for us; we would perish.

Our beast, the carcass monster, yet stood on wobbly legs. It screamed from a dozen mouths, and I closed my eyes and let myself sink into Ahès's power again, then deeper into the roots of my home.

I sank to the ground as her power coursed through me, even as I knew Ahès was dying. My whole body prickled with pain, as though covered in shards of glass.

I calmed myself, breathing in and out, the air cold and my breath so very hot. I did not fight as Coel held me; and somehow, it helped. Whether it was his power, far slighter than mine but disciplined, or simply the act of my surrendering, I do not know.

Our carcass beast rose and elongated, bones snapping into new shapes, as Ahès commanded it with a hoarse cry, reaching to the end of her reserves. From skin and sinew, it grew wings, leaking sizzling ichor to the ground below. We wove our power together, strands of destruction and death in a gyre of menace and nightmares.

The Glatisant turned her head toward our beast, eyes shining luminous vermillion and green, and then struck. Her great jaws clamped down upon the carcass beast's hind leg, and with a brutal wrench, pulled it apart entirely. Sinew snapped, popped, and leaked in its wake, as our spell began unraveling.

Ahès was powerful, but we were both exhausted. Had we been better prepared, perhaps we could have endured longer. The Glatisant was simply too strong, her magic too old to withstand. And it was just. She had endured great peril in her long life, and we were only more men looking to hurt her. Perhaps the only creature in the realm lonelier than I.

I grabbed Ahès by the hand and squeezed, giving her silent permission to stop. She sank back onto Coel and me, a defeated sound coming from deep within her chest, that expiration of breath I knew heralded the end.

We stood by the Maw of Death the next moment, veiled in shadow.

Ahès looked up at me, her face serene. "I'm sorry for deceiving you. But I was dying all along," she said, her body now shimmering and transparent as she prepared to cross. "The goddess—she guided my steps to you. I knew I had to give you my last. The blessing of Ys is with you now, the blessing of Avillion. Use it well, sister."

"I did not ask for this," I told her, my hands shaking and tears running hot down my raw cheeks. "I could have found another way to help you."

She was so young, goddess.

"I would choose no other bearer, Morgen le Fay. I go to sing with our ancestors, and to await your return."

Ahès turned away from me, and I held her hand across the threshold, my power leading where my heart could not.

When I blinked, I sat with her cooling body in my lap, fires leaping and the Glatisant screaming.

King Marqus's forces were fleeing for their lives, dispersing into the wood and away from Tintagel. There was small relief in that.

The two of us stood together, clustered, awaiting the final decision of the Glatisant. In the depths of the forest, I thought I heard a great roar.

I fell to the earth and buried my hands in the loam, probing deep for my power, fueled by my grief. Weary as I was, my mind felt changed from Ahès's gift, my body hot and strange and not wholly my own. I must dig here, beneath the ground—here lay some great mystery, soaked in the blood of my enemies and tempered with my own magic.

Power seized me, and I was distantly aware of Coel's voice and his hands on my shoulders, but much as I had done in my youth, I was taken by a holy vision on the wings of magic.

CHAPTER FORTY-ONE

LLACHLYN

LLACHLYN SQUINTED UP again at the curved edge of the tower, trying to absorb what she saw.

The quake had revealed another wall, hidden behind an interior wall, painted from ceiling to floor with thousands of drawings, words, and illustrations. Some were scribbled vignettes depicting daily life in the castle; others were verses carved straight into the stone with a hectic stroke that made Llachlyn uncomfortable.

Truly, it *all* made her uncomfortable, for more than one reason. Every hair on her body stood on end as she gazed at it.

"Is that our *graal*?" Percival asked, pointing to one of the center pieces.

There, indeed, was a blue pool surrounded by thickets, and in the middle, a silver object shaped very like the one they had all beheld in their shared dream. The *graal* of joy, it was called—a shield, to the spear and the cup.

Galahad, who had fallen to his knees, breathlessly said, "God in Heaven. What miracle is this?"

Llachlyn leaned forward to touch the scratched writing before either of them could stop her. The stone was cool and clean, the marks pointed in the center as if a dagger had drawn them. Indeed, toward the bottom of the wall, she saw splotches of what had to be blood, long dried to brown.

There were two great beasts carved along those blood stains, and two full moons painted in flaking blue and red paint. This close, she saw flecks of mica in the paint, making those heavenly bodies shimmer dully. Above them were two great stars, and in the middle, the *graal* floating atop the pool.

"It's an odd dialect," Percival said. "I can make out parts of it."

"What does it say?" Galahad asked, standing slowly.

Llachlyn did not need to know the words to know the meaning of the paintings. They were her *dreams*: the beasts, the moons, the two stars. Yet she could not find in herself the strength to say it aloud; fear had taken her voice and frozen her limbs. How could this be?

She thought of Vyvian, and of her mother, and wondered if they had ever seen this. If they had known. But no. This part of the castle was older even than they were.

"The words are mostly the names of plants and animals. Gorse and oak, hazel and woad. Snippets of old songs—familiar ones..." Percival said, half-muttering, and then startled and said, "Ah! There's a name here. Ganeida."

"Ganeida. I feel as if I've heard that before somewhere," Galahad said.

The name made Llachlyn shiver, and she did not know why. "We need to get the tonics back to the prince," she said, pulling away from the wall.

Percival continued on, no matter her protest. "'Ganeida'—sister? Yes—'sister of Myrddin'—that's Merlin's old name—'sister of Myrddin, kept here these—these seven years. Taker'—no, not taker—*keeper* of the Well of Joy.'"

Galahad had reached the wall by now and was staring at the depiction of the pool and the *graal*. When he spoke, it was softly, full of wonder. "Our dream, it was quite hazy to me. And that was before I knew of the place, of course."

"Galahad, what do you mean now?" Percival asked. Llachlyn thought he was shorter with the knight than he'd ever been. So continued their strange, unbalanced dance. "You're hardly the scholar among us."

The young knight reached up and put a hand on the very bottom of the *graal* image, which rose high up above their heads, covering most of the wall. "It's here. It's been here all along."

"The *graal* is here? In Carelon?" Llachlyn asked, glad to at least focus on something beside her doom-filled dreams—the dreams which, apparently, she shared with the mad sister of Merlin.

"It makes sense. We all dreamed it when we were together, after all." Galahad wiped tears from his face. "There are springs, tucked away, near an old, ruined temple. My father showed me. I felt an openness, a power, there. The *graal* of joy. It looks like, from this picture, it is kept at the bottom of those springs."

"We'll need it, I'm certain—to protect it," Llachlyn said, turning to Percival. "You need to get it—what I saw in the depths below the castle, my dreams. We shall need all the help we can get to keep it at bay."

How many things had she beheld since the last sunrise had changed the trajectory of her life? Her dreams had not been lies. Her life was not a curse.

"Do you think that's wise?" Galahad asked, even as Percival nodded in affirmation. "I ought to bring it to the priests—this would be a great boon to the Church."

"No," Llachlyn said, balling her hands into fists and walking straight over to him. If she'd had a mote of her mother's magic, she would set his hair afire with her fury. But she was so tired of Galahad always having the upper hand, always playing the commander and the arbiter of their plans. It was enough. "No, you stupid, *stupid* boy. That is the *last* thing we should do."

"Stupid? What makes you the great protector of the *graal*, Mallow?" Galahad asked, indignant and cruel. Though she saw—with some satisfaction—a twinge of fear in his expression. She had never stood up to him before.

Now she would.

"I come from an unbroken line of women who feel and see

and make magic. When I stood in the depths, when I spoke with the Green Knight, I realized I had let a curse decide who I am. I have been afraid my whole life—of you, of my mother, of my future. But that fear has stopped me from seeing. From *being*. From standing up for myself."

"Llachlyn, I—"

"No. You do *not* get to talk." She poked Galahad roughly in the chest, making him flinch. "I am the grandniece of Vyvian du Lac, who shaped the earth into the greatest weapons of the age, and she chose me to carry on her legacy; and I am daughter to Morgen le Fay, the greatest and most powerful sorceress to ever walk this earth—and I have *dreamed* this. I have seen this tower, and this message, and the gods know where I am needed. I can feel it." And she could. Inside her, a beacon, calling to her.

Galahad fell silent, blinking at his cousin as if seeing her for the first time.

"You should come with us," Percival said. "To the springs."

"It is not part of my story," Llachlyn said, securing the last of the potions in her satchel with a sigh. "Ganeida knew the castle would fall, and Mordred's life hangs in the balance. I need to trust you both. I cannot ride as you can, I cannot swim as you can. So, you and Percival will bring the *graal* to Hwyfar of Avillion after you find it, and no one else. And I will bring these potions to Mordred."

Galahad took in a breath, his gaze moving from Percival and back to Llachlyn again. "You are right. I'm sorry. I—Everything is so confusing."

"Simple answers are for simple times," Llachlyn snapped, quoting Vyvian. "And simple minds. Now, I must go. And if you slow me down, I will tell the King of your treachery."

"You would leave us, now?" Galahad asked, his eyes filling with tears. "Llachlyn—It has always been the three of us."

"Yes. But this is a path we cannot walk together. It is mine to take," Llachlyn said, hating how her face twisted in her sorrow. "There are places where I cannot follow. I love you both, more than I can properly say, but our lives are changing—Can't you feel it?"

Percival grabbed her in a fierce embrace, and after a moment's hesitation, Galahad did as well. They held one another, sniffling and weeping, until Llachlyn let them go.

Percival smoothed her hair from her cheek. Tears flowed fast from his eyes. "You are fast and small, and I know you can get these to Mordred faster than any of us. Only tell me—what does this say to you?" He pointed to Ganeida's drawings.

She placed her hand over his, cupping her cheek. She did not have to answer in words. He knew. He just had to think a little harder.

"Your dreams. These were always your dreams," Percival whispered. "The beasts. The moon! The end."

"It doesn't have to be the end," Llachlyn said, looking Galahad in the eyes. "Find the *graal*."

"We will find you," Galahad promised.

"I know."

"Llachlyn—"

He might have meant to apologize, but it did not matter. Llachlyn knew the matters of his heart, understood the wounds and bruises they gave to one another for so many years. They might have been cousins by birth, but they were siblings of spirit. For what were they without each other? Percival always was their balance. And right now, Galahad needed him.

Before she could hear what he had to say, Llachlyn was off through the rubble and on her way toward the King and Mordred.

WALKING AWAY FROM Percival and Galahad felt like a part of her was dying. Llachlyn's chest ached, her eyes flowing with bitter tears. The whole world, all the broken corners of Carelon, were sharper than they should be in the dark. Though dawn barely blushed the horizon, she moved through her sorrow and the rubble together, with a weight on her soul she had never felt before.

The castle was changed. She was changed. And now, their fate lay fragile between them. She wished Vyvian were here, but she supposed, in some ways, she was.

You hold the power in your hand, you must only decide how to shape it. Mordred had reminded her of her inheritance from Vyvian.

If the forge was not in ruins, she would have much work ahead of her. For now, her duty was to her family first.

As she approached the small side chapel where she last left Mordred, she passed more wounded knights and civilians, their eyes wide and lost and strange.

She did not dip her head, as she once might have, afraid to draw attention as Arthur's bastard. Now Llachlyn le Fay was newly forged.

The silence of the place, punctuated only by weeping and sounds of pain, was heavy and thick, like a dense mist.

Today she would not be a curse; she would bring hope.

A knight she did not recognize guarded the door; he allowed her entrance without any hesitation. The doors swung open, and she rushed forward.

Gawain stood immediately, Hwyfar still tending to Mordred. Father Olwein had fallen asleep but started awake on her arrival. King Arthur sat in a chair, pale and shivering, but he turned his eyes to her.

"Llachlyn," said the King, relief making his voice break. "Thank God."

"I brought all I could find," Llachlyn said to Princess Hwyfar, handing her the bag. "Galahad tells me Mordred was something of a potions expert, and thankfully he had quite a store."

"How did the lads fare?" Gawain asked.

Llachlyn gave her cousin a meaningful look. "They are well. I have sent them on a bit of a quest. We need a miracle this day, and I think they may deliver us one."

The King looked slightly perplexed, but did not question her. It was difficult to look away from him, knowing he was her father, knowing that her mere presence would cause him pain and—worse—shame. But she would not allow that to push her down any longer.

Hwyfar rooted through the potions and tinctures, opening some of them and smelling them, and outright ignoring others. Finally, she said: "Thank you, Llachlyn. These will help ease his pain."

It took a moment for Hwyfar's words to settle in Llachlyn's mind. "Ease his pain—can we not heal him?"

"His injuries are grave, Llachlyn."

"Let me help."

Hwyfar glanced up, her eyes shadowed with exhaustion and worry. "Llachlyn, you are untrained."

"I am my mother's daughter. And Vyvian's last apprentice." Every time she said the words, she could feel more strength, as if those storied women were somehow listening to her, responding to her insistence. "Mordred is—my friend. Let me *try*."

The princess drew a deep breath and took Llachlyn's hand. She reached her other hand to her husband, who took it without question or hesitation. She dropped her voice low, looking from one to the other.

"If you are brave, Llachlyn, give me what connection you have, and we may be able to combine our power to—"

She stopped, eyes wide, letting go of both their hands as if she had been stung by a nettle. Gawain was immediately at her side, confusion in his expression. Llachlyn hadn't felt a thing, and wondered if indeed her own power had somehow poisoned her.

"Tell me, love, what that was," Gawain said softly. "I felt it—I felt a breaking, deep within me somehow."

Hwyfar wept, her hauntingly beautiful face crumpled in sorrow, her hands on her mouth. "The Path. It is there, in us, but Gawain... Ahès and Modrun are dead."

CHAPTER FORTY-TWO

THE GRAAL

~ Percival ~

THE DEVASTATION OF the earthquake extended just past the castle grounds, where a massive, ragged slash in the earth opened wide through part of the tilting field. Percival had half a mind to explore it, to see if there were any clues as to what had caused this monstrous tragedy, but they did not have time. They had a purpose. A quest. Perhaps the greatest he would ever have.

He and Galahad rounded the stables and found two horses, neither injured nor too badly frightened, and rode out together in silence as they had done a hundred times before, as knight and squire.

The sunrise was unfairly beautiful, the skies streaked with puffy grey clouds limned in brilliant crimson. The fiery morning display seemed, Percival thought, a sign of their purpose, their promise—and he was part of that. For once, he was truly connected to the larger tale. It was a relief, in a way.

"You really think the *graal* was here all along?" Percival called ahead of him, where Galahad sat still as a stone upon his horse. "Right under our noses?"

The knight did not answer right away but glanced over his shoulder at Percival. No doubt, once again, he was deep in thoughts of guilt and shame. And Llachlyn had stood up to him, shown him the error of his ways, and it likely weighed heavily upon him.

"I know my father was drawn there, and I know what I sensed when I visited. While you were both gone, it was the only place in all of Carelon I knew any measure of comfort," Galahad replied. "Perhaps it was also what gave me strength."

"Warm water does tend to have a most soothing effect upon people, especially young men who routinely push their bodies to the limit," Percival observed. Ah, God, and he did enjoy watching Galahad do *anything* with his body.

Galahad huffed. "I know the difference, Percival. I've had many comforting baths before, with all manner of soothing herbs and oils and soaks and attendants. This is an experience beyond all others."

"Now I'm sorry I did not get to see it," Percival said.

The knight fell silent, not rising to his teasing. Percival should have curbed his tongue, but if anything, coming this close to death had made him reconsider his stance on their relationship. One tended to reevaluate one's life in the wake of tragedy; many men had come together on battlefields for that very reason. Theirs, he knew, was a gentler generation, and he had never had the opportunity to serve Galahad, on the battlefield *or* in their tent.

Though he did often picture what such a life might have been like for them, had they not been born into a world of peace.

"Are you still upset about the timing of the earthquake?" Percival asked, not unselfishly. He'd wanted to kiss Galahad again.

Galahad sighed, glancing over his shoulder at Percival. "I *am* troubled. God has set me a challenge, and a way to light my path. But the priests also tell us the Opposer can sabotage us with distractions and villains, and we must be wary."

Percival's irritation twisted in his heart again. "Are you calling me the Devil, Galahad?"

Galahad stilled his horse and at least had the decency to look embarrassed. His words surprised Percival, though. "I do not think you are any such thing. Quite the opposite, really."

Percival was not yet ready to accept such an oblique compliment. "Your language suggests otherwise."

"No, it is only—" Galahad sighed. "I believe the villain is, well, myself."

Of course they were back to Galahad's faith. Percival groaned. "And this is precisely the reason I have yet to commit to the new faith. Such self-hatred! I quite like myself most days, and though I have no delusions of my faults, I find the idea of constant guilt galling."

Galahad laughed, warming Percival to his toes, and he smiled in return. He had not meant to be funny; usually their conversations on religion were far from humorous.

Galahad reached out to touch Percival's arm gently, and his body responded immediately.

"I spent most of my life in my father's shadow," Galahad said softly. "And I didn't even know him. I remember thinking when we met, my life would change—I would finally understand who I was, where I belonged, what it meant. The way my uncle Hector talks about my father's deeds, you would think he could part rivers. Meeting my father did nothing but make me feel even more invisible."

"You could never be invisible," Percival said. "You should see the way people look at you." The way Percival himself looked at him, like he couldn't drink deeply enough of his face, his body, his mannerisms.

"I behaved in an unmannerly way when my brother Gareth tried to do the one thing I desperately wanted: he tried to bring me closer to the family. I didn't understand. I'd never had brothers—but now I see that doesn't matter. I was wrong."

"What changed?"

The cool breeze caught in their cloaks, which billowed and snapped about them. Galahad, cheeks flushed and eyes bright, looked every part the *graal* hero.

Galahad looked down at where he still captured Percival's arm. He squeezed gently. "I saw how brittle pride is. I do not doubt my father could have bested Gareth, but it would have cost him more than losing. Knowing he'd almost killed Gawain once—to see that almost happen again—I wondered which side I wanted to tread. Which side *God* would want me to walk upon. My brother Gareth, who seemed to want to know me? Or my absent father, who acted as if he did, but clearly did not."

Percival stroked his horse gently; she was starting to whicker as they approached a copse of hazel trees, and he wanted to calm her. But he liked listening to Galahad, the way he worked through his thoughts with language. It was a terribly vulnerable way of going about it, and he felt honored Galahad was letting him in.

"And which side did you choose?" Percival asked.

"My own." Galahad's words were dreamlike, breathy, almost as if he was afraid to give voice to them. "I cannot be the person my father was, and I cannot hide behind my brothers. I must make my own story. And I—I need someone by my side, someone who truly knows me."

That was quite unexpected—and Galahad was usually painfully predictable, even on a good day.

Galahad did not continue, and Percival did not reply, so shocked he was, but instead they dismounted their horses beside the old, bent chestnut tree. Once the horses were tied up safely, Galahad beckoned Percival through the brush.

And, truly, the closer they got to the spring, the more that sense of giddiness came over him. It was a heady mix of excitement and nervousness, not unlike how he felt thinking of Galahad when he wasn't around. Save that, now, Galahad stood right before him. He was close enough that Percival could see the small hairs at his nape darkened with sweat, and the flecks of brown horsehair on his pale tunic.

"You feel it," Galahad said with a chuckle. "I thought you would."

"How would you know?" Percival demanded in mock anger.

"You're *quiet*." The knight grinned as he pulled aside a curtain of dried vines, which snapped and crackled.

Percival would have made a clever retort, but he forgot all manner of speech the moment he beheld the place. Midmorning sun glinted across the small ruin—a flat building hewn from the rockface before the spring. Mist rose in an eerie layer above the crystalline water. It looked as if there might be stairs under the water, spiraling down. Bare-branched trees leaned over the spring as if in deference or curiosity, limbs twisting longingly toward their reflections. Golden leaves carpeted the walkway, and the smell of earth and brightness and salt permeated the air.

A deep, long-lost sensation rose up inside Percival and he had to steady himself on a smooth-barked beech. Somehow, he was weeping openly, the tang of tears in his mouth as his skin burned with the power of it. Everything he had ever wanted seemed achievable just then, within his grasp.

Joy. And Galahad. And this moment.

Galahad stood beside him, eyes closed as the sun dappled his face and skin. If he was moved or bothered by Percival's emotion, he did not show it. With the light on his hair and the color in his cheeks, Galahad looked like a great god of old, meant for the wild places and not the confines of court and armor and chivalry. He did not weep, but his whole body relaxed in a way Percival never knew was possible.

"I cannot count many gifts from my father that I treasure, but this is different," Galahad said, reaching for his tunic and pulling it over his head.

Percival never wanted anyone so much in his life as he did then. The desire to possess Galahad, to keep him, to protect him—though the latter was ludicrous. They had played this game between them so long, and Percival meant it when he said he did not want to be Galahad's shame. But with joy washing over him, another wonder to add to his adventures, he was willing to compromise.

"Galahad, you're not seriously considering swimming to the bottom of the well," Percival said, suddenly taken aback now that he had seen it.

"Of course I am." Galahad clapped his chest, then shook out his long, muscled arms. "It's a hot spring. I won't get cold."

The confounded man. "It's not the temperature that worries me, sweeting, but rather the limited circumference. You have no idea what you're looking for down there—you could get turned around, lose your way, end up drowning."

"I won't drown," Galahad said, shrugging off the rest of his clothes. "Have more faith in me than that."

Christ. Lugh. Whoever was up there, Percival needed an intercession. "This isn't a matter of faith, you lout. Don't be dim. You aren't invincible."

"No, but I am brave. And I believe God has given me this purpose; this was meant to be all along. He placed this before me. Before us."

"From what I gather, Lady Vyvian placed the *graal* before you, not God."

Galahad gave Percival such a piteous look that, if he were already not trying to keep from staring at his glorious naked body, he would have looked away. He was afraid if he gazed any lower, any more freely, he would endanger their entire mission by throwing himself directly at the young knight.

"Oftentimes, those outside of the faith do not realize they are doing the work of God. I have come to peace with it, Percival. I hope you can see that someday."

"At least take a rope."

"I have no idea how far down it goes, and a rope will be an impediment."

"Galahad, please."

"Percival, just stop talking," said Galahad with a chuckle.

And then, the young knight swept forward and kissed Percival, hard and firm and entirely brazen. No, *kiss* was far too simple a description; Galahad grabbed Percival's face, just under the angle of his jaw, and ravaged his mouth with his own.

Then he let go and jumped into the well.

* * *

~ *Galahad* ~

WATER RUSHED OVER Galahad's head, heat immediately suffusing his body as he sank lower into the well, lips still tingling from that kiss. Bubbles rose and obscured his vision for a moment, striking fear into his belly, banishing thoughts of that unbridled joy.

No, he would not be afraid.

The last months had been a long, confusing ordeal, toying with his heart and his soul. He had been aimless, without purpose, incomplete. Now, that had all changed. No, he could not see the entirety of the picture or his Fate. God, in His wisdom, kept it from him. It was part of the lesson, Galahad was certain: he must trust more in God's immediate plan rather than worry himself about the future.

The entirety of Carelon had nearly crumbled. And they were all helpless to do anything to prevent it. It should have terrified Galahad, ought to have made him feel despair and disconnection. Except it hadn't.

He had touched the edge of disaster and death—impossibly, it had looked him in the face and passed over, as if he was just a brick laid among the foundation. Galahad was nothing, and yet he was someone. His strength was great, but in the face of tragedy and such magnitude, it was naught.

And that had freed him. Deep inside of him, all the coiled anxiety and self-loathing, the pressure and the expectations... they all slipped away, leaving him laughing in his insignificance.

Only God's love remained, God's forgiveness and power. It did not matter if he was Galahad or a mouse in the field. God's love endured, in equal measure.

All these thoughts were too tangled to explain to Percival, who had clearly not come to the same conclusion after the earthquake. And that, too, did not bother Galahad. Their story was just beginning—he knew it as surely as he knew God's love and power.

Llachlyn was right. About so much. They would always be connected, the three of them, but for her to grow—and for Galahad to truly see God's love—their paths had to diverge. For now, at least.

Down Galahad sank, as the water darkened and clouded and cooled. If he looked up, he knew he would be able to see Percival and it might distract him, so he closed his eyes and pumped his legs harder, arms steering and stretching as he prayed for guidance, for strength, for humility.

He could feel the *graal* beneath him, calling and pulling at him. No wonder he had come here time and time again— no wonder their dreams had entwined with its song and its enchanting magic. As surely as he knew he loved Percival.

Galahad's heart pounded in his chest and neck and cheeks as he went deeper. For a brief moment, he thought he might turn back—doubt flitted across his consciousness like an inconstant fish. Then he gritted his teeth and forced himself even lower, noting how the well narrowed around his shoulders.

His hand hit uneven stonework, and he felt around in the dimness for a latch or a clue, some fissure or break in the rock.

Even with his eyes open, he saw only darkness. And damn it, but Percival was right: there was not enough space for him to turn around. He would have to float up, feet first, somehow, carrying his quarry.

If he could find it.

Frantically, Galahad ran his fingers around the edges and then down. From what he had seen in the tower ruin, it would be oval-shaped—surely if it was down here, it was within reach. God wouldn't have sent him here only to drown.

The elation of his sublime connection only moments ago began to subside, doubt creeping in. The Queen spoke often of God's punishment, His judgement. Had Galahad been too proud?

Blooming spots of red and purple spread at the edges of his vision as his lungs screamed for air. His legs cramped; his throat burned.

No! He would not concede to the darkness.

God, grant me Your blessing, Your kindness, Your gentleness. Let me see through this pain to find peace, to find joy.

Just as he was about to let go, to try and skitter up the narrow well in defeat, he felt cold metal under his fingers. Bubbles rose about him, moving the hair on his chest and his legs, as he fumbled with a small latch. The mechanism clicked, and he heaved with all his strength. A small box, about the size of his forearm, came loose. Far too small to be a shield.

When Galahad grasped and pulled again, the resistance grew even greater. Well, he would get a better handle on it and then try again.

Except he could not.

Invisible chains had wrapped around his forearm, his whole body going rigid with the force of its magic. Water whirled around him, his hair tickling his face and his sight dimming, even as he was suffused with the intensity of the *graal*'s unending joy.

Here was the end. The water began draining beneath him, his body lodged down from the suction, his heart thrashing in the cage of his chest.

He saw the next few minutes of his life played out before him as if from the eye of a bird high in the sky: Percival would be screaming for him above, would try to jump in, would not be able to. By the time he'd alerted the guard, they would find Percival curled up around Galahad's drowned body, having at last floated to the top of the water.

It was not fair to do such a thing to Percival. Not now. Not ever. There was no glory in such a death, even if God willed it. And Galahad could not believe He would.

That was when he felt a great tug at his foot. Someone was in the water with him—Percival! There was a rope around his foot. With his assistance, Galahad was able to dislodge himself, even as the water dragged at him. The water was not a force in and of itself, but was merely draining below—he had released it when he'd pulled out the box.

Percival half-dragged, half-hauled Galahad up the rest of the way. He was sobbing and shouting words Galahad could not make out, but he didn't mind. Sputtering, choking down air, the *graal* singing through his blood and Percival's hands on his body, he could not have experienced any more joy if he had sought it out on the Holy Mount itself.

CHAPTER FORTY-THREE

HWYFAR

GAWAIN AND LLACHLYN's help had indeed opened up the Path again to Hwyfar of Avillion, but with it came the bitter knowledge of loss. The Circle of Nine was broken even further: Vyvian, Ahès, and Modrun had all passed over the threshold of death, that shadowed, curious place Morgen had so often spoken of.

In that was a glimmer of hope, even amidst the bone-aching sorrow: Hwyfar could feel Morgen le Fay's magic along the Path, and in abundance—nowhere more than where Modrun and Ahès once stood. She was certain, though she did not yet comprehend, that Morgen had aided them across.

Ahès, her friend, who had helped her master the power of Avillion and tame the magic of Ys. The priestess who had challenged her, even before Hwyfar had taken her place as her mother's heir, who had been steadfast and true in the face of treachery at Withiel. They had seen each other every spring, when they could, and spoken for hours into the night, and later through letters and the Path itself. They were of an age. Theirs had been the truest friendship Hwyfar had ever had. And now she had slipped away to the distant shore of death.

Mordred stirred before her, and Hwyfar focused her attention back to Gawain and Llachlyn, swallowing her grief.

"Take my hands again. I am sorry, Llachlyn. The shock terrified me, seeing such death upon the Path," she said. "I do not know if you will be able to see what I see, but weaving my powers with yours has connected me again to the great Circle, to the Path, where all three strands of my power lie: the magic of Avillion, of Ys, and of Lyonesse. I hope they will guide my hands, and help us heal the prince."

Gawain closed his eyes and nodded solemnly, and although Llachlyn looked pale and wan, the look of determination on her face was all her famed mother's.

Hwyfar slipped into the three tides of magic within her, thinking of them not as separate sources, but streams from one pool. She could feel what remained in Gawain, the draw of Avillion, as well as her own powers, but also a keener power coming from Llachlyn that she could only identify as uniquely Morgen's. There was no time to follow her own curiosity, however, as the room fell away, and with it her sense of self.

Hwyfar floated through a grey expanse, loose robes billowing about her, the landscape shrouded in mist which delicately kissed her face with a strange coolness. High above her head, she could feel and see tethers to Gawain and Llachlyn.

I am here, love.

Gawain's voice.

Can you see where I stand? she asked him, plucking the string of their connection, that frail remnant of *carioz* that still lingered after they had chosen to let it go so many years ago.

I can see through your eyes. It was not entirely unlike the Path, which Hwyfar had traveled many times, but had a sense of incomparable vastness. It ought to have made her afraid, and yet it did not. She sensed the presence of magic everywhere, little pulses of consciousness, as if she stood upon a stage surrounded by thousands of people watching her. Hwyfar had always had a keen sense for when people looked her way, and it did not frighten her—it encouraged her. Besides, Gawain was with her.

If she focused, she could still feel her hands grasping to Llachlyn and Gawain, sticky with the prince's blood. She could still smell the dusty dryness of the room, the sweat from her husband's brow, the reek of wine on the King's breath. Those details rooted her to the living world, but did not keep her from seeing this strange other place.

Floating toward a tall pillar of fog, Hwyfar's feet touched the ground for the first time.

It smelled of Merlin's magic, but twined with what she now understood was Morgen's magical signature. The scent was citrusy and sharp, tinged with the smokiness of fragrant incense, or perhaps the sap of some tree unknown to her.

As soon as Hwyfar was sure of her feet, the mist around her shifted and she was looking directly into a room she was now quite familiar with: the Queen's chamber. It was full of figures, but none of them were drawn with particular detail, just vague grey shapes against a sparkling backdrop of swirling stars.

Gweyn's rooms? came Gawain's observation in her mind, his strength pulling slightly in her consciousness.

To her left, a tall woman stood at the foot of the bed, her features obscured. She held a sleeping babe in her hands, while she looked upon the figure asleep below the covers. He was crowned in an aura of blue and gold.

Hwyfar's breath caught in her chest, and she had to steady herself with great effort. This was where Mordred and Percival had begun, Anna Pendragon's treachery.

A vague green glow rose from beside Gweyn, and Hwyfar realized it was, indeed, another child. The green came from him—whether in warning or for some other reason, Hwyfar could not say. Green, touched by the Green Knight, or kindled by her green sight? Percival. It had to be.

Taking a few steps forward, the tall woman turned her head and Hwyfar saw a look of abject fear on Anna Pendragon's face. Haltingly, she gave the child in her hands to a shadowed woman, limned in purple. Then she sank to her knees by Gweyn's sleeping form.

The room flashed, and in a moment, Percival was gone, and the other babe replaced in Gweyn's arms.

Gweyn stirred, looking down at the child, and though she beamed at him, in love and relief, Hwyfar was sure she knew it was not her child. And yet she was not upset, not in the way one might expect with such a revelation.

She knew. She had to know, Hwyfar told her husband. *She had seen it.*

I am certain she did, Gawain said. *And yet she did not fight it.*

She trusted your mother, above all others. It must have broken her heart to know she had been so deceived.

The room flashed again, as if in a great storm, and Hwyfar now stood in another room: dark and rough and strange to her eyes. Outside, she heard a storm blowing, wind battening against the foundations, as the smell of the sea rose up around her.

This is Orkney, Gawain said. *A long time ago. That rug—I burned a hole through it when I was six, turning over a candle while I played with my soldiers. And—*

A little boy emerged from behind a chair in front of her, and she felt Gawain pull back slightly, as if in surprise or in sorrow. Unlike the figures of before, he was drawn in full color. And no surprise: it was her husband, Gawain, as a small, freckled child. His eyes glowed the same green as the child had before, but the figures around him did not seem to notice.

"Gawain, come out now. I promise you, your Uncle Arthur only wants a look at you," came a voice behind her.

Hwyfar turned to see Morgen le Fay. In the spring of her youth, her hair black as a raven's wing, the sorceress looked hardly more than a child herself. She couldn't have been twenty, and the likeness to Llachlyn was startling.

Arthur stood by Morgen's side, handsome and strong. His body was free of its current frailty, his face smooth and full of promise. He had been close to thirty the first time she had seen him, with none of the boyishness he held here.

Were we ever all so young? Gawain asked, his presence comforting and grounding.

Arthur looked upon little Gawain, who was barely walking

without assistance, with a mix of doubt and trepidation.

"I don't want to force him to come to me," Arthur said, squatting down so he was closer to Gawain's face. "I might frighten him, and then what would I do? He's my first nephew. The grandson of Uther Pendragon. First impressions are very important."

Morgen laughed lightly. "He has no idea he has such importance, Arthur. Gawain is just a child."

"A little child now, yes. But some day, he will be a great knight," Arthur said with certainty.

This appeared to help. Young Gawain peered out from behind a chair and then, a moment later, was standing almost nose to nose with his uncle. Hwyfar had never wanted children, and yet part of her ached to see this tiny, vulnerable version of her husband. It seemed impossible to imagine Gawain was ever so small. And yet all she knew of him was somehow visible to her: his stubbornness, his gentleness, his strength.

Then little Gawain raised up his hands and pumped his little fingers in silent request, as if to say, "Up, up, up!"

Delighted, Arthur scooped him up and held him aloft. The child did not giggle—he seemed quite serious for such an age—but his eyes glittered as the King twirled him over his head.

"I have never held a child before," Arthur said breathlessly to his sister. "He is so small! And yet sturdy. By God, he will be a force upon the field."

Morgen's brows lowered in reply, watching the scene before her with keen interest, but with concern, as well. Her words belied her expression, however. "We were all once so fragile, my lord. But it is true, Gawain is already twice the size of most children his age, here in Orkney."

Little Gawain threw his arms around Arthur's neck and would not let go. Arthur, stunned by the sudden affection, gently rubbed the boy's back, looking helplessly at his sister.

"Are most children so trusting?" the King asked.

Morgen stilled, her dark eyes shining just slightly. Were they tears? "You are family," she said simply. "Now, we are expected elsewhere. Gawain looks quite content where he is. I hope the future King of Braetan does not mind playing at the nursemaid for a little while longer."

It does my heart glad to see me so, Gawain said, though Hwyfar could taste his sorrow on her tongue. *Before my father began beating his will into me. Before his obsession with me becoming a king.*

Hwyfar went to speak again to Gawain, but she was yanked sideways and fell through some sort of magical tunnel, where a thousand sunrises and sunsets swirled about her.

Then, at the end, two blood red moons rose on the horizon; two wolves cried out. The ground shook. *The first child born of Arthur. The first child. Born of Arthur.* The voice came from everywhere and nowhere, familiar and ancient—Merlin's voice.

Darkness fell.

Hwyfar went to take a step forward, but came to an abrupt stop when the ground before her fell away to reveal a flight of stairs. Beside her, a window opened out to the sea: still in Orkney. The change of scenery made her head ached, and she did not know where or when she was.

She took two careful steps down, but froze at the sound of an old man, rutting... and a young woman—too young—telling him to stop. "You've such a plump and pretty mouth, Anette," said the voice, guttural and accented with the harsh burr of Orkney. "You would never deny your king, would you?"

That was my father's voice, Gawain said, his voice more distant. This had been too much, and she was no closer to finding healing for Mordred.

The room began to dim, and Hwyfar saw another scene: Anna, holding a young serving woman in her arms, sobbing. The cries were familiar—this had been the same woman from a moment ago.

There was a look of steel in Anna's expression, even though she caressed the girl so lovingly.

"We shall care for your child, and he shall live in Carelon, and

I will protect you, always," Anna said, and her words were all sharp as knives.

The vision faded and Hwyfar, heart pounding so hard she could feel it in her teeth, released her grasp on her husband and Llachlyn, shaking her hands. The pain shot up her arms, like a thousand stinging nettles, making it difficult for her to speak.

Gawain stood there, on the opposite side of the altar, his face a mask of concern. "You are overexerting yourself," he said, taking her gently by the shoulders.

"Llachlyn, are you well?" Hwyfar asked, noting how the young woman was now shuddering.

"I saw," Llachlyn said. "The moons—the wolves. I have dreamed those before."

Disoriented, Hwyfar steadied herself against the cold marble altar, fingers slipping against blood as she did so. It was good Gawain was holding her, or she did not think she would have managed. Her body felt bruised from the magic.

Was that Gweyn's power? Llachlyn's? Was that what it was to have the Eye? Did Gweyn's power still linger in Mordred, somehow, even if he had not been hers? Hwyfar's head pounded, and she welcomed the ale Llachlyn gave her.

"Where did we go, love?" Gawain asked, voice calm and familiar and welcome.

Hwyfar could still hear the young girl from the vision weeping down the stone corridor, and the hot, sick sound of the king pushing himself upon her.

Mordred stirred, his face crumpling in pain, lips parting as if to speak.

Carefully, Hwyfar leaned over and stroked the side of his cheek, pouring all the healing power she could find into him, willing him peace, strength, rejuvenation. He regained a bit of his color, but that was all.

"My prince," she said, pulling out another of the tinctures she knew would at least lessen his pain. "You have tasted far fouler than this, but I promise it will help with the pain."

He groaned, then shuddered.

"That's a good omen, is it not?" Arthur asked from across the room. He stood, aided by Father Olwein.

Hwyfar did not answer the King for fear of giving him any false hope. She was no skilled healer, but she was experienced in such grave injuries. Ten years living at Thistlewood had seen a fair share of their tenants hurt by cows, falling beams, and every manner of hunting accident. So often the body behaved in strange ways when it was exposed to vast amounts of pain, hiding the gravity of the injury behind a guise of hope.

Goddess, please. Hwyfar did not know which goddess she prayed to, or if she believed directly in her any longer.

She needed clarity, and answers.

"This is a grievous wound, Your Majesty," Hwyfar said. Goddess, she wanted to sleep for a year, her body was so weary. "It will take time, but I do not know that I have enough power. I am no Morgen, no Vyvian."

Just then, Mordred began convulsing. King Arthur cried out, Father Olwein falling to his knees praying—not, as she would have hoped, for Mordred, but a ward against evil directed at Hwyfar.

"She has nothing to do with this, you fool!" Gawain bellowed, before reaching down to touch Mordred, helping to still him.

"My mother used her blood to heal me once," Llachlyn said in a rush. She was smoothing Mordred's hair as he strained, his breath stuttering in his chest. "Because I was her child, because we were connected, she said, it would help. She cured me of a deadly fever that way."

Hwyfar knew what she was asking, what she implied. But Llachlyn did not know what Hwyfar had seen, and what she and Gawain had known about Mordred and Percival, and Anna Pendragon's terrible bargain.

How could Morgen ever manage this burden of knowing?

"Blasphemy," Father Olwein whispered. "Blood is sacred, and the prince's even more so. What would this whelp even know?"

"This *whelp* is a daughter of Avillion and my cousin," Gawain snarled. Hwyfar could feel his anger, hot as fresh iron and ready to combust. "Her blood is just as precious as his, and her mind far cleverer than yours will ever be."

Father Olwein covered his face with his hands. "I cannot be witness to this savagery."

"Would you prefer we allow the prince to die?" Gawain asked, rounding on the priest. "Because that is far easier than what we are trying to do. Unless you wish to just pray harder, aye?"

Father Olwein had the gall to cross himself and draw closer. Just at that moment, Mordred coughed up a clot of blood, and Hwyfar rushed to put him on his side so he would not inhale it.

There was so much blood on her hands, now.

Blood. Mordred's blood. Gawain's blood. She glanced down at her hands and saw that same blue and yellow shimmer, beckoning her.

That was my father's voice.

Yes, blood would help.

She was so tired of prophecies and of political machinations. Even with a decade's reprieve from Carelon, Hwyfar remained painfully woven into the fabric of these families, their legacies, their power. How did Anna live with herself, knowing what treachery she had wrought against these two children? As Gawain had said to her, it must have been a far more terrible power than either of them could imagine.

Glancing up at her husband, Hwyfar thought again of the vision they had shared, seeing Gawain so small and serious, relaxed and joyous in his uncle's arms. He'd borne him so effortlessly.

The first child born of Arthur.

Hwyfar glanced at Llachlyn, who was worrying her fingers together so much they might go raw, and understanding glimmered across her own magic—the Eye, the kenning, her sister Gweyn's gift, smelling of fresh daisies and upturned earth and newly hewn wood.

The first child borne of Arthur. She could hear her sister's voice in her mind.

The young woman weeping. The old man in Orkney Castle. The woman at the foot of the bed. Yes, there had been Llachlyn, and Loholt the bastard; there was Mordred, first in Arthur's heart, but not in his blood.

Hwyfar heard Arthur's voice again: *I have never held a child before.*

Arthur had not just held Gawain; he'd borne him aloft.

The first child borne of Arthur will bring his end.

CHAPTER FORTY-FOUR

GAWAIN

GAWAIN WATCHED HIS wife blanch again, staggering backwards. No, it was quite enough. He had managed to stay calm, but he would not stand by and have his wife fall apart before him. Not even for Prince Mordred.

"Hwyfar, this is enough," he said to her.

Mordred, mercifully, had quietened after his last bout. His breathing was slow, labored, and wet. Soon, deeper sickness would settle in. They had to act, or decide not to act and allow nature to take its course.

"Llachlyn is right," Hwyfar whispered. Her lips were almost white, cracked and dry, her eyes dark and fathomless. Magic still sizzled about her; he could feel it. "Blood would help."

She did not grab Llachlyn's hand, however. She took Gawain's, firm and without room for argument, and said to him: "The knife."

He knew what she meant. The knife they'd carried with them from Lyndesoires so many years ago, the one that blunted his own strength and power.

Gawain sensed the unease in his wife, and his throat constricted with concern and the threat of tears. They'd spent ten years in such a comfortable world, able to speak at leisure about nearly everything. Now, in the presence of the King and so many secrets, there was so much he could not say to her. So much he could not give her, though he wanted to.

Her expression spoke without words, and he felt it in the very center of his soul. *This is where everything changes,* she seemed to say. *All but my love for you. If you do not run, I will not falter.*

"I will give whatever I can to my cousin," Gawain said firmly, gesturing to the King to remain seated and calm. "I have more than enough blood to spare."

"But surely I should—" Llachlyn tried, but Hwyfar shook her head. The King looked horrified at the spoken implication. "As... as his..."

Hwyfar rescued her, even though her exhaustion was clear to all who saw her. "That is brave of you, Llachlyn, but the magic has shown me the path to take. And it is through Sir Gawain's blood that we may find enough healing for the prince," Hwyfar said, smoothly. She was *lying.* Gawain could not say how, but he knew it as surely as he knew the freckles on her shoulders.

"I do not like this at all, sire," Father Olwein said to the King. "It is unwise to practice such devilry here—and in the chapel."

Gawain worked to keep his breathing calm, ignoring the priest's prattling.

"My liege," he said to Arthur. "I will only do this with your blessing. But believe me when I say my wife's magic is powerful, second perhaps only to Morgen le Fay. She is the best chance we have."

Arthur looked so frail, so pained, and it broke Gawain's heart. The castle falling, Mordred in peril, his priest warring with a sorceress over his son's body. He understood that pain, but he also could not sit by and allow the priest's small-minded prattling take them from their focus.

Every hand, every breath, stilled in the room. Gawain could hear his blood rushing in his ears, the sweat prickling his skin, the flaring of his nerves through his body.

"Proceed, Gawain, Princess Hwyfar," the King said, sitting back down with a groan.

Gawain took out the cursed knife again, holding it to his wife.

Tenderly, Hwyfar took his hand in hers, stroking the fingers with her own, a line furrowing between her eyes as she concentrated. "We should not need much," she said quietly.

The knife cut quickly, surely. While the steel nicked his skin across the meat of his forearm, Gawain felt an echo of the same magic that had once rendered him utterly useless. Nausea swam up, a thousand cold fingers down his back, and he swayed on his knees slightly.

Then it was over, dark blood trickling into a small glass vial Hwyfar had procured. Her own hands trembled as she collected it, and he wished he could grant her all his strength, all his resolve—not that she did not have her own, but she was clearly on the brink of exhaustion. Since arriving at Carelon, the demands on her had been greater than anyone. And it was not fair.

Hwyfar drew a circle of blood upon Mordred's brow and at the bow of his lips, then one upon each of his eyes. When she finished, she took Gawain's hand and guided it to Mordred's chest.

"You are bound in blood," Hwyfar said to Gawain, and even he could tell there was more to her words than their immediate meaning. "Bone, breath, and body. You are woven of the same essence, bonded in power and in inheritance. May that power tie you together, and smooth the ills that have befallen us this day."

At first, nothing remarkable happened. Gawain felt the sting of his wound, but it was nothing time and a few salves would not fix. Mordred went still, though, lips pressed together against the pain.

Gawain was about to speak when an unmistakable tug in the very center of him jolted him, his breath going out like a snuffed candle. He jerked forward, and his vision dimmed and smeared like grease upon a window. He saw concern in his wife's face, but not enough to alarm him. Her cold fingers grasped his arm, rooting him in place.

"Stay here," she commanded, a hint of her occasional short temper. She used that tone with their hounds back home in Thistlewood.

Except Gawain wasn't trying to go anywhere. How could he? He couldn't even breathe!

Green filled his vision, then, and with it the calming sense of his great friend, the Green Knight, wrapped around him. It should have been cause for joy, as he always felt when they connected, but he knew they were inexorably pulling apart. His mouth tasted of loss and bitterness, the sting of long-shed tears and regret.

Time moves against you, Son of Orkney.

The Green Knight's voice resounded in Gawain's head, sharp and full of echoing whispers. It had sounded like that upon their first meeting; since then, their voice had always been a comfort or, at times, an annoyance. But not so full of dread.

I go across the Eversea, to rest in the great pool where Time cannot find me, and the doom of men has no teeth. For you must deny me forever and ascend. Do not fear, for I have prepared you both.

No! Gawain tried to reach out, to clasp his hand to the Green Knight. *Please—there is so much more you could teach us.*

Mordred. Of Orkney. The babe given in blood. He will begin the end.

Through this healing, your bond will be tested as never before, and the Crown will herald in the new age.

Hwyfar was there, listening—Gawain knew this. Her presence, their *carioz*, flared to life again with a sense of loss, duty, and at last, resignation.

He wanted to rage against the words, rage against the loss of the Green Knight. All was lost, all their years of peace and love— who would tend the fields of Thistlewood now? Who would call in the cows? Who would mend the fence? Had he truly ever lived in such simplicity? He had believed it would last forever.

Ever a man of action, never a man of strategy. He could feel his wife's sorrow, and it did not pull them apart. No, it brought them closer together, to this inevitable moment, where so many secrets were laid bare and the future of the kingdom splintered out before them.

He would give this gift to Mordred, even knowing what it would cost him, what it would cost Hwyfar. They had once mended the Green Knight, after all, with similar magic, and they had found their way back to one another, even so.

And she understood. He was not choosing this out of desperation or fear. No, they were choosing this together. *Carioz is a choice. I will choose you again and again and again, no matter what.*

The room sparkled into clarity again and Gawain held back the urge to vomit, his stomach acid churning. All the candles in the room, burning low but moments before, were now a vivid verdigris. It smelled of loam and fresh fallen rain, tinged with flux. Father Olwein was crossing himself, weeping fearfully.

Hwyfar cradled Mordred in her arms, tears of blood on her face, as he gazed up at her in wonder.

King Arthur rose with a shout.

"A miracle," King Arthur said. "Mordred…"

Mordred turned his head, teeth chattering through undoubted pain and disorientation. "Father," he said. "I dreamed the castle came down upon me and I died."

"The first part is true," King Arthur said, kissing his son desperately upon his brow. Mordred did not argue; he looked almost relieved at the attention. "But the second part, thankfully, is not. By God's grace, your aunt Hwyfar and uncle Gawain were able to help heal you."

Mordred tilted his head and looked at Gawain, a strange kind of recognition there. "I dreamed of a great knight," the prince said. "Green as new-sprung grass, clutching a great sword. They were not a man, and not a woman, but greater than both, I think." Mordred laughed. "I think they must have mistaken me for you, uncle, for they called me 'Son of Orkney.'"

CHAPTER FORTY-FIVE

MORGEN

IT WAS TINTAGEL, but it was not Tintagel. This was the castle of my childhood: vibrant and cared for, surrounded by green rolling hills and my mother's enchanting gardens. It was she who taught me herbalism and the language of flowers, and how to tend and use them without maligning their purposes. She who filled Tintagel with love.

Beautiful as it was, the castle was devoid of any inhabitants in this strange magical simulacrum. As I walked the perimeter, I kept anticipating I would see my sisters—younger, full of mischief—or my father, tending the climbing roses. Instead, I beheld only birds, bugs, and skittering mice. The air was fragrant, redolent of springtime, and without thinking I made my way to the solarium and the adjacent gardens.

Hope blossomed in my chest. My mother had to be there. Why else would I be given such a dream? What other reason to endure the tribulations of the recent weeks? Surely, in this perfect place, I might find a remnant of the woman I had loved more than any other and lost too soon. The woman whose tragedy had begun a chain of events that shook the foundations of a kingdom.

I shut my eyes, and imagined her, on her knees, fussing over the snails destroying her favorite patch of greens. Once again, I sensed her closeness, wrapping around me.

Yet it was not my mother who stood in the garden bed when I opened my eyes, but my father, Gorlois.

"Morgen mine," he said, his voice coming from the earth and the sky at once. The name he used to call me. "It's late. Where have you been off to today?"

Carefully, I stepped closer to him. He looked so young to my aged eyes. I was twice the age he was at his death; I had lived another lifetime. He had barely begun to go grey, only the subtlest touch of depth to his handsome face.

"I've been on an adventure," I said softly.

"I was hoping you might say that," he said, squatting down.

I realized, in this dream place, I was a child, still, in height and form.

As grief prickled at me, I held out my hands. "I've missed you so much." The words came out barely whispered.

He smiled, reaching up to tuck a wisp of a curl behind my ear. "And I missed you. But you are old enough you do not need me on your adventures. Tell me: what beasts did you see?"

"I lion," I said. "A cockatrice." My heart raced as I gazed into his dark eyes again. "The Glatisant."

"Goddess above, you are a warrior among princes to face down such foes!" my father said, all seriousness. He was the sort of adult who never spoke down to children, his voice full of wonder and respect.

"The lion became an unexpected friend," I said.

Then he held out his hand and I realized I, too, was crouching—I was no longer in the form of a child, but restored to my own, aging self, though my father remained the same. My vision shimmered as I stood, looking at him as an adult. I had never had the chance to do so while he was alive.

I watched as my father recognized the understanding in my face. "Do you know where we are, Morgen?" he asked.

"It looks like Tintagel," I said. "But I sense that is not the entirety of it."

He shook his head sadly. "When we die, we go back to the

center of the world, the place where magic and faith and love all abide together in peace. I am only here because a part of me yet lingers in the world. Trwth, the great boar who felled me, drank of my blood and, tinged as he was with Merlin's magic, still lives. For Merlin took that ancient creature's mind and set him upon me. So, too, part of me remains."

"Merlin is dead," I said. "Though 'twas no simple feat."

"His power is not dead, and you know it well. It threatens the very foundations of Carelon, even now. You taught your sister well, but she did not know the true cost of her vengeance upon the old mage."

I frowned, aware of the complexities, if only in part. I had allowed Anna access to magic she was never trained in, and had deluded myself into thinking there would be no consequences. "Be that as it may, there is little I can do from here," I said, holding up my hands helplessly. "I was thrown from the castle by a great power—the remnants of his power, perhaps. I believe Vyvian's magic was keeping it at bay somehow, but I do not think she knew it. I have been trying to get back, but I do not know what to do."

"That was not Merlin's magic, Morgen."

"You say that with such certainty."

My father smiled, the edges of his eyes crinkling. "It is simple. The goddesses brought you to the wilderness to learn. To grow. And you have."

"I do not have time for the whims and games of goddesses!" I shouted, anger searing through me like a living serpent of flame. "How dare they cast me out when I was needed."

"What is time, to the greatest sorceress of this greatest age?" He said the words so tenderly, they felt true. "Your name alone instills fear and wonder across the whole realm."

I let my head fall to his chest, and he gently rubbed my back, humming softly. Birds chirped overhead, shadows lengthened, and time itself held its breath.

"I am so tired of holding all of this in my hands at once. The responsibility, the guilt, the shame," I said, weeping into his tunic. It felt so real, so true. "I do not know where to start."

"Death has always followed you, Morgan mine. Begin there. If Merlin's power is not yet gone, it means he is not yet dead. Have you ever felt him across the threshold?" he asked.

"No," I said, quietly. "But I was always afraid to look."

"Well, now is the time to take the scales from your eyes: Merlin's soul still awaits on the threshold of the Maw of Death, twisted and broken from the magic he wrought and that which trapped him through your sister's will. And you must usher him across, or else Carelon will fall. For what remains is a hunger that will not be sated until it is vanquished. But, my love, you cannot do this alone. If you try, you will fail."

No, I could not bear that. I had been abandoned so many times in my life, relegated to the edges of others' joys and triumphs, that the bitterness clung to me. I had chosen loneliness—why should anyone heed my call?

And with the tide of anger and resentment came the overwhelming rush of abandonment I had cradled at the center of me for so many years. In my father's arms my resolve fractured.

For why should I do more to save Carelon? I, who had bled and lied and suffered in the shadows for decades?

"Perhaps Carelon deserves destruction," I said. "Perhaps I deserve it, too."

"You chose to uphold Uther's legacy to keep you and your sisters safe, and your mother along with you. You cannot change what he did, but you can preserve the best of Carelon for my granddaughter. For her friends. For the generation you shaped, both wittingly and willfully. They will need you."

"I have been a terrible mother."

"You still have time to change."

"*Tas.*" Father. "Don't go."

"I have never left you, Morgen mine. And I never shall." And it was not only my father's voice that called to me across the vast expanse of magic, but my mother's also.

My face was wet and warm, and in the distance, I heard the

familiar burbling of the stream I'd listened to every day for the first five years of my life.

I opened my eyes to see a pair of luminous brown eyes set in a golden face staring down upon me with clever interest.

Melic.

To hide my tears, but also in true joy, I threw my arms around the creature and buried my face in his mane. He smelled fresh and clean, like late-summer heath and honey, pulling me out of my strange dreams and into the living world.

Sunlight streamed in the room and, as I pulled myself from the dear cat's embrace, I took stock of where I was. Once again, I was back in the little cell I'd taken up residence in at Tintagel where Coel had given me counsel, and a good dose of insight into my own anguish.

A striking young woman sat across the room from me, and I did not recognize her immediately. She held a hoop of embroidery on her lap and sang softly to a lilting, joyous tune. When she glanced up at me, I finally placed her: Isolde.

"I'm glad to see you're awake," Isolde said, placing down her work and coming to stand by my little bed. If she was concerned by the enormous lion in the room, she showed no sign of it. In fact, her countenance was greatly improved from the last time I saw her, sitting blank-eyed and miserable in the great hall.

"Isolde. Goodness. How long was I asleep?" I asked.

Isolde smiled, dimples deepening her cheeks. "Just a few hours. You had a number of physical wounds, which I was able to attend to—but I'm afraid the kind of magic you and the priestess performed takes a heady toll that only sleep can mend. Coel carried you here after…" She trailed off, and the ache of Ahès's loss shattered me anew.

"She is truly gone, then," I whispered.

Isolde nodded somberly.

Ahès' gift lived inside of me. I could feel its newness and strangeness, like a blossoming flower. I felt my heart beating under my palm, almost surprised to feel it was just the same as ever before; I half expected to feel her heart trembling within.

The dream of my father lingered still, disorienting me enough that I half forgot what the presence of Melic meant.

"Is Sir Yvain here?" I asked.

"Indeed, he is," Isolde replied. "And it is to him, and his brother, we are indebted—Well, along with the great work you and the priestess did. He spoke with the Glatisant, and sent her away, promising to send her tribute. Can you imagine? A knight who speaks to animals."

I could imagine, indeed. Modrun's son had made us all very proud. "And Marqus?"

"He fled in shame, most of his force destroyed. When he emerges again, King Uriens plans to go straight to Arthur with his treachery."

"That is a relief," I said. "I am sorry for all you have endured."

"Such is the plight of women," Isolde said, her bright eyes rising to the window. Birds flew across the cloudy windowpane, the sound of their wings like a distant conversation. "But perhaps there is hope for us still, in this. Our love has been long fought, and even Tristan tires of it."

"King Marqus is a scourge and an insult to Cornwall," I said, wishing I was the sort of woman who might spit her curses.

"Yes, but he is a dangerous man, all the same, and I will proceed with extreme caution," Isolde said, her voice lowering. "But I feel safer here, with you."

I scoffed, wincing against the pain in my head. Melic pushed at my legs with his muzzle.

Rising, I went to the window to gaze out upon the courtyard and solarium. The signs of devastation were clear: half-eaten carcasses, rubble, and scars across the grounds from the great beasts fighting. Any human bodies had been removed from the premises.

And indeed, I spied soldiers wearing Uriens's black and white, both patrolling and at work—far more than we had arrived with. They must have changed their course, as Fate called to Yvain.

"We are working to restore what we can of the halls," Isolde said. "It was a travesty, what he did, bringing those poor dead beasts in. I knew him capable of so much cruelty, but it seemed egregious even for him."

My stomach growled and I laughed lightly, holding my hand to my side.

But the laughter was short-lived, for I saw a rider in the distance coming at great speed, the scarlet-and-gold banner of Carelon streaming behind him. The hand of the goddesses was still on my heart; I had a flash of prescience.

Now was the time to return home. To Carelon. To my tower.

I MET COEL and Yvain in the great hall, already in conversation with the messenger. I could see the look in Coel's eyes when he saw me, a mixture of relief and wariness he only let slip when he was at his most vulnerable.

"Lady Morgen," Yvain said, bowing courteously. He wore the clothes of a prince, his hair neatly braided down his back. When he smiled, it kindled inside me. I had missed him, I realized. Time in the sun had kissed his cheeks with a rosy hue, but his eyes remained cool and bright all the same.

"You found us," I said, taking his hand in mine. "How did you know?"

He grinned, comfortably and without hesitation. "Melic was restless our first day at sea, and by the second he was inconsolable. We made landfall so I could let him stalk about on land, and I heard of King Marqus's trek toward Tintagel. We followed his trail of destruction."

"We are indebted to you, Yvain," Coel said. "As, indeed, is all of Cornwall, I suspect."

"I did as any man worth his mettle might," Yvain said, touching his hand to his heart. "But it seems strange tidings are not solely reserved for Tintagel this day."

The messenger shifted uncomfortably. Tintagel had never looked worse, and we were a motley group of aging players standing in its old bones.

"What news from Carelon?" I asked.

A deep breath, and then the messenger blinked, eyes finally falling upon me, registering my face. Garbed as I was, disheveled and travel worn, it was not surprising it took them a moment.

"Lady Morgen?" asked the messenger.

"Yes," I replied.

"The King will be so relieved to find you safe and hale. And he needs you now more than ever before," they said, shaking their head in disbelief. "I was here to deliver the message to King Marqus, but—well, now you are the rightful Lady of Tintagel. So, to the point: Carelon was struck by a terrible earthquake, tumbling Merlin's tower and claiming many lives. Prince Mordred was gravely wounded. Mortally, we fear."

My world narrowed, calmed, focused. I ought to have cried out or wept, but instead a deep awareness opened up inside of me. It was not a sense of any goddess, nor of a saint or any specific entity. Ahès's power was illusion and connection, after all, and it felt as if she were standing beside me.

And for a moment I saw the ruins of Merlin's tower in my mind and, though the cost was great, I was relieved. And afeared. For I knew, without doubt, my daughter Llachlyn was there. And Hwyfar and Gawain, too. I could *almost* reach them across the Path.

"Morgen?" Coel's voice brought me back to the moment.

"What of the rest of the royal house?" I asked, thinking of Anna, of Bedevere, of Palomydes—and so many I counted as friends. "Arthur's knights?"

"Sir Gawain has returned from the North with his wife—the King proclaimed them all welcome at court," the messenger said, tactfully choosing his words.

"And who is his wife?" I asked, a hint of humor in my voice.

"It is Princes Hwyfar of Avillion and Lyonesse," the messenger replied. "They are attending the King and Mordred, last I heard. I rode as fast as I could, but the weather is turning."

Coel's hand on my back was reassuring, warm, and far from

unwanted. "Morgen, this is your choice," he said to me. "I know you are weary."

I was. Goddess alive, I was so tired.

It did not matter.

"We make for Carelon at once," I said, not stopping to ask permission. "Bring what men you have, and any supplies you know of. It is less than a day's ride from here."

Coel's answering look was a mixture of pride and purpose, and I was grateful beyond words. I was the Lady of Tintagel, now, duchess by birth and by the rules of chivalry.

Though I longed to linger, and rebuild, I also felt the responsibility of my father's words upon my heart. Perhaps Anna's spell had rid us of Merlin, but I had given her the key to that ruination—and if his power still lingered, and if it was, as I suspected, the cause of the earthquake beneath the castle, it was my duty to vanquish it.

Though, I did not hesitate to wish, briefly, for a younger body and a stronger constitution. My power was not yet returned, but *changed*, and I did not have the confidence I might once have had.

Yet, in the past I had been utterly alone. I looked from Coel's face to Yvain's, and felt Melic's soft, insistent purr, and understood the gifts I had been given without doubt. Perhaps I would not be able to repair the Path, or even conquer my own changed magics, but I had certainly built a new power, here.

PURPOSE SANG IN my body as we rose, fresh and welcome. In my youth I had traveled the realm near and far, but never at the head of a small force. Never as my own hero. Never in any form of command, though I certainly garnered respect.

This felt different. *I* felt different.

Perhaps I was wrong to feel hope amidst my worry and grief. Yet I could not banish it from my thoughts. So much in Carelon had been festering for years—so many secrets and subterfuge—perhaps now, with the earth itself rising up, people like Queen

Mawra might come to their senses. Perhaps Arthur would see how important his role as Mordred's father truly was. Perhaps Lanceloch would, for once, be happy in his place at court and not strive for more recognition.

And Llachlyn. She was meant to travel to the castle with Percival and Galahad weeks ago, no doubt distraught at my disappearance. Or relieved. I could not say. She was ever a timid creature, and I had never quite figured out how to speak with her as she grew. Did she hate me for what she was? Did she fear me? It was better, I reasoned, for her to think me distant and vague than meddling and tiresome.

Yet I had to believe if she'd died in the earthquake, I would have known. But I had been fighting monsters for so long, entrenched in my own self-pity, would I have even noticed? I knew well I did not think of my child often enough, nor did I feel even particularly maternal toward her. This was no doing of her own, but rather something lacking, or broken, or misaligned in me.

I kept these thoughts to myself, unsure what to do with them. Selfishly, I had hoped Vyvian's death might impact Arthur as much as it had me, drive him to action. Instead, he had withdrawn even more. He had never stopped mourning Merlin, but now the tower was gone, and I would ensure it was never built again.

And with Mordred in mortal peril, what would happen to all those frayed ends of Fate? Would Gawain rise to prominence in his uncle's stead? That was what I would have counseled, even though it would put him and Hwyfar in a position they had never wanted.

As afternoon deepened to evening, we pressed on. It would not do to fall asleep upon my horse; I could not bear the embarrassment. If I had time, I would have gathered herbs I knew would help keep me alert. Instead, I loosened my cloak to let the cold air in.

We initially made remarkable time, the wind in our favor, until the ground began to change, easy roads making way to a muddy slog as we forged our way north. Great rains had swollen the rivers and tributaries, and when we reached River Hafran, despair surrounded us.

"It's getting too dark, Morgen," Coel said to me. "I know we must continue on, but it would be unwise to continue in this weather."

I could not answer him, for I was too deep in my thoughts. Damn them all. Damn Vyvian for dying. Damn Merlin for his manipulations. Damn Arthur for his trust. Damn that I had relied on the Path so long and not thought to make my own way. Damn the goddesses for leaving me with this gift.

"I'm certain there are other healers at the castle helping the wounded," Coel offered when I could do nothing but pace back and forth behind the small, sputtering fire. "We could backtrack and find a ship to cross toward the bay, but I fear the sea looked angry."

"It is not simply the wounded," I said, harsher than I meant to. He did not need to bear the brunt of my anger, but he was there, and I did not know where else to put it. "I must get *below* Carelon, Coel. The root of the rot is there."

"I suppose there is no convincing you otherwise," Coel said. He took my hand, gently touching the back of my fingers.

And then he pulled me toward him, and I let him kiss me. I allowed his warmth, his affection, and his ardor to anchor me to the earth, felt the current of his own magic. This was no touch of death, but a reminder of life, of passion, of promises we had once made one another.

"Yvain tells me you flew into Brocéliande on the wings of crows," Coel said in my ear, his hand tracing my hair reverently at my back. "You slew a cockatrice, you confounded the Glatisant—you stood against a bloodthirsty king. Surely you can find the power in you to meet this foe."

"I don't even know how to summon the crows," I said, sinking into his warmth, grateful for the moment's reprieve. How I had yearned for this!

The trees rustled above our heads, in what I assumed was a passing breeze, but then Yvain, who had been watching us with a smirk upon his face, touched my shoulder and pointed up.

"Perhaps you ought to ask them," he said.

Dozens of green-eyed crows stared down at me from the branches, tilting their heads and flicking their tails.

"You travel with some odd friends," Coel said.

They had found me again. Messengers of Death, perhaps, but mine all the same.

I walked toward the largest tree, letting go of Coel's warm hands, that stillness opening in me again. I thought about what Ahés told me, that my old gifts remained—they were just quieter in comparison to my new powers. And I thought of her power, connecting me to them—and Ahés's strength, and her ties to the goddess.

Melic pushed into my legs, the sturdy warmth comforting. He purred lowly, almost plaintively, and a pair of crows spiraled down to stand before me.

They gazed up, canting their heads left and right.

I felt embarrassed talking to birds—but then, I had found myself speaking to Melic as if he understood me. And we had built quite the bond.

"Would you take me to Carelon?" I asked the birds. Knees cracking, I knelt down to hold out my hand. My nails were still dark in the moonlight from that strange curse, and between my wrinkles and veins I recognized the hand of a crone beseeching these birds of death.

The birds higher up let out a series of clicks and caws, and I tried again.

"You once took me to the great forest," I said. This time, I did not look at my hands, did not judge myself. "I ask you to take me back to Carelon, where you found me, so I may finish my tale."

I was Morgen.

Daughter of Death.

Queen of Mercy.

And these crows were my gift.

The world swirled away in a gyre of wings and feathers.

CHAPTER FORTY-SIX

LLACHLYN

LLACHLYN HAD FALLEN asleep in the nave of the church, hours after Hwyfar and Gawain had healed Mordred. She had anticipated being part of the healing magic, but it was not necessary, it seemed; not when Sir Gawain was there. At least she had been able to help in some way, with the ritual leading up to it, though she had seen nothing in Hwyfar's visions but a reminder of her own dream: the moons, the wolves, the crumbling castle.

She should have ridden out to find Galahad and Percival, but she'd gone so long without sleep that she'd collapsed in a corner, behind a fallen tapestry of Christ carrying the cross.

Her dreams meandered and twisted, and when she awoke with a start, she could remember none of them.

Percival stood over her, his eyes alight with mischief and relief. The tapestry fluttered behind him, blurs of crimson and gold flashing in the movement.

"There you are," he said to her. "I should have suspected you'd find the coziest, smallest corner in the keep."

Rubbing her eyes, Llachlyn took in her surroundings. "I must have fallen asleep. I didn't mean to."

"You must have needed it," Galahad said, coming down to sit beside her.

They both looked different. Clearer, somehow. As if she could focus on them better, or the light fell on them in a new way.

Much the same as how the world looked different depending on the angle of the sun and the season.

"Did you find it?" Llachlyn asked.

The young men exchanged a look, Percival nodding slowly. "We'd like to show you. Not here, though. The forge."

Anticipation prickled over Llachlyn's skin as they walked together to Vyvian's forge. It was the only place they could find relative quiet, and thankfully had been spared any serious damage. Llachlyn liked to think it was due to Vyvian's residual protection magic.

Aside from a few broken pieces of pottery, the forge was perfect.

"In the dream it was so large," Percival said as he closed the door behind them, words tumbling out as if he had been holding them back the whole time. "We were surprised to find it was so small—if I hadn't felt the miracle of it, I don't think I'd have even believed."

"I almost drowned," Galahad admitted, scratching the back of his head. His hair was still wet about the nape. "But Percival intervened."

"Percival can't swim," Llachlyn said. She could not stop worrying her hands together. "What were you thinking?"

Percival grinned. "I was thinking we might be able to save the realm. I was thinking I love Galahad, and living without him would probably ruin me."

He spoke lightly, but Galahad flushed at the words and Llachlyn felt the truth of them to her heart. And it was not sadness she experienced, not really, but relief. She had known it, since she was young: that their paths would diverge, that Percival would follow Galahad to the ends of the realm and beyond, because he loved adventure. He wasn't very good at it, yet, but with time, she had no doubt Galahad would rely on him—perhaps even see Percival raised to the station of a knight.

That was never Llachlyn's fate. Theirs was a borrowed time, no less precious for its brevity, nor less sweet.

She was surprised to find no bitterness in her heart.

Galahad reached behind him and produced an unassuming box, about the length of his forearm and half as wide.

"I can feel it in here," he said, awe in his voice. "We could feel it in the water—all through the springs. I know it doesn't look like a shield, but Percival was clever enough to point out that shields have all sorts of meanings."

"I suspect," Percival said, his scholar's tone rising, "that Vyvian was keeping it concealed by her magic, preventing its discovery. But upon her death, it called to us all—in our dreams."

The box was made of black wood, still damp from its long slumber in the depths, and banded with a thick metal Llachlyn had never seen before. It had perhaps been painted once, but time had eroded away all the details save a few flakes of color at the crevices. But she knew the make of that metal, as she knew the beating of her own heart: it was made by Vyvian, one of her very clever locks, imbued with magic.

"We want to show the King," Percival was saying. "But it's sealed in the box. Galahad found the handle—you see there, on to top—and pulled."

"It seemed best to come to an expert in metals," Galahad said, real pride in his eyes as he caught her gaze.

Reverently, Galahad passed the box to Llachlyn, hope in his expression.

Indeed, Llachlyn could feel the power intensify as her hand touched the box, and she gasped. Though she knew it was impossible, she sensed a living entity inside. The weight was imbalanced, shifting as she turned it in her hands. Tears sprang to her eyes, unbeckoned and strange, and he was both desperately sad and overwhelmed with joy.

It was as if Vyvian were standing there—as if, miraculously, the box held her heart. Or her soul. Some essential part of her.

"What do you feel when you hold it?" she asked, looking at her cousin and friend.

"Grace," said Galahad. "Pure and welcome and free."

"Delight," said Percival. "Joy. Freedom. And you?"

She closed her eyes and thought, basking in the warmth of the sensation. It was a mystery, and within that mystery was the sense that, no matter what happened in her life, no matter what she learned or was capable of, another horizon awaited. A horizon she would never see. And it was not a terrible thing, but a quiet, sublime reverence for her own insignificance. More than her own—the insignificance of all mortal kind.

It was, she realized, like looking into the fathomless eyes of the Green Knight once again.

At last, Lachlyn said: "Wonder."

"Can you break it open?" asked Galahad.

Llachlyn understood why they were so keen to get inside. Men forever saw such implements and sought to understand their inner workings. She was relieved they'd come to her first—though she did not doubt they had attempted to open it themselves first. They did not understand. Perhaps they never would.

Vyvian was always writing her about such concepts, telling her how shaping metal into new forms was a magic unto itself, and that in time, she could learn how to imbue her own work with power. With purpose. Llachyn had no doubt Vyvian had poured her own essence into this very vessel.

"The mystery is its power," she said softly, cradling the box protectively. "Perhaps there is a shield inside. Perhaps it is a weapon. Perhaps it is nothing. But the answer is not ours to find, right now."

"We are in a forge, Mallow—you can melt it," Galahad offered, as if Vyvian's magic could be thwarted by mere fire.

"It is a vessel," Llachlyn insisted, frustrated she could not find the words to explain it all correctly. Her mind was reeling, awakened. "I have spent countless hours with metal, studying Vyvian's own work, writing to her for years. There is no seam. No visible lock. The wood is very old, and I am certain she made this with her own hands and her own powers. She kept it closed for a reason."

"I don't understand," her cousin snorted. "What use is a *graal* if it is invisible to us? Why would Vyvian, who was imprisoned herself for twenty years, ever do such a thing?"

Percival clapped Galahad on his shoulder, sighing in the way he always did when Galahad was being particularly dense. "You forget she had twenty years to study locks and chains, sweeting."

"I won't open it. Not now," Llachlyn reiterated. "Not yet, I should say."

She would not be moved on the matter. So much of her existence was shadowed by her lack. This was no such thing. Llachlyn knew with absolute clarity what she should do. She knew what she *could* do. In that way, Vyvian had been preparing her all along. It had been frustrating to never get lessons on swords and armor, on the trappings of knights. For the longest time, she had questioned Vyvian's teachings, who had encouraged her to focus on forging small, but complex, locks and rings and charms. Vyvian had *known* it would serve her.

Now, Llachlyn understood. Purpose crystallized inside of her. She wished, for a brief moment, she could tell her mother. Morgen, who had always wanted more from Llachlyn but who could not coax it from her no matter how hard she tried. Morgen, the greatest sorceress to walk the earth.

"We must give this to Hwyfar. She has already carried a *graal*. And we must all go below the castle, as soon as we can," Llachlyn said, looking at both young men. They had fire in their eyes. "There is a power there, and I think it was behind the earthquakes. In the hands of a powerful wielder, the *graal* may help us understand."

"And you are that powerful wielder, I suppose," Galahad said, allowing his jealousy to get the better of him.

"I don't know," Llachlyn replied.

"And what of the King?" Percival asked, hesitating a bit, looking around as if someone might hear them. "He has long searched for a *graal*, only to find this one so close. If he were to discover we did not bring it straight to him…"

Llachlyn thought of her father, so pale and sad, unable to look her in the face. She turned the *graal* over in her hands, running her fingertips across the etched design, which she now saw was a vine motif. As it dried, the metal had taken on a verdigris hue.

Ascribing its power to the Green Knight made no sense, and yet she knew, without question, their power was interlinked, perhaps forged of the same magic. For the Green Knight was a smith, themselves. And indeed, as she continued to look at the metalwork, she was reminded of the remarkable armor and weapons Gawain and Hwyfar wore—gifts from the old god.

"There are two other *graals*," Llachlyn said slowly.

"There could be many more than that," Percival intoned, tapping the box with his finger.

"How do you mean?" Galahad asked.

Percival's posture straightened, ready for his lecture. "I mean, we have been told there are three. And three is an auspicious number—in both faiths. But what makes a *graal*? Hwyfar told us of the horn she used to travel great distances, and I once heard a tale of an enchanted chessboard. Could it be they give us power because we believe they do?"

Llachlyn considered. "Merlin sought their power, but he also sought to control them."

"Perhaps to lengthen his life, or to solidify the Pendragon rule," Percival said. "But even he was just a man."

Outside the forge, Llachlyn heard crows cawing as a whole murder fell upon the dry earth. She thought of her mother, and how she would always feed them from her window, yet claimed she did not like birds—or any animals, save cats.

Percival was lost in his discussion. "And who is to say there are implements only here in Braetan? Certainly, there are other kingdoms and queendoms, empires and realms beyond our borders. Our minds narrow to focus so keenly upon our own contributions—"

One of the crows let out a loud enough *crawk* to interrupt Percival. Llachlyn went to the window and found the bird had, inexplicably, made its way into the room. The pressure in the room changed, her ears popping, and it smelled of flux and loam and green, growing things.

Then there were three crows sitting inside the windowsill, their eyes glowing green, their beaks clacking and snapping.

"What in God's name?" Galahad asked, drawing his sword.

Drawn forward, Llachlyn cradled the *graal* with one hand, and reached out to the triune of crows.

"I won't hurt you," she said softly. "You're very pretty birds."

The moment Llachlyn touched the oil-black feathers of the closest bird, a gyre of black feathers poured into the room, a gale pushing her hair off her face and making her clothing billow around her. If she screamed, it was smothered by the flapping din. A smoky, musky scent filled her nostrils, and for a moment she was worried she might not be able to breathe. She went to grab for Percival or Galahad, but she might as well have been reaching across the abyss, for all was black feathers and glowing green eyes.

Llachlyn fell back, her rear hitting the hard floor with a crack that sent a sizzle of pain up her spine, but kept the *graal* firmly in hand.

It took a moment to make out what she saw, as the feathers and smoke cleared, all twirling and snaking out toward the flue. Llachlyn coughed, tears streaming from the smoke, her vision slowly blinking back to the present.

Standing in the center of the room, dressed in dark plain undyed wool, her white hair unkempt, was her mother. She wore none of her trappings of status: gone were her jewels, her embroidery, and her swaths of silk. Morgen's boots were made of thick-stitched leather, her belt of flax, and there were black feathers all in her hair. She looked mighty, relieved, and more regal than she had ever been to Llachlyn's eyes.

When their eyes met, however, Morgen's fierce mask shattered and she ran toward her daughter, enveloping her in a trembling embrace, speaking words too fast and full of emotion to make any sense.

Llachlyn shivered under the attention, not recalling the last time her mother showered her with such love. Her mother smelled as she always did, sweet and smoky with a suggestion of mint.

"Aunt Morgen?" asked Galahad from the corner of the room, where he and Percival were helping one another stand.

At last, Morgen let go, holding her daughter at arm's length, her dark eyes passing over Llachlyn's features.

"Where were you?" Llachlyn asked, failing to keep her angry tears at bay. "Why did you leave? You're too late! You're here, but it's too late."

Her mother's expression softened, her eyes shining. "I didn't mean to leave, Llachlyn. I swear to you I did not. And it is never too late." She took Llachlyn's chin in her hand and, tears flowing down her cheeks, kissed her forehead. "I would never leave without telling you. I know you and I have—no, I know *I* have been distant. I have been foolish, afraid. But for all that, you are my greatest treasure, and I would never have left you to the vultures alone if I could help it."

"People assumed you were dead. Like Aunt Vyvian," Galahad said.

"I know," said Morgen, bowing her head. "But I am here, and I wish I had gladder tidings. For I received word from a messenger from Carelon that the castle had fallen, and Prince Mordred was in mortal danger. Where does he now stand?"

"He is alive, but still gravely ill," Llachlyn said. "As for us, our quest has been rather unusual."

Llachlyn held up the *graal* vessel, gently and meaningfully.

Morgen, for the first time Llachlyn had ever seen, looked genuinely shocked. "By the moon, you found it. Tell me, where do we stand? How did your quest begin? We do not have much time, I do not think, but I must know."

They proceeded to tell Morgen of their adventures in the North, the deception of the Queen and du Lac, and the ruination of the castle. Percival, who had always been friendly with the sorceress, did most of the talking, while Llachlyn filled in the gaps. It was so strange seeing her mother among them, lively and focused, treating them as equals and not as children.

When they spoke of Merlin's tower, Morgen fretted and paced the room. A few crows still stood guard outside the window, and they watched her, their eyes shining with interest.

"Merlin spoke of using implements of power to enhance abilities, namely his. I believe his sister Ganeida may have been particularly deft at recognizing them, but she prevented him from attaining them all before she died. The story says she threw herself from his tower in utter despair. She was also a prophetess," Morgen explained.

Llachlyn took her mother's hand. "I saw the same vision. I—I have been having the same one, for years."

Morgen did not react other than to nod, then touched Llachlyn's face. "Tell me while we walk. We must find Gawain and Hwyfar."

"And the King?" Galahad asked. "Should we not go to him, first?"

Morgen avoided answering the question. "I cannot force you to withhold information. But, as I stand here, I see the great crossroads of our future, and to protect the stability of our realm and the strength of our King, we must consider the wisdom of keeping these secrets, as I have done for most of my life."

CHAPTER FORTY-SEVEN

MORGEN

My daughter and her remarkable companions had found a *graal*. That gave me some comfort, knowing how complicated bringing them into the world had been, how much scheming and lying we had done. Merlin had seen their outcomes, and I had not argued—for his ends were not always malicious. No doubt he imagined it would be him standing here, a breath away from the power he had so craved, and not me.

It gave me no small sense of satisfaction knowing his scheming might be his final undoing, and this next generation free of the taint of his whispers. For Merlin had known, somehow, that if Percival had been raised at court, he would not be the same man he was, could not have fit in with the tale in such a way. It was a terrible gamble, but also a relief to me that not all my subterfuge had ended in lies and death.

For this was not just any *graal*, but the very one that had cost Vyvian her freedom for decades, marooned on an island for her crimes against Merlin. For she hid it from him and would not give up its location. And my clever daughter knew this, as she told me in her recounting of the tale. Not only that, but Vyvian had prepared Llachlyn to wield and understand just this sort of vessel in her tutelage, at a distance.

I had no desire to make a grand entrance to Carelon, especially now in this time of despair and catastrophe. Perhaps, decades ago, when my pride and vainglory were at their peak, I might have seen myself as a savior, capable of inspiring wonder and loyalty. But no longer. I wished to remain as deep in the shadows as possible.

As we walked through the castle, the devastation shocked me, along with the lingering, coppery taste of magic rising from below. Every time I closed my eyes, I saw roots reaching, grabbing, climbing the walls. But it did not frighten me as it had before, when I had lost myself to the crows and to despair; no, I understood this rot, this power, for I had lived beside Merlin for half of my life, and I saw the shape of him even in this corruption.

But I felt, too, my sister Anna's magic, the power that had trapped him. The power that now demanded payment.

We encountered Sir Bedevere as we made our way toward where Llachlyn had last seen Gawain and Hwyfar. They would be instrumental in this fight, and for the first time in my long, storied existence, I was not ashamed to admit it. I sensed Hwyfar's magic, woven through the castle itself, and knew she must have exerted herself a great deal to leave such an impression. Powerful though she was, no sorceress in the realm could have prevented this disaster.

Bedevere looked pale and fearful, age lying heavily upon his lined brow, frosted by white curls. Even without my finery, he recognized me as I walked by with my young entourage.

"You are here at last," Bedevere said. "Thank God."

"You sound as if you expected me," I said.

The old knight's face winced in reflection of inner turmoil. He glanced at Llachlyn, Percival, and Galahad. "I had hoped. Wished. Begged God. Morgen, it's Anna…"

"Is she still ill?" Galahad asked, sparing him the pain of his secret. Perhaps, when the walls of Carelon had come down, so too had our endless lies.

Bedevere visibly relaxed. Too many ill-kept secrets, as I well knew, overwhelmed a person. The tryst between my sister and him went back to their youth, a connection no marriage or time or loyalty could break asunder. Galahad knew and accepted that his mother and father had never had a marriage of love. For where was Lanceloch du Lac, even now? Not with his wife, and not with his lover, but licking his wounds at the Joyous Guard.

Though I could not help but wonder at his part in all of this.

"Bors found the Lady Anna in the depths. She was unresponsive, and"—Bedevere swallowed, struggling—"she has remained so since. She shows no signs of injury I can see or treat, but has fled deep into her own mind. She was clutching a pair of large scales in her hands."

Scales. Indeed. I knew the rumors of what lurked below Carelon, but I suppose I had doubted their truth. There were so many myths about Merlin besting the great dragons beneath Uther's castle that I had dismissed them.

My sister Anna was the last witch to cross Merlin—I had no doubt the power he'd left behind had entangled her within its web. I felt the pull, myself. And if the specter of Merlin's power had also attached itself to the power of the great tree, it would explain the surge of magic all around us.

And if, like the Glatisant and the cockatrice, the wyrms below Carelon had awoken after Vyvian's death, then we were in great peril, indeed.

I sent off a prayer for my sister Anna and focused my energy on the present.

"Send the twins—your brothers Gaheris and Gareth—to keep watch over Lady Anna," I said to Galahad. "Her battle is on the spiritual plane." Galahad crossed himself, and thankfully, no such gesture could touch me.

I turned to Bedevere. "I need you to take me below, but send these three young saints onward to Gawain and Hwyfar." I turned to Llachlyn, measuring my words. "Tell the princess and her husband to come to me in their armor."

"I want to stay with you," Llachlyn said, her voice free of its characteristic tremulousness. "There is much I can do, I think."

"I need you ready at Vyvian's forge," I said to Llachlyn, cupping her freckled cheek and looking deep into her eyes. The eyes of the man who had broken my mother. The eyes I loved so much, now. "I will come to you once the foe is vanquished, but I need your skill to seal the *graal*."

"So, you intend to use it," Galahad said, the edge of suspicion in his voice. "To your own ends."

It was curious, how I stood there, staring at these three young, remarkable people, who I had spent so little time with, out of guilt and vanity, and I *knew*. The Sight had come to me more often in my younger years, but it had grown quieter as I'd aged, and was never as poetic as Gweyn's or that of the other priestesses of Avillion. Now, it was a steady warmth, like a guiding hand on my shoulder that said: *This young man, born of parents both noble and faulted, the son of Vyvian's own ward, your flesh and blood, touched by the Spirit; he has been called to this.*

"I shall not wield it. But you shall, Sir Galahad, when the time is right," I said to my youngest nephew, a frisson of power shivering down my spine at the rightness of it. "And in doing so, you will become a legend."

Percival laughed, genuinely amused. My heart swelled with pride to see him, finding joy and absurdity in even the most terrible situations. "The last thing Galahad needs is another chapter to his legend. His head is already swollen enough."

I had to chuckle with him, that delightful contrast of my Sight with his gentle humor.

But this was also the Sight. This was also Fate nudging me. Percival had the same lightness as his mother, the same gentleness; and he had the cleverness and humor of his father. Together, he and Galahad balanced one another. Their path had been long, together, and fraught at times.

"Then you will keep him humble, and you will wield it with him," I said, placing my hand on Percival's shoulder.

My inner eye opened wide at that touch, and I saw Gweyn across the Maw of Death, shimmering and waiting. She had not lived long enough to see her true son grow, nor even long enough to know Mordred, but my magic reached out to her, sensing this moment, the interlacing threads of Fate pulling tighter, tighter...

"Mother..." Llachlyn came to my side, taking my hand.

I shuddered as I was pulled back to the present. My magic was making me light-headed, batting me about like some uninitiated acolyte.

We sent Galahad and Percival onward to speak with Gawain and Hwyfar, they promising to join us as soon as they could, and then it was just the two of us alone with Bedevere, who looked longingly out the ruined window before us.

"Llachlyn," I said to her.

"Let me come with you. Please. I am so tired of being left behind. I know the castle well, and I am small and quick—if aught is amiss, I will run straightaway to the forge. But only I have been below. I can show you the way."

"Llachlyn, the magic there is powerful and deadly."

She squeezed my hand, taking a measured breath. "Bedevere should stay with the Lady Anna. She should not be alone."

I took Bedevere's sleeve, saw the fear in his eyes. For a man who had campaigned through unspeakable war, it was a harrowing sight. Death clung to him. My daughter was right. "Protect the Lady Anna, with her tall, fierce sons. Tell them all that my love and protection goes with you."

The haggard knight bowed his head and nodded, then grasped my hand as a warrior before fading away into the dark corridor, alone.

I wished I could have made a better end for them. I wished Fate had not been so cruel. But this was my fight now, even if it had been precipitated by Anna's magic, so many years ago. I ought to have protected her, ventured more often below the castle and checked on the great tree—but I, too, was afraid of what I might find lingering.

We continued on together, and Llachlyn guided me through the derelict passageways and safer corridors, her sense of direction truly a wonder, even despite the destruction. A good third of the castle was obliterated, and the devastation only increased the closer we got to the depths below Merlin's old tower.

"This is a great evil below," Llachlyn said, stopping us at the great threshold that led to the final descent. "I know you say I do not have the same powers as you, and I agree—I am different. But I heard it. Smelled it."

"What lingers was not always evil, Llachlyn. When Vyvian's protective spells fell, it awoke, desperate and hungry, and has been feeding upon the foul magics still lingering there."

Steeling myself, I touched the stone threshold to the passageway, and my vision swam with the Sight once again: I saw fragments of future possibilities flit across the walls, heard cries and voices, felt the anxiety and pain of a dozen generations. These possibilities stretched out before me, thousands of pathways branching and diverting. It was difficult to root myself in the present, to keep my mind from wandering those corridors of possibility with my magic so charged.

I thanked Ahès again, pressing my hand to my fluttering heart. My powers were not precisely as they had been before the goddesses' blessings had come to me, but nor were they wholly unfamiliar.

As Llachlyn led me further down, I had to stop often, rubbing my eyes to root myself in reality; the magic was everywhere, spilling out and confusing me. The Sight gave way to fire magic, a deep desire within me to light the torches—which I did, though I nearly burned my hair off doing so. I could feel life in the castle moving about me, distracting me.

Goddess, I needed to focus.

When I staggered and almost fell down the winding stairway, Llachlyn took my shoulder. "Are you certain you are capable of this?" she asked, not unkindly. I knew how I must look to her, so bedraggled and unlike myself. So old and thin and small.

"I must at least try," I said, taking her proffered arm. "But I need your help."

"How much time do we have?" she asked.

My magic settled into the walls, up and toward Anna's chambers, opening my eye to the power there. I could see her form, hovering above her body on the bed, as thousands of threads rose from her chest, blanketing the whole of Carelon Castle. The threads were not unlike those of the Path, but sturdier somehow. It was not magic I could recognize, yet it felt familiar. Perhaps it was akin to the *carioz* between Gawain and Hwyfar, but greater—across us all.

I slowly felt my way through the intermingled magics, and understood. She was protecting us. She was trying to uphold a simulacrum of Vyvian's own charms, though she was far from skilled enough.

"I believe Lady Anna is holding the worst at bay; somehow, she is filling every crack and blemish of Carelon with protection," I whispered. "Perhaps—perhaps Vyvian's spells can be reproduced. Perhaps there is a way."

"What will we do until then?"

"I will confront Merlin," I said simply, though my heart quaked. "Or whatever abominations now reside where his magic still stains the ground."

At the base of the stairway, I felt an abrupt shift in the magic streams moving around us. The Maw rose up inside of me, like a defensive shield, as I staggered back. My throat burned with bile, my eyes streaming.

Your base nature will diminish your power if you are not careful, Morgen. The longer you study with me, the more strength you will gain. I promise, I shall share the splendor of my knowledge in equal parts.

Merlin's voice. Merlin's words. He knew I was here.

My magic flared in alarm at those words, and I felt Anna's power slip away, the network of protection evaporating around us both, and I cried out in fear and in pain. She had been so close, so nearly there. If only she had been given the training, she might have had a chance—this time she could not win.

"Did you hear that?" I asked Llachlyn.

She frowned, shaking her head.

"Wait here," I told Llachlyn. "Please. I must do this alone. What lies beyond is madness. Danger. I do not want you to see what it would make me."

She nodded her agreement, though I knew it pained her. She had the heart of a knight but would never have the constitution.

I kissed her upon the forehead and turned to pass through the threshold, my bones crackling with energy the likes of which I'd never imagined. I felt like the Morgen le Fay so many believed me to be, infused with power and confidence and strength, even though my hands shook with fear.

Looking up, I swallowed a gasp as a great chasm opened up before me, empty and somehow terrifying in that void. The smell was sulfuric, metallic, like the very bowels of the earth, and my ears rang in warning.

I raised my staff before me and called light into the room. In a flash of bright crimson and violet, the true scale of what lay beneath Carelon made itself known. Two great beasts rose before me: dragons, massive wyrms, one azure and the other vermillion, locked in bitter battle. Their scales caught in the firelight, flashing opalescent as they writhed around one another in slow, unending, yet silent, agony.

No, they were not hurting one another—great vines, thick as tree trunks, had pierced their flesh and twisted around their massive bodies, releasing blood and fluid in streams across the expansive floor. It stank of decayed flesh and sulfur, and whispers ricocheted across the cavern in a thousand woebegone voices.

You are fit for nothing but the paltry life of a midwife. I will peel my secrets from your undeserving soul.

Anna had trapped Merlin and Nimue together in the great oak, the ancient tree which had stood for centuries upon this plain. I had thought it fitting, safe, and I'd let down my guard. I had misjudged the reach of the old conjurer's abilities. Perhaps it had taken twenty years, but by siphoning power from the sleeping dragons—those he had charmed into slumber himself as a child—he could indeed possess another life. And he had fed upon them both.

The hair rose on the back of my neck as I turned, feeling a soft gust of air behind my ankles, my magic warning me as the room shook and trembled again. I would have fallen to my knees were it not for my staff.

"You know, when I reflect on our time together, you must understand, I never wanted your body, not really," came Merlin's voice, echoing in my mind. "I wanted your *potential*. Your power. Your ambition. And how sly you were, crawling into bed with me and keeping me company all those years. But alas, for all your divine gifts, you squandered it."

His words were meant to infuriate me, to humiliate me, but I would not allow it. "Your prophetic musings made you hungry for power, and you stopped at nothing to gain it. And no, I was not brave enough to do the deed myself. But I helped guide the hand. Now, it is time I finish what my sister began."

"And yet the little spider did not see the fissures in the foundations, for she gave up the one protection granted to her," Merlin said, and I saw the specter of a ghostly hand. There, on the finger, was the ghost of the red-stoned ring I had refused after Vyvian's death. "Forged by Myrddin the First, fashioned in the cauldron, it would have given you enough power to easily root out my plot, to maintain Vyvian's protection upon the castle. Instead, you flew away."

Oh, by the goddess. What a fool I was. Modrun spoke true—I had stepped away from my duty and suffered the consequences. I had refused the ring, and my pride and grief had propelled me, and the Circle, into doom.

"It was no *graal*," I said. "I had no need of trinkets."

"Trinket? This *trinket* held the key to Carelon's safety, and you turned you back on it. On your brother, on your King. So it has always gone with you, Morgen. Mistaking affection for love, talent for power, and knowledge for wisdom."

"Vyvian would have told me if the ring were a key to her

protection," I said, letting his insults go to the winds. I would not tolerate his abuse, not again. "But it matters not. I demand you release Carelon from your wretched spell, or else you know the consequences."

"Do I? Do you suspect I did not see this day coming? You never asked—Oh, Morgen, so many terrible things I had you do, and you never questioned. Did you ever wonder if you were writing your own doom?"

"Fate is not inevitable. I have rewritten it again."

"Indeed, but sometimes it is useful. For if Percival had been raised at court, he would have died of croup at seven months old. If Percival had not lived, Galahad would never have gone to Benwick, and the Queen's grief would have shaken the foundations of court. Hwyfar would never have returned to Avillion; Gawain would have died at Loholt the Bold's hand; Lanceloch would have consoled Gweyn, and their treachery would have destroyed *everything*."

"There are infinite possibilities. You always felt yourself the judge, but you were also its manipulator."

He scoffed, so familiar and so *human*. He was gaining in strength; I could almost see his form at the edges of my staff's light. "As you know now, it is a tremendous burden to shoulder these possibilities, Morgen. I do not pretend these decisions were made lightly."

"The world is changing, Merlin, and I do not think it a friendly place for scheming wizards. And I will not be just another powerful woman discarded for your own gain."

"You overestimate your capabilities."

"Like your sister, Ganeida? Did you take her power, as well?"

"Gladly. Like you, she squandered her magic, so lost in her visions she made herself half-mad with them. By the time I pushed her from the tower, she was so lost in them she made no sense."

"And yet, her visions remain," I replied. "And I suppose she was just the first victim you bled dry."

"Oh, Morgen, Morgen. Do not try to wheedle your way out of this." He chuckled, for a moment like the dear old man so many knew. "I see the same power in you. Have you not taken power from others? I smell the forest and the sea upon you. And the deep wood of Brocéliande."

"Theirs was freely given, in the end."

"What difference does it make?" Merlin asked. "I always told you: One cannot burden themselves in ethical dilemmas. There is the power of magic and the power of force. Uther Pendragon had both, and he grew a new nation of peace and unity like no other. A world you now benefit from. A world you could hold in the palm of your hand if you just allow me to show you."

A world that had grown from the bones of my mother's ruined body and mind. A world where grief had given me a gift beyond measure, a window into death, a power that frightened Merlin still.

I was tired of his prattling, his constant need to defend himself, the hunger in his fevered eyes. My soul felt calm, swathed in the balm and quiet of death magic.

"And I will show you the face of death once again, old man. And she will claim you."

For although Merlin's work was great, he had walked alone, taking and never giving. It was the oldest and most sacred work among priestesses: power moves like the tides that guide the seas. Long I had given, I realized, but never had I asked for myself. Never had I gone into the well and asked the goddesses for power *for me,* for my Circle, for every soul I had touched with good intent while I did Merlin's corrupted work. I had retreated, again and again, into my own guilt, my own grief, and never pushed at the edges of my bower. Until I had lost it all. Until I was forced to see the world again.

I whispered to my birds, and my birds took flight.

CHAPTER FORTY-EIGHT

UPON THE PATH

WHEN HWYFAR, WEARY from healing Mordred and the constant nightmare of the last few days, opened her eyes to the world of dreaming, she did not expect to see her mother. And yet, there she was, Queen Tregerna of Lyonesse, standing before her on a great cliff overlooking the Narrow Sea. It smelled of fish rot and new life, a cool breeze lifting her mother's undone steely tresses. She wore pale silver armor, fashioned as if from moonlight, and it glinted as she moved.

"Mother," Hwyfar said, moving toward Tregerna, her legs frustratingly slow in this place. No matter how many steps she took, her mother was still out of reach.

Tregerna turned slowly, her icy eyes full of regret and love. Regret they had lost so much time to magic's corrupting force; love that never eroded away, no matter the deceit. They did not often speak of their separation, all those years while Lyndesoires was held captive, but Hwyfar could feel her mother's ache.

"Hwyfar," Queen Tregerna breathed, her shoulders sinking with relief. "At last."

They used to speak this way, before the Path fell, and even traveled, using the magic of Lyonesse to do so. But since Vyvian's death, that power had diminished and twisted and changed.

"I am in Carelon," Hwyfar said hurriedly. "With Gawain. There has been so much death—destruction. I fear the cost of

416

our peace was too great. I fear I have made myself too visible now, and all you gave up for me was wasted."

Tregerna held out her hand, and at last Hwyfar was able to grasp it. "My child, do not mistake the gods' timing for your own fault. You and Gawain are not to blame for this, nor your stolen years together. The Path will mend, but it is changing."

Hearing those words, Hwyfar felt part of her heart heal. She was not a superstitious woman, and yet she had feared somehow their love had contributed to the fissures opening wide in Carelon. Though she had nothing but distaste for the politics and intrigues of court, she found herself strangely protective of it, nonetheless.

"Mawra is broken," Hwyfar said. "And I do not know how to help. She denies me entrance, calls me spiteful names to her servants, and will not leave her rooms. It is bad enough the King is so ill, and the prince so wounded. She cannot act as Queen while her heart breaks."

"She is your sister. Do not forget that. She will listen to you— but you must be brave enough to face her."

"Her faith has twisted into a dangerous thing," Hwyfar said. "I fear she will die if she does not go to Lanceloch."

"This is why I come to you, Hwyfar."

The landscape shifted and they were now standing in the great hall at Withiel, the fortress in Avillion where Hwyfar and her sisters had been born. It was not the diminished thing it was now, but vivid and alive, hung with new tapestries, its frescos bright and bold.

Upon the dais, Hwyfar saw their whole family assembled, as they had been before Ymelda had corrupted their mother. King Leodegraunce was young and fit, his red beard bright as Hwyfar's own hair. Tregerna wore a thin circlet, looking so much like Mawra with her dark hair and piercing eyes, with little golden Gweyn upon her lap, plump and giggling. Hwyfar saw the younger version of herself, no more than four years old, standing patiently to the side, while Mawra gazed up at their father every now and again, a small white cat prancing about her lap.

"You sent me those visions," Hwyfar said, feeling the truth of the Path shimmer through her bones. "When I tried to heal Mordred."

Tregerna nodded slowly. "The Path remembers what we try to forget."

"I wish I remembered this," Hwyfar said, pointing to the scene before them.

"I was not a happy wife, but I was content with my children," Tregerna said from beside Hwyfar. "It is more than most queens are given."

Hwyfar's magic prickled at her mother's words, the air redolent with the uncanny sensation of prophecy. "I have already lost one sister to the misery of queenship, I do not know if I can bear another."

Tregerna turned to her eldest daughter, reaching out to touch the side of her face. In the dream she could not feel it, but deep in her soul she sensed the connection: tranquil, warm, and familiar.

"I will see you soon, Hwyfar, but you will be asked to bear that which you never desired, and for that you will be best suited—you will help the land heal again."

Hwyfar had been turning over the prophecy and her vision in her mind again and again, trying to make sense of it. "Arthur's end—Gawain is meant to be the harbinger of that promise. Not Llachlyn, not Loholt, not even Mordred—We are to rule."

Queen Tregerna looked so terribly sad when she began to back away, the edges of the dream already fraying. "Every end is a beginning. Every beginning, an end. Let your love guide you, especially where you do not wish to tread."

Two black crows flew down from the east, circling before they alighted in front of them.

Come, the Circle is needed.

GAWAIN HELPED THE King into a soft, high-backed chair beside Mordred's bedside in Galahad's own quarters. The journey had not been easy: Mordred's body was still perilously fragile from his injuries, and the castle a mire as workers tried to clear the rubble and tend to the remaining injured. But they had managed, and relief flooded his senses. He only wished Hwyfar were here, so they could comfort one another.

They had debated where to take the prince, but eventually agreed on Galahad's rooms, for they were close and not too badly damaged. It was strange to look about the once-familiar room, where he had grown from a stubborn young knight to a battle-hardy warrior. It featured far more crosses than it had, but it was otherwise the same.

As he watched the prince sleep, Gawain mused on the fragility of succession and the web of lies and deception that had brought about his own existence. He had no doubt this young man was not the blood of Pendragon. When they had connected through Hwyfar's power, he sensed no connection to it, only to Orkney.

It angered him and frustrated him by turns. He understood women had few tools to wield in politics, but gods, he wished his mother and his aunt had not entwined themselves so wholly in their intrigues, leaving him to sort through the scant clues.

There was no time to be personally affronted, though. Arthur had dozed off, and there were plenty of others to tend to Mordred.

Quietly as a man of his size and composition could manage, he went to leave, but Arthur took his hand.

"I must discuss an important matter with you before you leave, Gawain," said the King.

Gawain took his seat again, holding back a wince of pain. "Of course, Your Majesty."

King Arthur did not let go of his hand, but stroked it gently, reverently. "I need you to promise me something."

"You are my liege, uncle. I am at your service." Saying the words made Gawain's chest feel heavy, a lingering soreness from long-held wounds between them all. Or was it something else? If Arthur had known about his marriage to Hwyfar all this time, and had granted him protection, was this his way of seeking forgiveness? To say nothing of the damned prophecy.

But Gawain was far past believing in prophecies, given his experience with Hwyfar and healing Mordred.

"My kingdom balances on the precipice, and I fear I am unmoored." He squeezed Gawain's hand again, as if to give himself a reminder of solidity and strength. "In the case Mordred's wounds are grave enough, which I suspect they are, I wish to take him to Avillion."

The words surprised Gawain so much, he flinched back. "My lord?"

Arthur narrowed his eyes thoughtfully, watching Mordred sleep. The prince looked so young. "I know I am a Christian, but I also have lived in an age of magic. Merlin told me, many times, I always had a home in Avillion due to my mother's line, and if ever I was wounded, the healers of the Isle could help even when our healers could not. Well, both Mordred and I suffer without peace. I grow more frail with each passing season, and my priests have no answers for me. I do not wish to waste away upon the throne, Gawain."

"Your priests will not be pleased if you venture to Avillion," Gawain said, voicing the obvious. "The court is already fractured enough as it is."

"That is why I am going to name you as my regent," Arthur said.

The words hung in the air between them, Gawain's mouth open but words failing him. "Your Majesty, you cannot mean it. I've been away from court for a decade."

"You are my eldest nephew. And though you have been away, you are beloved in ways few others are. Not only are you a war hero, but you are an honest, just man."

"But the Queen, surely..."

The look of profound sadness in Arthur's expression was enough to make Gawain forget his own woes for a moment. "Your brother Gareth has been helping me these last months, providing me proof of what I knew all too well. In a week's time, the Queen will be charged with adultery and conspiracy against the throne, along with Lanceloch du Lac."

Gawain tried to summon up the anger he so often felt at the mention of that name, but he only found a well of deep regret and thorny pity where fury once lay. The words were spoken so softly, yet so distantly, they broke his heart.

"I am not a cruel man, however. Nor petty. I do not wish to bring these charges against them before the whole court. I will give them a chance at reconciliation—a last kindness. But I do not believe they will take it. And so, while I am gone, I will need to give the throne to one whose hands I will trust, who has a loving, powerful wife behind him. I cannot be a good ruler in the face of all this, and I do not wish to face the court much longer."

"It is the last thing I want, uncle. I am not a clever man, nor am I a Christian man," Gawain explained.

"Which is where I ask my favor," King Arthur said, looking Gawain straight in the eyes, now. "You must reject the old ways and be baptized in the chapel."

"My wife is—"

"A remarkable woman. Clever, powerful, and beautiful—perilously so. But to have a King Regent without the blood of Christ would put our entire kingdom at risk. I believe, however, you can manage the balance between you. I would advise you to give her the position Vyvian held, and Merlin before her. She would be Queen Regent and High Counselor of Braetan. That will protect her."

King Arthur took out a small gold object from his hand and held it out to Gawain. It was a ring, familiar to him in its legend: Merlin's ring. Thick, twisted gold encircled an enormous red stone, its face etched with two reared dragons.

Except, no. This was not the same ring. There *were* two dragons along the sides, but a unicorn and a lion carved beside the garnet.

"Give this to Princess Hwyfar; she will understand what it means," the King said. "I had Vyvian make this for me before she died—hoping we could start anew."

The King was not asking Gawain if he would assent to the regency—that was a command. He was asking if he would turn his back on the power he had discovered, nurtured, and experienced with his wife. Though not a man of faith, he was not yet the sort of man to take such a decision or action lightly. Gaheris and Galahad would be elated, of course—and certainly, putting Orkneys and Pendragons closer to the throne would ensure a much longer line of succession.

He wished his mother were here. Even for all her scheming, her coldness, her distance, he fiercely desired her counsel.

"How long will you be gone?" Gawain asked, gazing up from the ring.

King Arthur frowned, leaning forward to check upon Mordred a moment longer before answering. "As long as it requires."

"And when Mordred is healed?"

"You and I know he shares no blood with me," Arthur said, with a glimmer of mischief in his eyes. "Though no one would dare say it to me, and I found myself hopelessly, blissfully dedicated to the boy."

"My lord…"

"It does not matter to me. It never did. I told Gweyn as much, hoping she would find a lover, and she did. For what have bloodlines earned us in the end, my boy? Carelon is barely holding together. And our future is not promised, though once I felt it was. I am content to be the King who was, and not the King who endured."

Once again, words fled from Gawain's mind.

I go across the Eversea, to rest in the great pool where Time cannot find me, and the doom of men has no teeth. For you must deny me forever and bring in a new age of fate.

The Green Knight had known this moment would come, even if Gawain had doubted, thinking such a betrayal impossible.

A crow tapped upon the window, wings flapping in irritation.

Gawain slowly let himself down upon one knee, biting back the pain still harrowing his body two decades after its injury, and bowed his head before his uncle, his liege, and his King.

"I pledge to you, Arthur, King of all Braetan, that should the hour arise that I am needed, I will take up the Cross of Christ and serve in your stead, elevating Hwyfar of Lyonesse as High Counselor of the Realm, until I am no longer required."

Gods, Hwyfar might never forgive him. Thankfully, he had faith she would still love him, anyway.

ANNA WAS DYING.

Her dreams of late had been steeped in strange portents, winding passageways, and grasping vines. Just before the earthquake, she had followed whispers to the dark beneath Carelon, hearing Nimue's voice from below, and confronted the true cost of her magic.

Vyvian had warned her there was a chance her hold on that spell was incomplete, that Merlin was powerful and wily and not easy to eliminate. As the years passed uneventfully, she'd forgotten the warning and withdrawn into herself to help build the Path and keep her children safe. Gawain, Gaheris, Gareth, and Galahad—she was their fierce guardian, their protector, their unseen guide.

She would hold on, for them—she could protect them. Until she could no longer. She could find a little more strength, even now.

For she was not alone, and Morgen le Fay was calling out to her across the darkness, her voice feather-soft and full of strength.

CHAPTER FORTY-NINE

INTO THE DEPTHS

~ Galahad ~

A PAIR OF crows with green, glinting eyes led Galahad and Percival down into the lowest reaches of Carelon. He carried the *graal* before him, carefully wrapped in silks. It thrummed against his chest like an inconstant heartbeat, alive and moving.

Here beneath the dungeons, a stench arose like rot and carrion in the sun. Percival dutifully carried a lantern as they descended, but said precious little, concentrating on the hopping birds' progress and keeping pace with Galahad's more athletic stride.

When they arrived at an archway dug directly into rock—the old caverns the castle was built upon—Galahad nearly walked straight in without thought.

"Galahad," Percival called after him, firmly grabbing his shoulder.

Turning around, Galahad saw just how frightened Percival was. His eyes, always large and luminous, were exposed to the whites; his jaw clenched, his hands worrying the pommel of the dagger he carried.

"I'm sorry, I was getting carried away," Galahad said. The *graal* was a guiding force, and Morgen had asked *him* to wield it.

"I don't think you're sorry at all, but you might want to think twice about coming down here with me," Percival said.

Galahad reached to clasp Percival's shoulder. "I wouldn't be here with anyone else."

"I won't be able to protect you if anything happens," Percival said.

"You hoisted me from the well. You saved my life," Galahad pointed out.

"This feels more dire," Percival said. "And besides, I don't think my talents in knot-making will be of any service down here. You're always so prepared for conflict. I never know what to do."

Galahad gazed up at Percival, reaching for the right words. "I will protect you. But if I am to protect you, I need you with me."

With far less of an argument than expected, Percival relented. "Very well. You may regret it, though."

"I haven't so far," Galahad said, kissing Percival gently on the lips before turning down the next set of stairs.

And it was right, and it was good. Galahad did not want to barrel into danger without a kiss.

At last, they came to the lowest tier, where another bird stood guard next to Llachlyn. She sat before a massive archway into a vast room, looking down at her hands, her eyes red and raw from weeping. It sounded like a storm brewed within the caverns beyond them.

"Mallow!" Percival cried, scooping her up into an enormous embrace.

"Where is Aunt Morgen?" Galahad asked.

Back on her feet, Llachlyn brushed at her tunic. "She went in. We should help her, even though she said not to."

"Wise," Percival said. "Or foolish. Either way, I agree."

Galahad took out his sword, tucking the *graal* under his thick leather belt. It made his skin shiver with anticipation, fear quick on its heels. God had brought him here, along with the two people he loved most in the world, to perform this great deed. They needed his strength, his bravery. And he needed their hope, their cleverness, and their wits.

"I've been thinking about what you said, Percival, about the three *graals*. How many faiths believe in the power of that number," Galahad said, standing before them both. "And I think it may be because, no matter the faith, there is strength and significance. It is balance. I stand as a Christian, Llachlyn as a daughter of Avillion, and Percival in between, with no allegiance."

"I cannot argue with that sentiment," Percival said. "I have oft said as much."

"And I believe we must keep together, now, as we confront this pestilence," Galahad said. "I should have seen the power in that instead of fighting to change you both, ages ago. I'm sorry for not coming to your defense sooner. I wanted to be part of a greater story, but I failed to see I already was."

Llachlyn went forward, wrapping her arms around his middle. "You wretched creature," she said. "I love you."

"And I, you," Galahad said, squeezing her.

Percival enveloped them both in his long arms, and they swayed together.

"Together, or not at all," Percival said.

"Together, or not at all," Galahad replied.

They pulled away from one another as the sound of footsteps descending the staircase came behind them, sure and solid and strong.

It was Princess Hwyfar, alone, with a crow perched on her shoulder. She wore her magnificent green armor and had braided her hair into a flat-lying plait down the center of her head. She carried a dagger at her hip and a pair of axes.

There was no sign of Gawain.

"I have come, but without my husband," said Hwyfar. "Gawain will remain with the King and Prince Mordred."

Approaching the threshold, she placed her hand upon the stonework and went still. Galahad watched as she closed her eyes, her lips barely moving in silent prayer or supplication, he did not know.

* * *

~ *Hwyfar* ~

PARTING FROM GAWAIN had been painful, nearly as difficult as watching him confess the King's demand: Gawain would be Regent, and she a Queen. Even with her mother's warning and her own suspicions, it was a heavy burden. Especially given Gawain's promise to pledge his faith to the Christ.

A husband as regent, alive, and a Christian, was better than no husband at all. And she would be raised to High Counselor. There was so much good she could do. She supposed, if this was the price for their ten years of solitude, she would take it.

But, as Hwyfar knew well, tomorrow was not promised. Battle awaited them. Morgen le Fay awaited them.

At least here, in her armor and with her weapons, she could lose herself in the task. She did not have to consider her sister's plight or her husband's pain. Though both weighed upon her, they were but chaff in the great measure.

Seeing Percival, Galahad, and Llachlyn together gave her enough hope to push away the dread. That, and she recognized the imprint of Morgen's magic deep within the cavern, even through the oppressive weight of Merlin's power.

Hwyfar walked first across the stone archway, coming short as her eyes adjusted to the room before her.

Mist fell thick upon the cavern, pooling in corners and snaking around rock formations, a faint green and red glow coming from somewhere out of sight. Rising up out of the mist, high above their heads, were two sleeping dragons, entwined with thick vines of puce and scarlet. No, not merely entwined: impaled. The vines pulsed, pulling strength from those beasts like a monstrous leech. It was clear they suffered, for their muscles shook where the vines met their scales.

Hwyfar's armor kindled to life, a hundred whorls glowing green. She had only seen it do so once or twice in her life, and only in times of great peril. Today, she was glad to have Galantyne by her side, even if Gawain could not be.

"We must wait for Morgen's command," Hwyfar said, steadying her stance. Galahad shifted beside her, a pillar of anticipation.

She went to take a step forward, but gasped when her back leg met resistance. Turning, she saw shadowy vines wrapped around her calf. She severed them with her axe, but more came to replace them immediately. She was reminded of her fight in Lyndesoires over a decade past—was this magic connected to Ymelda's corrupted power? It felt similar.

Galahad roared as the vines pulled Llachlyn sideways, another trail of thorns dragging Percival down with her. More tendrils rose from the ground, some as thick as her own arm. Hwyfar strained against them, chopping blindly in every direction, gritting her teeth against the impacts. Sweat dripped down her face and into her eyes, and she groaned in frustration.

Galahad, still unencumbered, positioned himself before his dearest friends, hacking at every assault. The young knight was ferocious, deadly, and precise in his actions, clearing a path toward Hwyfar with astonishing swiftness.

Soon, they were side by side, protecting Llachlyn and Percival from the worst of the attacks.

One misstep and Hwyfar fell to her knees, pain echoing through her legs and into her hips as they struck the uneven stone floor. She reached into her stores of magic and came up empty. The last few days had been too much to manage. Her throat burned, her stomach roiled, as she tried again and failed to produce even a mote of magic.

But she would not bow; not now, not ever.

She would not run, and she would not falter.

~ Morgen ~

MY CROWS TRAVERSED far and wide, skittering down the Path, reaching allies and friends alike. Some heeded their call, while others were deaf to such omens. I did not need them all—I only needed a wider circle. I was born one among three sisters; I had created the nine; now I needed twenty-seven souls, the holiest of numbers to my goddess—one for each crow.

One by one they appeared—Tregerna of Lyonesse, Elayne of Astolat, Yvain, Coel, Isolde, and many more besides. Women I had helped in childbirth, herbalists I had instructed, potion-makers I had assisted with exotic and expensive ingredients. Even the humble innkeeper's wife Rozenn came to the cavern. I saw Hwyfar battling Merlin's vines alongside Galahad, Llachlyn, and Percival, heard their elated shouts as the space filled with new combatants.

They had answered my call. Never had I suspected they would come so quickly, nor with such focus and power.

But there were only twenty-six.

No matter, I would press forward.

Merlin laughed. "You risk the life of so many innocents, Morgen. What power could they possess that could endure against this ancient foe? Your Path? You believe it strong enough? They cannot see me. They will have to trust you. And you are the Mother of Lies."

I wished I had time to relay the whole plan, but it had come to me in shadows and whispers. Now they were waiting for me, for my command. I flushed both hot and cold, the weight of the moment pressing down upon me.

"Grant me your love," I managed to say, my voice reverberating around the cavern, even amidst the vines and gyrating wyrms. "And protect one another. No matter what you see."

THEN I FELT it: The *graal* was here. I felt a surge of power rise up through me, joy and gladness and abundant love, and I felt Merlin tremble.

Galahad let out a cry in the dark toward the entrance to the cave, and I watched as a great tendril plucked the *graal* box from his belt. My power flickered, but did not fail.

Percival and Llachlyn had managed to untangle themselves,

and they climbed up that treacherous tendril as my warriors went into motion all around me. Coel and Yvain charged forward to the heart of the cavern, immediately sawing and sundering the roots feeding off the dragons. Melic licked the wounds, using his own power to keep the dragons calm.

Percival grabbed the *graal* and twisted, managing to grasp it with his long fingers. Then he dashed to the side, narrowly avoiding a crumbling pillar as it fell behind him.

Merlin whispered in my mind. "You fool. You will disturb the dragons and pull down the entire castle!"

That was my greatest fear, and it held me back. I wanted to surrender to the trust of my companions, but my stubborn heart would not allow it. Merlin was correct: this plan was reckless and desperate.

As always, the fool.

"How many more must die for your selfishness, Morgen?" Merlin pressed. "Everywhere you tread, people die. For what? Your pity? Your forgiveness?"

Yes. That was the crux of my strength. Death was not to be feared. And my part in death was not its application, but in its mercy. For I could walk with the dying, side by side, and rescue them from their own loneliness. I could grant them the mercy they needed.

"No, Merlin. My mercy."

This was my greatest gift. *They* were my greatest gift.

I allowed mercy in. I released my grasp upon the Path. I surrendered my worries outward, relaxing my clenched fists. I stopped fighting and allowed Fate in, trusting my warriors, my friends, my family, to carry me.

~ *Llachlyn* ~

LLACHLYN WATCHED HER mother glow softly, blue dappled light emanating from her face and her hands. The cavern was overrun by more than just crows, as people had appeared from all corners of the realm. She knew how, for she had felt the call as well: her mother's voice, sent upon the wings of crows.

"Bring me the *graal*," commanded a voice inside her head. She looked around for the source of the voice, but she could not see it.

"Did you hear that voice?" she asked Percival, who was still trying to cradle the *graal* in his hands and make his way toward Morgen.

Percival went to run toward her, but tripped and fell. She watched helplessly as the *graal* took to the air and, instead of falling, began to fly toward her, as if pulled by an invisible hand.

Llachlyn dashed toward the *graal* and wrapped her arms around it. The invisible force was unmoved by her actions, and she had to grab on to keep a hold. Her feet left the ground before she was fully aware, and she floated toward her mother. Her mother, who was doing *nothing*.

She would not let it go, however. Not even when the *graal* dropped and left her groaning in pain upon the ground.

You know what to do. I trust you, Llachlyn. Do not listen to his lies.

Her mother's voice resonated in her mind, even though she could not see her face. Morgen le Fay stood still as a statue, eyes closed, and hands splayed.

No, she most certainly did not know what to do.

"Mother!"

Merlin, or the strange presence he had become, swirled around Llachlyn.

"Give me the *graal*, child, and I will bring peace to Carelon," Merlin said.

His voice was gentle and kind, terribly convincing.

And then there he was, standing before Llachlyn, an old man with a white beard and tattoos on his forehead. He leaned heavily on a staff, but was not entirely corporeal.

"You can't open it," Llachlyn said, holding up the *graal* vessel. "But I can."

* * *

~ *Percival* ~

GALAHAD WAS WINNING against the vines, but Hwyfar was struggling. Percival could not pursue Llachlyn now, but he had a duty to ensure the princess was safe, as well. Not that he was particularly adept at protection, but he was compelled to help her.

Stabbing madly with his dagger, he freed Hwyfar from another cluster of vines, which had tied her hands up.

"Thank you, Percival," she said, shaking her hands and wincing.

"Who are all these people?" Percival asked her.

"Friends." Hwyfar gestured to a pair of men dismantling the last of the vines protruding from the dragons. "Kind ones, as well. Morgen has called us together, to help her."

She cried out, wincing, and then took in a sharp breath as if in wonder or realization, and Percival helped steady her. "What is it?" he asked.

"I need to heal the Path—I think we can use it to secure the power here, to seal it in place," she said, half to herself. "But I am too tired. I am missing something."

"Can I help?" Percival desperately wanted to. Even if he didn't have magic, or strength. "I can regale you with a song or, perhaps, distract you momentarily with a dance?"

"You remind me of someone I loved and lost," Hwyfar said, grasping his hand. The touch was warm, but not what he expected. When their skin met, it tingled. "Perhaps that will assist me."

The dragons let out a low, gurgling sound which set Percival's hair further on end.

In a moment, a tall older woman with white hair and splendid armor came jogging toward them. She wore a simple diadem atop her braids, which glinted as she expertly cut through vines.

"Hwyfar," the woman said, and held her close.

"Mother," Hwyfar whimpered. Percival's heart ached to hear her so defeated.

"I am here, child. It is dire, but not yet time to concede. Who is this lad?" the woman asked.

"I'm Percival of... Well, just Percival is fine for now," he said.

"I am Tregerna," said the woman, inclining her head. She scrutinised him closely, as if he were an unusual portrait. "Hwyfar's mother."

"And Queen of Lyonesse," Percival said, awestruck. "Gweynevere's mother, too."

"We need to turn the Path's power upon this malfeasance—I know it will work," Hwyfar said, taking her mother by the hand. She grasped Percival's again. "I think we can do this, together. I believe, somehow, we were meant to, Percival."

Percival did not know how to perceive that comment, but he did like feeling important. "Show me what I'm meant to do," he said cheerfully.

~ Llachlyn ~

"I CAN FEEL it," Merlin said, glancing at the box, "but I believe you have spelled it somehow."

"I have not," Llachlyn replied.

Vyvian had managed to confound Merlin even after her death, and Llachlyn found immense pleasure in that.

"You have no magical prowess," he said.

"Not much, no." Llachlyn grinned at him. "Certainly not enough to confound you. Just trinkets, really."

Merlin's features were difficult to interpret, but Llachlyn had no doubt of his frustration. The vines ceased their attacks, the constant cracking sounds coming at last to a stop.

"I will show you," she said, preparing to open it.

But then she noticed: Her ring was glinting in the light.

The ring made of metal Vyvian had sent her, small and precious and imbued with more than what it seemed.

Glancing to Galahad, she saw the ring upon his finger, the posy ring she had made for him, glowing in response. And Hwyfar, carrying Galantyne, jumped back to see her sword blazing. A necklace around Queen Tregerna's throat glittered; one of the daggers belonging to the kingly fellow did the same. And was that charm upon the lion also shimmering?

Time slowed. Llachlyn understood. The Path was *here*. The path was in every little object between them, hammered and molded into trinkets, yes, but also swords. Llachlyn could feel their magic, their essences, mingling together, not just here but far beyond the reach of Carelon. Every piece of metal Vyvian had worked over fifty years.

Mordred had mentioned Llachlyn's unusual abilities to unlock Vyvian's puzzles. And so she had. The whole time, she had been preparing for this moment. For, to anyone else, the *graal* box was merely a sealed box, but she could read the Lady of the Lake's fingerprint. She had fashioned this *graal* vessel, and Llachlyn could undo it.

With a rush of breath, Llachlyn followed the glimmering lights connecting her to her companions and, in one smooth movement, she undid the mechanism upon the box and rolled, throwing the *graal* to Galahad with a great shout and all the strength she could muster—which was far more than she should have had, for it was the combined strength of them all.

Light filled the cavern, a spectrum of scintillating hues refracting against one another, as the pieces from within arranged themselves before Galahad. They were the elements of a shield: the boss, enarmes, and guards. In place of wood, a clear, faceted glass held each part within its shimmering surface. And the shield itself shone as bright as the moon.

In the light of that glow, Llachlyn saw every joy she had ever known: her mother's smile, Percival's laughter, Galahad's protectiveness, the smell of melting gold in the furnace, glowing embers in the dark, fresh braids of Una, cornflowers... So much joy, even in the face of so much sadness and loneliness.

Her mother's voice rang out. "Behold the joyless legacy you have wrought, Merlin, and prepare for your end."

CHAPTER FIFTY

THE MAW OF DEATH

THE PATH TWISTED, wound, and reformed around Merlin as he shrieked in horror at what the *graal* showed him: every time he had taken joy, every innocence he had ever robbed, every heart he had broken. The new Path, bright and terrible, twisted about him like a spider securing her prey, and his form shrank with each passing heartbeat, though he continued to fight until his muffled cries ceased all together.

Behind me, a cracking noise grabbed my attention as Yvain plunged a dagger into each of the dragons, their bodies slowly turning to stone. He had taken ichor from the cockatrice, knowing it might prove useful. The stone's progress continued through each remaining root and tendril, too, fortifying the foundation of Carelon at last.

I opened my eyes to the Maw of Death, the caverns beneath Carelon slipping away entirely.

What remained of Merlin's soul writhed upon the ground, a smoking worm the size of a housecat, hissing and whining. The thought of reaching down and touching it filled me with revulsion, but I did not know another way.

As a midwife of souls, it was not my choice when to usher others across the borders of life and death. Modrun and Ahès's deaths came at great pain, and I hoped I would be spared this time.

"Let me," said a voice.

I looked up and saw my sister Anna standing, arrayed in the muted grey of this place, and I gasped. "Sister, no, it cannot be."

So, a third soul I must usher across. I should have known. The twenty-seventh, the last of my flock. But not for long.

"I have been dying for a long time. But I am ready." Anna walked closer, her expression serene. She wore a silver gown flocked with blue, her long hair braided down on each side. "My revenge wrought this monster, and I ought to be the one to take him to his end."

She reached out a hand to where Merlin's form still twisted, and the shape of Nimue rose from him, separated at last. Her form was familiar, small and earthy and wild.

An unseen wind moved my hair and robes, and I watched in wonder as Nimue and Anna were reunited again.

"Anna, please…"

My sister took my hand and kissed it. "When I created Nimue, I left a part of myself in her. I was too cowardly to die, and foolish to think I would not suffer the consequences of such potent magics. Though I was not the only way Merlin found his way back in, I do not believe he would have been capable of such deeds had I not succeeded."

"The Path is rebuilding—there is yet a time for miracles," I told her, knowing how much time she had spent building and perfecting it, learning its secrets.

"I know. And my son, and his remarkable wife, will help lead Carelon into a new age. What else could a mother ask for? And you will help them, as you can. But you are no longer alone, Morgen. You never were."

"Thank you," I said to her, weeping bitter tears. "And I regret I did not foresee the cost then, when I gave you the key to this power."

"We cannot change what has happened, but together—all of us—we have ensured a safer future for our children. For behold, Llachlyn will be the next Spinner, for she has been doing the work already; Vyvian prepared her well." Anna sighed, her gaze drawn to the dark horizon beyond us. "I wish I could give you a more fitting gift, my sister. All I can do is bear this burden for you one final time."

"That is a greater gift than I deserve," I said.

"I love you, Morgen. You stood with me when I was alone. You helped me find my power—you gave me strength to become more. You were the sister I needed, and I will be forever grateful for that. You could have shunned me, for what I was to you, but you did not. It was not always easy between us, but sisterhood is a beautiful and perilous path."

Anna reached down to pick up the remnants of Merlin's corrupted soul. At her touch, blue light shone like a cold star and encapsulated what was there in a thousand glittering strands. The shape shifted, twisted, and where a formless mass once squirmed now nestled a small, grey owlet, blinking up at me.

"Find what joy you can in the time you have left, Morgen," my sister said to me. "Tell Bedevere I will wait for him. And tell my sons I loved them, to the end. I go now to meet their sister, to join our mother, and rest at last."

"I will do as you ask, sister," I said to her, trembling and taking her proffered hand. "I await our reunion on the other side of time."

I took Anna Pendragon's fair hand and helped her across the threshold, into what awaited her beyond. I prayed our souls would meet again, grateful for our love no matter how complicated it was.

A warm wind picked up, brushing aside the fog on the other side to reveal a field of stars in a deep azure firmament.

Through the Great Maw, I thought I caught a glimpse of the triune goddess, waiting patiently in the dark. Soon, I would travel this same path. And if I was lucky, someone I loved would guide me across.

AND HERE THE tale winds to the end, as much as these sorts of tales ever do.

When I returned to the cavern, my visitors had already been swept away to their previous locations by my crows.

Llachlyn returned the *graal* to its vessel, and I sent word to Arthur as soon as possible, assuring him we had addressed the threat and the castle was safe from further earthquakes. Yvain's clever thinking had ensured the castle would not fall again, and my daughter's power, the magic of little connections, was our saving grace in the end.

I visited Mordred and confirmed Hwyfar's fears: he needed the hand of Avillionian healers if he were to ever recover fully. And even then, he may never walk or be free of pain. So I wrote to King Leodegraunce, and secured a ship to depart as soon as Mordred had gained a little more strength.

Not long after, Queen Mawra was formally charged of adultery, the witnesses being young Percival himself and Lady Linette, her lady-in-waiting. Lady Linette detailed the Queen's confession to her sister, alongside months of incriminating evidence I later learned she had gathered with Gareth of Orkney. Arthur was inclined to be lenient to the Queen, arranging for her to go to a nunnery. Though she outwardly agreed to the terms, Lanceloch stormed the castle and rescued her. He took her to the Joyous Guard, and a handful of knights followed them, including my own nephew Gaheris.

The kingdom nearly broke apart then, but managed to endure.

In the end, Llachlyn did not doom the King. I understood the prophecy at last when I'd heard Arthur's decree: Gawain was to rule as regent. He was to be baptized upon Pentecost, and Hwyfar named High Counselor. Hwyfar reminded me of the many ways prophecies could unfold, and I scolded myself for allowing fear to narrow my interpretations. Gawain was the first child Arthur ever held, had borne upon his back. And indeed, Gawain eventually signaled the end of Arthur's reign. For even if he were to return, the world my brother built with Merlin's deceit and power had changed irrevocably.

I now believe the power in prophecies is more than their

outcomes. Sometimes Fate's design is as much of a reaction as an action, and we, ever thinking ourselves more capable than we are, stumble toward our greater stories.

As for the *graal* of joy, Llachlyn became its keeper, and eventually the Spinner of the Path. Though Galahad and Percival begged her to stay with them, as they sought to find the other powerful relics in search of a cure for Mordred's ailments, she understood her path diverged from them. It was Gareth who suggested she take up residence in Vyvian's old cottage on the lake, where she could work in quiet and concoct new ways to protect further *graals* and make her magical implements. She would not be far from court if needed, but I knew succeeding Vyvian as a smith was what Llachlyn wanted, and what she was always meant to be.

Percival never confirmed his parentage that I knew of, not wanting the burden. He did strike up a friendship with his father, Sir Lanval, however, and they oft rode together. In the aftermath of the earthquake, he was granted a full title as a knight of the Table Round for his bravery, after all.

Galahad became the most celebrated knight of the age, held sacred by the new church and the old alike. He and Percival rarely spent time apart, and whenever possible, they came to see Llachlyn at the lake. Though the fate of Lanceloch du Lac weighed upon him, Galahad's faith did not falter.

When the time came, I decided to accompany Arthur to Avillion. The realm had changed forever, and I no longer fit into the schemes of court. I was not surprised to find King Uriens, my Coel, waiting for me at the port, and I did not deter him from joining me, either. He and Yvain often visited court in those tumultuous months between Arthur's departure and Gawain's regency. I welcomed his counsel and his attentions. Too long had I spent denying myself love in the shadow of my own pain, and I would no longer do so. I would reconnect with Avillion and help tend to Mordred and Arthur myself. And Coel's love would help me through each day.

As the great barge pushed away from the shore, I watched my family and friends vanish into the mist. King Regent Gawain and Queen Hwyfar would usher in a new age of compassion, learning, and discernment. Theirs would not be a kingdom of magic and legends, but it would endure, even through the hardships to come.

For my part, I was content to let Carelon go, to let the realm go, and await my final days in relative peace. Yes, there would be pain and joy in equal measure. I would never truly retreat from Arthur's Braetan. But I would no longer fight alone.

As for King Regent Gawain and Queen Hwyfar, well, theirs was a just rule, if sometimes burdened with the scourge of politics and infighting. All who knew them spoke of their love, their mercy, and their compassion. Together, they found balance, and weathered wicked tempests, steered by his steadfastness and her cleverness. In time, they were beloved, even if all of Braetan held out hope that Arthur would return again, and Mordred take up the Crown.

Theirs was a reign of strength, their *carioz* expanding far beyond them, to bring about a golden age of peace and joy, tempered with pain. The Path continued, but in new ways, in smaller ways, though no less powerful.

And in the end, that is the greatest gift one can ask for: connection. No matter our power or prowess, life begins and ends for us all. When we face death—whether at the hands of a judgmental God or a three-faceted goddess—there is no greater mercy than to hold fast to one another, to walk with our fellow souls across the threshold. To stand in the darkness together.

For this is what I know above all: Those who go before us teach us how to die with grace; and so, we must teach those who come after us how to live with love.

THE END

ACKNOWLEDGMENTS

THIS SERIES HAS always been a tapestry, in my mind. It begins small, in the confines of a castle, but as more threads appear, the story becomes more apparent and the landscape opens up. But so, too, does it change. It is not a finished tapestry. There are unwoven ends, unresolved figures, and of course, a few *trompe-l'œil*.

Just as there is no single canon in Arthuriana, so, too, is there no true end. It is a genre of possibility, of love, of adventure, and of inclusion. Though this small arc comes to a close, so many stories linger on the edges of the tapestry, waiting for the next golden thread.

Writing Morgen as a woman in her sixties was something I had always wanted to do, but tackling her myth was no easy task. No, she is not an invisible woman in Arthuriana in the way of Anna and Hwyfar. But as an older woman, she experiences invisibility, as so many do, when society no longer sees her as valuable. This is a Carelon in decline, where the walls literally are falling down. In that space, she finds remarkable strength. In fact, when I realized Morgen's story was not about power, but about surrender, she truly came alive.

The deeper I got into her story, the more I realized Morgen's tale was merely finishing a corner of the tapestry, rising up as a powerful, flawed, wise woman, who had suffered abuse and manipulation, yet found magic outside the realm of the known.

No seductress, no vindictive vixen, this Morgen still holds many scars from her youth, enduring the worst so Arthur might have the best. I never could shake the story of Arthur's conception, knowing that Uther had taken Igraine against her will, and I always wondered what it would have been like for Morgen and her sisters to live afterwards.

This is also a story about religious trauma. I did not expect to find so much of my younger self when writing Galahad, but there I was: a closeted, zealous, emotional young person trying to balance their faith with their innermost desires. In fact, early drafts of *Queen of None* included no Christianity at all, which I now know was my way of running from subjects I was not yet ready to tackle. But then, suddenly, I was. And, as so often in the practice of writing, I healed a little part of me as I went through it.

And of course, we have the passing of the torch to Gawain and Hwyfar who, if I'm honest, I always knew would end up crowned (Lot was right about that, at least). As much as this story is about women, it is also about shaping Gawain into the man he needs to be as a king—a better king than his uncle. Not perfect, but vulnerable and real and compassionate. It also reclaims Hwyfar's tale, wherein she takes up the mantle of the warrior at the end of the story, yet her greatest act of strength is in accepting her next role as queen.

Then there is Anna. She began this tale and she ends it, too. I knew the price of her magic—shaping Nimue and murdering Merlin—would come due. It is a sad moment, for she never truly finds the peace of vengeance—but that is so often the case. Still, her tenacity and her fierce love for her children and refusal to let Fate tell her story for her, remains central to this particular take.

Thank you to all my readers who have followed me along on this journey. This is for you.

To my husband, Michael, who anchors me.

To my son Liam for making me a mother and giving me the courage to become a writer.

Natania Barron

To my daughter, Elodie, who was the fiercest of dragon slayers as a little girl and is now growing into a warrior woman with heart.

To Jenn, always. May we grow old together as twin crones.

To EJ, again, for the notes and the feedback and the patience.

Much gratitude to my editor David Thomas Moore, who took a chance on me and this series... and this somewhat unconventional conclusion, as well.

Much admiration to my audiobook narrators, Deborah Balm, Philip Battley, and Lucy Rayner. Your performances are such a gift to me.

Big thanks to the whole Solaris team, and especially Jess Gofton, for all the support.

To my intrepid agent, Stacey Graham. You rock. Thank you for everything.

To my amazing Patrons, thank you.

ABOUT THE AUTHOR

Natania Barron is an award-winning fantasy author long preoccupied with mythology, monsters, and magic. Her often historically-inspired novels are filled with lush description and vibrant characters. Publications include her 2011 debut, *Pilgrim of the Sky*, as well as *These Marvelous Beasts*, a collection of novellas.

In 2020, Barron's *Queen of None* was hailed as "a captivating look at the intriguing figures in King Arthur's golden realm" by *Kirkus*, and won the Manly Wade Wellman award the following year.

Her shorter works have appeared in *Weird Tales*, EscapePod, and various anthologies, RPG, and game settings. In addition, she's also known for #ThreadTalk, which dives deep into the unseen, and often forgotten, world of fashion history.

Barron lives in North Carolina, USA, with her family and two dogs. When she's not writing, you can find her wandering the woods, tending her garden, and collecting rocks.

🦋 @natania.bsky.social
📷 @nataniabarron
♪ @nataniabooks
🌐 www.nataniabarron.com

FIND US ONLINE!

www.rebellionpublishing.com

/solarisbooks   /solarisbks

/solarisbooks   /solarisbooks.
bsky.social

SIGN UP TO OUR NEWSLETTER!

rebellionpublishing.com/newsletter

YOUR REVIEWS MATTER!

Enjoy this book? Got something to say?

Leave a review on Amazon, GoodReads or with your
favourite bookseller and let the world know!

NATANIA BARRON

LOVE IN NETHERFORD
BOOK I

NETHERFORD HALL

PRIDE AND PREJUDICE AND WITCHES

Ⓖ SOLARISBOOKS.COM